BLOOD TO EARTH

The Ballad of the Songbird
Book 2

Jon Ford

Tepris Press
UK

Lil' Bubba

This one is for you.
Thank you for your love and your support.
I couldn't do this without you.
(*And I'm not just talking about the Instagram account!*)

Love Always & Forever

xXx

| The World of Songbird |

In 2016, The Rising shattered the status quo. Creatures that for centuries had been considered the creation of myths, legends, fables, and fairytales turned out to be frighteningly real. In just a few months, our world was irrevocably changed forever.

Rumor was that the Vampyrii started it. Tired of living incognito amongst us, they instigated a supernatural war between the Vampire races and Humanity. Humans became the hunted. Killed, turned, or enthralled in huge numbers as the Vampyrii took much of the United States of America and claimed it for their own.

They call it New Victus.

The Werewolves fought them, resisting their attacks along the former Canadian border. The Great White North is now known as Pack Nation and is Werewolf-controlled territory.

The remnants of the American and Canadian people now live on a slender piece of the West Coast, holding the San Andreas line. They call themselves the North American Alliance, and they want their countries back.

But The Rising was a worldwide phenomenon, not simply localized in North America. Across the Atlantic in Europe, the situation was dire until old magic, the Fae, intervened and put an end to the War.

The damage, however, had already been done.

Russia went dark. Incommunicado. They were abruptly segregated from western Europe by a new mountain range that appeared overnight, rumored to be the doing of the Trolls and Ice Giants who now govern the state of NordScania in partnership with Humans.

Africa was overrun and annexed by the more feral Vampire races that had long been legend in those countries. It is the one place where the War still rages. South America descended into feudal chaos, now run by corrupt crime lords. All except the tiny Independent State of Rio de Janeiro, which walled itself off from the rest of the continent.

The other nations of Europe came together as one united entity, the Federated States of Europa. Its capital nation is the United Kingdom, which now hides securely behind enormous coastal walls known as The Bulwarks.

As the Middle East descended into chaos, Japan and China closed their borders altogether. They rarely play on the world stage.

In the final days of the war, before the ceasefire, Iceland became disputed territory between the Vampyrii, Werewolf, and Human nations, each claiming a third. At the point where their claimed territories met, a settlement was established. Over the decades since, it grew to become Nexus City, perhaps the most important place on Earth.

Neutral ground.

A place where all the new factions of the world could come in peace to discuss their grievances rather than solve them with violence.

This time of peace has lasted an uneasy three decades.

The year is 2045 and everything is about to change…again.

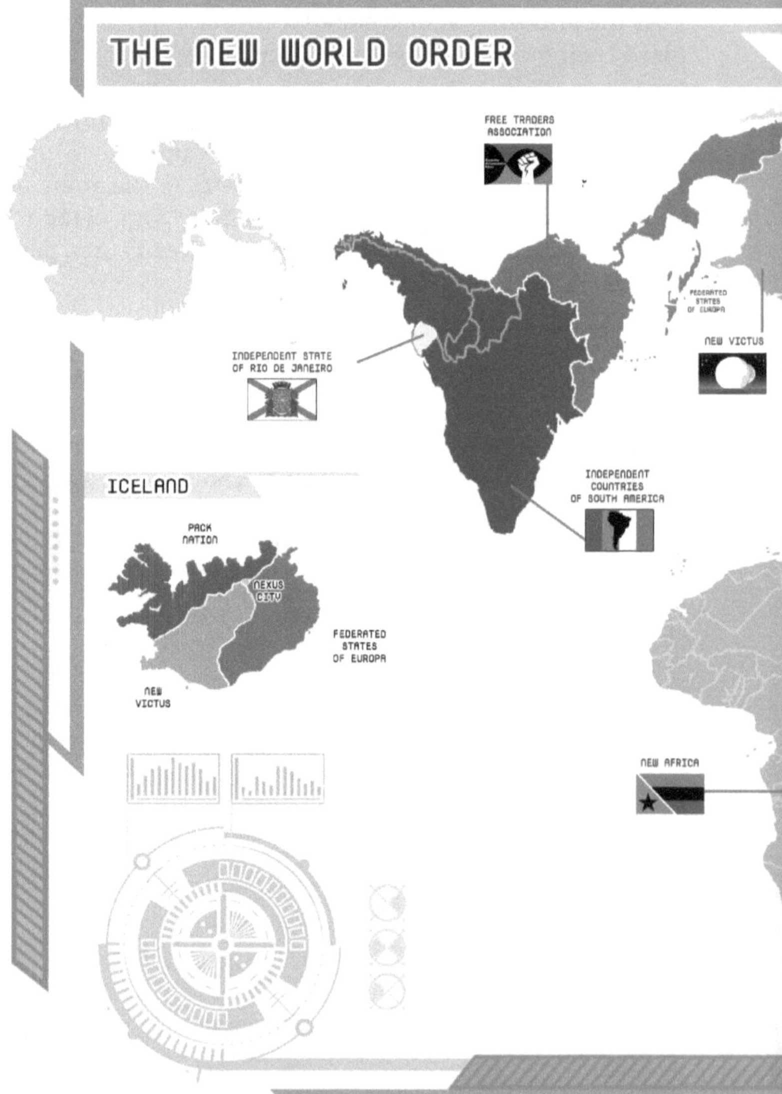
THE NEW WORLD ORDER
FREE TRADERS
ASSOCIATION
FEDERATED
STATES
OF EUROPA
NEW VICTUS
INDEPENDENT STATE
OF RIO DE JANEIRO
INDEPENDENT
COUNTRIES
OF SOUTH AMERICA
ICELAND
PACK
NATION
NEXUS
CITY
FEDERATED
STATES
OF EUROPA
NEW
VICTUS
NEW AFRICA

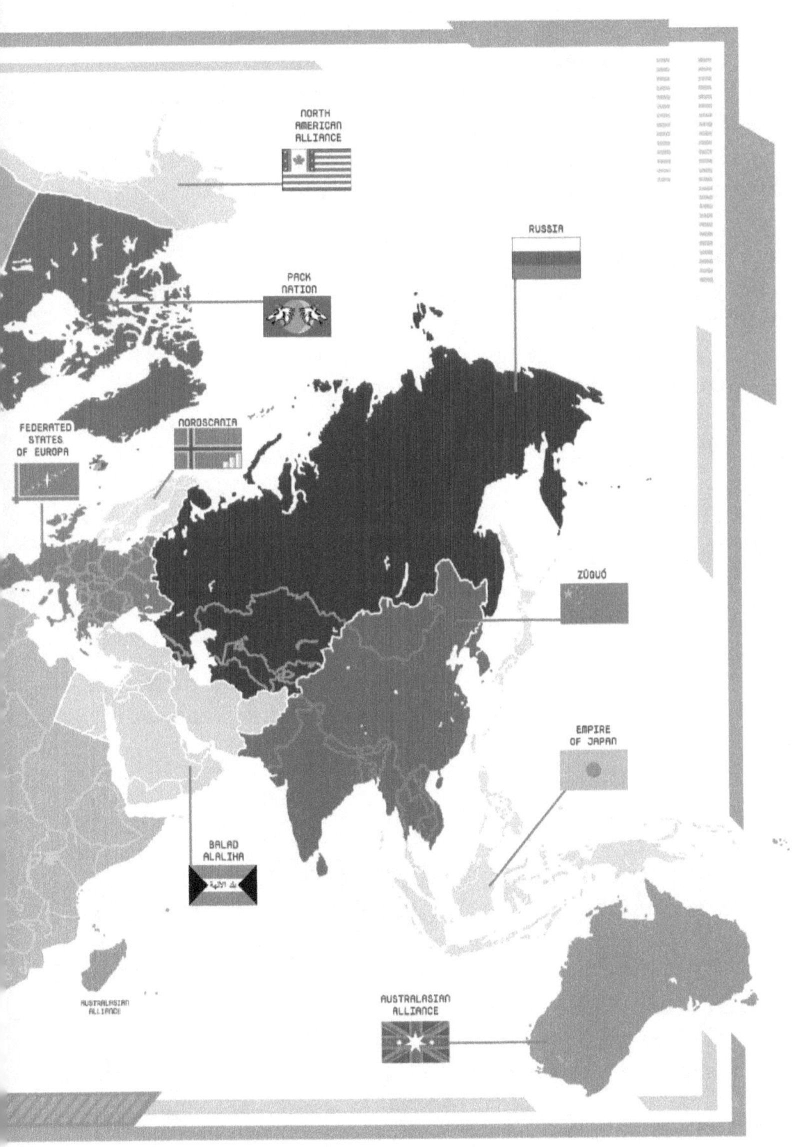
NORTH
AMERICAN
ALLIANCE
RUSSIA
PACK
NATION
FEDERATED
STATES
OF EUROPA
NORDSCANIA
ZHŌNGGUÓ
EMPIRE
OF JAPAN
BALAD
ALALIHA
AUSTRALASIAN
ALLIANCE
AUSTRALASIAN
ALLIANCE

| The Characters of Songbird |

Capt. Gayle Knightley — *Human/Fae hybrid*
Call sign '***Knightingale***'
Former leader of the 137th Hunters. Her team was KIA on a rescue mission referred to as 'Bloody Valletta'. Now assigned to the Human Fae Alliance (HFA) Academy, responsible for training the new cadets who will replace her team.

Allyson Knightley — *Human/Fae hybrid*
Gayle's younger sister. Former London cop, now Security Chief in Nexus City.

Carrie-Anne Knightley — *Human/Fae hybrid*
Youngest of the Knightley sisters. Journalist, intent on discovering why Russia has been dark since The Rising.

Serlia Knightley — *Fae*
Mother to the Knightley sisters. FSE Ambassador in Nexus City.

Jaymes Knightley — *Human*
Father to the Knightley sisters. FSE Ambassador in Nexus City. He was a victim of the bombing of the Nexus Peace Summit.

Capt. Lana Fordham — *Human*
Call sign '***Fordith***'
Gayle's best friend. Former pilot for the 137th Hunters.
Now assigned as Hand-to-Hand Combat instructor at the HFA Academy.

Sebastian StormHall — *Vampyrii*
The Grand Chancellor of New Victus, and allegedly the person who orchestrated The Rising.

Lyssa Balthazaar — *Vampyrii*
Head of House Balthazaar in New Victus. Lyssa is looking to

overthrow the regime of StormHall.

Mercy balthazaar — *Vampyrii/Human (half-blood)*
Lyssa's niece, best friend, and Military & Intelligence Officer.
She was a victim of the bombing of the Nexus Peace Summit.

Nykola Balthazaar — *Vampyrii*
Lyssa's younger sister and Chief Science Officer.

Damian Dane — *Werewolf (natural)*
The Wolf King. Leader of Pack Nation. He has been plotting
with Lyssa to overthrow the StormHall regime.

Capt. Michael Reynolds — *Human*
Call sign '*Rogue*'
Ex-North American Alliance Marine. Now assigned to the
HFA Academy, teaching alongside Capt. Knightley.

Alexa Reynolds — *Werewolf (turned)*
Call sign '*Zarra*'
Michael's twin sister. Ex-North American Alliance Marine.
Now plies a trade as a Bounty Hunter under the professional
alias 'Zarra Anderson.'

Becka Dawkins — *Human*
Alexa's business partner, friend, and pilot. Resident 'monster'
expert.

Lt. Amanda Forrester — *Human/Fae*
Call sign '*Zephyr*'
The only other member of the 137th Hunters to survive the
'Bloody Valletta' mission. Now assigned to the HFA Academy
as Firearms Instructor.

Alistair Torbar — *Human/Fae*
Call sign '*Firebird*'
Leader of the 136th Terminators, the rival squad to Gayle's
Hunters.

| **Prologue** |

FIGHT OR FLIGHT?

— Valentina Rodriguez —
— Thursday — Independent State of Rio de Janeiro —

She ran.

Her heart hammered painfully against her rib cage.

Terror? Or exertion?

Was there even a difference at this point? Fear *had* been the primary driver for her desperate flight through the almost impenetrable forest...but now?

She skidded to a halt in the tiny glade, and immediately bent over, heaving in ragged gasps as her exhausted body trembled uncontrollably.

Christ, help me! I'm going to vomit...

A shaking hand clutched at her stomach as if attempting to hold back the bile she felt rising, while the other covered her mouth. She swallowed hard, tasting the burning sensation at the back of her throat.

She was a slave to the rush of adrenaline coursing through her veins, unable to control the tremors shaking her body from head to toe. It surged into her system, making her faster, stronger, more alert. A natural steroid gifting her with the chemical turbo-boost she needed to do what had to be done.

But Valentina had no great plan.

Escape was the *only* word her muddled mind could conjure.

There was no miracle idea about what to do next.

It had all happened too fast.

Her mind was a whirling, confused mess of fragmented thoughts and memories. A spinning maelstrom she struggled to mentally process. She tried to focus, slow it down, and let her brain play catch up. Formulate a strategy. Valentina knew she couldn't keep running like this. She *had* to go back. Find her squad. Help them.

If they had survived...

Shaking her head in denial, she screwed her eyes shut and clenched her fists.

No! They have *to be alive. Have to be!*

They must have run, too. They were simply lost, just as she was, in this *fucking* forest. Her conscience wouldn't allow her to think otherwise, to believe she alone had fled and left her comrades for dead. Abandoned them.

How would she be able to live with herself if that were true?

How could she move forward knowing she was a coward?

But what more could I have done?

She just needed time. A moment to gather her wits and get her bearings.

Her hand desperately clutched at her side as a new pain stabbed her sharply like a relentless knife. She hissed a blasphemous curse under her breath.

Stitch.

She had become lazy, let her fitness slide. If she survived this, she vowed to get back into shape. To be ready to fight—not bent double and panting like a dog on a summer day.

Sweat dripped from her brow as she felt a fresh sting of rising bile. Valentina heaved, bringing forth a little vomit, which she promptly spat out onto the grassy floor. She coughed, struggling to clear her throat, but the vile flavor persisted.

Water. What I wouldn't give for a sip of water right now.

Trying to ignore it, she forced her eyes to scan the thick vegetation around her.

They *would* find her. It was only a matter of time.

From the corner of her eye, she saw movement. Her head

whipped around, adrenaline surging again. Her leg muscles tensed, readying her for a desperate flight into the rainforest once more. But her mind shackled her with dark notions.

What's the point? There's no escape.

Her hand reflexively reached for her hip, to the holster she already knew was empty. Her weapon lay miles away. Abandoned on the jungle floor somewhere. All she had was her boot-knife with which to protect herself. Snatching it from its sheath, Valentina brandished it toward the movement she had detected but knew instinctively that hand-to-hand combat was useless against what was coming.

The foliage parted.

Her time expired.

She ran.

| 1 |

THERAPY

— **Gayle Knightley** —
— *Friday* — *Nexus City, Iceland* —

"I imagine...you'd like to know what's been going on since we last saw each other."

It wasn't a question.

Gayle sat stiffly in her chair, left leg crossed over right, foot bobbing agitatedly. Her whole demeanor was one of barely disguised irritation. It was his reassuring smile that got under her skin. Projecting the soothing calm only a psychiatrist could.

"That would be a good place to start, yes," Dr. Griffin said in a measured tone that only served to compound her irascibility.

"Well, let's see," Gayle replied sarcastically. "After I got all my friends killed, my uncle made me an offer I *literally* couldn't refuse. Return to the Human Fae Alliance Academy to teach a bunch of kids to essentially be our replacements. A job I am cosmically ill-suited for. My father was in on this cunning plan which caused...a rift, of sorts, between us. We didn't get a chance... *I* didn't take the opportunity to make amends with him before..." Biting back the sting of tears she stared at the floor, gathering herself before continuing. "...before the bomb went off at the Nexus Summit. It took his life and the life of someone I had very recently considered a potential new friend." She glared at him. "So, yeah...life's been just peachy."

"It's not been an easy year for you."

"You think?" Gayle sniped.

Dr. Griffin quietly scribbled a few notes in his leather-bound notepad, which only served to escalate Gayle's level of irritation. On one hand, she didn't care what he was writing. The sooner these sessions were over and done with, the sooner she could move on with her life. On the other hand, she *really* wanted to know what notations he was making about her.

What psychological crap he was feeding back to her uncle.

Her eyes flicked to the clock on the wall, watching the second-hand tick quietly around the face, unaware that her foot was now bobbing in sync with it.

For fuck's sake! How can we be only five minutes into this bullshit?

"Maybe we should tackle each issue independently..."

God, she wanted to tell him to fuck off, but if she terminated this session before the hour was up, she wouldn't hear the end of it from her uncle, her sisters, her mother, Lana...the list was endless.

"Where do you want to start?" Gayle muttered in resignation.

"How's the knee?"

Her eyes glanced toward the healing joint. She hadn't expected him to begin there. There was nothing to see, of course. The bandages were safely hidden beneath the long black skirt she'd borrowed from her mother.

"Better." The lie was reflexive. She immediately corrected herself. "Better...than it was. I had a moment, a few weeks back, but it's okay now."

Why did I admit to that?

It was a rhetorical question; she knew why. Gayle had been skeptical counseling would be of any use, but she had promised her sisters, Lana, Amanda, and Gabe that she would be open and honest.

She'd promised her father.

"A moment?" Dr. Griffin tilted an eyebrow quizzically.

"I was running. Tripped and fell," Gayle clarified. "It took a pretty hard knock."

"How did that make you feel?"

"Scared," Gayle said truthfully.

"You thought you had re-injured it?"

She nodded. "Yeah, I thought maybe..."

He said nothing; simply left her to organize her thoughts, her feelings. Griffin knew when to push, and when to back off. He was good at that. Never putting words in her mouth, only prompting her to find her own answers.

"I have thirty-two physical scars on my body. That's a fact. I know...I keep count. Seventeen of those are from Valletta. I may have survived, but...my days of looking good naked are a long way behind me."

She brushed back her dark, candy-floss-colored hair, tucking it behind her left ear, exposing one such scar. It arced down the back of her cheek, running in a jagged crescent from ear to throat.

"This is the most obvious." Gayle gestured at it. "The rest are routinely covered up by my CombatSkin, or jeans and a long-sleeved jumper. But this one...this is the one I can't hide. Nobody ever mentions it. Honestly, I wouldn't care much if they did. Flesh wounds heal. They scar...but they heal."

"You talk about them like they're badges of honor."

Gayle bristled. It felt like an accusation aimed at making her feel shallow. Dr. Griffin was correct, though. Each mark *was* a kind of twisted souvenir of a job well done. Or, at a more basic level, of being a survivor. Only a moment ago she'd talked about how those scars had ruined her naked appearance, yet she wasn't shy about her body. She hadn't worried about running in a crop top and gym shorts that day with Michael when she tripped.

"Maybe," she shrugged. "Probably."

"So, why is this injury any different?"

"The knee..." she continued quietly, "it's not just cosmetic. It's...functional. It feels like...the end of something."

"Your ability to be a soldier?"

"Maybe. I certainly don't *feel* like an all-conquering, monster-slaying goddess anymore. I feel..." She knew the word she was looking for, but she didn't want to say it. The doctor filled in the blank.

"Vulnerable?"

She nodded. "For the first time since..." She drew a deep breath. "Since Valerio died. Valletta was a watershed moment. To lose my team...to see Amanda like that...to be *so* badly wounded I could barely stand, let alone walk... Yes, I felt vulnerable. I faced my own mortality for the first time. For years we...I...had considered life to be clear-cut. Victory or death. This injury showed me that things aren't so...uncomplicated."

"That your career may end not with death, but through disability?"

Gayle nodded again but said nothing.

"How did it make you feel when your uncle offered you the role at the Academy?"

"Hated it," she said honestly. "Hated him."

"Why?"

"They say those who can, do. Those that can't, teach. If I became a teacher, I was admitting I was washed up."

"But you took the job anyway?"

"I didn't have a choice."

"We always have a choice, Gayle. With your skills, you could have resigned and had a lucrative career as a freelancer." Griffin echoed the words she had spoken to Norbel back when he made the offer. For a moment, she wondered if he had consulted her uncle about any of this.

Fuck! Why does he have to be right every bloody time?!

"I suppose I could have, yes."

"So, why did you stay?"

"It's home," Gayle said simply. "I thought it would be difficult...to go back there. But it was actually harder not to."

"And how do you feel about it now?"

Her smile was small but genuine. "Honestly, pretty good."

"What changed?"

"I...met someone."

"In a romantic sense?" Dr. Griffin prodded.

"I like him." Gayle took a deep breath. "If I'm being honest, I like him more than I'd probably care to admit to myself. Of course, *that* comes with its own unique set of...problems."

"Why would it cause problems?"

Gayle arched an eyebrow at him.

"The issues you and I have talked about in the past were never rooted in you falling in love with someone," Griffin said pointedly. "Quite the opposite in fact."

"First day I met Michael, I tried to...manipulate him." She felt her cheeks burn. "To make him do things my way."

"Did he?"

"No." She shook her head and snorted with amusement. "Actually, he resisted...and I stopped when I realized what I was doing. Point is, I regressed. I did something I vowed I wouldn't do again."

"And how did that make you feel?"

"Like shit." She shrugged. "Disappointed...in myself."

There was a moment of silence between them as Gayle nibbled her thumbnail and gathered her thoughts. It abruptly occurred to her she was talking about much more than she really wanted to. But then that was his job, wasn't it? To tease out of her the things she wanted to repress.

"When you came to me eighteen months ago," Dr. Griffin finally said softly, "the problem you presented me with was not one of the heart, Gayle. It was something very different. A matter of biology. You say you like this Michael?"

"I...do. He's honest, fair, honorable, kind...generous with his forgiveness." She laughed lightly. "Basically, he's everything I'm not."

"So, you don't think you deserve the love of a man like Michael? What would he think?"

"He would disagree," she said immediately. "We had a moment, just before..." Tears started welling in her eyes. She bit her lip, trying to suppress them, but couldn't stop one from rolling down her cheek.

"The explosion," Dr. Griffin said with genuine sympathy. "I'm truly very sorry for your loss."

She had no words, simply nodded. After a few moments spent calming her emotions, she continued. "I love my father, but I was *so* angry at him...I didn't talk to him for weeks. I felt like a pawn in a game he and my uncle were playing. He tried to make amends, but I pushed him away. I wasted our time with an inability to see past my ego..." Her voice broke. She couldn't hold back the tears any longer, so she stopped trying. "For a brief moment...I thought maybe I could be happy. Maybe I *could* have something with Michael. I was looking forward to seeing Dad, to telling him about it. He'd have *loved* Michael and been so proud of me. Then the bomb went off and..." Her throat tightened and the words couldn't push past her sobs.

She couldn't tell him how she had arrived at the Nexus City hospital too late to say goodbye. How her siblings had met her on the landing pad as the Banshee touched down. How, as soon as Ally shook her head, she had known her chance was past. How she had fallen to her knees and wept as her sisters held her trembling form.

Dr. Griffin didn't push, simply let her sit in silence for a few minutes as she recovered her equilibrium.

"You mentioned you lost someone else in the incident? A new friend?"

"Mercy balthazaar," Gayle nodded.

"You grieve for her, too?" he said with a hint of surprise.

Gayle gave a shallow smile. "Yeah, I do. She was a good person. She didn't deserve to die like that. I'd only met her a few days before, and I'd been prepared to hate her. She was a Vampyrii, and I was a Hunter. I'd fought her kind all over the world for so long that I'd become indoctrinated to see matters in absolute terms. Humans and monsters. Meeting her was a *revelation*. She wasn't a monster, just a person. A friend.

"In a black and white world...she was a shade of grey."

| 2 |

AFTERMATH

— **Allyson Knightley** —
— *Friday* — *Nexus City, Iceland* —

"ALLYSON!"

Ally closed her weary eyes and massaged her temples, being careful to avoid the stitches knitting together her wound. She muttered a quiet curse before drawing a deep, calming breath. She held it briefly, then exhaled deliberately as she turned to greet her sister.

"Gayle. I've told you—repeatedly—you *can't* be here." It was impossible to keep the exasperation out of her voice.

"The fuck I can't," was the somewhat belligerent response.

She had seen her sister like this before—a seething mass of unbridled frustration looking for a suitable outlet. While Ally was reluctant to be on the receiving end of Gayle's annoyance, experience had taught her if *she* didn't bear the brunt of it, an unwitting member of the public probably would.

Fortunately for the general population, Ally had a conscience.

"He was *your* father, too," Gayle said accusingly, "so how come *you're* allowed to frequent the crime scene?"

As she spoke, Gayle gesticulated around the room at large, pointing out the destruction wrought on the World Council Chamber. Long, ugly cracks climbed up the crystal windows creating haphazard lightning bolt scars across their formerly flawless surface. Ally had no idea how they would repair those, though she was sure the Fae who had created them would have a technique.

Magic, maybe?

The elegant wooden beams that framed the crystal and arched gracefully to the apex of the dome had also suffered, their pale finish marred with dark charring as a result of the explosion's intense heat. Ally was no expert, but her police training had given her a basic knowledge of explosives. The incendiary device had been relatively small with a limited blast radius, aimed at killing people, not at destroying infrastructure. Hence, the damage sustained seemed mostly superficial.

The shallow-dished area that had housed the once magnificent AuthaGraphic holo-map now sat askew, the force of the detonation enough to tilt its base and fracture the crystal dome built to protect it. The holographic image inside stuttered through its broken animation. Ally stared at it, reflecting upon the metaphor it represented.

This incident would change the world.

Break it in ways she couldn't even fathom.

But then, that wasn't her responsibility. Piecing the world back together was the work of diplomats like her mother and...

She swallowed and gritted her teeth. Her voice coming as a growl. "Because I'm the Chief of Security here. *This* is my job. This is *my* investigation."

"Well, maybe I can help?" A more conciliatory tone crept into Gayle's voice.

But Allyson wasn't about to fall for that old trick. She cocked an eyebrow in the direction of her elder sister and sighed. "No," she said firmly. "What you'll end up doing is hindering. Anyway, I thought you were seeing your therapist today?"

"Just finished," Gayle exhaled heavily. "What are the odds that my therapist just happened to be in Nexus this week?"

Ally raised an eyebrow at the heavy sarcasm in her sister's

tone. "Luck had nothing to do with it," she replied flatly. "Uncle Norbel thought Dr. Griffin might be able to help with the trauma and grief counseling. That's why he's here."

"Then why haven't *you* been to see him?" Gayle shot back.

"Because I'm busy," Ally snapped.

"Well, like I said, maybe I can help. Look, I may not be an investigative journalist like Carrie," Gayle said, referencing their younger sibling, "or a 'master detective' like you, but I *do* have skills. Just tell me what you've found so far."

"You already know." Anger was seeping into Allyson's demeanor now. "And honestly, I shouldn't even have told you *that* much. My job is on the line here."

"Anything," Gayle persisted. "I promise you can trust me not to run my mouth off."

"That's not the point, and you're not listening." Ally felt her temper ratchet up another notch. "There's nothing new to tell you. We're still investigating."

"Still? It's been *days*!"

Allyson didn't want to hear another word. This whole conversation was a distraction from the job she was meant to be doing. Which was exactly her point.

"Okay, enough! Fucking, enough! I've *already* had to fend off the 'helpful' hand Carrie was trying to provide this morning. For fuck's sake, don't *either* of my sisters have any respect for me or my position? I don't swan into your lives trying to take over *your* job, do I? So, please...show some bloody courtesy for mine. If there was anything...*anything*...I thought either of you could do to help, I'd have sodding asked already. So, why don't you just *piss off* and leave me to get on with it?" She stabbed an accusatory finger at Gayle, invading her personal space.

The look on her sister's face was a study in surprise at the role reversal taking place. Gayle was the angry sister, Carrie the enthusiastic sister, and Allyson was supposed to be the calm one.

The rational one.

The room fell silent at her outburst, and she was suddenly acutely aware that all she could hear was the droning of the news channel which was being shown on the large displays in the chamber.

"And can somebody please turn those *fucking* screens off!" she shouted as she turned on her heel and angrily stalked back over to the area which had once been host to the Pack Nation delegation.

There was nothing there now but scorch marks and the splintered remnants of a once beautiful table and chairs. She felt a sharp pain in the palm of her right hand and realized she was clenching her fist so tightly her nails were digging into the soft flesh. Willing her trembling hand to unclench, she glanced at it, wondering if she had drawn blood.

There were marks, but no crimson stain to signify the breaking of the skin.

Allyson was so lost in thought she failed to notice her sister's approach until a hand squeezed her shoulder gently.

"I'm sorry, Ally. I know I am *freaking* the fuck out. Losing Dad… I forget you're grieving too, and I apologize for being a selfish bitch-sister."

Ally put both her hands over her face and screwed her eyes shut, trying to hold back the tears. She drew another deep, cleansing breath and held it. Exhaustion was making her emotional and that wasn't going to help anyone. She exhaled slowly between pursed lips, then turned to face her sister with a forced smile. She was about to say something when Gayle shook her head, interrupting.

"You're working too hard," she said gently. "You *need* to take some time to look after yourself. You're not doing the investigation any good by burning the candle at both ends. You need sleep and a shower so you can come at this with fresh eyes."

Of course, she was right,

"Yeah, I know. I'm sorry, too." Ally reciprocated the gesture and immediately felt some of the anger dissipate. "Truth is, Sis, I'm going over and over this in my head. What did I do wrong? What loophole did I leave open that allowed someone to bring a *bomb* into the Summit chamber?"

Her older sister threw her a sympathetic look as she responded. "We both know this is *not* your fault."

"Do we? Over a decade of Nexus Summits without major incident, and now the first time I'm in charge, disaster ensues."

"This has been on the cards for years. There are threats every year..."

"That's what Fran said. And Dad. But I had a feeling... I knew this was going to happen."

"Don't be ridiculous. There's no way you could have known. I spoke with Fran and she assured me your team did *everything* they should have. You really shouldn't take this personally."

"This *is* personal. They killed our father, Gayle. Our fucking dad. It doesn't *get* any more personal for me. I'm going to get to the truth of this, I swear to God."

She avoided looking at Gayle and instead cast her gaze back to the ruined remains of the Pack Nation area, trying to find some clue to lead her to the people responsible. Thus far, she had very little physical evidence to work with, the bomb having either obliterated or spread any trace remains all over the room. What she was left with were the high-definition camera feeds, which she had watched so many times the footage was scarred indelibly into her memory.

It felt weird, watching it and knowing she had been there amongst the carnage as it unfolded. The video seemed much more...real somehow.

Mercy balthazaar had stood from her seat behind the New Victus delegate table, an excited smile on her face, her auburn hair pulled back in a beautifully braided ponytail. She had picked up the official silver attaché case containing the bomb and walked out to meet Ambassador Sabadini of Pack Nation, heading clockwise around the walkway, skirting the holomap.

The next bit had been hard for Allyson to watch.

Her father had risen from his central seat at the FSE table as if bearing witness to the exchange. To his left, his aide,

Narissa, also stood and turned slightly to face the approaching Sabadini who was heading toward Mercy, hand extended. Allyson wasn't sure if he was looking to shake Mercy's hand or simply take the case from her. The answer was redundant. As Mercy walked past Allyson's father toward the Pack Nation table, the bomb detonated.

At that moment, the cameras had ceased functioning, the shockwave from the explosion rendering them instantaneously useless.

She was glad for that small mercy.

The force of the explosion had thrown Ally back into one of the supporting pillars, giving her a concussion, amongst other injuries. Her memory of the actual event was…fragmented. Blurry. It was one thing to know what had happened to her father in this room. It would be quite another to have to watch it again. The screen going blank was a kindness.

Allyson pushed her hand through her hair, smoothing back the mane of sapphire-blue and tucking it behind her ear while considering the state of her appearance. Since the attack, she'd had little opportunity for sleep or personal hygiene. Her hair felt tangled and greasy, and she figured the black dye was almost completely gone by now. The thought made her glance at the shattered mirror hanging askew on the wall to check. In it, she saw herself, and Gayle stood just behind her. For two sisters who were often mistaken for twins, the difference today couldn't be starker.

Her sister stood with her arms crossed over her chest. She was dressed casually in a white sweater, long black skirt, and matching boots, while sporting little makeup, as usual. Her long pink hair was down, tumbling across her shoulders. Ally, on the other hand, appeared disheveled in the same crumpled uniform she'd been wearing for days, and her hair looked flat and lifeless.

I look like shit.

Ally pursed her lips and cursed under her breath. Her father would be disappointed in her; this was no way for a Chief of Security to act. Gayle was right—she needed a few minutes to get back to her home for a shower and a change of clothes.

She gave a silent thanks to the fact that the chamber was now a closed crime scene. Off-limits to anyone but her security staff and a sister who didn't seem to respect those kinds of boundaries.

God forbid anyone important sees me like this.

"Is that who I think it is?" Gayle muttered quizzically.

Ally flicked her eyes in the direction her sister was looking and saw the well-dressed woman with the distinctive white stripe in her raven hair. She looked just as stunning as she had the night of the gala. Ally groaned, her embarrassment ratcheting up another few notches.

Typical! Of all the people to walk in right now!

"That *is* Lyssa Balthazaar, right?" Gayle continued as her phone beeped. "I think she's coming over here."

Conflicting emotions surged through Allyson's already crowded head. Just a few days prior, the woman approaching them had filled Allyson's thoughts, and dreams, with pleasant possibilities. A state of mind conceived on the night they had shared a bed together, a mere fortnight ago. Now, however, that mind was wrestling with grief and her need to find answers.

Lyssa being here complicated matters.

She took yet another deep breath and tried to steel herself for the inevitable awkward conversation. Gayle interrupted her preparation, looking at the phone she had fished from her pocket.

"Ally," she said seriously, gesturing at the screens that had not been turned off as requested, "New Victus is about to make a statement on the bombings."

| 3 |

THE BLAME GAME

— Sebastian StormHall —
— Friday — Nexus City, Iceland —

"Four days ago," Sebastian StormHall began, "our world was on the verge of something *truly* historic."

He surveyed the assembled throng of journalists, all eager for a soundbite to use for their news feeds. Within minutes, what Sebastian said here and now would be disseminated across the world. Pack Nation and the FSE had made their statements inside hours of the bombing, but he had bided his time. He made them wait for his remarks, stoking anticipation and speculation.

What was he going to say?

The truth, of course.

"New Victus intended to present a proposal at the Nexus Summit which would have opened negotiations with the North American Alliance and Pack Nation to transfer control of the western states. Our proposal was to relinquish North Dakota, South Dakota, Nebraska, Kansas, Oklahoma, and Texas back to the NAA. The proposition was to also include all the states between those and our currently disputed border along the San Andreas front.

"It was an initiative to *finally* bring the hostilities between our nations to a peaceful conclusion."

He paused for dramatic effect.

"There would have been demonstrable benefits for all of us. New Victus would contract, but my people would still have a country to call their own. The NAA would have a place to declare home again.

"The shortened border with Pack Nation would have allowed both countries to effectively deploy fewer troops, enabling our soldiers to return home to their families. We also hoped giving our neighbors to the north a common border with the NAA might encourage the establishment of a peaceful, three-way trade agreement to bolster all of our fledgling nations' economies."

Another calculated pause as he looked out across the silent journalists. Their faces demonstrated the shock at the revelation of his proposal.

"You were to have learned all of this by way of the diplomatic process. Our hope was this concession on our part might change the narrative on New Victus. I firmly believe we Vampyrii are a misunderstood race. As a people, we have long been seen as villains on the world stage.

"Tragically, our message of peace was supplanted by one of a very different kind. That of violence. A violence that I, as Grand Chancellor of New Victus, *cannot* condone. And yet a violence perpetrated against both the FSE and Pack Nation for which I must accept responsibility."

A murmur went around the room, each of the assembled press wondering if he was about to admit to bombing the conference. *That,* however, was not part of Sebastian's speech.

"I sent a representative to the Summit who I judged would be accepted more openly than if I had attended in person. I placed my trust in Ambassador Lyssa Balthazaar, an individual known to have opposed some of my policies in the past, but someone I felt was well placed to favorably push this proposal through.

"My judgment was flawed, for which I apologize to the families of Ambassador Sabadini, Ambassador Knightley, and FSE Ambassadorial Aide Narissa. They died as a result of this terrible attack on the Nexus Summit, a terrorist action we suspect was planned and undertaken by House Balthazaar."

The murmur in the room turned to a palpable buzz.

"Our investigation into the proceedings has thus far revealed House Balthazaar representatives were responsible for smuggling the explosive device both into the city and then into the conference chamber. The device was delivered to the Pack Nation delegation personally by Mercy balthazaar, Lyssa Balthazaar's first lieutenant. It is noteworthy to mention Ambassador Balthazaar herself was absent for the first day of the Summit due to...personal matters.

"At this time, it is our belief that the explosive was detonated prematurely, catching Mercy balthazaar in the blast radius and leading to her accidental death.

"While this matter is under investigation, all House Balthazaar representatives in Nexus are being arrested and held on suspicion of terrorism. At this point, we would urge both Pack Nation and the FSE *not* to harbor members of House Balthazaar within their territory. Furthermore, we extend this advice to the other embassies here in Nexus City."

Another dramatic pause. It was time to put the icing on the cake.

"New Victus remains dedicated toward global peace. To all the citizens of the world having a place and, more importantly, a voice.

"With this in mind, I am confirming, here and now, the proposal I detailed at the start of this briefing will still stand. I will personally be visiting with ambassadorial delegations for both Pack Nation and the North American Alliance to present this offer and directly negotiate in good faith.

"I will not let the violent actions of a small subset of our nation dictate our presence on the international stage. House Balthazaar does *not* speak for New Victus. *I* am that voice, and as such, I will put us on a course for peace and prosperity.

"Thank you all for your time and your patience during these difficult events.

"I will now open the floor to your questions."

The hand of every journalist in the room shot urgently into the air. StormHall's expression maintained a practiced look of compassion in the face of this tragedy.

This was all going according to plan.

| **4** |

SANCTUARY

— Lyssa Balthazaar —
— Friday — Nexus City, Iceland —

While the eyes of everyone in the room were now fixed on her, Lyssa's eyes were locked with Allyson's.

She'd had a vague plan to come here and try to talk with Allyson. To express her condolences. Then Storm's press conference had been broadcast on the large screens in the Summit chamber.

She had been afraid of the rumblings coming out of New Victus, the ever-shifting blame that was being unambiguously spread around. Some of the fingers were pointing to Pack Nation as the aggressors, while others were shading House Balthazaar as the culprits and, by extension, the other Progenitor Houses. Part of a conspiracy to overthrow the StormHall regime. Her fears had evidently been justified—StormHall had just laid the blame for all of it squarely at her feet.

Fortunately, she had already put plans into motion for this contingency. Her House would be secure. The question now became...could Lyssa find a safe haven for herself?

She stared at Allyson. Lyssa couldn't deny the attraction. They had shared far more than a bed that night. They had talked intimately and freely, and while they had only scratched the surface of each other's lives, Lyssa felt like Ally *knew* her. Like they had experienced decades together, rather than scant hours. She was confident Allyson wouldn't blindly believe the things of which Storm was accusing her. She was counting on the mutual connection they had made.

But Allyson had lost her father in the explosion.

In this very room.

This was a mistake...

Suddenly there was a far more pressing concern for Lyssa. New Victus security would be looking for her, to arrest her on Storm's orders. There were too many eyes on her; they would already know by now where she was. She had to leave and find somewhere to hide until she could be extracted to safety.

I'm so sorry.

She silently mouthed her words of apology to Allyson, then turned and fled the chamber, unsure of where she was heading. She just knew she had to get out before Storm's lackeys arrived. Her best option was to head into the FSE sector to find a way to contact Damian Dane. Surely, *he* would be able to help her.

"LYSSA!"

Stopping in her tracks, she turned to see Allyson running toward her, a serious look on her face.

"Ally, I..." She stumbled over her words, not sure what to say. "It wasn't me. Or Mercy. We didn't have anything to do with..."

Allyson shook her head, urging her to be quiet. "Lyssa, trust me when I say I don't believe StormHall's explanation for one second. But they've put an alert out for you to all security forces. NVSec is already on their way here. I'm supposed to detain you."

Ally frantically looked over her shoulder. The corridor they were in was empty. Lyssa knew what she was thinking—that wouldn't last long.

"Go to my apartment. Now," Ally said, pressing her key card into Lyssa's palm. "Do not be seen. Do not talk to *anyone*. No calls, no nothing. Just hang tight and I'll be with you as soon as I can. Then we can start getting to the bottom of what exactly is going on."

"Thank you," Lyssa said, a measure of relief plain in her voice. "Allyson, I need to get Mercy out of here, too. She can't be given over to Storm."

"We'll talk about it later—"

"Please! It's important," Lyssa insisted. "More important than my safety. *Please.*" Her last word was spoken in a pleading tone. She hated feeling like this, but in a matter of moments, Storm had put her on the back foot, isolating her in a place where she had no allies and nowhere to turn.

Except, maybe, Allyson Knightley.

"Dammit, Lyssa."

Lyssa watched her one-night lover rake a hand through her tangled hair.

Allyson looked stressed. "I'll see what I can do. Now go. Please. Before you're caught."

She felt Allyson give her an urgent push as she turned back toward the conference chamber. Time was almost up. Lyssa could hear footsteps approaching. She silently mouthed her thanks then turned and ran, clutching the keycard tightly in her hand, trying to remember where Allyson's apartment was.

The last time she had been there, she had been less than totally sober. The memory of how they'd gotten there was fuzzy at best.

It took an hour to make her way stealthily into the FSE sector, the route becoming loosely memorable as she trod it. The bridge they had stumbled over where Lyssa ditched her heels. The lamppost Allyson had leaned against when the alcohol left her feeling dizzy. Landmarks representing moments that, even in this darkest of times, brought a small smile to Lyssa's lips.

Finally, she let herself into Allyson's apartment, and the memories came at her in a flood of sensation. While her home looked vaguely familiar, it was the smells that linked the present to her recollections. She leaned back against the door as she shut it behind her, closing her eyes and breathing deeply through her nose. The sweet smell of honey permeated the air—Allyson's distinctive scent. She spent a moment basking in it, a welcome distraction from the events of the last few days.

Welcome...but fleeting.

She opened her eyes, suddenly aware of the fatigue sweeping through her. She had barely slept for three days now. Ever since the explosion. Her time had been spent coordinating contingency plans for her House. Balthazaar would have already been moved by now...Nykola would have seen to that straight away. She had a plan for the safety of her kin, but she needed time to take action. Time that was fast running out.

Now, I just need to figure out how I'm going to get out of this mess...

The current predicament was not something for which she had strategized. Keeping her family safe had always been the top priority. Protecting herself? Not so much.

Right now, though, she was too tired to think straight. She walked slowly to Allyson's bedroom, recognizing the large bed on which they had made love after the Nexus Gala. The linens were the same. Lyssa lay on the bed, curling up into a protective ball. The sheets had been cleaned recently, but there was still a trace of Allyson's scent on them; a scent that made her feel safe for the first time in days.

Within moments, she was sound asleep.

| 5 |

HOME

— **Gayle Knightley** —
— *Friday — Nexus City, Iceland* —

The old axiom was true—a home *was* much more than simply bricks and mortar.

Gayle had never really felt an affinity for her parents' apartment in Nexus City in the same way as she did for the farm back in Ely. She was a country girl at heart, preferring the tranquility a rural setting offered; city life was not for her. Still, this place *had* once felt like home.

However, without her father's presence, a huge piece of what made the apartment a home was absent. Something Gayle was struggling to reconcile.

She sat alone on the bed in the guestroom, conflicted. The room was comfortable enough, and it had the hallmarks of her parents' taste, but it was simply a guest room. There were no photographs of family, no personal knick-knacks. It was a blank slate to which she had no connection.

Yet, the rest of the apartment was filled with painful memories. The pictures of her and her sisters, her father's constantly mounting pile of books he always said he would get around to reading yet never did...

And now never would.

Her parents were good at creating homes, places where you felt you belonged from the moment you walked in. Now, though, it hurt to look upon those small touches that made it special, and the neutral décor of the guestroom left her cold.

Honestly, she didn't know which she preferred right now.

She heard the sliding door to the apartment whisper open then closed and knew by the absence of any other sounds it was her mother who had entered. Where Ally and Carrie would have made their presence known by their clumsy stomping, Serlia was light on her feet. Taking a cleansing breath and wiping away the tears, Gayle arose and braced herself to see her mother.

Serlia was in the kitchen, seemingly talking quietly to herself as she stood staring out the window at the Goðafoss...the aptly named 'Waterfall of the Gods.' As Gayle walked quietly out of the guestroom, she saw her mother give a small smile before turning to greet her.

"Sorry, Mum. I didn't mean to interrupt anything."

"You're not interrupting, dear. I was just enjoying the view. Jaymes lobbied hard to get this studio simply so we could wake up every morning to see this."

Gayle slid her arms around her mother from behind, hugging her tightly and placing her chin on her shoulder so she could admire the breathtaking vista with her.

"Dad always did have an eye for the spectacular."

"That he does," Serlia agreed.

"I thought Carrie was with you?"

"She was. She's not left my side since..." Serlia seemingly couldn't bring herself to say it. "I sent her on errands. I needed a little space."

"Do you want me to leave?"

"No," her mother said firmly, then repeated more gently, "no. You and I... It would be nice to spend some time with you. I know you're closer to your father than to me, but...I do love you, Gayle."

"I know, and I love you, too." She kissed her mother on the shoulder before extracting herself from the hug. "I think it's natural for a child to bond more closely with one parent or the other, but it doesn't mean I have ever loved you any less than I did Dad."

"You're right, of course. Carrie and I bonded similarly. Sometimes I feel for Allyson. As the middle child, I sometimes fear she felt left out."

"Allyson is fine," Gayle said reassuringly. "She's tough as old boots. Always the independent spirit."

"Good Lord, no." Serlia looked sideways at her daughter. "That was always you, my dear. You used to drive your father and me crazy with your need to be out on your own. Allyson, on the other hand…idolized you. You truly do not realize the profound impact you have had on her life. How much she modeled herself after her older sister."

"I'm not sure *that's* true." Gayle smiled sadly. "The way I screwed up my life… She's the role model. I'm the one in therapy, remember?"

Serlia glanced away from Gayle for a moment, as if listening to something, and then chuckled. "Life is fond of—"

"'—throwing us curveballs. It's how we swing the bat that makes us who we are.' Dad used to say that to us all the time. I feel like I've had more than my fair share of curveballs lately."

"Life has not been kind to you," Serlia acknowledged.

"Mostly my fault…if I'm brutally honest," Gayle sighed.

"What matters is where you are now. What you're doing about it. You made Jaymes extremely proud for taking the steps to make things better."

"Maybe it's a case of too little, too late, though."

"Now, you know this is *not* the philosophy your father taught you," her mother said sternly. "He passionately believes everything happens for a reason. That everything happens at the right *time*. The time it's supposed to."

"Even his death?" Gayle asked.

Serlia nodded. "Yes," she said softly, smiling sadly. "Even his death."

Gayle had never really engaged with her mother in deep philosophical discussion. She was right, of course—that was exactly what her father had always believed. To him, brooding on past mistakes simply stunted one's growth. Since life moved on, why live looking back? In her youth, she had also prescribed to this philosophy; however, somewhere along the way, she lost sight of it. Far too much time had been spent dwelling on the past and suffering for it. She bitterly regretted not letting go of her anger at him sooner, for his role in getting her back to the Academy.

With that in mind...

"I was thinking... Perhaps it's time I head back to London."

"Already?" Serlia was shocked.

Gayle nodded. "Truth is, I think I'm getting under Allyson's feet. You have Carrie—"

"—driving me crazy," Serlia interjected.

"Maybe. But at least she's still here for you. I can't help in any real capacity, and I just feel like..." She paused, searching for the words to describe how she was feeling. "I saw Dr. Griffin. It was...good."

"He's helping?" Serlia asked.

"Not at first," Gayle laughed gently. "But lately...I think I've had a breakthrough."

"Because of this man...Michael?"

Gayle looked surprised by her mother's casual name-drop.

Serlia gave a small chuckle and a dismissive wave of her hand. "Oh, *please*," she said. "Both of your sisters have mentioned your change in attitude lately. They attribute it to this Michael's influence."

Gayle recognized the look on her mother's face as a blend of happiness and pride. For a fleeting moment, she felt the slow dawn of that same blur of emotions. She may have been pushing thirty, but Serlia's words made her feel like a little girl again. It felt good to know her parents were proud of her. It was a moment quickly wiped away by a surge of sadness, erupting from deep within Gayle's broken heart.

"Dad would have liked him. He's...good for me. But going home is not about him. It's about feeling useful. I need to do something, and here, I just feel like a spare wheel. Ally has the investigation, Carrie is pursuing her story, while I'm...just loitering and waiting."

"Then you must go to London." Serlia hugged her daughter.

"I said I was considering it. But...I don't want to leave if you need me."

"I'm fine," her mother reassured her. "Honestly. I'm almost five hundred years old, and I have suffered through heartbreak and loss more times than I hope you'll ever know in your life. The specter of death is not one feared by the Fae; we have a different understanding than most others on aspects of life and beyond. While your father's physical manifestation was taken from us abruptly, I understand life moves ever forward, always flowing in one direction. Your father is the great love of my life, my one true soul-mate...

I shall love him for the rest of my days."

"You talk about him like he's still with us?"

Serlia just smiled enigmatically and looked at Gayle with love in her eyes. "For me, he will never be truly gone. Death comes to us all at our pre-destined time. This is the way of The River. Thus, we strive to live our lives to the best of our abilities so when the end comes, we have no regrets. I know your father has no regrets."

"What's 'The River'?" Gayle's curiosity was piqued. "I've not heard you mention it before."

There was a brief flash of something across Serlia's features. Surprise, like she had inadvertently told a secret that wasn't hers to tell. The River. Something about the term was familiar to Gayle, but she couldn't quite place where she had heard it before. Her mother's reaction simply fueled the questions smoldering within her. Serlia smiled and looked at her daughter.

"The River...it's a philosophical belief Fae have. The way of life. It flows toward your destiny. It shepherds your fate as you traverse it to your ultimate destination."

"To your death?"

"Maybe." Serlia shrugged delicately. "Maybe not. For Fae, death is merely a transition to another state of being. Simply because our physical form expires does not mean our journey is ended. Your father...his energy, his soul, still exists. He's all around us."

"I like that philosophy." Gayle smiled. "It makes me feel

better about... I still wish I could have—"

Serlia cut her off with a shake of her head. "Please. No regrets," she said. "You'll get your chance to say all those unspoken words when you meet again..."

"In The River?"

"Yes," Serlia nodded. "In The River."

Gayle looked out the window, staring at the falls while she contemplated her mother's belief. She liked it. It was a comforting thought.

"You've never really spoken to us about Fae philosophy. I'd love to hear more about it."

Her mother was silent for a moment, simply smiling. Gayle had known her mother long enough to read her expressions—she knew a fake smile when she saw one.

"One day," Serlia said quietly. "When will you be heading back to London?"

The change of subject was not subtle. Gayle wondered why her mother was being so evasive about what seemed to be something so benign, but she was empathic enough to know this was not the time to press the issue. Not while they were both grieving. It could wait.

Her instincts told her it was important, though. She had that feeling. A tingle in her subconscious. The feeling like she had just innocently been given a piece to a larger puzzle she couldn't quite see just yet.

| **6** |

SUITS YOU

— **Michael Reynolds** —
— *Friday* — *London, England* —

"It's just...frustrating." Michael sighed, lifting his arms to allow the scanner to whirl around his torso.

Though he tended to be tight-lipped about his feelings, he had to admit that sometimes it felt good to vent. So, it was a good thing his twin sister, Alexa, was doing a diligent job of patiently listening as she reclined in her chair, legs crossed and foot gently bobbing. Despite the tragedy leading to this moment, the circumstances *had* given them something over which to bond after their years of estrangement.

"I'm not sure what you can do about it," she replied with a shrug.

"I keep going over the plans I went through with her sister, Allyson..."

"Plans?" Alexa asked, looking confused.

"Gayle's sister Allyson is the Chief of FSE Security in Nexus City," he explained. "I was asked to review her security arrangements for the Summit, to see if anything had been overlooked."

"And was there?"

Michael shook his head. "No, not really. I made a couple of minor suggestions, but her strategies looked sound. Really good actually. She'd pretty much thought of everything. I've been wracking my brain to think of a detail I...we might have missed. But I can't see it.

"I wanted an answer...or something. Anything. I wanted to be able to look Gayle in the eye and tell her..."

"Tell her what? That this was somehow *your* fault?"

"No, nothing like that." Michael frowned, shaking his head. "More like... Honestly, I don't know. I just wanted to help."

"I don't know the woman personally, but from what you've told me, she's the type who doesn't let others share her pain easily. Look at what happened after she lost her team in Valletta."

Alexa had a point.

It had taken a while to break through Gayle's barriers. To glimpse the heartache and insecurities she was feeling deep down. He was worried this latest blow would lead her to rebuild those walls.

"She's had a rough time of it lately."

"She'll be back," Alexa reassured him. "And when she is, I'm sure things will slowly return to normal."

A series of chimes from the machine indicated it was now finished whirling around Michael, its measurement gathering routine now complete.

A female voice echoed over the room's intercom.

"Thank you, Captain Reynolds. You may step down. Your turn, please, Miss Anderson."

As Michael stepped down from the platform, he gestured for Alexa to take his place.

"I thought you might go back to using your real name."

"I considered it," Alexa shrugged. "But I've been trading on MercNet as Zarra Anderson for three years now. It has a cache of reputation attached to it."

"So, do I call you, Alexa...or Zarra?"

"Lexy is fine, Brother."

A sharp intake of breath drew Michael's attention to the room's arched entry. He turned to see a young woman with chocolate-hued hair cascading across her shoulders, frozen in place with a look of horror on her face. She was hugging herself against the chill in the air. It didn't help matters that she was dressed only in her underwear.

"Becka," Alexa addressed the newcomer innocently, "where are your clothes?"

"I..." Becka flicked her eyes from Michael to Alexa and back again. "I thought for the measurement thing we needed to be...you know...unencumbered. I mean, last time that's how..."

She stopped herself from saying any more as a crimson blush spread across her body. Practically unclothed as she was, there was no hiding it.

"The machine can read you through your clothes. Did I forget to tell you?" Alexa said, a hint of mischief in her tone.

Becka stared daggers at the now giggling Alexa.

"Mikey, this is my partner, Becka Daw—"

"So, you must be the brother Zarra *also* never told me about," Becka said, quickly interrupting Alexa's introduction. Despite her obvious embarrassment, her smile was warm.

"Michael Reynolds. Pleased to meet you, Becka."

"Becka here is my pilot and the logistical heart behind our operation."

Becka shook his hand firmly. There was something familiar about her... Something he couldn't quite put his finger on.

"Have we met?"

A look crossed Becka's face he couldn't decipher, but she shook her head vigorously. "Nope," she said firmly. "We've never met."

"How long have you been partners with my sister?" he asked, changing the subject.

Alexa had stepped up onto the plinth and was raising her arms to allow the machine to perform the same process it had just completed on Michael. A series of spindly mechanical arms started their choreographed dance around her, taking detailed measurements of her body.

CombatSkins were the bespoke battle-suits of the future. Each was custom-tailored to the individual's body and biometric requirements. Bulletproof and temperature regulating, they could also alter their form and color depending on the mission parameters. Additionally, they had built-in sensors which monitored the health and vital statistics of the wearer.

Michael had never worn one. State-of-the-art tech like this was *far* beyond the financial reach of the beleaguered North American Alliance forces. Gayle wore hers all the time, though, saying she found it wonderfully comfortable. Michael, after observing its body-hugging nature, thought it looked anything but. Even if it was, he doubted it would look particularly flattering on him.

Alas, it was mandatory equipment for FSE elite combat squads, which included the 137th Hunters. So, here he was, hoping to be proved wrong.

"Two years," Becka said thoughtfully. "I had just gained my freelancer license and was looking for my next step. I didn't have the resources to go solo, and Alexa had just bought a dropship and needed a pilot. So, we reached a partnership agreement."

"You bought a dropship when you can't fly?" Michael asked his sister.

"I *can* fly…a little," Alexa shrugged. "You need transport to get all the highest paid jobs, and since I'd just invested in her, I thought it best not to risk crashing *Diana* into the ground every time I took the controls."

"You called her *Diana*…" Michael said softly.

Becka grinned. "The Roman goddess of the hunt. I always thought it kinda apt."

"It was our mother's name," Michael added, looking closely at Alexa.

"Oh…" Becka said. "I'm sorry. I didn't know."

The moment of awkward silence was broken by the chimes signifying the end of Alexa's measuring session. The room's intercom sounded again with the same female voice as before.

"Thank you, Ms. Anderson, your measurements have been taken. We'll need to take your other measurements later to program the suit to accommodate your…transformation needs. Ms. Dawkins, if you would be kind enough to step up onto the plinth, please."

Alexa descended from the machine and sat next to her brother. Michael reached out his hand for hers. She took it and squeezed.

"I was surprised when they said they could accommodate for my other form," she chuckled. "They barely batted an eyelid when I asked them. I thought they'd notify the authorities or something."

"The UK entry ban only applies to Vampyrii," Becka stated matter-of-factly. "For instance, Pack Nation citizens can get special visas."

"How do you know that?" Alexa raised her eyebrow quizzically.

Becka shrugged evasively. "I, errr, must have picked it up somewhere... Anyhow, our MercNet credentials got us in, and I sorted the other red tape."

"Actually, talking about *my* 'other' measurements," Alexa said, turning to Michael, "shouldn't you be—"

Michael cut her off mid-question. "You named your dropship after our mother?"

Alexa sighed sadly. "I wanted to honor her in some small way. I named my Jeep after Dad."

"You have a Jeep called *Benjamin*?"

Alexa nodded again. "Yup, stowed aboard *Diana* just in case we need ground transport on a job. We call him *Benny*. Do you think Mom and Dad would have approved of our choices? Where our lives are now?"

Michael didn't have an answer to her question.

Their parents had been career military, so he knew they would be proud both he and Alexa had also served.

However, the events of the last few years were more of a grey area. He chose to think they would have realized their children had made the only choices they could to survive in a dangerous world. There was, however, one thing he knew they would have been disappointed about.

"They'd have been pissed we spent so many years apart," he said eventually.

"I meant to ask..." Becka said from the plinth, arms outstretched. "Why *did* you guys stop talking to each other? Zee never even mentioned she had a twin brother."

An awkward hush descended. Some things should be kept private. This was one of them.

"It was...a family matter," Alexa said sadly. "My fault."

Michael shook his head. "I'm just as much to blame. I've known you were freelancing for a long time. I could have built the bridge myself."

Becka flicked her eyes from Alexa to Michael and back again. "I can see the family resemblance."

The chimes signaled an end to the measuring. Michael was surprised at the brevity of the scan.

"Thank you, Ms. Dawkins," the voice came over the intercom. "So much easier to get a clean scan without clothing being in the way. You can step down now."

She stepped off the platform and headed to the door with a smug look on her face.

"Who feels foolish now?" she asked as she strutted past the two siblings.

Michael laughed at Alexa's surprised expression as Becka exited the room, clearly in a hurry to get back into her clothes, despite her vindication. As she passed him, he got the faint scent of her perfume. Sweet on the air.

Like honey.

| **7** |

TRUTH

— **Lyssa Balthazaar** —
— *Friday — Nexus City, Iceland* —

"Lyssa..." The voice was soft with a hint of urgency. Her brain locked onto the familiar tones and let them lead her back to consciousness.

As her eyelids cracked open, a smile curved her lips at the sight of Allyson Knightley kneeling beside the bed wrapped in a towel. Her dripping hair evidence of the shower she had just taken. Lyssa felt fingers softly stroking her face.

"Allyson..." she mumbled, a stale taste in her dry mouth. "How long—"

"—Have you been asleep?" Ally smiled. "It's been about six hours since I saw you in the chambers. StormHall's conference kicked up a shit-storm I've been trying to deal with all afternoon. How are you feeling?"

"I'm fine," she lied.

That's the question, though, isn't it? How do *I feel?*

Conflicted. That was probably the closest description for the emotions churning in her stomach.

While Lyssa felt profoundly concerned about the safety of her family, she had done as Allyson instructed and not spoken to a soul since they had parted company in the corridor. She knew her family would be worried about her. Nykola was probably already assuming Storm had caught her.

Yet, here in Allyson's apartment—in her bed—Lyssa felt oddly safe. Untouchable. Because here...she didn't feel...alone.

She rubbed at tired eyes, trying to focus on Allyson. The bath-sheet left little to the imagination...including the litany of purple bruises across Allyson's arms, legs, and shoulders. A neat row of stitches sealed a nasty-looking cut on her left temple.

"Oh, Gods, Allyson..." she reached up to gently touch the wound, but Allyson's hand intercepted it en-route.

Ally smiled. "I'll survive."

The expression, body language, and tone of her voice indicated she didn't want to dwell on her injuries, so Lyssa changed the subject. "What's happening out there?"

"NVSec descended on the conference center looking for you. They went home disappointed. StormHall is applying pressure to the FSE to have you extradited if you're found in our territory. Fortunately for us, the current FSE Ambassador is *not* in a frame of mind to be acquiescing to his demands right now."

Lyssa realized Allyson was referring to her mother, Serlia. A wave of awkwardness washed over her. She was a fugitive on the run, hiding in the home of the daughter of the man she was accused of killing through a bungled terrorist attack.

"I am sincerely sorry about what happened to your father..."

Allyson shook her head gently. "It's *not* your fault," she said, a firm certainty in her voice.

Lyssa tilted her head slightly. While she was grateful for Allyson's confidence in her innocence, she did not understand where the belief was coming from. Simply because they had shared one night of passion?

"How can you be so sure?" she asked curiously. "I mean, it's not. I promise you that Mercy and I had nothing to do with it...but how can you be so trusting?"

A smile spread across Allyson's face, and she shifted position to sit cross-legged while tucking an errant strand of her wet hair behind her ear.

"My sisters and I have...gifts, if you can call them that.

Gayle has this natural…charisma which allows her to pretty much talk anyone into doing just about anything. Carrie has an instinctive nose for the story. It's why she became a journalist."

"And your gift?" Lyssa prompted.

"I have a sixth sense for when people are being dishonest. Basically, I'm a human lie detector, which comes in really handy in my line of work. When I was young, my sisters nicknamed me 'uncanny Ally.'

"Watching StormHall's conference…my alarm bells were ringing. He's *full* of bullshit. You, though…you've been honest with me since the night we met."

Lyssa nodded. "I have."

"I know," Ally said softly. "Mercy, too. I haven't had even a hint of dishonesty. I liked her. There's no way I could see *either* of you wrapped up in this."

"And you've *never* been wrong?"

"Are you trying to talk me *into* your guilt?" Allyson laughed lightly.

"Tellus, no!" Lyssa exclaimed. "I just wondered if you're always right."

Allyson considered for a moment and then shrugged. "No," she admitted. "Maybe not *always*. When you deal with criminals regularly, sometimes it's not clear *what* they're lying about, unless you ask a direct question, which is sometimes difficult when you don't know the exact question to ask. But I *can* always tell if they are lying about something to me. With the innocent, though, it's clear cut. You're a flat line on my lie detector—not so much as a blip. StormHall on the other hand…"

"Most of what he said *is* true, though."

"Well, my sense is *less* of a lie detector and more of a sense of when someone is being…deceitful. It's hard to define… So, which bits were true?"

"The proposal mostly," Lyssa admitted. "We *were* offering to cede the Western States back to the NAA, a course of action *I've* been advocating for years. Hence the logic in giving me the responsibility to present it. I also *did* drop out of the conference's first day for personal reasons."

"Which were?"

Lyssa said nothing. Did she want to tell Allyson about her dark family history?

"Lyssa," Allyson said softly, detecting her discomfort. "The more I know, the better position I'll be in to help us find the truth."

Still Lyssa hesitated. "It's a long story..."

"We have time."

Time.

The word touched a nerve with Lyssa, and she jolted upright on the bed.

"Allyson," she said urgently, "Mercy... I need—"

Allyson shook her head, placed a hand on Lyssa's knee, and smiled calmly. "Don't worry. I've sorted it. Mercy's body is in stasis in the FSE Security morgue. I can sneak you in to see her before the autopsy—"

"No, you don't understand," Lyssa said desperately. "No autopsy! I need to get her body back."

Ally frowned at her. "Why? Even *if* I could stop her examination, where are you going to take her? StormHall has declared your entire House blood traitors. I honestly don't know what our options are."

"I need..." Lyssa wracked her brain for a moment. "I need a phone. Not yours, not mine. Can you get me one?"

Ally continued to look confused. "Who do you need to call?"

"It's...another long story," Lyssa repeated, cringing as she heard the cryptic nature of her statements.

"Lyssa," Allyson said plainly, "as much as I believe you're not lying to me, I'm still not going to give you free rein on the back of a one-night stand. You need to give me more."

"Was that all it was to you?" Lyssa said, slightly hurt. "A one-night stand?"

"I think we're getting sidetracked into other topics. But yes...no... I honestly don't know. I don't do one-night stands. But...you're a Vampyrii, and I wasn't even sure if we would ever see each other again...in a personal context. Look, can we get back to the matter at hand?"

"Sorry," Lyssa said quietly. "Of course."

She stood and walked to the glass wall, looking out across the city. It was beautiful at night. The Goðafoss was lit up, and the streetlights twinkled in the light rainfall. She wondered where to start, how much to say.

Be honest. Start at the beginning.

"Roughly two years ago I made contact with Damian Dane."

"The Wolf King?"

Lyssa smiled. "He hates being called that, but yes. Storm's reign over New Victus was problematic for us both and was only going to get worse. I had already contacted some of the other Progenitor Houses, tentatively forging a plan to overthrow his regime."

"To stage a coup?" Ally confirmed.

"Yes. But we needed allies. Hence my efforts to broker peace with Pack Nation. I asked Damian if he would help."

"He agreed?"

"After a fashion." Lyssa hesitated. "We were plotting a coordinated military offensive between the Progenitor Houses, Pack Nation, and hopefully, the NAA forces to the West. My plan hinged on gaining an audience with the NAA and dangling a carrot for them to help us. Essentially offering the same thing Storm is offering them now. The return of the Western States."

"When was this going to happen?"

"There wasn't a date in mind," Lyssa admitted. "But it wasn't far away. The NAA was the last ally we needed. I'd hoped your parents might be able to broker a meeting at the Summit. A few weeks ago, however, things started to go askew..."

"In what way?"

"My sister..." Lyssa took a deep breath; this was not going to be easy to talk about.

"What happened to her?"

"My sister has...had a genetic disorder called Hypersexuality."

"Sounds fun." Allyson raised her eyebrow.

"It's not." Lyssa shook her head. "That's the medical term, but in Vampyrii society, women like my sister are called succubi. It's an illness that makes it challenging to live a normal life. Succubi feed off sexual energy and are driven to..." she winced, "harvest it. The condition also gives them a measure of telepathic aptitude and the ability to target their victims with pheromones designed to arouse and make them suppliant to their will.

"Succubi are *very* rare."

"So, what happened?"

Lyssa sighed. "I kept her medicated and under house arrest in Burlington. She escaped. Freed by, of all things, a Werewolf incubus who led them on a murderous rampage through the forests of Montreal. They were eventually stopped by a bounty hunter Damian hired."

"An incubus?"

"The male equivalent of a succubus," Lyssa explained. "*Also* exceedingly rare."

"What are the chances of that?"

"Exactly what Mercy said. She was suspicious of both the timing and the nature of Vanessa's escape partner."

"Vanessa was your sister?"

Lyssa nodded. "She was killed in the attempt to capture her. Her body was returned to me in New Victus the day I was due to leave for Nexus. I asked Mercy to oversee the early Summit duties on my behalf as I tended to her funeral ritual."

All at once, Lyssa saw a reflection of her own state of mind. There was a sadness in Allyson's eyes that she profoundly recognized. Grief. They had both lost family, yet the woman staring at her with such empathy was holding her life together so much better than Lyssa thought she herself was.

"I'm sorry about your sister," Allyson said quietly.

"How do you do it?" Lyssa whispered. "How can you be so together? So strong after losing your father? I... I feel like I'm drowning."

"Did you not *see* me earlier? Trust me, I'm a complete mess, too."

She stood and gestured around her apartment.

"The last few nights I've been here alone, and I can't sleep," Allyson said softly. "I cry. A lot. Then the alarm goes off, I drag myself out of bed, and head to work. Work helps. Concentrating on helping you helps.

"But, until today, I am ashamed to say my personal hygiene routine had slipped significantly. If my hair had gotten any greasier, it would've been classified a fire hazard."

Her self-deprecating comment elicited a chuckle from Lyssa, which in turn brought about a smile from Allyson.

"You look fine," Lyssa said.

Allyson raised her eyebrow. "Just fine?"

"You look beautiful," Lyssa corrected. "Better?"

"Better," Allyson said. "Now, the way I see it, we have four items to check off our agenda. First, we need to get you a way to communicate with your people. Second, we need to get Mercy's body out of the morgue and out of Nexus. Third, we need to get *you* out of the city to safety."

"And the fourth item?"

"Find the truth about who bombed the Summit and make them pay for what they've done," Allyson said, steel in her voice.

Before Lyssa could respond, she was interrupted by the chime of the apartment's doorbell.

| 8 |

PERSONAL INTERESTS

— Allyson Knightley —
— Friday — Nexus City, Iceland —

"I sincerely hope I am not interrupting anything."

As her uncle crossed the threshold into Ally's apartment, he peered around the lounge as if expecting to find something. There was nothing to see. Lyssa was safely secreted in Ally's bedroom out of sight.

"Not at all, Uncle." Allyson smiled congenially. "I was just taking a shower to freshen up before getting back to work." She gestured toward the towel wrapped tightly around her bosom and the dripping of her still damp hair.

"I have to admit, I was becoming concerned about you. You have been working almost *obsessively* hard this past week."

"It's all under control," Ally assured him. "I just needed a few minutes to freshen up. I'll be back to it within the hour."

Norbel looked at her with an uncomfortable expression. Evidently, his visit wasn't entirely one of concern for his niece.

"That is actually what I came here to talk to you about," he said gravely.

"That sounds disturbingly ominous…"

"I am here in a professional capacity, Allyson. To relieve you of your duties in the investigation." His intonation was flat and emotionless.

Ally stared at him as her mouth dropped open in shock. The words that had just left his lips were the last things she had expected to hear when he walked through the door.

"I..." She searched for a response that wasn't based on profanity. "You just said it yourself—I'm working so hard on this. You can't fire me now. Besides, this is *not* your decision to make. I'm employed by the FSE, not the HFA."

"FSE President De Villiers requested my assistance, temporarily, with matters here in Nexus. Typically, your parents handle such concerns; however, with the current situation being as it is, it was thought my presence may relieve some pressure. Your mother should be allowed to concentrate on items other than matters of state."

"This all seems highly unorthodox..." Allyson said hesitantly.

"These are unorthodox times, Allyson. I will state for the record, no one thinks the inability to prevent this bombing is your responsibility. I read through the report Captain Reynolds wrote for the NAA regarding your security strategies, and I am satisfied every precaution was correctly taken. The action I am implementing is not about blame." Norbel sat on the sofa in Ally's living room and spread his hands in supplication. "Also, to clarify, I am not relieving you of your post as Nexus Security Chief. I am simply doing something that should have been done days ago. As the daughter of one of the victims, you should never have been allowed to run this investigation due to a conflict of interest."

Well, if he's expecting a fight, he's going to get it!

"Conflict of interest?" Ally said in disbelief. "This is my *job*. Investigating is what I do."

"Your father was one of the victims," Norbel stated. "Tell me, Allyson, what would you do if you were in my position? If it was the father of one of your subordinates who had been killed."

Shit!

She couldn't argue—his point was solid. In his position, she *would* be the first person to yank one of her staff from a case if there was a chance personal interests could cloud their judgment. Even so, she could still feel the resentment building within her. There was *no one* better to take on this job. No one better suited to get to the truth of what exactly happened at the Summit.

"General…" She addressed him by his title now that this was official business. "You know I have unique skills that can be of use in this investi—"

Her uncle cut her off with a wave of his hand. "Allyson, I have no doubt whatsoever about your skills," he said. "Furthermore, I agree with you. However, I am now your superior officer. Questions would be asked of our professional conduct if I were not to remove you."

Ally slumped into one of the armchairs. There was no point in continuing to debate the matter. The decision had already been made.

"Well…fuck," she muttered under her breath.

"For what it is worth, Allyson, I am sorry," her uncle said.

Ally sighed. "It's okay. I get it. I'm pissed about it…but I get it. Who's taking over the investigation? Fran?"

Her deputy, Francesca Romano, was competent enough. At least in her hands, Allyson would be reassured the work would be thorough. Her uncle looked at her, his face inscrutable, but the awkward clearing of his throat indicated he was about to deliver more unwanted news.

"At the insistence of Grand Chancellor StormHall, the investigation has been turned over to New Victus Security."

"Are you *joking*?" Allyson almost choked on the words. "*Please* tell me you're joking. NVSec are taking charge?"

"No humor is intended," Norbel said quietly. "They consider this an internal matter."

They sat in awkward silence as both of them searched for something to say. Small talk seemed inappropriate at this point, and all Allyson wanted was for him to leave so she could be alone. She almost laughed at the thought, recalling she *was* actually harboring a known fugitive in her bedroom.

Her mind turned to Lyssa and her promise to help. How was she going to do that if she was removed from the investigation? Ally started to process a plan of action for moving forward, a plan that required a level of freedom she currently did not possess.

"If I'm going to be off the case, then I'd like to take a leave of absence. I don't think I can be here while the investigation is happening and just ignore it."

"Certainly. Consider it granted," Norbel said immediately. "What will you do?"

Ally shrugged. "Maybe go to London, spend some time with Gayle. Maybe go back to the farm in Ely. Just somewhere that's not here."

Norbel nodded his understanding as he pushed himself up off the sofa and straightened his uniform jacket. "I think that would be an excellent course of action," he said with a nod. "Allow yourself time to grieve, Allyson. No need to get up. I shall see myself out, leave you to dry and dress."

He walked to the door and slowly opened it to leave the apartment. Just before heading out into the corridor, he paused. Ally watched him turn slightly, his eyes flicking around the apartment again. After a moment, his gaze met Allyson's.

"I am truly sorry about your father. If there is anything I can do—"

Ally cut him off. "I know."

"One final word..." Norbel looked her in the eye. "Please do not be foolish enough to investigate this yourself. If I were to discover you taking matters into your own hands..." He trailed off, but his sentiment was clear.

"Understood, Uncle."

He nodded and exited the apartment, pulling the door closed behind him. Allyson waited for a minute or two to make sure he was clear of the immediate vicinity before she dashed to the bedroom.

"Lyssa?" she whispered as she entered the apparently empty room.

The closet door cracked open and a hesitant Lyssa poked her head out.

"Coast is clear," Ally said, forcing a smile.

Lyssa moved into the room and pushed the closet door closed behind her.

"I heard what happened," she said gently with a look of sadness.

"In hindsight, I'm surprised I lasted this long," Ally shrugged. "It *is* protocol after all; he wasn't wrong about that."

"So, what happens next?" Lyssa asked. "I understand if you're no longer in a position to help me. I'll find another way."

Allyson was vehemently shaking her head. "No," she said firmly. "I said I'd help, and I will. Just because I'm officially off the case does *not* mean I'm dropping this. It just means I'm going to have to be a bit more...sneaky about it."

"Sneaky?" Lyssa said with a furrowed brow.

"Sneaky," Ally confirmed as she grabbed her cellphone off the bedside table.

She hit quick-dial and raised it to her ear waiting for the call to connect. It rang only a handful of times before it was answered.

"Hey, Sis. Yeah, I'm good. Look, I need a favor..."

| **9** |

NEW FACES

— **Damian Dane** —
— *Friday — Domaine Saint-Bernard, Pack Nation* —

Both physically and metaphorically, Damian was standing at a crossroads.

I must be crazy.

Releasing a long-held breath, he watched the convoy of trucks with heavily tinted windows kicking up clouds of dust as they rumbled up the road toward him, the first of the refugees to arrive. The Exodus Initiative had been a last-ditch contingency plan if things went disastrously wrong. He had never expected them to *actually* need it.

Truth was, he had dragged his feet somewhat in finding a safe harbor in Pack Nation for the evacuation of Lyssa's people. If his people knew Vampyrii were being harbored within the borders of their country, there would be hell to pay. Hence his reluctance.

It was with a certain irony that Lyssa's family were now arriving at Domaine Saint-Bernard. Twenty years ago, Eloise, a former lover, had come here looking for safety and protection for her family. Today, the family of another former lover came here to find the same shelter from danger. Hopefully the outcome would be less tragic this time around.

Damian glanced back at the lodge that had been Eloise's home, and a stab of grief ran through him. He had failed to keep her out of harm's way. He had made this area off-limits to his people, considering it a safe haven for her. Confident no one would stumble across her little community, he had been somewhat less than vigilant when it came to her security. He may not have been the person who killed her, but he shouldered a share of the responsibility for her death.

He would carry that burden to his grave.

As he returned his attention to the approaching trucks, he consoled himself with the knowledge that Eloise would be the first person to offer help to those in need. It would please her to know something positive came from the heartbreak of the massacre here.

The first of the large eighteen-wheelers shuddered to a halt next to him with a squeal and a hiss of the airbrakes. As the engine continued its deep rumble, a pale-skinned woman with a sparkling nose piercing and short blonde hair poking out from beneath a baseball cap leaned out the window on his side.

"Damian Dane?" she said, a hint of hope in her voice.

He nodded. "Welcome to Domaine Saint-Bernard."

She pushed the door open and hopped down out of the cab, her diminutive stature taking Damian by surprise as her sturdy boots thudded onto the ground. She extended one hand toward him in a gesture of greeting, while her other hand pushed her dark sunglasses up on her nose. Even under the cap and behind the shades, her face bore the distinctive features of her family line.

Her handshake was firm. "Nykola Balthazaar. Where can we park the trucks?"

"Pick a spot. Your people are free to use any of the buildings. There's no one else here. Nykola...you're Lyssa's sister, right?"

She nodded and grinned widely. "One and the same. Guess she told you about me?"

"I'm fairly familiar with your family tree," Dane replied

Nykola laughed. "I'm *sure* you've barely scratched the surface."

"I know Lyssa was the fourth daughter..."

Nykola nodded. "Yeah, the eldest surviving. I'm number six. Hold that thought..."

She climbed back up the steps and poked her head into the window of the truck. From the ground, Damian could hear her directing the driver to park the truck near the buildings Damian had told her to use.

With instructions issued, she hopped back down and watched for a moment as the truck shifted into gear and slowly pulled away. As the convoy rolled past them, he noticed her paying careful attention to the first three tractor-trailers that were painted matt-black and markedly newer than those that were following. After they passed by, she turned her attention back to Damian.

"Now, where were we?" She grinned.

"We were dipping into your family tree."

"Oh, yeah. So, I'm daughter number six of fifteen," Nykola stated. "Don't get me started on our brothers...of which there are many."

"Your House has been around a long time. Big families come with the territory."

Nykola nodded. "That they do. Lyssa told me what happened to the people who used to live here. I'm genuinely sorry for your loss."

"Thank you." He appreciated the sentiment. "We tried to clean up as much as we could for you, but honestly, the extent of it..." He spread his hands in a gesture of apology.

"Say no more," Nykola reassured him. "We're just grateful for somewhere to go. Somewhere safe. Would you mind if we get out of the sun?"

"No, of course. My apologies." He gestured for her to follow him to the Kuchar Pavilion near the lake, a short walk away.

As they stepped under the freestanding roof and into the shade, Nykola took off her cap and glasses and ran a hand through her disheveled hair. When she looked at him again, he noticed her eyes were a very pale green—unusual for a Vampyrii—and matched the gemstone in her nose-stud.

"Long trip?" He offered up small talk.

"You could say that," she sighed. "We've been cooped up

in those trucks for almost three days because of the numerous detours we had to take to avoid StormHall's search parties."

"Not the most comfortable of situations," Damian agreed.

"I'm *dying* for a shower and a bed, to be honest." Nykola laughed gently. "But I have to say..." She paused, squinting heavily as she peered out across the lake toward the mountain and the forests beyond. "...it was worth the trip. This place is...*breathtaking*."

Sunlight reflected playfully off the gentle ripples of the lake waters as the soft breeze teased the placid surface. Behind it, the blue sky framed the mountain and the lush green of the trees. It was so quiet here. Peaceful. In his grief, he had forgotten the reason why Eloise had chosen it as the place for her family almost two decades ago.

It *was* quite special.

"Yes..." he said softly. "It truly is."

"I thought there would be more of your people here," Nykola commented as she slipped her dark sunglasses back on to protect her sensitive eyes from the dazzling reflections.

"While Lyssa and I were working on contingency plans in preparation for her rebellion, we hadn't got that far down the road yet. Convincing my people to give refuge to Vampyrii rebels was *always* going to be a hard sell."

"So, we're here in secret?" Nykola pursed her lips.

Damian sighed. "Only I and a few of my trusted senior staff know you're here. For now, at least. I need to handle this *very* carefully to prevent a civil war of my own."

"Understood," she nodded. "We'll try and keep a low profile."

"Thank you." He took a deep breath. "Hopefully it's only a temporary situation."

"Our being here?" Nykola asked. "Or our being here in secret?"

"Both, really," he admitted. "I'm working on the latter, but if this is the somewhat premature start of the rebellion, then maybe it won't matter in the long run."

"Unless we lose."

She had a point. If they failed to overthrow the current

New Victus regime, thousands of Vampyrii would be in a gravely desperate situation, something Lyssa had been very concerned about.

"It won't come to that," he said firmly. "Have you heard anything from Lyssa?"

She shook her head. "Since StormHall's speech, I assume she is lying low and trying to find a way out of Nexus City without being caught."

"Easier said than done," Damian said.

"She'll be fine," she assured him.

He hoped she was right.

| 10 |

TAXI

— **Gayle Knightley** —
— *Saturday* — *London, England* —

The strap of the bag Gayle had borrowed from her sister was starting to dig uncomfortably into her shoulder, making her wish she'd just bought a rucksack in Nexus City to pack her stuff for the trip home. Dropping it to the pavement, she wondered how she had managed to fly out in an FSE Airforce Banshee wearing nothing but her CombatSkin, yet was returning via commercial flight, burdened with clothes and toiletries. It wasn't as if she still had her CombatSkin either; that was currently in Allyson's hands for God knew what purpose. She glanced at her watch—another new addition to her wardrobe—and noted the time.

Lana was late.

As if on cue, Gayle heard the familiar rumble of a V8 engine. The sound brought a small smile to a face that had seen far too much sadness the past few days. The snow-white convertible rolled gently to a stop, her driver grinning inanely.

"I *love* this car," Lana said breathlessly.

"The top down? Really?" Gayle arched an eyebrow.

"Hey, I *never* get the chance to drive her! You rarely even take her out of the garage!" Lana protested.

"And for that, I have very good reasons," Gayle said. "One of which is that all my friends want to have a go."

"So, you'll trust me to fly you into combat, but *not* to drive your Mustang?"

"Do you know how hard it is to find parts for a 2011 GT500 in the FSE?" Gayle asked rhetorically. "I spent years restoring *Sally* to her former glory only to have you drive her to Stansted, with the top down in the rain."

"It's okay," Lana smirked. "I drove fast so I barely felt it."

Gayle threw her luggage into the back then wearily pulled open the passenger door and got in.

"How was the flight?" Lana asked.

"Fine," Gayle said succinctly.

"And how are you feeling?"

That's a very good question, isn't it?

The truth was she simply felt numb to all of it at the moment. She knew she should be broken up and grieving, especially as this *was* her father, but there was...nothing. Maybe she was somehow becoming accustomed to loss. Or maybe she just hadn't processed it yet.

"I'm fine."

Lana threw the car into gear and smoothly pulled away, frowning at Gayle as she did so. "You don't look it," she commented.

Gayle leaned back against the headrest and felt the wind tousle her hair. She sighed.

"Honestly...I don't feel much of anything right now. Just tired."

"How are Ally and Carrie coping?" Lana asked while steering the car around a roundabout a smidgen too quickly, making the tires squeal on the wet road as they struggled for adhesion.

"Carrie is the worst affected, weirdly. I think this is the first time she's faced death like this. I dunno, Lana. I think—as awful as this sounds—what happened in Malta a year ago has kind of tapped me out grief-wise. And Allyson..." Gayle paused. "I'm not sure. An outsider might think she's being cold and uncaring, but I know her better. She's just thrown herself into her work. She's driven to find out who did this. I'm worried about her, frankly."

"How so?" Lana asked.

"Uncle Norbel took her off the case," Gayle explained.

"Ouch. I bet that did *not* go down well."

"You'd think, but no." Gayle rubbed her eyes and yawned. "She simply accepted it. Maybe she was expecting it. But then I got a call from her asking to borrow my CombatSkin."

"What for?" Lana said curiously.

"That's what I asked. She wouldn't say." Gayle shook her head. "But she won't let this lie. She won't give up till she gets answers."

"I saw StormHall's speech blaming Lyssa Balthazaar. The news outlets say she's gone into hiding. You think she's to blame?"

Gayle shook her head. Lana prodded the accelerator and the car gathered speed as it joined the motorway.

"Nope," Gayle answered. "Certainly not after talking to Mercy. I think she's being set up. What's more, I'm pretty sure I know where she's hiding."

Lana looked sideways at her, prompting for an answer.

"I think she's shacked up with Ally."

"Why on earth would Ally take in the fugitive accused of killing her—your—father?" Lana said, gobsmacked.

"Because...sister dearest is sleeping with said fugitive."

"Holy shit!" Lana exclaimed.

"I kid you not." Gayle thought for a moment. "But she has her 'uncanny-Ally' thing, so she must believe Lyssa is on the up-and-up."

Lana shook her head. "Sleeping with the enemy, though..."

"She's not the enemy." Gayle glanced at her friend. "Not that I've met her, but from what both Ally and Mercy told me..." Her comment trailed off as she sank into thought.

"You liked her, didn't you?" Lana asked quietly. "Mercy."

Gayle nodded. "I'm not exaggerating when I say she *significantly* moved the needle on my feelings about Vampyrii. I wish I'd been able to tell Lyssa Balthazaar that. I'd like to have gone to the funeral...or whatever it is Vampyrii do."

"Speaking of which," Lana said, "when's your father's? You know I'll be there, right?"

"Not sure. It'll be back home. Soon, though, I'd think."

"You wanna talk about it?"

"Nope."

"Gayle...you *have* to talk about it at some point."

"Not today I don't."

"I spoke to your mum, and your sisters," Lana confessed. "All of them said you're not talking about it. That you've barely shed a tear..."

"I cried. I'm grieving," Gayle said moodily. "Just because everyone expects me to be broken again, like after Valletta..."

"That's not what we're saying." Lana shook her head. "We just think it would be healthy if you opened up about it."

"Maybe." Gayle took a deep breath. "Look, Lana, when I'm ready... I'll come talk to you, okay?"

"Fair enough. That's all I'm asking. Oh, and FYI, I found my own place, at last, and moved out of Ally's. So, she'll be able to have some privacy when she comes back for the funeral. I'll message you the address later, so you know where to come...when you're ready."

They drove in silence for a while as the Mustang devoured the asphalt of the M11. The rain had stopped, and the autumn sun was stealing a peek through the gunmetal clouds. Gayle sniffed and pulled her jacket snugly around her to ward off the cold air that was now blowing her hair into a tangled mess. She swept it behind her ear and stared accusingly at Lana, who just grinned.

"When do I *ever* get the chance to drive a convertible?" she laughed.

"*My* convertible!" Gayle retorted. "I'll let you borrow it in the summer."

"I'll hold you to that," Lana replied. "By the way...I think someone has missed you very much."

"Who?" Gayle asked, though she knew the answer.

At least...she hoped she knew the answer.

"The other piece of American muscle in your life," Lana laughed. "He's asked me how you're doing just about every day since you've been gone, and he's terrible at making it seem casual."

Gayle said nothing, simply relaxed against the headrest and allowed herself a small smile.

| 11 |

ASYLUM

— **Lyssa Balthazaar** —
— *Saturday — Nexus City, Iceland* —

She was safe.

Her sensitive hearing confirmed there was no one coming or even close by. Still, Lyssa couldn't help glancing nervously up and down the empty corridor. Her heart was racing as she reached up and lightly rapped her knuckles thrice on the hardwood door. She prayed her knock had been loud enough to attract the attention of the apartment's occupant, yet not carry down the passageway. Just in case her senses betrayed her.

Please be in. Please be in.

The seconds dragged by, and Lyssa started to doubt her present course of action. But it wasn't as if she had many other viable alternatives. Lyssa could continue to hide out in Allyson's apartment, turn herself over the NVSec, or do what she was doing now.

Which was to knock on the FSE ambassador's door in order to ask a grieving widow if she would grant asylum for her and her other family members now hiding underground in the city.

What the fuck *am I doing? This is a bad idea.*

Suddenly, a wave of second thoughts flooded her. Why would the ambassador even *consider* such a petition from the very person Storm was blaming for this tragedy?

Lyssa felt vaguely nauseous.

She was on the verge of turning to scurry away when the door silently opened, and the serene visage of Serlia Knightley greeted her.

"Miss Balthazaar," she said quietly. "I think you had better come in quickly, don't you?"

Lyssa had to admit to being a little taken aback by Serlia's calm demeanor, but she gratefully accepted the invitation to hurry inside from the exposed corridor. The Fae woman closed the door firmly behind them.

"I am *so* sorry to have come here, Ambassador," Lyssa croaked, her throat dry. "I need to tell you...I *swear* on my father's life I had *nothing* to do with what happened to your husband. I can only offer my deepest condolences..."

"Lyssa," Serlia smiled. "Please...I have never for one single moment held the belief that you were involved as anything more than a pawn in a broader narrative. I personally believe you are as much a victim in all this as I am. I am truly sorry about your niece. Jaymes tells me she was delightful. I wish I'd had the chance to meet her myself."

Relief flooded from every pore of Lyssa's being. She felt tears welling but refused to let them coalesce into the rivulets they wished to become. Instead, she swallowed and set her jaw, steeling her emotions.

"Ambassador—" she began but was cut off before she could speak any further.

"Please, call me Serlia. I'd like to think we're on friendly terms. Besides, I *think* I know why you're here and, if I am correct, then this is a conversation I believe we should have hypothetically, as friends first, before you say anything...official."

"Okay..." Lyssa hesitated, not quite knowing where to go next.

Fortunately, she was conversing with a woman who had decades of experience in the art of speaking diplomatically. Serlia beckoned for her to move to the lounge and sit. As Lyssa perched on one of the large leather sofas, Serlia reclined into a comfortable-looking armchair, crossing her legs elegantly.

"I assume that if this *were* an official conversation, you would be here to ask if I could grant you and your family asylum in Europa. Would I be hypothetically correct?"

Lyssa nodded slowly. "Yes. There are a few of us here in Nexus. Since Storm has declared my House to be blood-traitors, they...we have all been forced to go into hiding."

"I don't think I need to ask where you've been...'lying low,' I believe is the term."

"I..." Lyssa's cheeks flushed hot.

Serlia waved her hand dismissively. "I saw the connection you had with my daughter the night of the Summit Gala. In truth, it was wonderful to see Allyson enjoying herself again. And while I have my own opinions about you, which are positive I might add, it is Allyson's trust in you that reinforces my belief in your veracity. You see, Allyson has a skill not many others possess—"

This time it was Lyssa's turn to interrupt. "She told me. 'Uncanny Ally.'"

"Quite." Serlia smiled. "Suffice to say, she would not be...associating with you if she thought you were lying about any of this."

"I *know* Storm is behind all this. Somehow," Lyssa said quietly. "He played me like a fiddle. Preyed on my optimism to set me up for the fall. Now my family is being hunted. You're right—I came here to ask if—"

Serlia held up a hand, bringing her entreaty to a halt. "Let's keep this hypothetical, remember. I want to make sure you fully understand the ramifications of your request."

"I know the ramifications," Lyssa said resolutely.

"I'm not convinced you do," Serlia countered. "Hypothetically, if you came to me and formally tabled your request, I would, by law, have to take your petition before the FSE Council. Though we project a singular voice to the world, we are in fact a union of the remaining European nations. Each nation has a voice. The other voices on the Council do not know you as I do...and with the bombing and StormHall's address fresh in their minds..."

"You could not guarantee a favorable outcome." Lyssa sighed and nodded her understanding. She closed her eyes and massaged her temples. "Monsters. You'll *always* think of us as monsters..."

"I'm not sure that's true, Lyssa." Serlia shook her head. "Attitudes change, but it takes time."

"And you, Ambassador?" Lyssa opened her eyes. "What do *you* believe?"

There was a knowing twinkle in the Fae woman's emerald eyes. "Ah, I do not have a belief. I have knowledge," she said cryptically. "But I'm afraid not everyone on the Council will be so...enlightened. Convincing them to accept an asylum petition from a Vampyrii would *not* be an easy task. Many of the Council members draw no distinction between the races. Vampyrii, Werewolf..."

"...we're all monsters." Lyssa nodded. "I wish I didn't understand...but I do. Look at what we did to the world, to this country. It's hard to undo the damage the War did."

"Which brings me neatly to my next point. You realize the consequences of my accepting a petition should you officially make one?" Serlia said. "If you were to ask that of me, and I could convince the Council to acquiesce, then I would be inciting a diplomatic incident between the FSE and New Victus.

"My brother has already turned the investigation over to New Victus Security and stated our intention to comply with their process. If I was to now offer you haven within the boundaries of our territory, it would not only be seen as a slight on the Grand Chancellor and New Victus—who have neatly positioned themselves as the innocent party in all this—but also as an internal disconnect between the senior ranks of the FSE."

"I can see how that would be awkward," Lyssa conceded. "But I would only be asking for a temporary haven for my family members within Nexus City. I have plans in motion to create a more long-term solution to this...situation."

"May I enquire, off the record, as to what those plans are?"

Lyssa hesitated. Did she want to reveal the scope of her designs to a woman she trusted, yet barely knew? On the other hand, at this point was there anything to lose in at least telling Serlia a portion of the truth? It wasn't like things could get any worse.

Could they?

"My family in New Victus is already evacuating to a safe location." She hesitated, taking a deep breath.

In for a penny...

"Some years ago, I made contact with Damian Dane."

She paused for effect, but oddly Serlia didn't look in the least bit surprised.

"He and I," she continued, "have been formulating strategies to end Storm's regime. Much of our plan hinged upon approaching the FSE and the NAA to offer them the western half of the country back if they would ally themselves with us militarily to overthrow his forces. I have the support of many of the Progenitor Houses, and with Pack Nation engaging from the north, the NAA from the west, and us from within, we could oust Storm from power once and for all."

Serlia looked thoughtful. "How close were you to bringing this scheme to fruition?"

"Close. I was planning to use the Summit to get an audience with yourself and the NAA ambassadors. State my case."

"Your case for starting a war?"

Lyssa shook her head. "No. My case for correcting an injustice. The War should never have happened. Storm pursued a personal vendetta to gain a power he never should have had. I can't turn the clock back thirty years, but I *can* help restore a little piece of the United States to its rightful owners. To bring some stability to that part of the world.

"I don't need you to *start* a war with Storm. I need your help to *end* it in a way that is beneficial to us all."

Serlia sat contemplating for a minute or two, a period of reflection Lyssa didn't want to interrupt. Her perfect face was inscrutable, not a flicker of emotion to give away her frame of mind. She had expected the Fae woman to be showing some outward sign of her heartache, but there was none. Odd when you considered her recent loss. Lyssa still felt the keen sting of what happened to Mercy, but maybe Fae dealt with grief differently to Vampyrii.

"If you were to ask for asylum, I'm afraid I would not be able to grant it," Serlia finally said.

Lyssa's heart sank. She sighed, standing, this meeting apparently at an end.

"I understand your position, Ambassador. I had to ask. Or not, as it turns out."

Serlia regarded her with an amused smile. "But...I didn't say I wouldn't help you. While officially my hands are tied, I'm not without...'unofficial' means. Please sit. I think we still have much to discuss."

Lyssa eased back down onto the sofa.

"When we first learned the Grand Chancellor was to send *you* as his replacement, my husband said he had a gut feeling something was wrong. Why send an adversary to be his advocate? StormHall's reasoning made logical sense considering the plan he was tabling, but Jaymes was still suspicious. My husband was a superb diplomat because he had excellent instincts...and he trusted them.

"I have little doubt Grand Chancellor StormHall orchestrated this tragedy and while, as the Ambassador for the Federated States of Europa, I can't help you officially, I'll be damned if I will sit back and watch this man cause any more pain and suffering.

"Are you working on the theory StormHall discovered your plans to instigate a coup?"

"I don't know," Lyssa admitted. "I don't think so. We were *very* careful. It's more likely this is the result of my standing in opposition to him during The Rising. Storm is the type of man who holds a grudge.

"However, saying that...it's certainly possible."

Serlia steepled her fingers thoughtfully. "I *can* find a place of safety for your family here in Nexus City."

Lyssa furrowed her brow, confused. "But you just said—"

"My dear," Serlia interrupted, "the FSE is not my only resource. Can you contact your people?"

"I have means," Lyssa nodded.

"Excellent. Of course, this is all...unofficial. If anyone finds out about this, I will be forced to deny it."

"I understand. Thank you. Sincerely."

"Lyssa, my dear, there is no need to thank me for doing what is right." Serlia smiled enigmatically. "Besides, this is only a stop-gap to tide us over until the day I *can* help you in a more official capacity."

Lyssa furrowed her brow.

What did the ambassador mean by that exactly?

| 12 |

PRIVATE EYES

— Allyson Knightley —
— Saturday — Nexus City, Iceland —

The aurora borealis danced gracefully in the sky overhead, casting its emerald glow through the crystal glass of the domed roof. On any other day, Allyson would probably have sat and watched it for a while, but tonight she had other things on her mind as she crept through the empty World Council Chambers. It was dark in the devastated amphitheater and quiet as a graveyard. She cursed mentally at her poor choice of words. A gentle scuff alerted her to the approaching security guard before she saw him, slipping into the shadows to conceal her presence. The slow shuffle of footsteps approached, and the flick of a torch-beam panned across the room as Kristopher Johannson came into view and did his checks.

Good, Allyson thought. *They haven't changed the rotation.*

She liked Kristopher but knew he wasn't her most diligent security officer. He was close to retirement, a little overweight, and preferred to take his time on his rounds. Thus, her last act before relinquishing her post for her leave of absence was to amend the duty roster to ensure he was on patrol tonight. She knew he would also spend at least twenty minutes after his first circuit getting a tea and resting in the security office before beginning his second sweep, allowing her ample time to do what she needed to do without interruption.

She made like a statue as he passed by, holding her breath and trusting her borrowed CombatSkin to do its job concealing her presence. The surface of the suit rippled briefly, changing color, chameleon-like, to blend her into the shadows, as Kristopher walked past mere feet away without suspicion. When he exited the chamber, Allyson exhaled slowly then moved with stealth toward the spot where the bomb that killed her father had been detonated. She paused and looked around, biting her lip and contemplating her first move.

Where do I begin?

Forensics had been all over the crime scene, finding little to provide a solid clue as to who was to blame for the attack. The blast had been small, but significant. Enough to obliterate most of the trace evidence. Yet Allyson was convinced if she took just one more look, she would find *something* that had been missed.

I've got to.

She paced the area carefully, the sound of each footfall absorbed by the soft soles of the stealth-enabled outfit. So, when she heard the subdued sound of someone surreptitiously approaching out of the darkness, she knew it wasn't her own footsteps she was hearing. Her initial reaction was the assumption Kristopher had broken with habit and returned early, but a moment later she realized the pattern was distinctly...different. Lighter, less...shuffling. Someone else was here, trying to hide in the blackness, just as Allyson herself was.

She dodged back into the shadows again. Ineffectively, as it happened.

"Allyson?" A voice whispered.

Ally closed her eyes and cursed under her breath.

"Ally," the voice said again. "You *do* know I can see you right?"

She stepped out of the darkness and into a shaft of moonlight, staring angrily at the newcomer. "Lyssa, what the *actual* fuck!" she hissed.

"I came to help."

"You can't help—you're a fugitive! Wanted by just about everyone for what happened right here!" Ally said, her hushed voice getting higher pitched by the second. "Don't you think it's a tad irresponsible, considering the personal risk I went to letting you hide out in my home?"

"I'm sorry, but I *can't* just sit by and do nothing," Lyssa hissed back. "Not while the people who did this to Mercy are still out there and no one is looking into it."

"*I'm* looking into it!"

"You know what I mean," Lyssa sighed wearily. "They've handed the reins of the investigation over to NVSec, who are in Storm's pocket. Which means, since I'm the named person of interest, they won't look any further."

Can't argue with that.

"Regardless," she said, shaking her head, "you *should* have stayed safely hidden."

"I was out and about anyway."

"LYSSA!" Ally hissed.

"I went to see your mother. About asylum for my people here in Nexus."

Allyson stared wide-eyed at the beautiful Vampyrii. She moved her mouth to say something but changed her mind before the words came out. After a moment, she went with a simple question instead. "What did she say?"

"She couldn't offer assistance officially," Lyssa admitted. "But unofficially she's helping me hide any family I have here. Which, while it is less than I hoped for, is significantly more than I expected. Anyway, being as I was in the vicinity and knew you were coming here, I thought I could help."

"I don't need help!"

"Nevertheless, I think I can."

"How?"

Lyssa looked around the room and then shrugged. After a beat, she looked Ally up and down with a lascivious look. "Well, while I love the outfit..."

"Uh...thanks I..." Allyson glanced down self-consciously at the figure-hugging catsuit.

"...Unless it comes equipped with some sort of night vision—"

"—It comes with a pair of custom tactical-glasses," Ally interrupted, then sighed, "but...Gayle didn't have them with her."

"—then I'd wager I can see in the dark far better than you can."

Fuck, she has another point.

"Fine. Help then. Look around discreetly—and quietly—and see if you can find anything my people missed."

"Where do you want me to look?" Lyssa asked.

That's a very good question.

The forensics team had been widening their search when NVSec was put in charge. True to expectation, it didn't look like StormHall's cronies had advanced the investigation any further thus far. The room looked *exactly* as it had yesterday. She pointed back toward the Pack Nation area.

"You'll see the markers where our team picked up trace evidence...work beyond those. Let's see if the explosion threw any clues further out. The teams haven't investigated that far yet, so it's fresh territory."

Lyssa nodded and made her way over to where Ally had indicated, slowly sweeping her eyes back and forth as she searched. Allyson headed to the New Victus area and flicked on her torch. It was a tiny unit, no bigger than a lipstick, but the beam was powerful and confined. She carefully panned it around, paying close attention to listen for the sounds of a returning Kristopher.

Ten minutes later they had found nothing, and Allyson was acutely aware time was running out. She was quietly cursing this dead-end under her breath when something glinted as her torch-beam panned over it, drawing her attention. She flicked the light back and forth briefly, trying to pinpoint its location, and spotted a small, silvery object. She picked her way over the debris to the hardwood panel separating the viewing gallery from the conference floor and found a tiny sliver of what looked like circuit board embedded into it, definitely as a result of the explosion.

She tried to recall if any of the ambassadors who had been caught in or near the blast had been carrying electronics. She wasn't one hundred percent sure—she would check later—but she was confident there had been none. So, if that was true, then where did this shard of microchip come from?

"Did you find something?"

The voice startled her. Ally spun around, accidentally shining the powerful torch beam directly into Lyssa's face.

"Motherfucker!" Lyssa exclaimed as she was temporarily blinded.

Realizing what she had done, Ally pivoted the light away from the Vampyrii's sensitive eyes.

"Fuck!" Ally hissed. "I'm *so* sorry! Are you okay?"

Lyssa was blinking furiously, her eyes streaming tears. "I'll survive," she whispered and then cursed under her breath again.

"This is the worst attempt at a stealth mission ever..." Allyson shook her head in dismay.

Lyssa laughed lightly and put her hand on Ally's shoulder to steady herself as her vision cleared. "What would your sister say?"

"Gayle?" Ally giggled. "She'd have a field day with this. She already thought it was weird I wanted to borrow her CombatSkin. The fact I'm stumbling around without any night-vision glasses and I've just blinded the only one of us who can see in the dark would amuse her no end."

As Lyssa placed a hand over her mouth to stifle her laugh, Ally was abruptly struck by the notion that, while Lyssa was many times her age, she rarely showed it. She looked in her thirties and acted no differently to Allyson herself. They had only shared one night, but the memory of that experience lingered. Her sisters' warnings regarding the impracticality of pursuing a relationship with Lyssa popped, unbidden, into her brain. They were right. There were *so* many obstacles that would prevent them from ever being together.

A girl can dream, though, right?

But tonight, as she looked at this Vampyrii who had centuries on her and was currently blinking furiously to clear the tears from her eyes, she suddenly had an epiphany.

The fantasy wasn't totally unattainable.

"So, what was it you found?"

For a split-second, Ally, caught in her moment of distraction, wondered what Lyssa was talking about, and then she remembered why they were standing in the dark in the World Council Chambers.

"I...errr...found a," she hesitated, "...a something. Something embedded in the wood here."

"Where?"

"You can see again?"

"Well enough," Lyssa confirmed. "Show me."

Allyson pointed to the spot on the panel. She couldn't see it herself now without the torch on, but Lyssa apparently could, and she started to reach her hand toward it.

"Wait!" Ally snatched at the hand.

"What?"

"Don't contaminate the evidence. Here use these. And put it in this."

From the pouch on her belt, she pulled out a pair of latex gloves and a clear plastic bag.

"Your sister carries these?" Lyssa asked.

"The CombatSkin is hers, but the belt is mine. I'm a cop, remember."

"I thought you were the Security Chief?"

"Fine...ex-cop," Ally whispered and proffered the gloves. "Put these on before you touch it."

Lyssa pulled them onto her elegant hands and then set about prying it slowly from the wood. After a couple of minutes of gentle wiggling and tugging, it came free, and she dropped it into the open bag Ally was holding.

Just in time.

"Someone's coming!" Lyssa hissed urgently.

"Then time's up. Let's get out of here and see what we've got."

Ally's mood was buoyed somewhat by their find. She knew there was a strong possibility it was nothing, but her gut told her maybe this was the clue to finding out the truth.

| 13 |

GOODBYE/HELLO

— **Michael Reynolds** —
— *Sunday — London, England* —

The evening sun slid leisurely toward the horizon, throwing long shadows across the lounge as brother and sister embraced. She hugged him so fervently that he felt his ribs might crack under the strain. But this was a *good* hug. The kind he had feared he would never feel again. It saddened him that he was about to start missing these hugs all over again just when he was getting reacquainted with them.

"Gonna miss you, Mikey," Alexa said into his shoulder.

"You too, Lexy," Michael reciprocated. "I can't believe you're goin' again *already*. You've only been here a week!"

His sister chuckled, relinquishing him from her embrace and reaching for her coat, draped haphazardly over the back of a chair.

"After being estranged for so long, I thought it best we not overdo it."

"As Dad used to say, that's a loada bull."

Alexa shrugged on the jacket, preparing to leave. "I think *those* are more Mom's words than Dad's."

Michael sighed. Did Alexa *truly* remember their parents? Or was she simply hypothesizing based on hazy sepia-hued nostalgia? They had no photographs from that time, so even their parents' faces were indistinct. Fuzzy. A wave of melancholy briefly washed over him. On their tequila-fueled night of brutal honesty, he had told Gayle that, while he and Alexa were twins, they never shared the psychic connection that was stereotypical. However, sometimes there was an uncanny sense of understanding between them.

"I know," she said simply.

Michael took a deep breath and forced a smile. "So...what are your plans?" he said, changing the subject. "I thought you'd decided to get some RnR?"

"And that plan," Alexa nodded, "has not changed. Our CombatSkins won't be ready for a few weeks, and *Diana* needs servicing—"

"—Which I can arrange to be done by the Academy flight engineers—"

She interrupted his interruption with a vehement shake of her head. "No. I promised Becka some down-time and her idea of that doesn't include hangin' out in London for too long. She *definitely* doesn't like bein' here. I get the impression something happened..."

"Like what?"

Alexa shrugged. "I have *no* clue, and she won't talk about it. Anyhow, when I asked her where she'd like to go, she proposed Rio."

"Rio de Janeiro?"

"The very same," Alexa laughed.

"Can you even get in there?"

"I have contacts. The perks of being a licensed MercNet Agent. Besides, it suits me because the work to *Diana* will require some...unusual parts, which I doubt your engineers would have here."

His sister's use of the word 'unusual' probably meant 'black-market.' If so, then he understood why she would not want official HFA ground crew crawling all over her dropship and finding all the likely illegal custom additions she had made.

"Fair enough," he smiled. "When will you be back?"

Before she could answer there was a knock at the front

door.

"That'll be my ride," Alexa sighed. "I promise I won't leave it too long this time, Mikey. We've got to come back in to pick up the CombatSkins anyway, so probably three or four weeks at a guess."

She hoisted her kitbag onto her shoulder, chuckling as she saw Michael staring wistfully at it. He remembered a time when they had practically lived out of bags like that.

"Yeah, I know," Alexa said as if she'd read his mind. "You can take the girl out of the army, but you can't take the army out of the girl. But...I guess it *would* be nice to settle down somewhere."

He glanced around his new home. "Yeah, it kinda is."

Alexa reached the front door and twisted the handle to open it. As the door swung inward, the figure waiting on the doorstep beyond wasn't the person they had both expected it to be. Standing silhouetted against the pink and orange-hued sunset sky was a decidedly nervous-looking Gayle Knightley.

"Hey," Gayle said hesitantly while staring at Alexa. "I'm sorry. I just got back and... I apologize if I'm interrupting...something."

She looked almost shy, something Michael had never seen in her before. Then suddenly—as she tucked a windswept strand of candy-floss hair behind her ear while her eyes flicked from him to Alexa and back again—he realized why. All Gayle saw was a strange woman she'd never met exiting his house with what looked like a large overnight bag.

"Oh, shoot, you two ain't met yet. Gayle, this is Alexa. My sister."

"Oh," Gayle furrowed her brow for a moment. "Ohhh, when you said you had a twin called Alex, I assumed... I thought it was a dude. Now I feel like a fucking idiot!"

Alexa smiled and extended her hand which Gayle duly accepted.

"Common misconception. Everyone hears the word twin and assumes identical. It's a pleasure to meet you, Captain Knightley."

"Gayle, please."

"Gayle it is then," Alexa smiled. "We were supposed to be introduced a week ago, but... I'd like to offer my deepest condolences on your father."

"Thank you," Gayle replied.

An uncomfortable silence descended over their little group. Michael was about to say something in an attempt to break the tension when there was a honk from the taxi that had pulled up unnoticed. The rear door opened and Becka stepped halfway out before abruptly stopping. Her gaze wandered from Alexa to him and back again, but Michael could have sworn she was avoiding eye contact with Gayle. For her part, Gayle was staring at Becka with a puzzled look.

"That's my ride," Alexa smiled. "It was nice meeting you, Gayle. Sorry, it was so fleeting."

"Don't worry about it," Gayle said distractedly. "We'll do something more conducive to getting to know each other next time you're in town."

"I'd like that." Alexa turned to her brother, arms outstretched. "See you soon, Mikey. Be back before you know it."

"I thought we already hugged this one out?" he chuckled.

"Well, forgive me for wantin' to make up for lost time." Alexa laughed and wrapped him in another vice-like bear hug, which he reciprocated in kind.

"Love you, Sis."

"Love you, too."

With that, she relinquished her hold, walked over to the taxi, and hopped into the back next to Becka. Within moments, the car had pulled away, and with a final wave, she was gone, leaving Michael and Gayle stood on the doorstep looking at each other in another awkward silence.

| 14 |

BETTER DAYS

— **Gayle Knightley** —
— *Sunday* — *London, England* —

"So...hey," she squeaked, a little higher pitched than she had meant it.

"Hey," he reciprocated.

Gayle bit her lip and swallowed nervously as she rocked on her heels. On the flight back, she had caught herself more than once cracking a shy smile at the thought of seeing Michael again. While the emotional trauma of the past week had been a dark cloud hanging over her, the thought of Michael and how they had left things felt like a hopeful ray of sunshine peeking through the grey. She'd been looking forward to this moment, mentally rehearsing their reunion ad-infinitum.

Now that she was in front of him, those practiced words were taken from her. Stolen by the genuinely warm smile on his handsome face.

Fuck, this is kinda awkward.

"Welcome home." His baritone voice was a salve to her nerves. "How are you feeling?"

Gayle let out a sigh and considered his question for a moment before responding.

"I'm...well...I'm good. Thanks. For asking that is," she stammered. "You know. I'm doing okay."

Michael rubbed his chin thoughtfully. "I'm...I wanted to

contact you. Wanted to give my condolences, but…"

"It's okay." Gayle smiled. "I wish you could have met him. He'd have liked you."

"I didn't expect you back yet. I figured maybe you'd need a little more time."

She shook her head. "No. I'm done with moping around Nexus. I need to get back to work. Take my mind off things. There's nothing there but questions with no answers. I wanted to be somewhere more familiar." She shrugged. "Here in London, with my home, the Academy, Lana… You."

She flicked her emerald eyes at his chocolate brown ones and for a moment they held each other's stare.

"I'm here," Michael said quietly, before adding, "and, of course, Lana and…everything. Ready and waiting for you."

Her eyes stayed locked with his. "Ready and waiting?"

"Waiting," he nodded. "And ready."

The subtext was deafening, but even so, Gayle hesitated to assume what she thought he was hinting at.

You know the old saying about the word 'assume.'

"I errr…" she began, before pausing to formulate her query. "Thought maybe the…when you came to the classroom the day…"

The day her father had died. She couldn't bring herself to say it, but he nodded, knowing what she meant.

"I kinda thought maybe you'd come to ask for another date. I mean, not that the tequila night was a date, of course…"

"No," he said in agreement. "Of course."

What the fuck does that mean?

"I dunno. I think perchance I was a little caught up in the heat of the moment…"

Perchance? Okay, now you're just talking nonsense.

"Actually," Michael said, looking a little awkward. "I was on my way to come introduce my sister to you. But then I ran into Norbel, and he told me what happened…"

"Oh…" Gayle felt like the wind had been stolen from her sails.

"I mean, that's not to say I wouldn't…want to ask you out on another date…or non-date," he said quietly. "It's just Alexa wanted to meet you."

"She seems nice." Gayle nodded in the direction where Alexa's taxi had been. "Really...and the family resemblance. Not identical, I know, but you can tell."

Michael stared at her for a few seconds; a stare that started to make her feel uncomfortable. Then he laughed. Gayle furrowed her brow, wondering what he was finding so funny.

"I'm sorry," he said eventually. "I honestly don't mean this to be so awkward. Maybe if we start over?"

"Fuck," Gayle nodded. "And maybe if I could come in?"

She almost laughed at the look on Michael's face as he realized they were indeed still standing on the doorstep.

"Oh, jeez, yeah. Of course. Come on in."

It felt weird, being there and walking down the hallway toward Michael's lounge. It took her a moment to realize why, and then she remembered the last time...when she had been carried down the corridor in his arms. Under her own power, it was an oddly different perspective. The thought made her chuckle.

"Two cents for them?"

"I was just recalling the last time I was here..."

"Ah, the damsel in distress routine," Michael laughed.

"It was no 'routine.' I was *genuinely* hurt that day," she protested. "No word of a lie. However, I do have a confession to make."

Here goes. And the truth will set me free!

"Now, that sounds vaguely ominous..."

"I meant to tell you before..." she couldn't say it, but he knew what she meant. "So, I'm sorry this is so late. I need to talk to you about our tequila night."

"Ah, you want to talk about the kiss." Michael nodded.

"Well, yes...and no." Gayle sat down on the sofa and slumped wearily back. "It's more than that."

"If you're about to apologize for a drunken kiss, then please don't—"

"—No, you don't understand. That's exactly it...I *wasn't* drunk that night."

Michael chuckled in disbelief. "Girl, we put away the better part of two bottles of tequila between us. There's no *way* you could have been sober that night unless there's some Fae trick I don't know about that neutralizes alcohol."

"Not exactly."

"Meaning?"

"Ugh." Gayle leaned forward. "Pass me that." She pointed toward the empty hi-ball glass that sat on the coffee table. Michael reached down and plucked it up.

"It's dirty," he said, confused. "Alexa was using it this morning."

"Doesn't matter." Gayle took it from him. "Watch."

She held the glass in her hand and waited till his eyes were focused on it, then she closed hers and took a deep breath. It had been easier that night—her powers fueled by the happiness of the moment. In the light of day and the wake of her father's death, it was harder to summon the positive emotion needed to utilize her water ability. She thought about the kiss. Tried to recall the giddy feeling of joy that moment had fired within her. Her eyes opened to see Michael looking wide-eyed at the now full glass of pure water.

"Sorry," she shrugged.

"So, if I'm understanding this right...you never drank the tequila that night. You just replaced all your drinks with water?"

"Guilty as charged. Admittedly, it's why I picked blanco tequila..."

"So...you were *acting* drunk?"

"Kind of..." Gayle closed her eyes again. "It's really hard to explain..."

Michael raised an eyebrow. "I feel like I need more than that."

"And I will provide. Just...not yet, okay?" Gayle sighed. "I'm not trying to be evasive. It's just... Fuck. You know I see a therapist; I'm working through something. When I'm ready, I promise I'll tell you. I just didn't want to lie to you anymore, or have you think I was intentionally trying to deceive you, or take advantage of you. I genuinely just wanted a nice, normal evening out with you. Simply that. But the truth is I'm a re-covering addict...and I...I can't drink."

"You're an alcoholic?"

She shook her head. "No, it's not that." Gayle searched her brain for an analogy. "It's more like..."

"I get it. Like you just need to avoid anything that could be addictive."

"Yeah. Something like that. I promise you I will explain everything when I'm ready. But I wanted to come clean, so our next date is above board."

"Our *next* date?" Michael said with a smile.

"Can we change the subject?"

"You brought this up!" he laughed.

"And now that I've got it off my chest, I'd like to talk about something else." Gayle smiled, shaking her head. "How're the kids?"

Michael took the hint and shifted gears as requested. "They were concerned about you. The Nexus thing has been on the news all week. It's been impossible to keep them away from it. I think they know better than to be asking you questions when you come back. Now, honestly, I'm not trying to rush you, take all the time you need, but any idea when you might be ready?"

"I'll be in tomorrow."

"You sure?"

Gayle nodded. "I need something to do to take my mind off things."

"Okay, then. That's good. You still want to chaperone Lieutenant Forrester?"

"Oh, fuck!" Gayle slumped back again, covering her face with her hands.

She had totally spaced on the fact that Amanda was joining the Academy the next day. It had been one of the last things she had arranged before leaving in a hurry for Nexus. The paperwork, however, had now been sitting for a week waiting for Gayle to complete and file it.

"Don't worry about it," Michael said with a chuckle. "She got in touch when she realized what happened. We worked out the details, and I've filled in and filed all the paperwork. Her security clearance is sorted out. It's all taken care of."

"Thank you," Gayle exhaled slowly before a stab of unwanted jealousy pierced her relief. "You met up with her?"

"No, not yet. We did everything over the phone and by email. She did say she wasn't up to anything strenuous just yet—which I said wasn't a problem as we just need a firearms instructor. She's more than happy to do that. She as good as her reputation?"

"Better," Gayle muttered under her breath, her mind on an entirely different reputation than the one Michael was referring to.

"Excuse me?"

"She's better," Gayle said, forcing the other thoughts from her mind. "Put it this way...have you seen the Academy shooting records?" Michael nodded. "Then you'd see they *all* belong to her. What you may have missed is they all have an asterisk and a tiny 's' next to them."

"You're right—I never noticed. What does the 's' stand for?"

"'Suppressed.' It means she set those benchmarks while her abilities were shut off using a Power Access Dampener."

"Okay, I get it, but why the distinction?" Michael shrugged and sat on the sofa next to Gayle. "Why does it matter if a PAD was used?"

"Because it was unfair competition. I mean, she's a fucking goddess with a gun anyway, but unsuppressed Amanda *never* misses the bullseye."

"Never?"

"Never," Gayle confirmed. "With her powers in effect, she was money...every single time."

"I don't understand. Everyone misses sometimes."

"Not Zephyr. You remember our conversation about how my powers work?"

She saw the smirk on Michael's face and realized she had just inadvertently looped the conversation back to the aforementioned tequila night. She cringed, knowing exactly what he was about to say.

"Well, I'm not sure how much *I* remember," he said sarcastically. "At least one of us was pretty drunk that night."

"Hey, I said I was sorry!"

She smiled as he laughed. A part of her had known he would be okay with her little deception. He had forgiven her worse transgressions. Still, it was the kind of thing that—in her albeit limited experience—could have been held over her head in a less than teasing manner. In her time with Torbar, there's no way he would have let it go. It would have been another point scored for him in the unhealthy relationship game they were playing at the time.

Pot and kettle. You did exactly the same thing to him whenever he fucked up.

Which was true. Back then, in that mutually destructive partnership, she would have. Michael was different, though, and he inspired *her* to be different. Hence, why the dishonesty had been eating away at her, compelling her to come clean.

"Anyway," she continued, "you remember you asked what dictated which powers we could use? And I said it was usually natural affinity or hereditary? Well, that's not *quite* accurate. In truth, almost all hybrids can channel all four abilities, but we tend to be stronger in one or two. Those are the ones I was talking about. Amanda, however...she could only really control one."

"As her call sign is Zephyr, I'm assuming that power was air manipulation."

"And you'd be correct in that assumption. She's what we—kind of cruelly—referred to as a 'one-trick-pony.' But it was the one trick no one else in the unit could duplicate. Not even me."

"I thought your powers were 'off the fucking charts?' And that—I think—is a direct quote."

"Well remembered," Gayle laughed. "But Zephyr isn't about power. She is all about finesse. She manipulates tiny currents and micro-gusts of air to guide the flight of her bullets. Any projectile, really. Bullets, knives, soccer balls, tennis balls...you name it. If it travels through the air, she can influence it."

"How is that even possible?" Michael said. "I mean, bullets travel at what...?"

"Zephyr's custom sniper rifle clocks at fourteen hundred meters-per-second at the muzzle. Which was why no one else could do it—none of us. The bullet had hit its target before we could even *think* about using our powers. But, for Amanda...it's an instinctual ability. We never really figured out how it worked, but she always thought she unconsciously prepared the trajectory before pulling the trigger.

"Anyway, she was a natural for the squad's sniper. We had total confidence in her ability to provide cover fire because she never missed a target."

"So, why set the records under suppression?"

"Because she knew her raw power was the weakest in the unit. Firearms were her equalizer, so to speak, so she chased that skill. Mastered it with or without powers. She was the only one of us to regularly carry guns into combat; a routine she tried to get us to follow, too. We probably should have fucking listened."

Maybe if I'd insisted we all carry sidearms, things would have been different in Valletta...

Gayle felt her mood slipping toward a darker shade and shook her head to clear it. Forcing a smile, she stared at Michael, his face holding a look of deep sympathy. He slipped his hand over hers and squeezed it gently. No words, just the simplest of gestures. Such a seemingly tiny thing, but to Gayle, it felt huge.

This was what she'd come home for.

She returned his grip, squeezing his hand harder than was polite. She couldn't help it...she was broken.

"Michael...my dad..." She sobbed and could say no more.

She screwed her eyes closed and felt his arms wrap around her as she succumbed to his embrace. Feeling his hand on her hair, tenderly cradling her head to his chest as she shook. Months of bottled-up emotion came flooding out. The loss of her team, her father, her injuries, frustrations...all of it suddenly burst through the dam with the touch of his hand on hers. For a moment, she wondered why...

Why now?

Why couldn't she have done this with her sisters? Her parents? Or Lana? Even her therapist? Then it hit her like a brick. The realization that with Michael, the monsters couldn't hurt her.

"It's okay," Michael whispered. "It's gonna be okay."

He was right. For the first time in what seemed like so long...she finally felt safe.

| 15 |

LEARNING JAPANESE

— **Lyssa Balthazaar** —
— *Sunday — Nexus City, Iceland* —

Lyssa watched as Allyson scampered around her apartment feverishly searching through drawers and cupboards. It was starting to look a lot like her home had been tossed by burglars as she neglected to close said drawers and cupboards before moving on to the next potential hiding place for the sought-after object.

"If I knew what you were looking for, maybe I could help?" Lyssa ventured as Allyson wandered past her toward the bedroom while muttering under her breath.

Following in her wake, she walked through the door to see Ally kneeling on the floor, her head and shoulders under the bed, and her ass in the air.

"It's here somewhere..." her muffled voice muttered. "Aha!"

She dragged out a fancy gift box, then sat on the floor cross-legged, nestling it in her lap. Unceremoniously discarding the lid, Ally began rummaging through the box. To Lyssa it looked like a memory box, full of nick-knacks and greetings cards. As Ally tossed a few of them onto the floor, Lyssa snatched one up to examine it.

"'Congratulations on your new job!' These were..." Lyssa started.

"Leaving gifts and cards from my cop job," Ally explained distractedly. "The guys thought it would be funny to give me an old-fashioned detective kit...including...got it!"

She snatched out the object triumphantly and held it aloft for Lyssa to see.

"A magnifying glass?"

"A very *good* magnifying glass. No cheap plastic shit from my ex-colleagues." Ally jumped up and swiftly headed back to the lounge.

Lyssa dropped the card back into the box and followed suit, finding Ally in the lounge trying to unplug her reading lamp. The power cord was wrapped around one of the legs of her reading chair and wouldn't pull free.

"Help me..." Ally urged Lyssa.

She lifted the chair to allow Allyson to untangle the mess beneath.

"Can I ask what you're doing?"

"I want to take a closer look at that fragment we found." She stalked off into the kitchen, lamp in tow.

"Would you slow down for a minute..." Lyssa said, struggling to keep up with her fast-moving lover.

Allyson was already plugging the reading lamp in at the kitchen counter and angling the powerful LED light toward the black surface. She paused before activating the brilliant glow. "I just need to use it for a minute or two..."

Lyssa understood what she was hinting at. It occurred to her how it was the little things that were going to catch her out as she tried to adjust to being exiled in a human world. Back home, her kind generally slept during the day, and all their windows were polarized to keep out the bright sunlight. During the night, she would pad around her house in the dark, her eyes more than capable of seeing clearly. Any lights they did have, had very low wattage bulbs.

The world Allyson lived in was a lot more vivid. Brighter.

Painfully so at times.

Lyssa nodded. "I'll be fine. I'll just look away."

"Sorry," Ally said apologetically. "I'll be fast as I can. I promise."

Lyssa laughed in response. "At least you didn't just blind me without warning this time."

She turned her back to Allyson and closed her eyes. While the ambient light from the reading lamp actually wasn't too bright, her eyes were still overly sensitive from the earlier incident with the torch.

"There's something here…" Ally muttered.

"Tell me. What is it you're seeing?"

"Writing. Looks…I dunno. Chinese? Japanese? I don't know…I can't read either language. Could be Martian for all I know."

"Can I see?" Lyssa said. "I read a little Japanese."

"How do you know Japanese?" Ally asked.

"I probably shouldn't admit to this…but New Victus obtains a fair amount of black market tech from the Empire." She shrugged. "And I'm honestly more guilty than most on that front. Over time, I've learned a little of the language, both spoken and written."

"Okay, then, you come take a look."

"Turn the light off so I can turn around."

Ally obliged, and the kitchen returned to the lower ambient light level Lyssa could tolerate. She took the magnifying glass and the evidence bag containing the fragment they had recovered from the World Council Chamber. Pulling the clear plastic taut, she focused her stare through the glass. The magnified view confirmed what Ally had said—a fragment of circuit board. A corner piece, by the looks of things. She squinted at it, moving the glass in and out in an effort to focus on what she could see was indeed Japanese lettering.

"What does it say?" Ally asked impatiently.

"It doesn't say anything…"

"So, it's *not* Japanese?"

"Yes, it's Japanese…" Lyssa said. "But it's not writing. It's a manufacturer logo, I think."

"Do you recognize it?"

Lyssa placed the magnifying glass down on the counter, shaking her head. She may have purchased items from the Japanese Empire, but she was hardly an authority on the manufacturers. In actual fact, it wasn't strictly a manufacturer's logo at all. Things had changed since the War.

"No, I don't. Sorry. The Japanese Empire is very…secretive. Information about them is hard to come by. We know they've made strides in technology that is second only to the Fae. We're not sure how they achieved that level of expertise, but we do know the tech comes out of a number of what they now refer to as the TechMasters."

"What are TechMasters?"

"It's not a what. It's a who," Lyssa explained. "The only logo I recognize is that of TechMaster Saito who built my flyer. This isn't it."

"So, who is it?" Ally asked.

Lyssa shrugged.

"Can we search NewNet for it?"

"You can try," Lyssa sighed, "but I doubt you'll find anything."

"But you just said it was on your flyer back home, so surely there must be a record of these logos somewhere?"

"I never said it was on my flyer. I said it was TechMaster Saito that built my flyer. I had to pick it up at a secret rendezvous in the middle of the Pacific. She arrived on an aircraft carrier, which was where we exchanged the money for the merchandise. Then I flew *Tawaic'iya* home from there."

"*Tawaic'iya?*"

"The name of my flyer," Lyssa explained. "It's a Lakota word. It means to be free, or to be one's self."

"I like it." Ally smiled.

"The ship flew under two flags. One was the flag of the Japanese Empire, the other was a stylized Japanese S in a kind of three-dimensional cube. TechMaster Saito's, I assume. I don't know any of the others, I'm afraid."

The two stood staring at the little plastic evidence bag containing the tiny clue. Their only lead to uncovering the truth behind the bombing and who was responsible for what had happened to Allyson's father, and to Mercy.

She would know.

Lyssa vocalized what she was thinking. "I bet Mercy has

intelligence files on all of the known TechMasters back home in New York."

Allyson sighed. Her shoulders slumped.

"Well, getting you back to New York under your current fugitive status is going to be impossible," she mused. "I'd wager FSE Intelligence probably has that information, too, but I don't have any unofficial contacts there. Maybe Gayle can help. Or maybe even Carrie. She has her ears to the ground and knows people who know people. She might have even done some research on this for a story."

Suddenly Lyssa had a brainwave. "Getting into *New York* might be impossible...but getting into New Victus isn't."

"I think you'll find it pretty much is," Ally laughed. "There's two-and-a-half thousand miles and the North Atlantic between us and New Victus. There's no way we can get a flyer, and a boat would take days even if we could get to the Icelandic coast...so unless you've got a handy teleporter lying around..."

Lyssa shook her head. "Allyson, you're not thinking. There's less than a mile between us and New Victus. It's a fifteen-minute walk."

"Lyssa, that's not much better. We've still got to somehow sneak across NVSec's border control, and I know how difficult that's going to be as I worked closely with them in my role as Security Chief."

"Which means you know the weak spots. You can get us in."

Ally placed the evidence down on the kitchen table, and after a brief last look, she walked back into the lounge to slump onto the sofa and stare at the ceiling. Lyssa followed and sat down next to her, likewise reclining and joining her upward gaze. She didn't say anything. She could tell Allyson was deep in thought about something, likely trying to figure out if it was indeed possible to sneak past the border. After a couple of minutes, she pivoted her head to look at Lyssa.

"Okay, so, *maybe* I can get us over the border and into New Victus territory. Where would we go?"

"We go see Bob the Broker."

Allyson burst out laughing. "Bob the Broker?"

Lyssa nodded. "It's more like a working pseudonym, I guess," she chuckled. "Bobbi Akhza is my black market contact in Nexus, the one through whom I arranged the purchase of *Tawaic'iya*."

"So, you want us to sneak across the border to visit a dodgy broker of black market information, goods, and personal flyers?"

"You have a better idea?"

"Actually, yes! I ask Gayle or Carrie," Ally said. "Maybe they'll know something."

"I don't like the 'maybe' in that statement. Bobbi *will* know."

The look on Allyson's face was pure skepticism. Lyssa knew what she was thinking. Generally, if a person is willing to walk along the tightrope of legality, then how trustworthy does it really make them? Lyssa was a wanted fugitive, and Ally would be illegally crossing the border into another nation's sovereign territory. If they got caught, the consequences would be severe. Bobbi could turn a tidy profit if she was tempted to sell them out to StormHall.

"How do you know you can trust them?" Ally asked.

"Because Bobbi is family..."

"Your tone doesn't do much to reassure me."

"My mother is Perlania Akhza—she's Akhza's second daughter. She had Bobbi in a union with Braska Haggari, the fourth son of Haggari. In Vampyrii culture, the child takes the house-name of the most senior sire, in this case, Akhza..."

"Whoosh!" Ally made a motion with her hand over her head.

"All you need to know," Lyssa reassured her, "is that Haggari is a House that has a reputation for loyalty. Bobbi has kept my secret for years, even though I'm sure it would have been exceedingly profitable to betray me to Storm."

"Fine. I trust you...so, if you trust Bobbi, then I'm good."

Lyssa jumped up from the sofa, ready for action. "Let's go then. Sooner we get answers the better."

Ally shook her head. "No, not tonight," she said, and then

held up her hand to stop Lyssa's protest before it began. "I'm tired and need sleep. Plus, you know as well as I do the New Victus sector will be crawling with Vampyrii at this time of night. As much as I want a quick answer to this, I also don't want to get caught. So, we take it carefully. We get a few hours of sleep then we try and hit the border at sunrise. Hopefully, that will be the quietest time. The FSE sector waking up while the Vampyrii start to turn in for the day. If we can sneak across during that sweet spot, we stand the best chance.

"Plus...we really need to change your look."

"What?" Lyssa said. "What's wrong with my look?"

"Nothing at all. I think you're hot, remember," Ally laughed. "But...that white stripe is pretty distinctive. It'll have to go...for now. We'll need contact lenses, too. And maybe something else to accessorize..."

Lyssa laughed nervously, wondering what on earth an Allyson Knightley makeover would look like. Her lover was right, though. She had always been a well-known face in Vampyrii society, and now with her visage splashed all over the news, everyone in Nexus would know her.

"Fine," she said with a sigh. "Do your worst."

"Don't worry, you're in safe hands."

Lyssa smiled. Suddenly things didn't seem quite so desperately bleak anymore.

| 16 |

NEW JOB; OLD LIFE

— **Alexa Reynolds** —
— *Monday* — *Independent State of Rio de Janeiro* —

"Oh, my," Becka whispered breathlessly as *Diana* banked to glide gracefully over the coastline. "Would you look at those beaches…"

Alexa peered out of the co-pilot's window to see the golden sand and cerulean waters of Copacabana that had mesmerized her partner pass lazily beneath them. She smiled. Those beaches and those waves were the very reason Becka had chosen Rio as their destination. It wasn't just *Diana* that needed some tender loving care. It was time for the two of them to take that relaxing break they had earned.

"Welcome to the Independent State of Rio de Janeiro. First time here?" she asked.

"Mmmhmm," Becka nodded. "I've always wanted to visit. To see Christ the Redeemer ever since… Well, a friend used to talk about it in revered terms. I just never had the chance—or frankly the money—to actually come here."

"Yeah. It ain't a cheap destination, but this one is on me," Alexa said with a yawn. "November's a little early for the peak temperatures, but it's plenty warm enough for you to be a beach bunny."

"You're kidding, right?" Becka laughed. "This is positively tropical compared to the English autumn I'm used to."

"We're *in* the tropics, Becks."

Her partner responded by laughing. "*Exactly*. Anyway, what are your plans while I'm sunning myself on the beach?"

Alexa shrugged. Rest and relaxation *had* originally been on the cards until a few days ago when she was contacted by Marshal Carlos Braga. The message simply referred to something urgent he needed to talk to her about and to meet him upon landing at the International SkyPort.

"Depends what Braga wants, I guess," she said with a shrug.

"Want me to come with you to the meeting?"

Alexa shook her head. "That's not necessary. I'm fairly sure it'll be nothing," she lied.

Becka glanced over at her as she adjusted the flight path to start the descent into the SkyPort. She casually threw a couple of toggle switches on the control panel, causing *Diana* to shudder momentarily as the engine pods shifted into landing mode, tilting to angle their thrust down rather than aft.

"That's *not* what it sounded like on the message he sent you," she said. "It sounded like he knew you…"

"Braga? He was the reason I quit the marines. He's ex-NAA military. He was a Colonel at Fort Miramar when Michael and I were stationed there. After I got bitten in Sawtooth, he… Well, let's just say he doesn't much like Werewolves and took the dim view that getting turned was somehow *my* fault. Made my life a misery for two years until I eventually…resigned."

"So, a bit of a dick then?" Becka said deadpan.

Alexa couldn't help but burst out laughing. "Sure, you could say that. Anyway, now he's the Marshal of the ISRdJ Military, predominantly responsible for the defensive walls."

"Do you think we'll get to see them while we're here?"

"The walls? I'm sure it could be arranged." Alexa looked bemused. "Not sure why you'd want to."

She felt the landing gear deploy as Becka hit the switch on the console, prompting another gentle shudder and an audible whine. The repulsor-jets increased in their intensity as *Diana* slowed on her final approach.

"I've seen the Bulwarks around the UK. I'd love to see how they compare."

"Rio's are bigger. Taller," Alexa said as *Diana* settled onto the asphalt of the landing pad. "But then they need to be. The Independent Countries of South America coalition is still pissed Rio declared its sovereignty. The situation has been volatile for a *long* time now. They also have a big problem with The Cartel smuggling contraband in and out of the State through ISCA territory."

Becka shut down the engines and cycled through the final checks before turning off *Diana*'s systems. Alexa unbuckled her harness and started to get up out of her seat.

"Well," Becka mused, "I doubt this is about international relations. So, do you think Braga wants to talk to you about tracking smugglers?"

Alexa shook her head. "Not really my area of expertise, is it?"

It was a rhetorical question. Alexa left the cockpit and clambered down the ladder into the cargo bay before following the short corridor to her quarters. Both she and Becka had already packed, so it was a simple case of collecting her kitbag, lugging it down the cargo ramp, and stepping out into the South American sunshine.

She was signing over control of *Diana* to the ground crew who were going to perform the overhaul when Becka appeared carrying her luggage. She'd changed clothes—jeans and a plain white T-shirt. As she reached the bottom of the ramp, she nodded toward a trio of men approaching them in a jeep at speed. Military uniforms, serious expressions...it wasn't difficult to guess who they were. Alexa dropped her kitbag and took a deep breath.

"Alexa Reynolds," Marshal Braga said with a smile as he extended his hand in her direction. "It's been a while."

False familiarity.

A far cry from their last meeting, the day Alexa had quit the NAA marines. On that occasion, he had been less than polite. Today, though, he was buttering her up with pleasantries.

This is a bad sign.

"Five years, Marshal," she said, playing along and shaking his outstretched hand. "You've risen to high places, I see. This is my partner, Becka Dawkins."

Becka stepped forward with a smile and shook the marshal's hand. "Pleasure, Marshal."

"Pleasure is all mine," he replied smoothly. "If you ladies would like to get in the jeep, we'll take you to HQ where I'll brief you on the job."

Becka looked at Alexa, confused. "The job?"

He beckoned for them to get into the vehicle while his aides picked up their kitbags and deposited them in the back. Apparently taking no for an answer was not going to be a valid option.

"I need your expertise," he said.

"There are hundreds of mercs for hire," Alexa countered. "We're just here for some RnR and to get my ship overhauled."

Braga looked undeterred by her argument. "Your maintenance work will be done at my expense, and you'll also be handsomely paid for your time. It has to be you due to your recent...experience."

The jeep accelerated quickly, pushing Alexa back in her seat a little.

What recent experience was the marshal referring to? He couldn't possibly mean the job they'd just wrapped up in Pack Nation. While it *had* been an official MercNet job, she knew Damian had been pretty cagey with the details. There was no way this could be another succubus.

Could it?

She glanced over to see an equally confused Becka shrug at her.

Alexa didn't press for details, simply settled back into her seat and endeavored to enjoy the ride. Becka, meanwhile, was staring dolefully out of the vehicle's grimy windows as the destination she so desperately wanted to explore passed rapidly by. A depressing way to see a city of such beauty.

Sorry, Becks. I promise I'll make it up to you.

Twenty minutes later, they were sitting in a modest briefing room staring at a digital map of the ISRdJ territory on a huge, flatscreen monitor.

Across the briefing table sat a very nervous-looking young woman wearing an olive-green military uniform. Her name patch said simply 'Rodriguez,' and if Alexa was reading her rank stripes correctly, she was a corporal. She looked distracted, biting her thumbnail and staring at her blurry reflection in the gleaming tabletop. As the marshal sat himself down at the head of the table, he didn't bother to introduce them.

Now, there's the Braga I remember.

"How much do you know about Rio?" Braga started when they were all settled.

"Well," Becka pointed to the screen, "I know it doesn't *just* refer to the city anymore. It's the surrounding area, too. Everything within the walls. Roughly ten thousand square kilometers...if memory serves."

Alexa looked at her partner with a raised eyebrow. She wondered—not for the first time—how Becka knew some of the information she did. She turned to Braga and shrugged.

"All I know is you have the richest population per capita in the world. Which is how you could afford to build the wall that guarantees your independence and how you fund your pretty extensive military."

The marshal leaned forward onto the conference table and spread his hands. "The Independent State of Rio de Janeiro keeps itself independent from The Cartels and The Coalition using the Parede de Fronteira..."

"The Boundary Wall," Alexa helpfully translated.

"It's a series of fortifications linked by a forty-foot wall armed with automated gun emplacements, and it's patrolled constantly. It's worked well to keep undesirables out of Rio for the past twenty years. Until now.

Alexa nodded. "Which, I'm guessing, is why you need our help?"

The marshal gestured to the screen. The walls glowed yellow on the satellite image forming a boundary around the area with Rio de Janeiro at its center. With another hand movement, the view on the monitor focused on a smaller area around the northeast. A marker on the map was labeled 'Bom Jardim.'

"Two weeks ago, we started to get reports of…disturbances near the Fort situated at Bom Jardim. It's one of our more remote stations in the Tijuca Forest. We're used to having trouble out there. Relations are frosty at best with ICSA. Additionally, we're in a constant battle trying to stop drug trafficking by The Cartel. Day to day, we have our hands full.

"This time, however…it wasn't *either* of those problems."

"So, what was it?" Alexa asked, her curiosity piqued.

Braga gestured to the woman across the table. His manner almost dismissive, instantly grating on Alexa. Who was this young lady and what had she done to deserve such disdain?

"This is Corporal Valentina Rodriguez," he said brusquely. "She was part of a squad sent out into the jungle at Bom Jardim to investigate. She was the only one to come back."

So, that's it then. She disappointed him. Just like I did.

Alexa instantly felt a bond with the woman. A kinship. The haunted look in Valentina's sunken, sleepless eyes was a look Alexa knew well. She remembered seeing that very expression staring back at her from the mirror for weeks in the aftermath of Sawtooth.

Valentina was searching for answers, and suddenly, so was Alexa.

What happened to her?

Braga pointed to the screen. "Her team was dispatched to investigate after we saw this…"

On the screen, a video began to play. The detail from the camera was incredible. The jungle looked gorgeous. Vibrant shades of verdant green crowded the screen, and the foliage looked so dense it made Alexa question how The Cartel insurgents could penetrate it. She was also wondering what they were *supposed* to be seeing when a subtle movement in the lower right of the screen caught her eye.

A ripple of burnt-orange and black fur, barely visible through the vegetation.

Becka spotted it, too. "Tigers?"

Braga nodded. "At first we thought, somehow, we actually

had a tiger problem. Escaped zoo animals that had bred, maybe. But then we saw this…"

While the footage on the screen continued, a series of other glimpses of fur could be seen moving through the forest. As Alexa watched, she counted what must have been at least a dozen of the animals.

What is a group of tigers called?

However, it quickly became clear these *weren't* simply tigers. One of the creatures started to shift form, and a moment later, the tiger had been replaced by the figure of a large man.

A man Alexa recognized.

She sat back in her chair, shaking her head. "That's…not possible…"

It was Becka who put the pieces together first. "The Havana job? That's what you meant by us having experience. You have a Harimau Jadian problem."

"But…we caught him," Alexa continued. "We handed him over to the FSE authorities in Nassau. It *can't* be the same man."

Could it?

She glanced at Becka, who nodded. "It is. I can't explain why he's now prowling the forests of Brazil, but it's *definitely* our Cuban bounty."

It *was* a mystery, that much was certain, but Alexa couldn't help but wonder why exactly they were being dragged into this. Granted, she had a history with the man in the video, but Braga couldn't have known that. And besides, that one hunt was the limit of her experience with the Harimau Jadian. Becka was evidently thinking along similar lines.

"Marshal," Becka said slowly, "what *exactly* is it you want us to do? I mean, we managed to subdue *one* of these buggers, but the footage shows maybe a dozen of them…"

"I don't want you to subdue them, Ms. Dawkins. I want you to talk to them," Braga said. "We think they've established a settlement in the forest somewhere not far from Fort Bom Jardim. We'd like you to go find them and talk to them."

The pieces were starting to fall into place for Alexa now. She glanced between Braga and Valentina, then sat back in her chair, her eyes narrowed.

"You already sent the corporal here, didn't you?" she said. "But it didn't go according to plan..."

The marshal regarded the young soldier with barely concealed disdain. "Tell them."

Valentina's eyes flicked nervously toward Braga before subsequently focusing on Alexa. There was a visible nervousness. Sadness, too. Yet also a strength Alexa recognized. She didn't know what Valentina had faced out in the forests, but the woman had *survived*.

Braga may not care about that, but Alexa did.

When she opened her mouth to speak, Valentina's voice was hoarse, her words almost a whisper. Her hands trembled as she clasped them together and placed them on the tabletop. "My squad was ordered to find the Harimau Jadian. We were to..." Her eyes flicked toward Marshal Braga. "To try and...find out why they're here. To negotiate with them."

Alexa didn't need a polygraph to know the girl was lying. You don't sign a peace treaty with a hammer. Sending in soldiers was what you did when you wanted to eliminate a problem, not negotiate with it.

"We tracked them to their settlement and attempted to make...peaceful contact. But they attacked us. They came out of the jungle, all around us... They were so fast.

"I...I tried to talk, but they wouldn't listen. My squad was outnumbered. There were dozens of them." She took a deep, shaky breath. "So many. We weren't trained to fight tigers. We were trained to fight men...people. The Cartels. Not tigers..." She trailed off, lost in whatever memory she was reliving.

"Corporal Rodriguez..." Marshal Braga started, his voice tinged with a warning tone.

Alexa interrupted the marshal with a soothing voice. "Please continue, Valentina. What happened out there?"

She would not let him bully Valentina like he had browbeaten her after the events of Sawtooth.

"I ran," Valentina whispered. "I panicked. I dropped my weapon... I ran. We all ran. Different directions, just trying to escape. To get away with our lives. But it was so confusing.

"I stopped, trying to get my bearings. I had no reference point…no landmarks. I looked around. I thought maybe I'd lost them…maybe I could backtrack and find my squad. Maybe they were alive, and I could save them. I *wanted* to save them.

"But the leaves moved. They found me. I thought they were going to kill me."

"But you're here," Becka said.

The girl nodded slowly. "I was surrounded. So many of them. Huge. Black and orange…teeth bared, claws out…" She hesitated. "I thought I was dead, but then…she arrived."

"She?" Alexa prompted.

"She was…beautiful." Valentina's voice was still hushed, but now there was a sense of awe. "White and black… Her tail flicked. Like a cat does when it's angry…"

"White tiger?" Becka asked.

Valentina shook her head for a moment, then shrugged. "Yes…but she was a woman…naked. Her skin was covered in white fur…like snow. With black stripes, like a tiger… Her hair was so long and white. And she had the ears…cat ears…"

"And the tail?" Alexa confirmed.

Valentina nodded.

"Mid-shifter," Becka conjectured, referring to a shapeshifter's ability to maintain a form between human and animal.

"She walked out of the jungle…graceful like a dancer. Barefoot. So quiet. She was angry. I could tell she was very angry at us. At me. But she stopped and spoke… She said it three times…slowly. Carefully. I remember the words. I'll never forget the words…

"'Kami hanya ingin hidup dengan aman. Tolong, kami memerlukan bantuan anda.'" The words were uttered, awkwardly. It was clear she had no idea of the language she was speaking; she had simply learned to relay them phonetically.

Alexa turned toward Marshal Braga. "I assume you've translated this?"

"It's Malay. "'*We only wish to live in peace. Please, we need your help.*'"

"Help with what?" Alexa asked.

Braga shrugged.

"None of this explains why us?" Becka said. "I mean...we've never come across this...tigress before, and the one Harimau Jadian we *have* met... Well, we didn't exactly leave him on good terms with us when we dropped him off in Nassau."

"Maybe not, Ms. Dawkins, but I think he *respects* you. I put my intelligence staff to work, finding out all I could about these things. They respect strength, and you, Ms. Reynolds, beat one of their best in one-on-one combat. And you did it without using...your other ability. If anyone has earned their respect...it's you."

"So, because Alexa kicked the arse of one of their boys, you're hoping they'll listen to us, where they wouldn't listen to you?"

Marshal Braga nodded. "That is the theory."

"Okay," Alexa leaned forward, "assuming they will listen to me, what do you want me to talk to them about?"

Braga looked at her seriously and raised an eyebrow. "I want to know why they're here," he said, "and more to the point...what they want us to help them with."

| 17 |

SNEAKING AROUND

— **Allyson Knightley** —
— *Monday* — *Nexus City, Iceland* —

"You're *absolutely* sure about this?" Lyssa whispered.

"Just tie the blindfold around your eyes. Tightly. It's almost time."

The sun crowned over the horizon, birthing a fresh dawn, slowly erasing the night one shortening shadow at a time. As the darkness departed, so did the citizens of the New Victus sector. While the rest of the city awoke to a bright new day, the nocturnal Vampyrii hid away from it. This was their time to sleep. Which made it the perfect time for Lyssa and Allyson to make their move.

Ally knew how the border between the FSE and New Victus sectors was patrolled and monitored. New Victus had constructed a wall to segregate themselves from the rest of the Nexus City community. There were only a few gates, and all were closely guarded.

However, one of them *did* have the tiniest of flaws that could be exploited if they were very fast and exceptionally lucky.

This has got to be timed perfectly.

"You want to explain this to me again? Just so I'm straight."

Allyson sighed. "No time. Just keep hold of my hand and

be ready to go on my signal, okay?"

The blindfolded Lyssa looked nervous but nodded, her hand gripping Allyson's tightly.

They had left Ally's apartment just before sunrise making their way as quickly and as surreptitiously as possible to their current vantage point. Hidden in the disappearing shadows of an office building sitting about fifty meters from the New Victus wall, Ally could see the small guard post manned by one Vampyrii leading into a cargo transfer holding area.

This was a guard post Allyson knew *very* well indeed.

It had been the subject of a continual stream of petty complaints from a particular NVSec Security Officer. Sergeant Vizkar Khirion objected to the fact that, every morning at dawn, the Nexus SkyPort would system check the 'Triplets,' the large radar tracking dishes sitting atop the control tower. Each of the dishes would go through a series of motions designed to evaluate its scope and range, ensuring it was working and correctly aligned.

Vizkar's issue was that during the process, each of the dishes in turn would bounce the dazzling morning sun off the polished parabola and directly into his guard post. He pointed out that this was a potential security breach, as for those thirty seconds or so every morning, he—or whoever was stationed there that day—was effectively blinded by the reflected sunlight.

Vizkar requested the SkyPort change its maintenance routine and do their checks later in the day when the sun was in a different position. The SkyPort said it was too expensive to change their schedule and told Vizkar to invest in blinds for his windows. Vizkar argued they already *had* blinds for the windows that shielded them from the rising sun. This was a problem specific to the focused beam of light from the Triplets.

And thus, the argument went around and around.

Allyson had read the brief, and while she sympathized and agreed with Vizkar's assessment, she had bigger fish to fry than the fact that a small cargo checkpoint on the arse-end of the city had a little inconvenience once a day for a few seconds. Her focus had been on the security of the Summit, and anyone sneaking in past NVSec this way would still be caught by one of the Conference Center's security checkpoints. Conversely, anyone sneaking into New Victus territory would, of course, be dealt with by NVSec if they were caught.

Which made it somewhat ironic that today she would be the one using the security flaw she had once called 'trivial' to do *exactly* what Officer Vizkar had warned her about.

"You know the plan, right?" Ally whispered. "We'll have a thirty-second window, so you'll have to run."

"Fine for you," Lyssa hissed. "You're not wearing a blindfold!"

"I'll guide you. Trust me." Ally squeezed her hand.

"I do. I do trust you."

"Good, because we're up...any second..."

She stared up at the Triplets and heard the distinctive whine of their motors as they started their checks. Each one would rotate in turn from left to right, individually reflecting a shaft of focused sunlight their way. She watched as dish one started its pirouette, the beam moving slowly in their direction. Just as it was about to play its light across the guard post, she pulled on Lyssa's hand.

"NOW!" she growled and broke into a run.

Lyssa didn't hesitate, following her blindly as they covered the open ground from the building to the gate. They were approaching just as the reflected radiance from dish two took over from its sibling. Ally scrabbled to a stop, bringing the blinded Lyssa crashing into her back.

"Over the barrier," she whispered urgently while placing Lyssa's hand on the metal pole that barred their way.

It was a low obstacle, and it took her only a moment to hop over, but a blinded Lyssa had a little more trouble, clambering clumsily as her footing slipped on the other side. She knew the second dish would have spent its light on them by now, and they were being hidden by the third and final shaft. Time was running out. She grabbed Lyssa by the hand again, urging her to her feet.

"We gotta run!"

The light passed by, no alarms sounded, and Ally found herself leaning against the shadowed side of a cargo container, hidden from view, panting. They'd made it. As relief set in and she realized what they had just done, it manifested as a giggle. She clamped a hand over her mouth to try to stifle her amusement.

"Shhhh!" Lyssa whispered between her own suppressed laughter. "Vampyrii have excellent hearing— we'll get caught!"

"Come on," Ally said. Taking Lyssa's hand, she led her deeper into the shadows.

Finally, she brought them to a stop between two containers a good distance from the guard post. She sat on the ground and looked at her hands. They were shaking with the rush of adrenaline. Taking a deep breath, she closed her eyes, trying to calm herself. Lyssa finally removed her blindfold, crouched down next to her, and put a hand on her shoulder.

"Are you okay?"

Allyson nodded. "Sorry. About the giggles. I was just struck by the *absurdity* of what we were doing. I'm a cop, or former cop, but the last few years were just detective stuff. I didn't have to run around like this. I'm so out of shape. All this...this is my sisters' forte, not mine. Both of them. Carrie is the one always sneaking into places she shouldn't be for a story, and Gayle is the one with the covert ops training. I'm just winging it while wearing her CombatSkin."

"You look good in it," Lyssa said with a wink.

"Is this you flirting?" Ally laughed quietly. "Or your way of calming me down?"

"Consider it both. Look, Ally, you got us this far—which is something I couldn't have done. Now leave the rest to me."

Ally nodded in response, not telling her partner exactly what was going through her mind. If this all came to light, her career was over. She had been ordered to step back from this investigation due to the personal conflict it represented. Not only had she not done that, but she had also taken in a wanted fugitive, stolen evidence from an active crime scene, and now breached the New Victus border illegally with the aforementioned wanted fugitive to take their stolen evidence to be looked at by someone who trafficked in black market goods.

She looked across at Lyssa, the woman for whom she was risking it all.

The truth. That's what this all boiled down to at the end of the day. Allyson *needed* it. Lyssa was telling it. Of that she was certain.

"You didn't have to do this," Lyssa said softly.

"Yes, I did. We both know it."

"Maybe, but I could have done this alone. You could have told me where to cross and when—"

"—and you could have stumbled around in the blinding sunlight till you were caught. Plus, you're wearing my sneakers, so if you got caught, I'd be up shit creek anyway."

"I could've said I stole them."

Ally laughed. "Yeah, and left your boots in my apartment in exchange. No, there's way too much forensics evidence in my apartment for me to ever innocently say you just broke in and absconded with my footwear."

"Well, I'm grateful for the sneakers." Lyssa chuckled and sat down on the floor next to her. "For what it's worth, I'm not used to this sneaking around either. This is Shadowwraith work."

Ally frowned. "What work?"

"Shadowwraith," Lyssa repeated. "You've never heard of them?"

Ally shook her head.

"They're a genetic offshoot of the Adze. Storm uses them for covert work from time to time because their skin works like a chameleon. A little like your CombatSkin."

"So, they camouflage themselves?"

Lyssa nodded. "They're good pretty much anywhere, but because of their Adze traits, they tend to prefer working in the dark. They're practically impossible to see when blending into the shadows, hence the name."

Something tickled at Allyson's brain. A feeling of a memory she couldn't quite recall. Something recent.

"*Practically* impossible?" she asked.

"Some people say you can sense them when you look in their direction. Even if you can't see them, you get a feeling of something being wrong or out of place. I've never experienced it myself. Just heard the stories."

"Gayle once said the Adze are a bit like that," Ally said thoughtfully. "She said watching them move felt unnatural...like a stop-motion effect come to life. Made her feel uneasy, agitated."

"I know what she means. Seeing Adze always makes the hairs stand up on the back of my neck. Shadowwraiths, though...I've never seen one myself. Just heard the stories."

Ally's hand drifted to her nape, gently stroking the skin there.

What am I forgetting?

"I suggest we wait a little while before heading onto the streets. Give my people a little time to get to bed. It'll be a lot quieter then and we'll be able to move a little more freely."

Ally nodded, distractedly agreeing with Lyssa's assessment. But in the back of her head, she was still trying to chase the memory that was eluding her.

| 18 |

MARK OF THE EMPIRE

— **Lyssa Balthazaar** —
— *Monday — Nexus City, Iceland —*

Lyssa knocked—three times softly. No immediate answer was forthcoming, not that she'd expected one. She glanced at the security camera affixed to the wall above the nondescript-looking door, and then back over her shoulder nervously. Allyson's face mirrored her anxiousness by at least a factor of ten. Illicit meetings in the back alleys of New Victus were new territory for her. Fortunately, Lyssa was experienced with this kind of subterfuge, even if being a fugitive did give an apprehensive edge to this particular rendezvous.

A minute or two passed, but finally, the doorway cracked open a few inches. From the shadows beyond, a square-jawed face peered at them suspiciously before suddenly changing to recognition.

"Fuck me! Lyssa, babe, is that you? Are you fucking insane? What are you...never mind. Get your arse in 'ere. Quick. Before someone eyeballs you!"

The door was hastily opened wider, and the woman with the strong Cockney accent beckoned them in before quickly closing it behind them, locking it securely. Her gaze flirted briefly over Allyson then turned once more to Lyssa.

"*You*...are a wanted woman, Lyssa Balthazaar. Do you realize the tremendous pile of *shit* we'll both be in if they find you here?"

"We won't stay long, Bobbi. I promise," Lyssa said. "We just need a few minutes of your time...and a small favor. Then we'll be out of your hair."

"Babe, you *know* I have all the time in the bloody world for you." Bobbi grinned. "I'm more concerned about *you* than me—"

Lyssa held up her hand to interrupt. "If you've seen the news, then you know that I *can't* be in any more trouble than I already am."

Bobbi chuckled and shook her head. "You know, for a moment there, I 'ave to admit, I almost didn't recognize you. Not the best wig, to be brutal, but being a redhead suits ya. The nose ring, too...is that the genuine article?"

"Clip-on," Lyssa admitted. "We thought it best to come in disguise."

"The contacts are a nice touch, too," Bobbi chuckled gesturing to Lyssa's eyes.

Lyssa blinked. "They are *not* the most comfortable things to wear..."

"I feel your pain, babe. Come on, you can take them out downstairs," Bobbi replied. "Honest, when I saw you on the security cam, I wondered who the *fuck* was knocking on my door. Took me a minute to recognize you..." She paused for a moment, her eyes moving to Allyson. "...'specially as you have such high-profile company."

Allyson extended her hand in a friendly gesture. "Allyson Knightley," she said by way of introduction.

"I know who you are, *Chief* Knightley. What I couldn't figure out when I saw you on the camera was why the fuck the FSE security chief was standing on my bleedin' doorstep. Then I saw this bitch," Bobbi jabbed her thumb at Lyssa, "and figured if you were with her then there was probably a bloody good reason. Color me curious, but I had to find out what that reason was."

"Ally is helping me," Lyssa said. "You can trust her, Bobbi. She got me safely across the border."

Bobbi stared at Ally, her eyes narrowing slightly. Lyssa

knew Bobbi prided herself on being an excellent judge of character; she had to be considering the business she was in. She'd seen her half-sister do this before. The stare, she called it. Bobbi had once said—jokingly, she assumed—that she could peer into people's souls and reveal the truth in their character. While Lyssa was *fairly* sure that was hyperbole, there was a small part of her that wondered if it was true.

"I don't know *you*, Allyson Knightley...but I am familiar with your family. Met your dad once. Came across as one of the most unprejudiced and uncomplicated people I'd ever had the good fortune to meet. I admired him. He was good people. My sincerest condolences on your loss." Bobbi grasped Ally's outstretched hand and firmly pumped it up and down. "Scores a bunch of brownie points with me that you're helpin' my sister out when by rights you should be grieving."

"Thanks," Ally replied in a subdued tone.

"Reckon we're gonna be good mates, you and me, Allyson," Bobbi said with a grin. "Right, follow me."

And with that she was off again, leading them down a hallway, past a number of beautifully furnished rooms. At the end of the corridor, Bobbi ran a finger over a mundane-looking section of wall, which was evidently more than it seemed. A secret entrance rolled open to reveal an elevator car. A moment later they were slowly descending.

"So, Lyssa, how's that little flyer I hooked you up with doing?"

Lyssa nodded. "Perfect. Just as advertised."

"Never doubted it. So, what can I do for you today? I assume you're looking for safe passage out of Nexus?"

"Can you arrange that?" Ally asked.

Bobbi chuckled. "I can arrange *anything* you desire, luv. Just call me the genie of the fucking lamp."

Lyssa sighed. "Can you arrange it for Mercy?"

"Mercy?" Bobbi's brow wrinkled. "I mean... Isn't she... Didn't she—"

Lyssa interrupted her. "I *need* to get her out of the city before NVSec starts to do anything with her."

Bobbi said nothing for a moment and then recognition

dawned. "I'm betting this has something to do with Nyk's secret little side project and the weird shit she's been sourcing off me lately?" Lyssa's face stayed stoic. Bobbi chuckled. "Fair enough. Well, it's difficult but doable. Can your new friend here get us access to her body?"

"I think so," Ally nodded.

"Then if you don't mind a few...questionable ethics being used, then yeah, I can get her out of Nexus. So, my next question becomes...where do you want to go?"

"I need you to get Mercy to Montreal."

"Montreal?" Bobbi smiled slyly. "So, you're not done with the Wolf King after all then?"

"Can you do it?" Lyssa pressed.

"Course I can. But what about you and the sheriff here?"

"Well, I need to get back into the FSE sector. Don't suppose you have an easy way to do that, do you?" Ally said.

"Darlin', gimme a challenge, please! Getting you back home...piece of piss." Bobbi laughed as the elevator doors opened out into a basement room adorned with an impressive array of computer technology. "I know technically you're the Old Bill, but by being here *illegally* and with your...relationship to my half-sister, I'm assuming I can trust you to be discreet about my methods?"

Ally nodded. "I've crossed lines today that there's no going back over. Your secret is safe. I promise."

"And you, Sister? Where do you need to go?"

Lyssa considered the question for a moment. Honestly, she had no idea. She needed a plan, but first, she needed the information for which they'd come.

"I'll think on that, but the real reason we're here, Bobbi, is because we need help identifying something we found."

She beckoned to Allyson who passed the evidence bag containing the microchip fragment to Bobbi. She peered at it closely, pulling the plastic taut to get a better look.

"I don't think I need to ask where you found this," she said and then winked at Allyson. "Going rogue and pursuing your own investigation, are you?"

Allyson looked surprised. "You might say that, yes."

Bobbi chuckled. "I got ears to the ground all over Nexus. I don't just deal in tech; information is a commodity too, luv. I *know* your uncle threw you off the big case. Of course, the bigger clue was you risking your career to hop the border with a fugitive to visit an illegal black-market broker…"

"No pulling the wool over your eyes," Ally laughed.

"As I said, information is my business." Bobbi turned back to the microchip. "But as to what this is… Not a fucking clue."

Her face turned serious as she scrutinized the tiny piece of circuitry for a moment before walking almost absentmindedly toward a workbench filled with a collection of computer equipment. Seating herself on a worn office chair, she lifted the lid on a piece of apparatus Lyssa didn't recognize and carefully placed the evidence inside before closing it up again. Seconds later, an enlarged picture of the computer chip fragment flickered into view on the wall monitor. The three stared at the magnified image, all of them tilting their heads to get a better view of the logo that needed identifying.

"Well," Bobbi said eventually, "I can tell you this *is* a bio-chip… Whether there's enough of it left to identify its function I couldn't say. Maybe someone with the right diagnostic equipment could help… But I refer to my earlier statement— I've got no fucking clue."

"Bio-chip?" Ally asked.

"Bio-organically engineered," Lyssa explained.

"That said, while I can't tell you *what* it does, I *can* tell you who manufactured it." Bobbi smiled. "That logo…that's the mark of TechMaster Takahashi. Which is, in itself, more than a little bit interesting."

"How so?" Ally said.

"For starters…this would have been some expensive fucking shit. Takahashi doesn't usually sell. Believe me, I know. I've tried to acquire his designs for years and never got further than a rejection from his assistants. So, for someone to *actually* get their hands on a piece of his tech—"

"—Means they're either very rich or well connected," Lyssa interrupted.

And who do we know that's both?

"Or maybe had something Takahashi wanted in return," Bobbi shrugged.

"Or maybe someone stole it—" Ally started before Bobbi interrupted.

"No one steals from the TechMasters. *No one*."

"Okay," Ally changed tack, "so, maybe he didn't *sell* at all. Maybe this is Takahashi's doing."

Lyssa considered Allyson's comment for a moment. It didn't seem likely, but that didn't mean it wasn't possible. Or true. Was she *so* biased toward Storm that she was predisposed to pencil him into the role of villain at any given opportunity?

No.

She *knew* he was behind this. She felt it in her gut.

"I don't think the Japanese Empire is behind this. Storm procured this tech...somehow and used it in the bomb. Don't tell me how I know...I just know."

"Well," Ally pursed her lips, "as a former cop, I tend to rely on this little thing called 'evidence,' and this...just isn't enough. All we have is a piece of Japanese technology that may or may not be related to the bomb, and there's nothing linking it to StormHall."

"And you're not bloody likely to find anything either," Bobbi muttered. "Face it, Lys. If dear old Sebastian is behind this, then there's no *way* he left a trail leadin' back to him. He's too fucking smart."

"So, what are you saying?" A hint of frustration shaded Lyssa's question.

"I'm saying," Ally sighed, "that at this point, we don't have anything more than spurious leads to follow. Nothing solid. We need to find someone who can tell us what this thing does...or did. We need to know if it's connected to the bomb or just random debris wasting our time—"

"—I'd say having Takahashi's logo on it is evidence enough that this is not random debris."

"And you're probably right," Ally agreed. "But that's *not* enough. We have to know for sure."

"Maybe we could talk directly to Takahashi himself?"

"No chance of that, Sis," Bobbi snorted. "Takahashi is a recluse. I don't know anyone who's dealt with him directly. As I said before, all you get are his assistants, of which there are *many*."

Exhaling heavily, Lyssa sagged into one of the nearby chairs. She felt deflated. She had been so sure coming here would provide the answers she wanted, but instead, it had raised more questions. What she needed was a justification for going after Storm with everything she had, but it remained irritatingly out of her grasp.

Ally squatted in front of her. "Lyssa, I know you wanted definitive answers. Believe me...I did, too. But honestly, take it from someone who knows— investigations rarely go quickly. To get to the truth, you have to observe the three Ds. Be diligent, detailed, and determined. We found one clue, now we have two. We still have to find out what this chip is, but now we know who made it. Maybe *you* feel like we've not made any progress, but *I* know we've taken a big step forward. We'll find the truth. I promise.

"And I think I know a way to get the next clue..."

| 19 |

GREEN-EYED MONSTER

— Lana Fordham —
— Monday — London, England —

"You're late," Lana said as Gayle came running into the staffroom.

"Don't!" Gayle retorted, throwing her jacket over the back of a chair and snatching open her locker.

"And you didn't go home last night…"

"How do you know?"

"Because I dropped your car back and you weren't there."

"Maybe I got home late!"

Lana raised an eyebrow. "Maybe. Except when I couldn't give you the keys, I drove *Sally* back to my place and then tried again early this morning—"

"Ah…" Gayle suddenly looked a little embarrassed.

"—and you still weren't in. So, I brought *Sally* here. She's parked in the courtyard. So, where were you?"

"I stayed at Michael's."

"Then…is this a walk of shame?" Lana exclaimed excitedly. Gayle's head poked out from behind her locker door, and she stared at her friend, a look of annoyance on her face.

"What? *No!*" she hissed. "I…we talked, and I lost track of the time. I grabbed a taxi home for a change of clothes and…other things, before heading here."

Lana closed the book she was reading and placed it down

on the coffee table, turning her full attention to her flustered friend. Something was clearly eating at Gayle this morning and—knowing her friend as she did—she had a pretty good inkling of what it might be.

"What did you talk about?"

"Just...stuff..." Gayle said distractedly.

"I'm going to need more than that."

"I told you. Stuff."

Lana, however, was not going to be placated with generalities. "Gayle, stop doing whatever it is you're doing, and come over here and sit down. I mean it."

With a sigh, Gayle shut the locker and looked at her friend. Which was when Lana noticed the tell-tale signs that confirmed at least one of the items she suspected was getting under her friend's skin.

"This is about Amanda, isn't it?"

"What?" Gayle looked at her like she was mad. "Don't be ridiculous."

"Oh, *I'm* being ridiculous, am I? Let's see...you've shunned the CombatSkin this morning—"

"Ally borrowed it. Never returned it."

"Even if that's true, I know for a fact you have more than one," Lana said, rejecting her explanation. "But that's not all. The freshly styled hair. The make-up you don't usually bother with. You've even got the 'girls' out."

Gayle glanced down at her modestly cut top and frowned. "I have not!"

"Maybe not to your former...extremes. But in your current incarnation, this is the equivalent of putting the goods on Front Street. This is you competing with Amanda all over again."

Gayle opened her mouth as if about to protest, but instead, she shut it and slumped down into the chair opposite. Lana didn't say anything else; just waited for her to confess the truth.

"Okay, *fine*," Gayle eventually muttered, throwing her arms up. "I admit it. I am a little freaked out today."

"Why on earth would you be freaked out? You two have always been rivals. But this isn't like it was before. We're not going bar-hopping to pick up men. I think we know you're far more interested in... Oh...of course."

Suddenly she realized what insecurities were running through Gayle's head. This wasn't like their Academy days when the men they met at the bar would be fair game for both Amanda and Gayle to compete over. This was far more personal. She watched Gayle swallow and take a deep breath.

"Lana, when Michael and I were talking yesterday, he reminded me Amanda was starting today. So, I asked if he'd met her yet, and he said they'd only communicated by email or phone or something. Not face to face."

"So?"

"So?" Gayle repeated. "Look up the word bomb-shell in a dictionary—"

"I'm not sure that's a specific word..."

"—and you'll see a picture of Amanda Forrester next to it."

"She's attractive, yes—" Lana started.

"Attractive?" Gayle spluttered. "She's fucking gorgeous. That hair, those eyes, those legs, those curves..."

"You're starting to sound like your sister."

"Lana, you know what I mean," Gayle sighed. "When did I *ever* beat her in a straight-up fight for a man?"

"No." Lana shook her head vehemently. "Don't you go comparing your current situation to picking up men for sex in Barnun. It's *not* the same. I'd be the first to admit Amanda turns heads, and yes, she often got her pick of the bunch. But this is Michael. We both know he feels something *real* for you, and he doesn't seem to me to be the kind of man who will have his head turned by a pretty face—"

"—or perfect breasts?" Gayle muttered.

"Stop it. Right now. Just think about this rationally for a minute."

Gayle let her head rest on the back of the chair and stared at the ceiling. "I'm being stupid, aren't I?"

"No," Lana said with a smile. "You're being in love is what you're being."

"Fuck off."

"You keep denying it, but it's obvious to everyone who spends any time around the two of you. And the feeling is mutual, so it's time you—both of you—start to take it seriously and stop avoiding it."

"I did! We did. We went on the tequila night date."

"That wasn't a date," Lana laughed. "That was a *pre-cursor* to a date."

"Well…" Gayle's shoulders slumped. "I thought we were going to…that he was coming to ask me about a second date on the day…before Nexus. Since then, things have been…muddled."

"Okay," Lana said. "So, you lost the momentum of that night, but the feelings haven't changed. Just seize the initiative back again."

"I tried last night. But…"

"But what?"

Gayle exhaled heavily and sat forward to look straight at Lana. "I admitted I wasn't drunk the night of the kiss. I didn't touch the tequila."

"Did you tell him why?"

Gayle shook her head. "Not the whole truth…no."

"Why not?"

"I don't know. Baby steps, I guess. Then we started talking about Zephyr and he asked about her skills. I told him she may have only had the one real skill, but she excelled at it beyond anything I could do. I told him she was always badgering us to wear sidearms, just in case. But we were too cocky to listen.

"And then I started thinking about Valletta, and whether if we had been armed… And…then the floodgates opened."

"Your dad?"

Gayle nodded but said nothing.

"I *knew* you were lying to me on the way back from the SkyPort saying you were emotionally tapped out and not feeling anything.

"You know why you were the leader of the 137th? Why you got the nod and not Gabriel? Because you already *were* the leader of the team. Even before you got the shiny rank pin to make it official. We could all see it. So could your uncle. Even Gabe knew he would only ever play second fiddle to you.

"If any of us had a problem, you were there. If any of us were falling behind, you helped us keep up. *You* were always our strength. Mags used to call you our 'mother hen.' Stands to reason when you went to Nexus in the wake of your father's death, you'd be the one picking up the pieces and supporting your sisters and your mother.

"You have a nasty habit of suppressing your own trauma to deal with everyone else's. Which is why the Malta thing hit you so hard. You don't know how to deal with this stuff."

"I deal with it just fine," Gayle protested.

"Really?" Lana raised an eyebrow of disbelief.

"Fine...maybe you have a point. I mean, I did just break down and spend most of the night crying my eyes out with Michael. Which is also why I'm fairly sure any attraction he may have had for me is now gone."

"Bullshit. Doesn't the fact that he *just* sat up all night with you—"

"Not all night," Gayle shrugged. "I fell asleep on his sofa in the early hours."

"Gayle, my point is he cares for you. And that emotional bond is worth more than Zephyr's pretty face."

"Yeah, right," Gayle laughed. "Hot brunette bomb-shell versus pink-haired emotional disaster zone."

Lana sat back in her chair. "You know I'm right."

Fate chose that exact moment to have the man they were discussing enter the staff room. With his nose buried in a sheaf of paperwork, Michael slowly made his way toward the kitchen area and the percolating coffee machine.

"Ladies," he acknowledged absently as he grabbed a mug.

"Good morning, Captain," Lana reciprocated as Gayle made a move to get out of her chair.

She strolled over to the kitchen area herself, grabbing her mug and starting the process of making tea. Lana watched with great interest as the two of them went about their beverage making in comfortable silence, both occasionally taking side glances at each other when they were confident the other wasn't watching. Finally, Gayle picked up her steaming mug and turned to head to the door.

"What time is Lieutenant Forrester arriving?"

"We arranged to meet on the gun range at ten-hundred," Gayle answered Michael's question. "I'm heading there now to get in an hour or so of practice, so I don't look like a complete muppet when she arrives."

"You need the practice?" he asked.

"Zephyr trained me; kindly gifted me her old guns. I got to be pretty good. But I haven't fired a shot in over a year. I'd like to get my eye in a little."

"Tell you what," Lana chimed in. "I'll meet our girl when she arrives and tell her where you are."

"Sounds like a plan." Gayle smiled.

"I have the kids this morning for Phys-Ed," Michael said as he stirred his coffee. "Maybe I'll drop by and introduce myself afterward."

"Okay, sure." To Lana's ears, Gayle's reply sounded a little less than enthusiastic.

Gayle walked back to her locker, put the tea mug on top, and retrieved her gun belt. She strapped the twin holsters to her hips and gently—but firmly—slid the two Beretta 20-20 *Firestorms* in them. Reclaiming her steaming mug, she headed for the door.

"See you on the range," she said.

"Will do," Michael said looking at her with a smile. "By the way...you look real pretty today. You do somethin' different with your hair?"

Gayle looked at him. Her face lit up with a smile. "Nothing special," she said and walked out the door.

Lana raised an eyebrow and looked at Michael, who looked back at her and shrugged.

"Nicely played, Captain," she said.

"I honestly have no idea what you're talkin' about."

"Of course you don't. But nicely played anyway."

Michael picked up his mug of coffee and paperwork and, with a knowing smile, walked out of the same door Gayle had used moments earlier.

| 20 |

BACK HOME

— **Lana Fordham** —
— *Monday* — *London, England* —

"Zephyr, can I ask you a favor? It's kind of an odd one."

Amanda Forrester was smiling—obviously enjoying walking the familiar corridors of the Academy once more—but her brow furrowed beneath her wavy brunette curls as she turned to regard Lana.

"Sure," she said. "What do you need?"

"I need your help...with Gayle."

"Gayle?"

While she *had* made significant strides over the last few weeks, it was clear to Lana that Gayle's further progress was hampered psychologically by something Lana couldn't fully understand. As much help as Michael was being, there was a ceiling to how far his unique form of rehabilitation was able to take her. Neither he nor Lana would be able to help her over that final hurdle because neither of them could truly understand what she was feeling.

Because neither of them had been there in Valletta that fateful day.

But Amanda had.

She might be the only one of us who can get through to her.

Lana stopped walking.

"Okay, so, what's up?" Amanda asked. "We had a long chat

when she visited me in hospital. She seemed a lot better."

"She is," Lana agreed. "Very much better. But there's been a setback on that front..."

"Jeez! Of course...her father." Amanda put her palm to her face. "I'm such a dipshit sometimes."

Lana chuckled. "She's grieving, obviously, and there's still an undercurrent of anger bubbling away in there... but she's coping. Helped, no doubt, by the fact that our girl is smitten—"

"About bloody time," Amanda interrupted. "Who's the lucky fella?"

"I'll fill you in later, but that's not what I need your help with. There's one problem area that still isn't resolved, and I'm not sure I'm qualified to tackle it..."

When it turned out none of the 137th could fly a dropship with anything more than basic competence, Lana had been recruited for the job. Though she had skills, she wasn't a hybrid like the rest of the Hunters. It was her job to drive the bus, then get to a safe distance and let the team do their thing. None of them had ever made her feel like an outsider, but the truth was she didn't have powers...and they did.

Which, to Lana, was the crux of Gayle's issue.

Somebody needed to convince Gayle to use her powers again, to properly teach the kids how to use theirs, but whenever she tried to broach the subject, Gayle had been openly dismissive.

Amanda's return to the Academy was akin to getting reinforcements at the most opportune time. Better yet—it was reinforcements who had shared experiences with Gayle. Zephyr had powers and was the only other surviving team member from that fateful Malta mission. Maybe that would give Amanda an insight Lana didn't have.

"She won't teach the students how to use their powers," Lana sighed. "And it's starting to cause friction with the kids."

Amanda shrugged. "Maybe she has a plan. You know what it was like when we were here. We developed too far, too fast and it led to... complications."

"And that would be understandable," Lana agreed, "if it

were true. But Gayle won't teach them to use their powers...because she refuses to use her own."

"I was afraid of this."

"You were?"

Amanda put her hands on her hips as she stood for a moment, biting her lip and thinking carefully about what to say next.

"I had plenty of time to reflect on what happened in Malta while I was laid up in hospital. Not just Malta, but also about events leading up to it. As much as we'd like to blame the loss of our frie..." she couldn't bring herself to finish the word, "...the team on being caught with our pants down, we can't ignore the years that led up to that point.

"We were irresponsible with our abilities. Wildly irresponsible. You wouldn't put a drunk driver in charge of a sports car, yet that's essentially what we were. Pissed behind the wheel, and we steered ourselves right over a cliff. Gayle was the best of us...and the worst of us. And she knows it.

"She is riddled with the insecurity of that knowledge. Knowing that, not only did she make the decisions that led to that final battle, but she never did anything to reel us in *before* it got to that point."

Lana shrugged. "I don't think any of us knew where that path was taking us."

"Lana, please don't take this the wrong way, but...you're not like us. And maybe that's a good thing. We knew. Like the junkie who knows they should quit drugs before it kills them, we knew what we were doing, and we did it anyway."

Lana considered Amanda's words, and then her attitude. She didn't look or sound like someone who was suffering through the same demons that tormented Gayle.

A lot of time to think... That's what Amanda said.

"So, how did you move on?"

"Me? Well, I didn't have the burden of leadership on my shoulders. That's *got* to account for a shitload of guilt. But mostly...the realization our powers can be used but shouldn't be abused. It's easier for me because I'm the 'one-trick-pony.' My powers were never overt. I can do a little fire and a little air, but my use is subtle.

"Gayle, though...hers are much—*much*—stronger."

"Off the fucking charts." Lana smiled. "As she likes to re-mind us."

Amanda's face didn't change; there was no humor on her features as she shook her head slowly. "Oh, Lana, you have no idea. None of us had any idea."

"I don't know what that means," Lana said.

"Lana, if the addiction is proportional to the power level..." Amanda shook her head. "What I saw her do in Valletta wasn't just *off* the charts...it obliterated the fucking charts."

The two of them stood in silence for a moment as Lana tried to absorb what Amanda was telling her. She leaned against the corridor wall and exhaled heavily.

"I'll talk to her," Amanda said finally. "Maybe this is about moderation rather than abstinence. I'll try, okay?

"I'll try."

| 21 |

OLD FRIENDS

— Alexa Reynolds —
— Monday — Independent State of Rio de Janeiro —

"So, we're picking up strays now?" Becka muttered.

"I picked up you, didn't I?" Alexa shot back with a wry chuckle.

Becka, however, didn't seem in the least bit amused. She had been keeping a wary eye on Valentina—who was sitting in the back of *Benny*, Alexa's old Jeep Wrangler. The young woman had said barely a word since they'd left the city. She simply stared distractedly into the passing forest as they bounced down a track that, even on its best day, would not have been worthy of the name. As he squeaked and rattled over the bumps, Alexa had to admit *Benny* was coping with the terrain pretty well considering the Jeep was likely older than both Becka and herself combined.

They had left the relatively smooth asphalt road far behind them hours ago, branching off into the trees and following what appeared to be an overgrown footpath rather than something frequented by vehicles. Fortunately, the trees to either side were set back far enough to allow *Benny* passage, but Alexa couldn't help wondering how long that would last.

If my luck follows my usual track record...not much longer.

As if on cue, the vegetation began to get significantly denser. The forest canopy crowded in, obscuring the sun and forming a dappled effect all around them. Alexa gently slowed the Jeep to a crawl as they navigated the increasingly uneven ground.

"Besides," Alexa continued, "she's our only witness to what happened out here. Maybe this little excursion will jog an important memory. Something she forgot."

Becka looked dubious. "I don't think that's likely, Zee."

"It's just…" Alexa didn't want to talk about this in front of the young Brazilian and was a tad frustrated Becka hadn't realized why she had brought the girl along for the trip. "Look…Valentina is *you*…before you met *me*. Understand?"

Becka furrowed her brow, glancing back at their passenger.

The track narrowed significantly as it turned a blind bend, the foliage whipping against the windscreen momentarily, obscuring Alexa's view of the way forward. As the branches peeled back from the vehicle, Alexa reacted immediately to avoid a collision, hitting the brakes hard. *Benny* shuddered to a halt, throwing his passengers violently forward in their seats.

"What the fuck…?" Becka exclaimed before looking through the windscreen and seeing what they had narrowly avoided colliding with. "Shit!"

Alexa sighed. "Shit, indeed."

Lying across their path was the trunk of an enormous fallen tree, a good meter in diameter at least. It manifested out of the forest on one side and disappeared into the identically thick undergrowth on the other. Its length made it impossible to tell which end was which, not from the driver's seat anyway. She turned the key, shutting off the rumbling V8. While the Jeep had a good reputation as an accomplished off-roader, there was no way it was getting over *this* obstacle, and the forest was too dense on either side to drive around.

"Maybe we can move it?" Becka muttered. "Or chop through it?"

"That might be our only option," Alexa agreed.

They had axes in the back of *Benny* for emergency use, so with three of them—and a little elbow grease—they could do it. It would take a while, though.

"Does this happen a lot?" Alexa asked their passenger in the back.

"Trees fall," Valentina shrugged.

"Just our bloody luck..." Becka grumbled. "Is there another route?"

The young Brazilian shook her head sullenly.

"Well, nothing gained by just sittin' here," Alexa said.

She pulled the handle to carefully open the driver's door. It didn't get far before it was pressing against the undergrowth. Still, there was just enough room for her to slide out. Becka did likewise, and the two of them walked to survey the fallen tree impeding their progress. Alexa could now see it had fallen from the left. The tree's branches were clearly visible to their right.

Yet something was tickling that part of her brain that sensed trouble...

"So, what did you mean back there?" Becka said quietly. "About her being me?"

They were far enough away from the Jeep to talk without being overheard, so as Alexa inspected the roadblock, she explained her earlier statement.

"If I'm being honest, Valentina is me, too. After I got turned, I returned to Fort Miramir, and as I told you earlier, Braga was a complete douche-bag about it. He...he made life practically impossible for me to continue to serve. No place for a dog in a Human army. Especially not for a soldier who lost her unit. That little nugget did me no favors in his eyes.

"He made me an outcast, and he'll do the same to Valentina. I guaran-fucking-tee it. I saw the way he looked at her in that briefing room."

"So what? Come on, Zee...you *know* I get it. But she's not the first, and if I'm reading Braga's dickhead credentials right, she won't be the last. You can't rescue them all."

Alexa shrugged as she walked slowly toward the root end of the fallen tree. "Maybe not," she admitted, "but I'm here. Now. And I'll be damned if I let Braga..." Her voice tailed off.

Valentina's statement had led them to assume the tree

blocking their progress had been a natural fell. Alexa thought they would find the earth eroded around the root system to a point where it could no longer support its own weight.

That, however, was emphatically not the case.

As she pulled the foliage aside to clear her view, she could see with crystal clarity this tree had not fallen. It had been felled.

Deliberately.

"Fuck..." she cursed under her breath.

"What is it?" Sensing something was wrong, Becka's voice had now inherited a harder edge.

This wasn't the work of a chainsaw or axe. The trunk on the felled side was a litany of what Alexa instantly recognized as deep claw strikes. The bark had been torn away haphazardly, and the wood struck repeatedly with sharp claws that tore deep enough for the weight of the tree to do the rest.

This wasn't an accident.

This was a trap.

"Back in the truck. Quickly," she hissed.

"Why? Zee, what are you...?" Becka never finished asking why Alexa had suddenly, and quickly, started shedding her clothes. It took her only a moment to deduce the facts of the situation.

Damn, I can't wait to get that custom CombatSkin! This is humiliating!

Her guns were in the Jeep, uselessly sat holstered in the gun belt hanging over the back of the driver's seat. She cursed inwardly for being so stupid. Fortunately, she had other weapons on which to rely. Razor-sharp ones. Teeth and claws. So, it was either strip naked or let what she was about to do ruin the only clothes she had with her.

"I can fight. I can—" Becka started, only to be interrupted by Alexa who was now down to her underwear.

"—It's not about whether or not you can fight. You know that I *know* what you're capable of. But I hope it doesn't come to that. Show of strength, remember?" she said urgently. "But if it all goes wrong, then you're my ace in the hole, Becs. I don't want to tip our hand up front. I need you in my back pocket.

Understand?"

Her partner begrudgingly nodded and collected Alexa's abandoned clothing, including the newly discarded underwear. Without another word, Becka headed back to the vehicle where a confused passenger was starting to disembark.

"Is she naked?" Valentina muttered. "Why is she naked?"

"Because she can't do what she's about to do without trashing her clothes," Becka answered curtly. "Get back in the Jeep. Now!"

Alexa closed her eyes and willed the transformation. She felt the endorphin rush spread through her, almost orgasmic in its intensity as her body prepared itself for the transition from woman to Wolf. Nature's painkillers rendered her temporarily oblivious to the world as her bones rapidly rearranged themselves and her skin stretched over this new form, sprouting her distinctive snow-white fur as it did so.

Now that she had made her peace with her true nature, the change was welcomed. Yet, accepting it did *not* mean it was easy. Damian had once told her the more she transitioned from one form to another, the easier and more fluid it would become. But she wasn't there just yet. The transformation wasn't a trauma anymore. Not like that virgin moment. It was just that the change sometimes left her with a kind of headrush. Like standing up too fast. In Mont Tremblant, the immediate life or death nature of the situation had focused her, but today the sudden sensory overload threatened to overwhelm. She forced herself to concentrate.

Dammit. Sometimes I hate being right!

The forest air cycling through her lupine nostrils told the tale of just how correct she had been.

When chasing the Harimau Jadian in Havana, she had been in Human form, and while her senses were still somewhat enhanced, they could perceive only a fraction of what her Wolf form could detect. She inhaled deeply, her nose twitching as it deciphered the scents being carried to her. The distinctive markers were all there. Keener now, though. More defined.

Definitely Harimau Jadian.

Not just one…

Multiple scents, overlapping. It took her a moment to sift through them to arrive at a number. Five. Four males and one female, and her previous bounty from Cuba was amongst them. They were close…and getting closer.

Alexa heard the door of the Jeep slam shut and turned her head to check. Becka and Valentina were safely back in the vehicle, neither looking particularly happy about it. It didn't matter. The only thing of concern right now was they were protected, not that the car would hold out for long against an attack if the Harimau Jadian decided to get…aggressive.

Soundlessly, they appeared out of the trees one by one. A pair to the left of her, another pair to the right. Alexa snarled, baring her teeth as she gave a low warning growl that would have terrified most people to witness. The four Harimau Jadian were unmoved by her display. They knew as well as she did that tiger trumped wolf every time.

Each was a sinewy, prowling mass of pure muscle. Large feline heads with huge teeth that were easily a match for her own. Paws as big as dinner plates padded along the ground, housing those razor-sharp claws that had shredded her shoulder in Havana.

Factoring in that she was outnumbered four-to-one, Alexa started having serious second thoughts about taking on this job. She fervently hoped it wouldn't come down to a skirmish, but as she glanced left at the one Harimau Jadian she recognized, she recalled she had expressed that sentiment before.

It always comes down to the final stand, and they always decide to fight.

With the clear advantage of numbers, would he follow the same pattern of behavior this time? Or would their previous fight earn her a little respect?

The four big cats stopped, holding station.

Waiting.

A moment later *she* arrived.

The tigress made her entrance, hopping easily up onto the fallen tree and dropping into a crouch. Alexa's hunter instincts kicked in and she calmly evaluated this surprising newcomer. Unlike the males, she was mid-shifted. Maintaining a mostly Human form but with feline characteristics. She was naked. Her body was covered with short frost-white fur, striped in the distinctive black bands of the tiger. Her hands and feet were furnished with the same, albeit smaller, vicious-looking claws her brethren wielded. Her black and white striped tail flicked to and fro as she regarded Alexa carefully with her stunning bright blue eyes and their catlike pupils.

Nerves? Or anger?

Alexa waited. She wanted to let this newcomer make the first move.

"Adakah awak memahami saya?" the tiger-woman said slowly and carefully.

Alexa recognized the language. She'd heard it spoken by her quarry in Cuba, and then again from Valentina in the briefing room earlier. Yet recognition did not equate to translation. She slowly shook her head to show her lack of understanding. The female Harimau Jadian tilted her head. Her feline ears twitched.

She spoke again, hesitantly, in a broken accent. "You...speak...English?"

Alexa nodded.

"I am...my name Rahanah..." the woman said slowly. "I am...Queen...of Harimau Jadian. Mine are... My peoples need your help. Please...Zarra Anderson, agent of peacekeeping...will you listen?"

Alexa stared into Rahanah eyes, startled to hear the creature address her by name. There was no aggression.

Only desperation.

| **22** |

HOME ON THE RANGE

— **Gayle Knightley** —
— *Monday* — *London, England* —

Gayle had to admit, spending time on the shooting range was somewhat therapeutic. It was easy to block out the other thoughts that crowded her mind and let herself get absorbed into the routine Amanda had tried to instill in them years ago. She called it 'tantric gunplay,'...the almost ritualistic art of losing oneself—body and mind—into being one with the weapon.

She had been genuinely honored when Amanda had gifted to her the custom *Firestorm*s. Of course, her friend was passing them down because she had splashed out on the newer upgraded version, but even so, the gesture had touched Gayle. It was only now she realized maybe it had been Zephyr's subtle way of trying to prod her into taking better care of herself.

She hadn't listened.

None of them had.

Gayle had been to the range, fired off some rounds, and become competent. Yet it was really just paying lip service to something she had never taken that seriously. Like the other non-Zephyr members of the 137th, she considered her powers to be all she truly needed to see her through. She remembered vividly how she had looked at the beautifully crafted *Firestorms* sitting in her locker before shipping out and made the fateful decision not to take them to Malta.

To her credit, Amanda never said 'I told you so.'

It simply wasn't her style.

Taking unpowered self-defense seriously was something long overdue, which was why she was planning to attend Lana's martial arts classes and was being far more diligent on the gun range. Thus, upon arrival, she'd started following the routine Zephyr had taught her.

Removing the *Firestorms* from their holsters, she carefully unloaded them and stripped them down. Before long, she was absorbed in the ritual of meticulously cleaning each component, lubricating where necessary, and then painstakingly re-assembling them, step by step. She could do it in a hurry if she needed to, but that wasn't the point here. The point was to use this as an exercise to bond with the weapon and clear the mind of distraction.

The next step was to reload the clips, fastidiously clipping each micro-bullet into place in the spring-loaded container. After that, she loaded micro-tips suitable for the gun range before sliding the clip into the handle of the pistols, feeling and hearing them seat themselves with a satisfying, and reassuring click.

Her mind clear, she donned her ear defenders and stepped into the gun range alley.

The *Firestorm* was perfectly balanced in her grip as she pointed it down the range, sighting it on the bullseye of the target twenty-five yards away. She focused on her breathing. Slow measured breaths. In. Out. Her mind was clear, her heartbeat slow, her hand rock steady.

She gently squeezed the trigger.

A single shot.

The bullet hit the target the moment she felt the recoil, slicing through the paper just left of the bullseye.

Bollocks!

She felt her shoulders tense up and forced herself to relax, closing her eyes for a moment to center herself.

Deep breaths.

She slowly raised the *Firestorm* once more and opened her

eyes.

Another squeeze of the trigger. This time her bullet tore through the bullseye. Still not perfectly centered, but good enough for her.

"Not bad," came a voice from behind her. "But it's painfully *obvious* you've not been practicing what I taught you."

Gayle smiled, flicking the safety on the gun and placing it down carefully before turning to greet her old friend. "*You* are a sight for sore eyes."

"It's good to be back." Amanda nodded at the target. "You pulled the first shot a little but corrected well with the second."

"Well, I didn't think that was too bad. Haven't fired a gun for almost a year, so..."

Amanda unclipped her holster and pulled out her gun while raising an eyebrow. "Neither have I," she laughed. "And *I've* been laid up in a hospital bed for almost eight months of that. So, let's put bullshit excuses aside, and what's say we see if I can *still* outshoot you?"

Gayle smiled. "No powers, right?"

"No powers."

"I'll turn on the fucking PAD if I get even a *hint* of cheating."

"No powers. I promise." Amanda made a motion to cross her heart. "Not that I need them to kick your lazy ass."

She drew her weapon, spinning it gunslinger style around her finger till it slapped into the palm of her hand.

Gayle flicked up an eyebrow. "Show off," she chuckled.

"Firestorm 2020Cs, the best Beretta has to offer," Amanda said with a wink. "Lighter and with a built-in stabilizer."

"That's hardly fair competition!"

"If it makes you feel better, we'll use *your* gun to level the playing field. Mines not loaded anyway... Unless you changed the biometric safety?" Amanda chuckled

"Nope," Gayle smiled. "Your DNA is still encoded."

"Awesome. You want the first shot?"

Gayle flipped the weapon and offered it to Amanda, grip first. "Oh, no, please, be my guest."

She beckoned toward the range, stepping aside to let Amanda up to the firing line. She watched as her friend took a deep breath and raised the gun toward the target.

A sense of normalcy came over Gayle. For the first time in weeks, this finally felt...familiar. Having Lana here had created an initial surge of homeyness at the Academy, but the truth was, Lana was there to serve a different purpose from her original job description. A year ago, she was their pilot. Today, she was a teacher. It was good to have her back, but it didn't feel quite the same.

Amanda was also there to be a teacher, but right now she was stood on the range baiting Gayle into a shooting competition just like she had over a year ago. It was the most comfortable feeling of déjà vu. There was just one thing missing.

Let the games commence.

"Jesus, Zephyr," Gayle muttered as she shook her head. "From back here that CombatSkin makes your arse look huge!"

The jibe was timed perfectly to coincide with Amanda pulling the trigger and had the desired effect. Ordinarily, the comment wouldn't have distracted Zephyr in the slightest, but today she snorted in amusement. The bullet whistled through the paper target, barely grazing the top of the bullseye. She turned her head slowly and glared at Gayle, but the eyes gave away the true emotion she was feeling.

Humor.

"It looks like resting in that hospital bed *has* dulled your prowess somewhat."

"Oh, you'd love that, wouldn't you?" Amanda laughed, carefully setting down the *Firestorm*. "But I'm just warming up. Now shut up and take your shot."

Gayle stepped up to the firing line and picked up her gun, training it toward the target. Behind her, she heard Amanda maneuvering and was expecting the distraction before her friend even opened her mouth.

"Jesus, Knight, I wondered why you were dressed in civvies, but with an arse *that* big, I'm figuring you don't even *fit* in your CombatSkin these days."

It didn't bother her. This was the game they played, and after so long, she was just happy they were still playing. She squeezed the trigger with a smile on her face and the micro-bullet thudded through the bullseye.

Dead center.

"Your insult game is weak, my dear," she said as she placed her gun down on the counter before stepping back with a smile. "Time to acknowledge the *new* queen of the gun range."

"Oh, this is *not* over yet, Knightley," Amanda retorted. "Watch...and learn."

She walked up to the range, and picked up Gayle's gun in one swift motion, pointed, and fired three shots in quick succession. To the untrained eye, it looked like she had missed the target entirely, but Gayle knew better. There were no new bullet holes in the paper target because all three shots had tracked directly through the hole Gayle's bullet had already left. She shook her head in mild disbelief and chuckled wryly.

"Cheater!"

"I don't know *what* you're talking about," Zephyr laughed. *God, I've missed this!*

Relief flooded through Gayle. The guilt she had felt about what happened in Malta, for the injuries Amanda had sustained, started to ebb away. For a long time, she had wondered if her friend would ever walk again, let alone shoot. But the wonders of Fae technology had gifted her with a cybernetic implant that mimicked the signals that had previously been sent up and down her now ruined spine. The casual observer wouldn't even know she'd been close to death ten months prior. To know Zephyr still had access to her abilities was a massive relief.

"You know *exactly* what you just did."

Amanda holstered her weapon and tilted her head sideways as she looked back at Gayle. "You can do it, too," she said seriously.

Gayle shook her head. "Nope. We've tried this, remember? There's not much I can't do power-wise, but that is *not* in my skillset. Never was, never will be."

"It is," Amanda said deadpan. "I saw what you did in Valletta."

Gayle's mood quickly shifted toward something darker. "Well, whatever I did…I don't remember it."

"Doesn't change the fact that I know what I saw. Why don't you just try?"

Gayle breathed out heavily and stared at the floor.

Do I dare try?

She thought back to the classroom a couple of weeks ago, when she'd demonstrated her ability to manipulate fire for the kids. She'd felt the negative emotions slipping away, the power flowing through her, calming her, relaxing her. Her breathing had slowed, and she had been on the verge of letting herself slip deep into the comfortable embrace of oblivion.

That was just the first step.

Fortunately, Dylan had spoken to her, breaking the spell. If not for his interruption, she would have let herself be sucked deeper down the rabbit hole that day. Lost herself to the bliss.

"I… I can't."

Amanda was staring at her, an expression of sympathy on her face. Gayle hated that look. She didn't want to be pitied. It didn't last long before Amanda's face hardened.

"Try," Amanda said, holding the *Firestorm* out for Gayle to accept. "The Knightingale *I* know would not pussy out like this."

Gayle couldn't help but laugh. "And the Zephyr I know would *definitely* bully me into doing something I didn't want to do *exactly* like this. Fine. Fuck it. I'll give it a shot."

She took back her sidearm and stepped up to the firing line once more.

| 23 |

JUST THE TWO OF US

— Amanda Forrester —
— Monday — London, England —

"Take a deep breath..." She spoke softly, trying to soothe her friend with her words.

Amanda had *never* seen Gayle quite like this. Her breathing was ragged, and her hands trembled uncontrollably. More distressing, though, were the tears streaming down her face. She knew they weren't tears of sadness or despair—nothing so mundane. This was something else. Something she understood but had never truly felt.

Not to the extent Gayle did.

This was the 'hit.'

That first chunk of the chocolate bar. The first taste of something wonderful.

Something addictive.

Amanda sat on the floor next to Gayle supportively holding her hand. Gayle gripped it as if it was her lifeline.

"Jesus, Gayle. Lana said it was bad, but... How long has this been happening?"

"Since Valletta."

It broke her heart to hear the tremor in Gayle's voice. To see her screwing her other hand into a white-knuckled fist. Amanda didn't say anything in response. She didn't know what to say. She picked up the fallen *Firestorm* off the floor where Gayle had dropped it and cradled it in her lap. They both sat in silence, their backs against the wall, as Gayle brought herself under control.

"I'm sorry. I should never have pushed you into this…" Amanda hesitated. "I thought maybe I could help."

"Believe me, I wish you could," Gayle laughed bitterly. "I don't know what happened to me, but Valletta *really* fucked me up somehow. Every time I use my abilities…I feel it. The craving. The need for more. I can't have sex because of this. And I can't drink to drown my sorrows because getting drunk—"

"—inevitably leads to sex," Amanda said ruefully.

Gayle nodded. "You were here a year ago, Amanda. You saw what it did to me."

"You weren't alone on that particular runaway train, Gayle."

Gayle shook her head vehemently. "Maybe not, but you guys didn't abuse it like I did."

"I wouldn't be so sure about that," Amanda laughed. "I became positively slutty—"

"—No, you were already mostly in the gutter anyway," Gayle interrupted, which got her an elbow in the ribs from Amanda.

"Hey! I resemble that comment!"

Gayle smiled before her face turned serious again. She wiped away an errant tear.

"The point is that you and the others realized it was a means to an end. You just treated sex as…fun. Which is what it's supposed to be," Gayle sighed. "Which for the rest of the team was fine. Most of them were either married or in steady relationships… But for me, it's an addiction. It took me a while to realize it. Actually, it took me *therapy* to realize it."

"I think we were all a little addicted," Amanda said softly. "We all felt that rush. Sex before a mission became…routine."

"There's a difference, though, between feeling that rush and *craving* it. It played to my worst, most base instincts. To be the best. I always *had* to be the best. And when I found out that sex was like pumping nitrous-oxide into our powers…"

Gayle sighed heavily and closed her eyes. "I chased that fucking dragon *hard*, Amanda. There was *nothing* like the hit I got from feeling that power flow through me. I know you understand, but I can't describe it to anyone else... Just a rush. I'd feel like...the most powerful person in the whole fucking world, and the feeling was...*is* addictive.

"And it got so much worse when things between me and Alastair went so far off the fucking rails..."

"Torbar's a wanker," Amanda interjected.

"Maybe so, but after he and I broke up, I was so pissed. There was *nothing* I wanted more than to wipe the floor with him and his precious Terminators. To do it, I needed to be better, stronger, and faster than him.

"I *needed* that hit. I needed that high, that feeling of ecstasy because I felt so fucking miserable. God...I needed it in the worst way possible just to forget, just for a little while, how hurt I was."

"I know," Amanda said softly. "We all knew. When we realized how much you were drinking...and that you were..." She tailed off, but Gayle knew what she was referring to.

"...That I was sleeping with just about anything that had a pulse? Don't remind me."

Amanda watched her friend hang her head in shame, staring at the floor. "I wasn't going to say that, but...yeah. That was why we decided to stage the intervention. You needed help."

"And you were right," Gayle confessed. "I started seeing a therapist, Dr. Griffin, who—admittedly—is really helpful."

"You still go?"

Gayle nodded. "I pay more attention to him now. Back then I was talking, but I wasn't listening. I wasn't *doing* anything about it. I know now in order to quit an addiction you have to go cold turkey. But a year ago...I was still hunting for the hit, every fucking night. I was buzzing on the Malta mission, so much so I got everyone killed."

"No," Amanda shook her head. "No, you didn't. I'm not going to let you take all the blame for that. As your seconds, both Gabe and I would have objected had we thought anything was wrong. We'd disagreed with you before. We knew the situation, and honestly, we concurred with you...we needed to rescue those people."

"But Ghost... She felt it. She knew"

"No. Don't go there, Gayle. I *mean* it." Amanda shook her head vehemently. "We all knew what Maggie's feeling represented. But we also knew every time we went on a mission it might just be our last. Like Valerio, we might not come back alive. We accept that fate because we *are* the thin line between life and death for those who can't fight for themselves.

"The mission parameters for Malta were clear. Civilians that needed evacuating—"

"—There were *no* civilians—" Gayle interrupted.

Amanda cut off her interruption. "—But we didn't know that at the time. All the information we had told us people needed rescuing. One of the first things your uncle taught us right here ten years ago—'Humanity is an endangered species, and you are the thin line between their survival and their extinction—'"

"'—This is a dangerous job, and you're not special to do it. Special implies you're better than everyone else. More valuable than everyone else. You're not. It's that last remnant of humanity that is special. It is your job to protect them.'" Gayle laughed as she finished the quote.

"What's so funny?" Amanda asked quizzically.

"I gave the kids the same speech in their first lesson with me...more or less."

"I'd wager your version was a tad less eloquent?" Amanda offered with a grin. "Maybe a swear word or two thrown in?"

"I did my best," Gayle shrugged. "I did warn anyone who would listen that I wasn't cut out for this job."

"That lesson is still as true today as it was a decade ago," Amanda said.

"Maybe. Anyway, even if what you're saying about the team is true," Gayle sounded unconvinced, "the buck still stops with me. This, though, the craving, it's gotten worse."

"Since Valletta?"

Gayle nodded her confirmation. "I'm fucked if I know why.

I'm not having sex, or drinking, or doing anything that would trigger my addiction. But if I do use any of my powers, the craving hits me *hard*. It overcomes me. I can't think straight. I can't concentrate. I shake uncontrollably... Amanda, it scares the shit out of me."

"Knightingale...scared? Never thought I'd see *that* day."

"Well, that day is here. Look what *just* happened when I accessed even a little of my power."

"You hit the target at least." Amanda smiled. "You'll probably hate me for saying this, but the look on your face... I mean, you aimed your gun, concentrated, summoned your air powers, and then...your eyes kind of half-closed and...orgasm face."

Gayle stared at her for a moment and then burst out laughing. Amanda smiled to herself. Maybe this was exactly the approach she needed to take to reach Gayle. Humor could be a salve to all kinds of ills.

"I'm sorry," she chuckled. "I just thought we needed a little levity. Seriously, though, I think something happened to you that night in Valletta. You don't remember anything at all?"

Gayle shook her head. "I've read your report, but I don't remember anything past..." She stopped talking, seemingly unsure of what she did recollect.

"Do you remember us walking into the fort?" Amanda prompted softly.

"No. Not really," Gayle sighed, her brow furrowed in concentration. "Everything, the whole mission, is just fuzzy or blank. It feels like I short-circuited my brain or something. And ever since then..." She let the statement hang.

"Maybe, that's not far from the truth," Amanda said slowly.

"What do you mean?"

"Well, *you* may not remember it, but what I saw you do that night...that was next-level shit. I've *never* seen you display power like that before. Maybe something *did* change in your brain. Maybe this isn't a psychological matter. Maybe this is physical..."

"You're saying I should see a doctor?"

"Could it hurt?"

Gayle shrugged. "Probably not. All I know right now is everyone wants me to teach the kids how to use their powers. But whenever I try and use *mine*...I end up like this. So, tell me, how am I supposed to teach them to use theirs when I'm so fucked up that I can't even control my own?"

"Honestly...I don't have the answers you want," Amanda said as she squeezed Gayle's hand tightly. "But I promise you there's nothing to be afraid of. We'll find a way to get you through this. To face your fears head-on. You, me, and Lana. 'Stronger together,' remember?"

Gayle nodded, recognizing the motto of the 137th. Looking back, Amanda realized it was something they had all lost sight of before the ill-fated mission to Malta. It was high time they started paying more than just lip service to it. She watched as her friend exhaled heavily and put her head back against the wall to stare at the ceiling.

The two sat in silence for a few minutes before the sound of footsteps started to echo down the corridors outside the range.

| 24 |

STILL GOT IT

— Gayle Knightley —
— Monday — London, England —

Bollocks.

Gayle was experiencing a conflict of emotions.

On one hand, Amanda had been her friend for the better part of a decade. She was trusted implicitly and loved like a sister.

On the other hand, Amanda was the competition. The long, wavy brunette curls and the big eyes with the long lashes. Where Gayle was tall and athletic, Amanda was a little shorter and enviously curvy. She was—and always had been—a head-turner.

Emotional-Gayle feared one of those heads might belong to Michael.

He entered the range with what looked like the entire class in tow. Word had spread regarding Zephyr's arrival, and the cadets opted to spend their free period checking out the new teacher.

Michael proffered his hand in greeting. "Lieutenant Forrester, welcome home."

She extended her hand toward him, grasping his firmly in a shake as she started to stand. He kept hold and helped pull her up, then likewise offered the hand to Gayle. She smiled and gratefully accepted it, favoring her injured knee as he

144

slowly took her weight.

"It's good to be back, and a pleasure to finally meet you face to face, Captain."

"I'm glad you accepted Captain Knightley's proposal."

Amanda smiled and then gestured toward the cadets with a chuckle. "Is the range usually this popular? Back in our day, trying to get the team to come out here with me was like trying to pull teeth."

"Your reputation precedes you," Michael said. "Word got around this morning that the infamous Zephyr was here."

"Large as life and twice as ugly!" Amanda laughed self-deprecatingly.

"Ugly is the last word I'd use." Gayle nudged her friend.

"Can't argue with that," Michael said.

Gayle felt something. A twinge.

Okay... So, he thinks she's pretty.

"Thank you both." Amanda smiled. "But I'm not the infamous one around here. I'm *fairly* sure that specific title belongs to Gayle."

Gayle laughed. "Fuck, no," she said. "These kids are *not* here for me. I dispelled the illusion of my infamy very early on."

"So, you're saying the bar has been set very low then?" Amanda nodded thoughtfully.

"You'd have to dig a pretty deep hole just to find the bar," Gayle admitted.

She watched as her friend stood idly spinning Gayle's *Firestorm* around her finger, gunslinger style. A habit she had picked up years ago, but one that made their current situation seem eerily, but also comfortingly, familiar. Usually, Amanda would finish with a flourish and slide the firearm back into her holster in one slick motion, but today her gun-belt was occupied with her own weapons. Hence, the gun just continued to spin lazily.

"We'd love to see a demonstration of your skills." Michael smiled, nodding toward the rotating weapon. "If you'd oblige us."

"What?" Amanda blinked blankly, then realized what he

was referring to. "God, no. This is Gayle's gun now. Not mine."

"It used to be yours," Gayle interrupted. "Give them a show."

"You sure?" Amanda stopped spinning the gun.

Gayle nodded. She had already struggled to move past *her* blown first impression with these kids. But there was a solid chance Amanda could make a good impact right from the jump.

A sly grin spread across her friend's features. Gayle couldn't help but admire the courage, strength, and determination it must have taken to come back from the horrific injuries she had suffered. The surgery to repair her back had been long and arduous, and yet here she was, the same bubbly personality Gayle remembered. She felt ashamed of how distressed she felt thinking about Amanda's injuries. How she had been too scared to visit her in her time of need.

Unforgivable.

Yet Amanda *had* forgiven her. Immediately.

More than anyone, she knew what Gayle was going through. Knew the extent of her problems even before that disastrous day. She also understood the depth of her grief.

Still, in Amanda's position, would Gayle have been so magnanimous?

Her thoughts drifted to her father and the petty argument they'd had before he died. She would *never* be able to mend that fence. That would haunt her for the rest of her days.

"Okay," Amanda nodded. "I'll do it."

Michael signaled to the cadets. "Gather round, all. This is Lieutenant Amanda Forrester. I'm sure you all know her better as Zephyr."

A murmur of excitement circulated through the gathered trainees at the official introduction to someone who was considered a legend on this very gun range.

"Lieutenant Forrester will be your new firearms instructor," Michael continued. "She'll start officially next Monday, but this afternoon she has graciously agreed to give you a demonstration of her skills."

He bowed out and left the floor to Amanda who stepped

up to the firing lane, approaching the panel on the right-hand wall. She prodded it with a finger before swiveling her head to face the congregated cadets.

"Okay, give me a distance."

The kids looked at each other, but none of them spoke up.

After a few seconds, it was Michael who gestured toward the panel and offered a suggestion. "Fifty meters."

"*Please*," Amanda frowned. "At least give me a challenge!"

"One hundred meters?" Michael laughed.

"With my eyes closed." Amanda smiled. "Try again."

As Emotional-Gayle watched the friendly interplay between them, she couldn't help feeling like it was flirting. Reaching deliberately between them, she placed her finger over the control panel ready to input what she considered a real test for her fellow Hunter. "How about three hundred meters? Is *that* a big enough challenge for you?"

Petty much? Inner-Gayle chastised her more sensitive counterpart.

"Three hundred?" Michael looked surprised. "That's rifle distance, surely? We'll have to use the virtual range..."

Gayle flicked her eyes sideways at Amanda in a sly look. "She can nail it. Can't you, Zephyr?"

Amanda spun the *Firestorm* on her finger and snapped it into her hand, pointing it down the virtual range.

"Dial it up," she said confidently.

Gayle brushed her finger over the touchscreen. The paper target withdrew, and the range darkened. A holographic representation of a target with a simulated distance of three hundred yards appeared. Reaching to the receptacle just above the panel, she plucked out the range glasses and handed them to Amanda who pushed her long brunette waves over her shoulder and slipped them on.

Tapping a button on the side of the glasses, Amanda zoomed-in her vision to see the distant computer-generated bull's eye. Staring at it for a moment, she closed her eyes and slowly raised the *Firestorm*. Deep breaths. Gayle recognized the process of preparing the trajectory—the same method Amanda had tried to teach them at one time, yet none of them had been able to master it.

Her eyes flicked open.

When the *Firestorm* released its load on the squeeze of the trigger, it sounded more like a series of muted cracks.

One.

Two.

Three.

Silence.

The trio of shots in quick succession were followed by an equally rapid series of dings from the range, registering the micro-bullets had hit their virtual objective. As Amanda removed the glasses, a holographic representation of the distant target manifested above the firing line, complete with statistics.

A buzz went around the cadets when they saw the results.

There were three tiny holes through the bullseye.

"Holy crap..." Michael whispered under his breath.

"Yeah," Amanda tilted her head sideways, "not my best shooting. I'm out of practice."

"You're kidding, right?" Michael said. "That's three center shots...with a handgun...at rifle distance!"

Amanda shrugged. "At my best, there would only be one hole."

"Honestly, I'm impressed," he laughed. "Hell of a first impression, Lieutenant Forrester."

Gayle bit her lip as she watched them. It irritated her. It was so easy, the banter being passed back and forth.

When Gayle had first met Michael, she'd been a total bitch. The second time had not been much better—trying to manipulate him using her Fae pheromones had been a mistake. She had needed to work hard to get back into his good graces, to make him see her as *more* than a burden he'd been saddled to work with.

Now, here was her beautiful friend hitting it off on her first meeting with Gayle's...

What exactly?

What are we to each other now?

They'd talked about a date, but thus far they hadn't been

on one yet. She had no claim on him.

So why did it feel like her friend was suddenly trespassing on her territory?

Gayle turned to the cadets.

"So, now you've seen how it's done, and you've all satisfied your curiosity. You're with me for Enemy Recognition and Intelligence after lunch." She gestured toward them and their current disheveled state. "And I swear to God, if you turn up to my class covered in that muck, I will assign you so much homework your asses will be stuck in study hall for the rest of the month. I suggest you all go grab showers and a *very* quick bite to eat. Dismissed, one-three-eight."

Even she could hear the note of irritation in her voice.

Oh, for fuck's sake. Simmer down. Inner-Gayle strived again to be the voice of reason. *Amanda's one of your closest friends, remember? And this is just Michael being nice. Because he is nice.*

There were a few grumbles as Gayle watched the kids slowly file out of the range. Before long, it was Amanda, Michael, and herself. Now that Amanda had stopped twirling it, Michael was staring at Gayle's *Firestorm* with great interest.

"I've never used a *Firestorm* before. I've heard good things about them," he said.

"Best handgun money can buy," Gayle chipped in.

"Certainly can't blame the weapon for my earlier shoddiness," Amanda nodded. "Give me a few weeks to practice sans powers...*then* I'll impress you properly."

"I don't doubt it. Even so, I'd love to know how you did that," Michael said pointing at the target.

"Sorry, hybrids only. But I might be able to give you some pointers on your technique..." Amanda offered.

Michael shook his head. "I don't think there's anything wrong with my technique."

"Spoken like a typical man," Amanda shot back, but it was clear by her tone she was teasing.

Gayle did *not* like this one little bit. This was openly flirting. Frankly, it felt unprofessional.

Hypocrite much? Inner-Gayle commented. *Did you conven-*

iently forget the fact that you tried to use your pheromones to manipulate the good captain on your second meeting?

Gayle's *Firestorm* spun swiftly in Amanda's hand, and faster than the eye could track, it was suddenly being held grip-out toward Michael. "Show me your moves then, Captain."

But...that's my *gun!* Emotional-Gayle whined.

He hesitated for a moment and then took the gun from her, accepting the challenge. Stepping up to the firing line, he gripped the gun in his large hands and raised it to point down the range as Amanda prodded the control panel to switch the target back to its conventional mode. A paper target dropped into the line of fire twenty-five meters away. She tutted when she saw his grip.

"What's wrong?" he said, brow furrowed.

Amanda leaned in close, sliding her hand atop his to guide it. "Relax your hold a little. The *Firestorm* isn't like other guns you're used to. Hold it like a lover, gentle but firm. Caress the trigger with your finger..."

Gayle bit the inside of her lip...hard. As she watched, Amanda slid her index finger up a little and placed it on a small glass circle on the side of the *Firestorm*. She held it a moment and the weapon bleeped twice. The first was it recognizing her DNA print, the second was enabling voice commands.

They were touching now...

They're using my gun as a flirtation device! And why are they touching?

She could feel Emotional-Gayle's anxiety rising within her, but she wasn't sure at whom or what she was anxious. Mostly the situation. Which made her feel...childish.

Yeah, because you're acting childish! Inner-Gayle responded. *Neither of them are doing anything wrong. Michael is just being friendly, and Amanda is just being Amanda. She's only being flirty because she doesn't know how you feel about Michael. Maybe deal with this like an adult for a change?*

"Temporary biometric override," she said flatly.

"*Voice command Zephyr recognized,*" the gun intoned in a familiar voice.

"Is that you?" Michael chuckled.

Amanda nodded. "I wanted Gayle to have a reminder of me," she laughed.

"I tried to change it," Gayle lied.

She'd never even attempted it. Mostly because Amanda was more correct than she knew. Post Valletta, Gayle had been worried Amanda wouldn't make it. She had sometimes sat alone, listening to the voice of Amanda coming from the *Firestorm*. Like she was a part of the gun. She thought for a while it may be the only way she would hear her friend's voice again.

"Okay, now..." Amanda said softly while still standing too close to Michael for Gayle's comfort, "take the shot."

Michael pulled at the trigger and the *Firestorm* barked as the bullet leaped from it, instantly tearing a hole in the paper target just below the bullseye.

"Dammit." Michael shook his head.

"Honestly, that's not bad for your first *Firestorm* shot," Amanda chuckled. "You're used to a conventional handgun, so you're bracing for the kick, but—"

"—there's almost none," Michael nodded. "It's astonishingly light, but also has a heft to it. Feels solid in your hand."

"You get used to it," Amanda reassured him. "Your second shot will be better."

Grateful though she was, she had witnessed enough of the obvious chemistry between Michael and Amanda. This was the *wrong* kind of familiarity, the kind she had been afraid of. She knew Inner-Gayle was right about how she was feeling right now, but Emotional-Gayle was firmly in the driver's seat. Her heart sank.

"Well, maybe you should let him try *your* gun," Gayle interjected. "Anyway, if you'll excuse me, I have a class to get to."

She could hear the brusqueness in her tone and wished it weren't there, but she couldn't help it. Jealousy had turned to anger, and as Michael handed her the *Firestorm,* she snatched it from his hand a little more abruptly than she had meant to.

"Are you okay, Gayle?" Amanda asked with a furrowed brow of concern.

"Fine," Gayle shot back. "I got kids to teach. I'll leave you two to have fun. Welcome back, Amanda."

I give up. Inner-Gayle sighed and threw up her metaphorical arms in disappointment.

She stalked from the room, not daring to look back at Michael and Amanda.

Afraid of what she'd see on their faces.

| 25 |

THE TIGER-QUEEN

— **Alexa Reynolds** —
— *Monday* — *Independent State of Rio de Janeiro* —

Benny had been left far behind.

Except for Becka's occasional complaints about her aching feet, they trudged slowly through the forest in silence. Being surrounded by Harimau Jadian had revived traumatizing memories for Valentina, who seemed more withdrawn than ever. Alexa was far more concerned that they were now unarmed. Rahanah had insisted their weapons remain locked in the Jeep, assuring them no harm would come to them while they traveled under her protection.

Such assurances did *not* make Alexa feel any better.

Though she had taken the opportunity to change back to her human form and get dressed again, Alexa still felt somehow naked. The absence of her *Freelancers* and their reassuring weight on her hips made her nervous as they were escorted single file through the unfamiliar forest to an unknown destination.

Being outnumbered by powerful Harimau Jadian, however, Alexa had felt refusing Rahanah's 'invitation' would have been a particularly misjudged decision.

Never start a fight you can't win.

Regardless, she still didn't like their current predicament one little bit.

She glanced around trying to make it look like nothing more than a casual passing interest in the flora when what she was *actually* doing was surreptitiously checking on the relative positions of their escorts. Two of the muscular jungle cats flanked them as a third prowled down the track a few meters ahead. Alexa reflected briefly on the irony that the bounty she had once pursued in Cuba was the one that remained behind to safeguard her Jeep.

Rahanah herself was quietly padding in Alexa's footsteps. The soldier in Alexa hated the fact that she was effectively surrounded. Trapped. She clenched her fist in frustration, a gesture that didn't go unnoticed.

"I made a promise, Zarra Anderson," said Rahanah quietly. "You are safe. We are no threat."

Alexa paused, letting the 'Queen' of the Harimau Jadian sidle up alongside her. The two looked at each other, momentarily holding their mutual stares.

Finally, Alexa flicked her right eyebrow upward. "Well, your English has certainly improved quickly," she said with a slight smile.

Rahanah's expression remained deadpan. "I have known English all my life. Was taught it as a child," she said. "It has been...much years since I have used it. My use is..."

Alexa could see her searching for the right word, struggling to find it. "Rusty," Alexa finished. "Your use is rusty."

Finally, Rahanah cracked a smile and laughed lightly, drawing the attention of her feline companions who glanced over to check on their queen.

"Yes, yes," Rahanah said enthusiastically. "Like a car that is not used. Rusty. Thank you, Zarra Anderson."

"It's Alexa, actually. Alexa Reynolds."

Rahanah furrowed her brow, clearly confused. "Ashraff...he said you are Zarra Anderson. You told him you are Zarra Anderson. Agent of peacekeeping."

"Ashraff? It was him I captured in Cuba?"

"Yes, Alexa Reynolds," Rahanah confirmed with a nod as her tail flicked. "My younger brother. One of our best warriors, and you won him."

"I 'won' him?" It took Alexa a moment to work out what Rahanah meant. "You mean I *beat* him."

"Beat, won, yes."

"Well, he certainly didn't make it easy. Anyway, Zarra is my...professional name."

Rahanah nodded. "I understand."

They walked shoulder to shoulder in silence for a while. Despite Rahanah's words, Alexa couldn't help but stay alert, her keenly attuned hunter senses noticing things around her she doubted Becka or Valentina would spot.

For starters, this path was well-trodden. The flora was regularly trampled and sparse along the forest floor. The fact that they were still pushing aside high-level vegetation indicated this was an animal track, *not* one frequented by humans. She suspected Rahanah would prefer to be prowling this trail in her full tiger form than mid-shifted and walking upright with Alexa.

Additionally, while Alexa wasn't sure *exactly* where they were going, she knew, despite the path winding naturally around the trees, curving unpredictably and making it almost impossible to establish a bearing, they were definitely heading east. She had been able to deduce that using the few glimpses of the sun's position the dense canopy allowed.

While her baseline senses in her human form were far more sensitive than those possessed by Becka or Valentina, they were still limited. Alexa found herself wishing she had remained in her Wolf form. *Those* senses would have been extremely useful in trying to determine whether there truly was any threat lying ahead of them.

"You say we're in no danger, Rahanah," she said, finally breaking the silence, "but we have no idea where you're taking us. Where are we going?"

Rahanah tilted her catlike face sideways as she regarded Alexa. She could practically see the Tiger-Queen weighing the pros and cons of revealing their intended destination. Finally, for whatever reason, she made her decision.

"Home," she said simply. "This forest is our new home. For now, at least, Harimau Jadian live here. It is a big risk I am taking. But...I need you to see and understand. So, you will help us."

"Help you? Help you with what?"

Rahanah locked her eyes with Alexa's, her stare intense. "Help to save Harimau Jadian. I will explain soon. We are close now."

True to her word, a handful of minutes later the trail came to a natural end. The tiger leading them didn't stop, however, simply slipping through the foliage and out of sight. Becka, who was following closely behind, paused for a second before moving to nervously push through the leafy branches herself. Valentina followed suit, likewise disappearing from view.

As Alexa reached out her hand to move aside the undergrowth, she heard a scream. Her heartbeat increased. She knew the shriek wasn't Becka, so it must have been Valentina. Her eyes flicked toward Rahanah.

"You said we would be safe," she said as she broke into a run forcing her way through the vegetation, wishing she had her *Freelancers* with her.

She was on the verge of shifting to her Wolf form when she stumbled into the huge clearing beyond, and her mouth fell open.

What she found was not at all what she had expected.

A sizable artificial clearing had been created; there was evidence of felled trees all around. The wood had been put to good use for the construction of several buildings around the edges of this tiny hidden village. Makeshift tables and benches were scattered around the center, where a number of campfires were burning.

There were people here. Harimau Jadian, like Rahanah. Dozens of men and women. Some were fully human, others mid-shifted like their queen. A few were still in their tiger mode, prowling or lying in the sun.

There were also six Humans dressed in the military uniforms of the ISRdJ, and Valentina was crying and squealing with joy as she moved between them, embracing each in turn. They were unarmed, but unharmed, and seemed in good spirits. Not at all the horribly mutilated bodies a part of her had expected to find. Not even seemingly captives who weren't allowed to leave. They looked more like honored guests than prisoners.

"We never intended any harm," Rahanah said as she walked up behind Alexa. "Our intention was only to defend our secret. To stay hidden. In truth…once we captured these soldiers, we were…unsure of what to do with them next. But I assure you, killing them was *never* an option." She pointed toward one of the wooden domiciles to the left and smiled warmly. "Please," she continued, "we have set aside a shelter for you and your companions. You will find water, shade, and beds. We have walked far, and the forest is very hot today. Rest now. My people will prepare dinner this evening, and we will discuss matters further."

Before Alexa could reply, Rahanah walked away. Becka sauntered over, hands in her pockets. The two of them stood side by side and watched the regular village life of the Harimau Jadian for a few minutes, and the interplay between a clearly relieved Valentina and her comrades. Becka gave a wry chuckle that elicited a sideways glance from Alexa.

"I was thinking," she said, "when you were chasing that tiger through the streets of Havana, did you *ever* in a million years think you'd be standing here, right now, witnessing this?"

Alexa smiled and shook her head slowly. "You are not wrong," she said softly.

The rest of the afternoon played out in a very casual manner. Becka and Alexa took advantage of the time to rest in the shade and clean themselves up. It was strange, but Alexa felt very much at ease, despite being surrounded by a race of people she had just a few weeks ago considered a dangerous enemy. The way of life they had was…peaceful. As she sat and watched them go about their daily business, she was struck by how easy it all seemed.

How relaxed.

As dusk arrived, their hosts lit lanterns in the huts, and the golden hues of the setting sun gave way to the flickering shadows of the campfires. The aroma of freshly cooked meat permeated the air of the glade. She wasn't entirely sure what they were serving, but Valentina said it was Capybara, which was considered a delicacy in certain parts of South America. Apparently, it tasted somewhat like pork. Rahanah confirmed Valentina's assertion. A hunting pack had brought back a number of them earlier in the day, enough to feed the whole streak plus their guests.

Alexa unfurled her legs from their crossed position and stretched them out in front of her. The campfire crackled and lit up their faces with a flickering dance of amber light. She took a deep breath, closing her eyes for a moment. Memories of camping with Mikey and her parents bubbled to the surface of her mind, making her smile a little. Her hunter's instincts were quiet. There were no jangling nerves and the hairs on the back of her neck were calm, despite the dozens of Harimau Jadian surrounding them.

Reopening her eyes, she looked around the clearing at their hosts. Some were sleeping, both in Human and tiger form. Others were holding their own quiet conversations around other fires or cooking the spoils of their hunts. Alexa's stomach rumbled with hunger. She closed her eyes again briefly, savoring the fragrance. More childhood memories crept from her subconscious, a fleeting reminiscence of her father tending a smokey barbeque...

"Do not be concerned, friend Alexa." Rahanah approached smiling a toothy grin. "My people are generous. Food will be shared shortly. Our hunt was bountiful today."

"Was it that obvious?" Alexa chuckled.

"I heard your belly rumble from across the village," Rahanah laughed and pointed at her cat ears. "Harimau Jadian have excellent hearing."

"Good to know," Alexa said.

True to her word, they were soon invited to join Rahanah's people around the large central campfire and enjoy the spoils of the hunt. Valentina was right about the flavor, too, and Alexa couldn't help but groan with pleasure as she tore into the perfectly cooked meat. It tasted delicious. As she tried to delicately nibble around the stick piercing the center of her morsel, it amused her to watch their hosts tear into the food with animalistic abandon.

They made small talk for a while as they ate, but eventually, when Alexa was licking her fingers clean of the last trace of Capybara, Rahanah finally broached the subject of why they were there.

"We are hunted," she began simply. "You know this, Alexa Reynolds. You hunted Ashraff in Cuba. Captured him. Took him to the Federation."

Alexa nodded. "I'm a licensed Freelance Peacekeeping Agent. And *as* a duly registered FPA, I make my living by taking jobs off MercNet—"

"—MercNet?" Rahanah interrupted, looking confused.

"The Federation Warrant Service," Alexa tried to explain. "It's a kind of brokering service for mercenaries—like myself—to find jobs like the one in Havana. The file provided a picture of Ashraff and an apprehend and return order. Dead or alive. Generally, I prefer to take my bounties in alive as the contracts pay out more."

"But Ashraff did nothing." Rahanah shook her head. "Why would the Federation hunt for him?"

"It likely wasn't the Federation hunting Ashraff. Pretty much anyone who has the money and the credentials can list a job on MercNet. Honestly, I never check too closely on the originator of the warrant itself. We take the job for the money, which is guaranteed by the Federation Warrant Service. We tend not to ask too many questions regarding the tasks we take on."

"Who paid for Ashraff?"

Alexa shrugged. "I'm sorry, I don't know," she said. "Could I ask you a question? How did Ashraff escape the custody of the Federation in Nassau?"

"Ashraff did not escape in Nassau. I rescued him. Here." Rahanah's explanation only added to Alexa's confusion.

"Here? In Brazil?"

"In Rio," Rahanah clarified.

Alexa leaned forward. "Maybe we're going to need some

clarification of the events leading up to...this."

The Tiger-Queen nodded. "Then I will do my best to explain."

| 26 |

PLEAS AND THANK YOU

— Damian Dane —
— Monday — Domaine Saint-Bernard, Pack Nation —

"D!"

His name—or rather a much-abbreviated version—being shouted from across the commune brought his weary trudge to a halt and a genuine smile to his lips. His first in a rough couple of days. The generals were breathing down his neck as rumors of the Vampyrii being harbored here in Domaine Saint-Bernard started to spread. Thus far, Damian had refused to comment, not wanting to outright lie to his people.

This strategy, however, was only fanning the flames of the already hot gossip.

It wasn't a problem that would resolve itself anytime soon, regardless of how hard he sought a solution. Nykola didn't have the answers any more than he did, but her company was, at least, a pleasant distraction from the shit-storm he was trying to navigate daily.

"What can I do for you, Nykola?"

She jogged across the courtyard, slowing as she approached. "Lys sent a message. She wants to talk to you."

"I hope it's good news," he muttered. "I'm not sure how much *more* bad I can handle."

Nykola smiled warmly. "Aw, come on, D," she said with a sly, sideways glance, "it's not *all* been bad."

Damian snorted with amusement.

She's not wrong. Things haven't been all bad.

If he were being honest, working with Nykola had been a joy. She reminded him of Lyssa in some respects. Same work ethic, diligence, and attention to detail. There were, however, many refreshingly different aspects of her personality.

The little nicknames, for example. She had them for *everyone*. The usual form was a mandatory shortening of their names. Lyssa became Lys, Damian became D, and so forth. For a while, she insisted he call her Nyk, but his mother had brought him up to be respectful of others, and that meant the use of proper names in more formal relationships.

He had used nicknames before.

Alexa had been Lexy.

Eloise had been Elly.

For Damian abbreviations were a sign of intimacy. The crossing of a line to a more personal place where secrets were shared, and pet names were common.

This was not a place he and Nykola were currently at.

"I'm not sure you understand the position I'm in right now..." he said slowly.

She smiled sympathetically. "Tell you what D, go have your pow-wow with Lys, and if you're sticking around tonight, then come find me in the lodge when you're done. I'll cook up something nice for dinner—"

"You cook?"

"It has been known," Nykola laughed lightly. "While we eat, you can unburden all your problems. Maybe I can help."

"I'm not sure you can. It's...political."

"Okay, admittedly I don't have a whole lot of experience in matters of that nature..." she shrugged. "Honestly, that's more Lyssa's or Mercy's area."

"I thought Mercy had been in charge of your intelligence service?"

Nykola nodded. "Amongst other things. She has a military background, so she coordinates our meager armed forces, too. She also has a knack for strategy, both military and political. There's a reason she's Lyssa's right-hand woman."

"I wish I'd got to meet her..." he said, genuinely. When Nykola didn't respond, Damian decided a change of subject was in order. Though they had extensively discussed the evacuation and logistics of getting as many refugees into the area around Domaine Saint-Bernard as possible, he realized he knew little of Nykola's background *before* she had arrived here. "So, what's your area of expertise?"

There was a brief hesitation, and her eyes flickered almost imperceptibly toward the three large black trailers parked neatly in a row alongside the lodge. He had assumed they were a modular Mobile Command Center. However, since Nykola arrived in them, they had been sitting there, quietly doing nothing.

Almost innocuous...if you disregarded the discreetly situated armed guards that were constantly within proximity. He hadn't mentioned his curiosity to Nykola simply because they currently had bigger fish to fry.

"Science," she said simply. "I'm Lyssa's science advisor. In charge of science projects... That kind of thing."

"Science then?" He smiled.

She rolled her eyes at him. "Yeah, science. All the science."

While they were now having good-natured banter about her overuse of the word, the way she had first said 'science' struck Damian as too...casual.

There was more to her role in House Balthazaar than met the eye, he was sure of that.

This hadn't been his first clue either.

She had made some unusual requests over the past week for chemicals Damian didn't readily recognize. His initial assumption was they were something to do with Vampyrii funeral rites. The 'Blood to Earth' ritual. Lyssa had spoken of it when he returned Vanessa's body to her. He suspected she would be trying to get Mercy's body back—by whatever means necessary—to perform the same ceremony.

Now, however, he wasn't so sure that was the correct conclusion.

Nykola had been nothing but charming and forthright in

general, except when it came to questions regarding the nature of her requests. Those answers were always...vague. A waved hand and talk of some form of research followed by a change of subject. She was pretty adept at diverting the conversation.

Not that Damian was concerned. He'd checked, and the items she was asking for were pretty commonplace and not dangerous at all. Most could easily be obtained from any ordinary pharmacy. She probably would have acquired them herself except for the fact she was a Vampyrii in Pack Nation.

That and the quantities she requested had raised more than a few eyebrows.

Anyway, a mystery for another time.

"So..." he prompted. "Lyssa wants me to contact her?"

"Oh, yeah...right." Nykola looked startled, like she had momentarily forgotten why she'd flagged Damian down in the first place. "We set up a communications center in the Wheeler Pavilion down near the lake. Head over and my guys will link you up."

"Thanks."

"And think about my offer," Nykola said, turning to leave. "Dinner and my sparkling company await the correct answer."

As she strode away from him, he *was* already considering her offer.

While the thought of enjoying an evening in Nykola's company was an enticing prospect, Domaine Saint-Bernard held unpleasant memories for him. In truth, it was painfully bittersweet being here.

He had loved Eloise. Hope had blossomed in his heart that she would be the one. He had considered offering her his gift—turning her so they could spend their extended years together.

Of course, it wasn't to be.

He had been warned. Both close friends and family alike had expressed their concerns. Eloise had only just entered her twenties. She was too immature, too flighty to settle down as the recognized paramour to the Prince of Pack Nation. He hadn't listened, and they had been right.

Only one other woman had ever come close to inspiring a similar depth of feeling in him.

"Hello, Lyssa," he said as Nykola's staff connected the communications link.

The image on the screen smiled. "Damian. How are things?"

"You want me to answer honestly?" he chuckled. "I think a more pertinent question is how are things with you?"

"I'm good…" she said, and then paused.

"…for a wanted criminal?" he asked with a wry smile.

Lyssa nodded and sighed. "Thank you for taking in my people. I know we had discussed it as a contingency, but I hoped we'd never have to use it. Unfortunately, I come bearing a larger request…"

Damian slumped his shoulders. He had been expecting this from the moment he heard StormHall's address to the press. Declaring Lyssa a fugitive was, by default, making House Balthazaar traitors to New Victus. He hadn't said as much, but StormHall knew as well as anyone, Lyssa's House was fervently loyal to her.

But those weren't the only Vampyrii loyal to Lyssa.

Many years of planning to overthrow StormHall's regime had led them to the realization they would need allies. To wit, Lyssa had been discreetly feeling out the loyalties and sentiments of the other Vampyrii Houses.

"This attack accelerates our timeline. The clock is ticking, Damian. I have House Akhza firmly on our side, but I need to touch base with the heads of Houses Skarling and Haggari. I think they'll join us; they were always at the top of my list."

"What makes you think they'll help?" Damian asked.

"Because they're the last of the Houses who still have a living Progenitor. If StormHall is willing to threaten Balthazaar, then how far behind can the others be? He knows full well the Progenitors endanger his power base. He'll want them neutralized."

Damian could see Lyssa's logic but wasn't about to throw his limited forces into a war based purely on conjecture.

"How can you be sure they won't simply make a deal with StormHall?" he countered. "They may view that as a safer alternative than civil war."

Lyssa looked down, deep in thought, her lips pursed slightly. A moment later she locked her eyes with his. "I didn't want the War or anything to do with it," Lyssa said quietly. "Back then, I wanted House Balthazaar to stay clear of anything Storm had planned. We had a good life. Most of us were happy living alongside Humanity. But a few wanted more, and he was a lightning rod to them."

"This is nothing new to me, Lyssa. We've talked about this before..."

"Yes, I know." She nodded. "And I told you how guilty I felt that I didn't stop Storm politically *before* he got into power. Afterward, it was too late. When the Rising started, I stood House Balthazaar down and all the other Progenitor Houses followed suit."

"Again, ancient history," Damian said, impatient for Lyssa to get to her point.

"But what you don't know," Lyssa said, "is *why* they stood down."

He shrugged. "They followed your example."

Lyssa shook her head. "No. Most of them were going to side with Storm. I personally lobbied for them to stand down. First I asked my mother, Perlania, to ally House Akhza with us. She petitioned Akhza herself who agreed *not* to commit to Storm's cause. After she agreed, we moved to the others, one by one, convincing each to peacefully abstain from Storm's war."

"All twelve agreed?"

"All except House Jareb. But then six months after the war ended...Akhza died. She was the first of the Progenitors to pass away. Since then, another *seven* have died."

"How?" Damian enquired.

"Not obviously..." Lyssa paused. "But what would you say are the chances that *eight* practically immortal beings all died of 'natural causes' within a twenty-five-year span?"

"I didn't know," Dane said with mild surprise. "I mean, I

knew many *had* died, but I never even considered it was less than above board. I remember the big funerals, but no one ever said anything about it being—"

"Murder?" Lyssa finished for him. "Some have speculated maybe what we're seeing is the limit of the natural Vampyrii lifespan, but I don't buy that at all. It's Storm's doing—I am convinced of it. But there's no evidence, no trail leading back to him. Only the suspicious order of their deaths..."

"Order?"

"Their deaths have been in the *exact* same order as I persuaded them to turn their back on Storm. This is his petty vengeance for being abandoned. Jareb, Haggari, Skarling, and Balthazaar are all that remain. All are in hibernation for their safety, and we protect their sanctums at all costs. Which is why we need to go ahead with our plan to rid New Victus of Storm *now*."

"We're not ready, Lyssa," Dane said slowly.

"Ready or not, we *have* to," she said. "Storm thinks Balthazaar's chamber is deep below Hearst Tower. Nykola followed protocol and locked it down before she left, but eventually, Storm will gain access and find out he's not there. We moved him weeks ago, after Storm visited us in New York."

"Where is he now?"

Lyssa paused, grimacing at the screen before speaking. "Balthazaar's move was the primary focus of the Exodus Initiative..."

Her voice trailed off as she left Damian to put the pieces of the puzzle together himself. The Exodus Initiative. A week ago, the members of House Balthazaar started to arrive. Three days ago, Nykola Balthazaar had appeared with a convoy of rather large trucks.

By the gods, Lyssa! What did you do?

Wide-eyed, Damian shook his head. "You brought him *here*?"

"What else were we supposed to do? He's safe there with you and Nykola. As safe as he can be. But Haggari and Skarling are *still* vulnerable. We need to get them out of New Victus before Storm moves against them."

"Lyssa, I can't have the Progenitors in Pack Nation!"

"Why not?" she snapped back.

"Because if my people find out..." He closed his eyes and rubbed his temples, suddenly fighting a stress headache. "I'm having a tough enough time fighting the *rumors* of Vampyrii crossing our border—"

"—They're not rumors," Lyssa interrupted. "We *are* crossing into Pack Nation."

"Yes, but I'm not ready to tell my people that truth. Do you understand how precarious our position is?"

"I get it. I do," she said forcefully. "But we *need* the Progenitors. We need what's left of The Twelve. The reason Storm has been so patient in eliminating them is because he fears them. Most Vampyrii are deeply religious, and the Progenitors are almost worshipped like the gods. Our little Houses may pale in significance size-wise against Storm and his followers, but we survive because our religious importance far outweighs our numbers.

"If the surviving Progenitors come out against Storm, then other Houses will follow. If we're talking about a Vampyrii civil war, then we *need* that swing in allegiance. It's the only card we have left to play.

"Dane, you *know* this. We've talked about this before. We *need* the religious vote."

"The religious vote..." Dane shook his head and laughed lightly.

Lyssa cast him a look that was a mixture of confusion and annoyance. Laughter was the last thing she was expecting at a time like this.

"I'm sorry," he said, looking slightly abashed. "It's just...with all we've done together, the subject of religion never came up. I mean, I get the importance to your people, but I was just struck by how totally in the dark I am about the history of your religion."

"I'm not sure now is the time to be taking a bible lesson..."

"Do you have a Vampyrii bible?"

"Well...no," Lyssa replied. "But that's not the point..."

"Maybe not," Damian admitted. "But...both our cultures

are heavily religious. Maybe there's something in there that could help me sell all this to the packs. I need something to bring them around to our way of thinking, and currently I'm drawing a blank. It's almost like Werewolves are genetically coded to distrust Vampyrii at a cellular level."

On the screen, Lyssa sighed and rubbed her temples wearily. "Yes," she said eventually. "I know exactly what you mean. Okay, well... We, the Vampyrii—or at least those who believe—worship the Six Gods."

"Go on..." Damian looked intrigued.

"There is Solista and Nocturne, the goddesses of the Sun and the Moon, respectively. They're represented on the New Victus flag. Then there's Tellus—"

"—The Earth god," Damian interrupted.

"I thought you said you didn't know anything about Vampyrii religion?"

"Oh, I don't," Damian said. "But those are the same gods we worship in our religion, too. You remember the mural in my Great Hall?"

Lyssa nodded. "Of course. '*The Children of the Stolen Sun.*'"

"Well, I generalized, calling them the gods of the Sun and the Moon," Damian said, "but in our *actual* legends, they too are Solista and Nocturne. Though, for us, Nocturne is masculine."

"What are the chances?" Lyssa muttered.

Damian nodded thoughtfully. "What indeed?"

While they had been busy sleeping together and discussing current events and future plans, he and Lyssa had never looked back toward the past. Yet, now that he considered it, it was peculiar. The cogs were turning in Damian's head. There were undeniable parallels between their two races.

The question became...why?

And why did it suddenly feel important to know the answer?

| **27** |

GROUND RULES

— Amanda Forrester —
— Monday — London, England —

There was no sign of her in the classrooms, her office was empty, and the Officers Lounge was likewise deserted. Amanda had searched the Palace from top to bottom and nothing. She had been contemplating widening the scope of her hunt to the local bars they'd been known to frequent; however, a peek in the car park revealed the presence of a distinctive white Mustang.

Gayle Knightley *was* still here.

Somewhere.

If she hasn't left...where would she go?

Her friend was a contradiction. Gayle often wore her emotions on her sleeve but conversely kept her private affairs very much under lock and key. To get to the root of what was troubling her was like milking a cow with a crowbar.

Staring at the muscular convertible, Amanda tried to recall the places Gayle would hide away to brood over her troubles.

One potential spot sprang to mind.

She traversed back through the Palace, heading for the rear of the grounds. As she ambled across the grass in the direction of the lake, she glanced toward the landing pads where *Artemis* and *Minerva* would usually sit, being fettled by their ground crews. This evening, those pads were empty.

The horseshoe-shaped lake curved around a modest copse of trees. To get there meant circumnavigating the water; not that Amanda minded. Spending close to a year lying in a hospital bed unable to use your legs gave one a new perspective on the simple act of walking.

Her convalescence had been an almost soul-crushing experience. Twelve long months of staring at the ceiling of her spartan room broken by the occasional wheelchair jaunts around the Stoke Mandeville site had left her craving the world outside her window. Amanda desperately missed the fresh air, the sounds of nature, and the simple pleasure of feeling the gentle breeze on her face.

After all, Zephyr *was* her call sign.

And, truth be told, the Academy grounds did provide a beautiful backdrop for a promenade. Of course, these grounds had once belonged to the Royal Family, and Amanda knew for a fact a handful of the older groundskeepers had been cultivating these gardens since before the War.

They took great pride in their work.

As it dipped toward the horizon, the sun cast dusky shadows amongst the trees while the relative silence made it feel oddly spooky at the edge of the Palace grounds. Keeping a brisk pace and taking in the pleasant evening, Amanda followed the path skirting the water and meandered through the trees. The cloudless autumn sky was a breathtaking blend of orange hues, as the setting sun slipped ever closer to meeting the horizon.

I'd forgotten how pretty it is here...

It didn't take long to reach the clearing for which she was aiming. Sure enough, Gayle sat in the quiet glade all alone. Amanda sauntered over to the bench and sat down beside her friend. The two rested in silence for a few minutes.

Gayle looked...adrift.

"So..." Amanda said, finally breaking the tranquility. "Do you want to tell me what your little temper tantrum on the range was all about?"

"There was no temper tantrum."

"I beg to differ. I've known you for ten years, and I've seen *that* reaction before."

"No idea what you're talking about," Gayle denied, but the truth was in her tone.

"Yeah," Amanda continued. "The first time was eight years ago. You got pissed Peter Harrison preferred me after we'd both been trying to pick him up in Barnun on the night of your twentieth birthday."

"It was *my* birthday," Gayle shrugged.

Amanda chuckled. "I was competitive."

"Yeah, well... It would have been nice for you to let me win *sometimes.*"

"It was just *sex*. It's not like you were short of suitors yourself."

"It doesn't matter, Amanda," Gayle sighed. "Water under the bridge."

Amanda peered sideways at Gayle with narrowed eyes which slowly widened as she figured out what was going on.

"Oh..." she said quietly, then repeated it louder. "Ohhhh. This is... This is about Captain Reynolds, isn't it? Holy *fucking* shit."

Gayle said nothing.

"Fuck, I'm so stupid..." Amanda cursed as she continued to piece the puzzle together. "Lana said you'd fallen in love—"

"Why does everyone keep saying that?" Gayle growled.

Amanda ignored her and continued. "—But she never said with *who*. It's Captain Reynolds!" She stared at Gayle. "Ohhhhh, and I was... On the gun range... With *your* gun..."

Gayle still wouldn't meet her eye. She simply stared at the six irregularly shaped paving stones set in a circle on the ground. "It's not a problem. I overreacted to.... Don't worry about it."

Amanda shook her head. *How did I not notice?*

The styled hair, the make-up, the modestly revealing top... All these things were contrary to how her friend normally presented herself. Gayle usually didn't give a damn about trying to impress anyone with her looks, but today she had felt she needed to make an effort.

Oh, my, God, she's feeling threatened...by me!

Gayle slowly turned to look at her. "I like Michael," she said quietly. "I like him a lot, but I've only known him a month..."

Amanda shrugged. "People fall in love fast all the time."

"We had one date...not even a real date," Gayle sighed. "What's more, I've fucked up and lied to him so many times... I'm not sure I even deserve—"

"No," Amanda interrupted firmly. "You can stop that line of thinking right now!"

"Why? Amanda, I'm a pink-haired freak with a reputation for being difficult to deal with. I'm broken both physically and emotionally.

"Then you sashay in, all big eyes and brunette curls, being flirty and showing off your gun skills. I see you hitting it off immediately and... I mean, it's pretty fucking obvious who he should pick—"

Amanda could feel herself getting annoyed. "Okay, slow your roll, Gayle. I'm *not* going to apologize for being who I am. Yes, I'm a flirt, but that doesn't mean I'm out to sleep with every man I bat my eyelashes at..."

"I know..." Gayle sighed. "I know, and I'm sorry."

"No," Amanda said firmly. "Stop being sorry and be...Gayle. The Gayle I remember from before. Going back to the Peter Harrison incident for a moment, while you were pissed at me that night, the next day you were over it.

"I might have the 'big eyes and brunette curls,' but *you* had *swagger*. We all wanted to be like you. To have the innate confidence *you* had from the first moment we laid eyes on you."

Gayle rolled her eyes. "Oh, please!"

"Fuck, no. It's true," Amanda said. "Day one. We were all sat in the classroom, and when you walked in, the conversation *stopped*. You had your hair in that short, scruffy bob, no makeup, and you were wearing ripped jeans and a black T-shirt with some bloody sci-fi reference on it nobody understood..."

"USS *Sulaco*." Gayle smiled. "It's from the movie Aliens."

"As if that means *anything* to me," Amanda laughed. "Anyway, you dropped your kitbag, and the room went silent. Then you grinned and said—"

"—'Fuck, this is going to be fun!'" Gayle said with a nod. "I can't believe you remember that day."

"Clear as fucking crystal. You walked into a room with eleven strangers and every eye in the room was *drawn* to you. You had something...something none of the rest of us did. We all recognized it immediately.

"Throughout our training, we *all* had doubts about ourselves, our abilities. Me more than most. I used to laugh it off, but that 'one-trick pony' stuff used to hurt. At first, at least. I *longed* for your power levels, your skills..."

"I'm sorry, Amanda." Gayle's face fell. "I never... I should have been more..." She was searching for a word which wouldn't come, but Amanda shook her head and grasped her hand.

"No, Gayle, it's fine. *You* were the one who pushed me to use what I had to my advantage. You had confidence—not just in yourself but in us. You pushed every single one of us to be better. Yes, the 'one-trick pony' slight bothered me at first, but after a while, I started to wear it like a badge of honor. I found my role on the team, doing something *no one* else could do...and believe me, I tried to teach you all!"

"Well, I could see it was what made you special..." Gayle shrugged.

"And what makes *you* special is that insight. That confidence. You need to find that again. Use it with these kids."

"I don't think it's in me anymore..."

"What you said a moment ago is true, Gayle. You *have* been hurt. Both mentally and physically. Believe me, I know. I was there, too." Amanda's tone was hard. "But you came to Stoke Mandeville to see me before my surgery. You assured me it would be okay. Told me to have faith.

"Consider *this* as me returning the favor. If you like Michael...and you *want* Michael... Then go and *get* Michael. I am not competing with you on this one. We're not twenty anymore, and this is not a Peter Harrison situation. I can see Michael *means* something to you, so I am going to help you in any way I can to land the big handsome bastard."

Gayle looked down at the ground and smiled shyly. "He is handsome, isn't he?"

"Oh, I definitely would," Amanda declared firmly.

The sentence was incomplete, but Gayle knew the missing words were 'fuck him.' She laughed and slumped back on the bench, staring at the sky for a moment. She had the look of someone whose burden had been lifted from her shoulders. Once the laughter faded, she turned toward Amanda and pulled her into an embrace, which Amanda gratefully accepted. The hug was tight, but not *too* tight.

Amanda whispered into Gayle's ear. "I'm not going to break. The new spine is technically stronger than the old one."

Acknowledging Amanda's assertion, Gayle constricted her arms, intensifying the hug.

"Better?" she said.

"Much!" Amanda replied. "Now, let's discuss your seduction strategies. I'm thinking you've got to stop trying to be me. It's time for you to be more...like you."

"I'm not sure what that means..." Gayle laughed and let her friend out of the bear-like grip in which she had been holding her. "It's been a while."

"Well," Amanda said with a grin, "that's why I'm here to help you figure it out."

| 28 |

BONDING

— **Allyson Knightley** —
— *Monday — Nexus City, Iceland* —

Bobbi strode into the room and sat herself down in the chair across from the sofa on which Ally had been napping. "You look knackered, luv."

Allyson glanced up at Bobbi with a wry smile. "It's been a...hectic week."

She exhaled heavily as she swung her legs around to sit up.

"You're sellin' yourself short. By all accounts, you've had a fuckin' awful week. Did you sleep at all?"

Ally nodded wearily as she worked to massage the kink out of her neck.

"Good. I saw the news footage. Quite a knock you took." Bobbi gestured toward the band-aid covering the stitches on Ally's temple. "'Tween that and those bruises—sorry, I couldn't help but notice—you need the rest, darlin'."

Ally regarded the Vampyrii curiously. She wasn't at all what Ally had imagined. To be honest, Lyssa saying they were half-sisters had kind of colored her expectations.

Bobbi was taller than Lyssa by at least six inches and broader across the shoulders. They shared the same strong jawline, but there wasn't a hint of the Native American ancestry in Bobbi's features which was so prevalent in Lyssa's.

Bobbi was attractive, but where Lyssa was pretty, Bobbi was more...handsome.

"Thanks, Bobbi," Ally said, stifling a yawn. "Lyssa is constantly bugging me to take better care of myself..."

"She's right. You should listen."

Ally nodded and yawned. Bobbi's foot jiggled as she sat, studying Ally, this stranger who had been thrust into her midst. Ally didn't feel like she was being judged, but the intensity of Bobbi's scrutiny was a little unnerving.

"So, you've spent time in London?" Ally asked, trying to break the awkward silence.

"What was your first clue?" Bobbi snorted with amusement.

"The accent. And...the swearing," Ally chuckled.

"You can take the girl out of the East End, but you can't take the East End out of the girl." Bobbi laughed. "I lived in Whitechapel before StormHall's fucking War. The bloody 'Purification' forced me out of the UK."

"You'd get on great with my sister. She has a propensity toward the profane, too."

Bobbi cocked an eyebrow. "Ah, yes. Big sister, Gayle. The infamous Knightingale. Mercy had a lot to say about her. Have to admit...I'm keen to meet her. Maybe one day we could make it happen, eh?"

Ally nodded. "Maybe."

An awkward silence descended as the two of them regarded each other. Bobbi's intimidating physical presence was enhanced by the very well-tailored black pants suit she wore. Even the height of her shoes was daunting to Ally who rarely wore anything with a heel.

Suddenly Bobbi uncrossed her legs and leaned forward in the chair, not taking her eyes off Ally. "Can I ask you a question?"

"Sure."

"I have spent the last four hours with my half-sister, trying to figure out what the fuck we're gonna do next. Approximately once every five minutes, your name enters the conversation. 'Allyson this. Allyson that.' I don't have to be a bloody mind-reader to know you girls have been fucking—"

"—We slept together twice," Ally interrupted.

"Well, she's quite the smitten kitten. But she also has a metric fuck-ton of responsibility weighing down on those pretty shoulders. Regardless of how much she wants to do the horizontal tango with you, that responsibility is taking her back to New Victus because she sure as shit is gonna kick StormHall's arse out of power.

"So, my question is...what are *you* going to do, Allyson Knightley?"

Ally slumped back on the sofa. Bobbi had cut right to the core of her dilemma. She closed her eyes and sighed.

"I *really* want to help, but..." She paused, trying to find the right words. "I'm a cop at heart, Bobbi. Someone set off a bomb and killed people on my watch. Killed my dad. No offense, but you and I both know NVSec won't solve this..."

Bobbi laughed. "New Victus Security couldn't solve a crossword puzzle if you gave them a fuckin' thesaurus! Just 'cause they're Vampyrii doesn't mean I hold them in high regard, luv. You're right, though. NVSec is in StormHall's pocket, and it's in *his* best interests to keep the finger pointed at Lyssa and only Lyssa."

"Which means," Ally continued, "if I want to bring the people behind this to justice, I'm going to have to do it myself—"

"—Which is hard to do when you're the FSE Security Chief, *and* they've removed you from the investigation," Bobbi finished.

Ally nodded.

"So...you're gonna quit," Bobbi stated matter-of-factly.

"I'm considering it."

"But that, in turn, gives you another dilemma, don't it?"

"Why do I feel like you're reading my mind?" Ally chuckled, shaking her head.

"'Cause I am...a little," Bobbi admitted. "You know about Lyssa's sister Vanessa, right?"

Ally nodded. "The succubus?"

"Did she tell you Vanessa had low-level telepathy?" Bobbi

said quietly.

"She did. I'd always thought that was an old Vampire myth. Like garlic and holy water."

"Well, those two *are* bullshit, yeah. But telepathy...nah, that's real. It's fuckin' rare, but it *is* a Vampyrii trait. Vanessa could not only read minds to a degree but also put her thoughts into your noggin, too. Now, I can't do the latter, but I do have some skill surface-reading a mind. Which is bleedin' useful in my line of work. It always helps to know who I can trust.

"I trust *you*, Allyson Knightley."

There was a sincerity to Bobbi's words that touched something deep in Ally. Before she knew it, she was talking openly about what was on her mind.

"I feel...torn, Bobbi. I want to go with Lyssa. I want to help. But at the same time, I have to find out who killed my dad."

Bobbi reclined in her seat and smiled sadly. "I get that. I'd want to do the same thing. There's a substantial part of me that wants to steer well fucking clear of this war Lyssa is gonna start. It's bad for my business to be seen taking sides. But, in this case, I don't have much of a choice.

"What Lyssa is about to do is bigger than anything I've *ever* done. For me and her, this shit is personal on a level most people don't understand. StormHall doesn't tolerate diversity. If you aren't pure-blooded and male, then fuck you. Lyssa threatens him because she's a powerful woman. That's the first big no-no! She's also bisexual, which is strike number two."

"Bi-sexual?" Ally whispered.

"You didn't know?"

"I guess I assumed she was like me. Gay."

"She doesn't publicize the fact, but yeah, she swings both ways."

"You said this was personal for you too, so you're saying you're...what? Gay or bisexual, too?" Ally said with a frown.

"Oh, darlin', I am *way* more complicated!" Bobbi said with a laugh. "I was born in London, to the bells of St. Mary-le-

Bow. Cockney from my first days in this world. My birth certificate tells the world Perlania Ahkza gave birth to her son Lucius, 14th May 1932. I grew up on the streets of London during the blitz, playing in my cap and vest with the other little boys. Cute as a button, but...different."

"You were born male?" Ally couldn't keep the surprise from her voice.

"Still am, biologically speaking," Bobbi shrugged. "But I identify female. This is me. I like me as I am. Sooner the rest of the world catches up with the fact people can be whatever they fucking want, the better off we'll all be."

"So, when did you become Bobbi?" Ally was now leaning forward again in rapt attention.

"In the 1960s I truly found myself. But those were the early days of really understanding this shit. Society wasn't that tolerant back then.

"Roll forward fifty years and things were looking much better. I moved to the US—San Francisco—and became Bobbi. Felt fucking wonderful to just be who I am. Then 2016 happened and fucking StormHall ruined everything. Reset the whole sodding world back to the fucking dark ages."

"Yeah, he doesn't seem like the most enlightened of people," Ally commented.

"He's not. He's a homophobic, xenophobic, racist bastard...but suddenly, he was the big dog in Vampyrii politics. Wasn't just him, though. When the Rising happened, the world closed its doors to our kind, understandably so. Since then, racism and intolerance have taken on a new aspect. It ain't just color, race, gender identity no more. Now it's species, too.

"So, here I am, ticking all the fuckin' prejudice boxes. My only choice was to move here and go underground."

"Shit..." was all Ally could muster. "I'm sorry, Bobbi."

"I'm not tellin' you all this to get your sympathy, Knightley," Bobbi laughed. "I'm a fuckin' saleswoman; think of this as my pitch. I'm tellin' you this because Lyssa is the *one* person in the world who can *fix* this shit. But she can't do it alone, and I'm not just talking about allying with the big guns. She needs help on a personal level, and I'm fucking hoping you'll be that person.

"Me? I'll negotiate a price for just about anything. Lys...she gives her love easily and freely to those who deserve it. I know you got shit to do yourself, and I get that. You want closure on who killed ya dad. Just, maybe once you've got your peace of mind...please consider helping her."

Allyson nodded. "I will. I promise."

"I've got a good feelin' about you, Knightley. A *really* good feelin'. There's something about you; something I can't quite put my finger on... I know we're more alike than either of us realize."

Ally wondered what Bobbi meant by that, but before she could say anything further, Lyssa swept into the room, full of energy. She appeared well-rested and the steely look of determination was back in her eyes.

"What are you guys talking about?" she said with a smile.

"Just chatting..." Allyson said innocently.

"Glad you two are getting on. Have you decided what to do next?" Lyssa asked.

Her question prompted Ally and Bobbi to exchange a look, but Lyssa didn't notice as she sat on the sofa and grasped Ally's hand. The hold was firm but tender.

"I need to get back to the FSE sector before I'm missed. And get Bobbi's people into the morgue to get Mercy out. You said there's a way?"

Bobbi nodded. "I have no idea how you got across the border, but if I'd known you were coming, I'd have let you use my passage...and that's *not* a bloody euphemism, darlin'!"

As she laughed, their host walked to the back of the room, reached up, and tapped her hand against a non-descript looking section of wall. A secret door whispered aside revealing a passageway.

"It's a bit of a hike, but this tunnel will take you right under the border wall and back into FSE territory. It exits in an office I rent through a third-party source. I pay good money, and they don't ask awkward questions. That's all you need to know. I'm trusting you with this because I like you. Even if you are the fucking FSE Security Chief."

"I don't think you'll have to worry about that too much longer, Bobbi," Ally said cryptically.

"I can't come with you," Lyssa sighed. "There are too many people looking for me. Besides, I have business to attend to. Arrangements to make with Damian. Plus, I'll need to talk to the other Progenitor House leaders. Bobbi, can you get me a conference call with Skarling and Haggari?"

"I'm fucking insulted you should even have to ask that question, Sis!"

"Okay," Allyson said, "so that's sorted. Communications aside, Lyssa, you lie low here till I get back."

"What are you going to do?" Lyssa asked.

"What I need to do," Ally said firmly.

| 29 |

THE ESCAPE

— Rahanah —
— Monday — Independent State of Rio de Janeiro —

She gazed into the dancing amber of the campfire, transfixed by the shimmering embers at its base. The rainforest was peaceful tonight, and around her, everyone was silent. Waiting. Rahanah wondered where to begin. After a beat, she decided to start where all stories do.

At the beginning.

"My people have no memory of how we became. Simply stories passed down through generations. Our legends tell of six brothers and six sisters, where every family line of Harimau Jadian originated.

"For centuries we prospered, hidden in the jungles of Malaysia. We were many. Outsiders consider our animal form to be a predator, but that notion is *far* from what it means to be Harimau Jadian. The path delivers purpose, harmony, and truth to those who follow it. My people lived peacefully on the winding path for many, many years.

"Then...the war came."

"The Rising?" Becka asked.

The term was unfamiliar to Rahanah, yet the young auburn-haired girl who traveled with Alexa looked at her as if those words should mean something. Fortunately, the She-Wolf could sense Rahanah's confusion.

"The Rising," Alexa explained, "was the term used by the media outlets in the West for the upheaval sparked when the Vampyrii started their war with the Werewolves. The effects were global."

"How many years past?" Rahanah asked.

She watched as Alexa did the math in her head. "Twenty-nine."

Rahanah considered it for a moment.

Has it truly been so long?

"This term is not familiar to me," she said slowly. "But the time…sounds correct. It was the beginning of what my people call the 'Dragon War.'"

"The Dragon War?" Becka said quietly.

Rahanah nodded. "I do not know all of the details. My simple understanding is China expanded quickly and…unexpectedly. The Empire moved to intervene, acting to preserve and protect the countries China was annexing.

"Thailand and Malaysia became disputed territory…there was *much* fighting. We hid deep in the jungles and forests, hoping we would not be noticed, but my people were caught in the crossfire. Many died as our jungles burned under the assault of the Chinese Dragon-Riders. Japan fought back using their machines—"

Alexa held up her hand, stopping her mid-sentence. "—Woah, hold up there, cowgirl!" she said, her eyes wide.

"I am a tiger! Not a cow…" Rahanah replied, confused by Alexa's choice of words.

Alexa shook her head. "No, I mean slow down for a moment. There's a lot to unpack in what you just said."

"Chinese *Dragon*-Riders?" Becka said quizzically.

Rahanah nodded.

"Like…real, *actual* Dragons?"

Rahanah shrugged as she answered. "Harimau Jadian have poor eyes, our sense of smell…is not great. But ears… We hear things *very* well. The Dragon-Riders came without warning. Like a whisper on the breeze. We only knew of battle when we heard the sound of the Japanese flying machines." Rahanah pointed up into the night sky. "They would fight high above us. In the clouds." She paused for a second, remembering the terror she had felt upon hearing the sounds of distant battle.

When the forest is your home, there is *one* thing you fear above all. One horrifying element which would destroy your habitat without compunction. That would kill your kin in the most horrible way, without mercy or remorse.

"As they warred, the fire fell on the jungle. Unnatural fire. The trees of the forest in which we lived were filled with flame and smoke. Our homes burned in seconds. Many of my kind died slow painful deaths. We had no choice but to leave if we were to survive.

"It was not easy. I managed to gather as many of my kind as could be found, and we trekked through Indonesia to AustralAsian territory. Once there, we stowed away on a large cargo ship carrying trade goods to Costa Rica."

Alexa whistled under her breath. "Must have been a hell of a sea trip."

The tigress nodded sadly. "Many of my people did not survive. We were created to roam the jungles, not the oceans. When we finally arrived, we thought we would be safe in Federation territory...and for a while we were. Then the hunts began."

"The hunts?" Becka asked.

Rahanah nodded. "Fifty-seven Harimau Jadian survived the journey to our new home. We settled. Started to make a life for ourselves...but six months later, one of our number went missing. We didn't know why but did not assume a problem. A week later, another went missing. And another two weeks after that. All gone. No trace. We were being targeted. Afraid for our lives, we moved again."

"To Cuba?" Alexa guessed.

Rahanah nodded. "For a little while, it seemed safe there. Even so, I told my people to be in pairs at all times. We were in Havana trying to buy provisions when you found us, Alexa Reynolds."

"Pairs..." Alexa suddenly made a leap of intuition. "You. You were with Ashraff in Havana."

"Yes," Rahanah said with a nod. "In the bar where you

found Ashraff. He ran to protect me. I followed, unsure of what to do. Other hunters, when they had been forced to fight *two* Harimau Jadian…" She couldn't finish the statement, but she hoped Alexa would understand what she was trying to say.

"I'm sorry," Alexa said softly.

"I watched your fight with Ashraff," Rahanah said with a sad smile. "He is bigger, stronger than you. I saw the wounds to your shoulder, and I was sure you would kill my brother in self-preservation. Yet, when you shot at him, you aimed only to warn or impede him. Even when he had his teeth to your throat, you spared his life."

"I try not to kill unless I have to…" Alexa shrugged.

She had tried to make it a nonchalant gesture, but Rahanah could see the pain in Alexa Reynolds' eyes. She, too, had seen much unnecessary death in her life, of that Rahanah was certain. She reached over to place her hand gently on Alexa's knee.

"That is a very rare trait in people of your profession." Rahanah smiled. "I thank you *deeply* for sparing my brother's life."

"You're welcome…" Alexa said hesitantly.

Rahanah turned slightly to address Becka. "I was about to try and retrieve Ashraff when your flying machine landed. I watched you help Alexa up the ramp. There was much blood. While you were away, I tried to carry Ashraff, but he was too heavy to move quickly or easily. I knew you would come back for him, so I hid beneath the ramp of your craft. As you loaded him, I crept aboard and concealed myself. I thought I would revive Ashraff while you were busy, then we would escape. But I could not wake him."

"We used a Stasis-Grenade on him," Becka explained. "We call them Icers. They freeze their target, paralyzing movement and putting them to sleep for up to twenty-four hours."

"Yes, I saw the blue light when you fought." Rahanah nodded. "I did not know what it was, but I knew my brother was still alive.

"I stayed hidden until you landed in Nassau. Alexa was

sleeping when you took Ashraff to the Federation men. I followed, waiting for a time to stage a rescue. I stayed in hiding nearby. Waiting patiently. But the guards were alert and well-armed. There was no time to free him.

"Two days later, another aircraft arrived. Ashraff was loaded aboard with other prisoners. I hid on board again. I could hear them talk about another pick-up, and they flew to Brazil, landing near a town. As they left, I seized my moment and freed Ashraff. We fled into the forest to safety. After eight days of walking, we found this place."

She watched the faces of her guests. They were all held in rapt attention by her tale.

It was Valentina, the young soldier, who spoke first. "Why did you attack our outpost at Bom Jardim?"

"It was not an attack," Rahanah protested softly. "Ashraff and I needed to communicate with our kin. We had a long-range radio at our camp in Cuba. We had hoped we could use your radio at the outpost to reach them. Tell them to join us here."

"You have a radio?" Valentina looked taken aback.

Rahanah laughed. "Do not mistake a simple life for an un-educated life. We can use technology; it's just that we choose not to. When we infiltrated your outpost, we were spotted. Your people reacted...badly. Jumped to conclusions. Very much like you did, Corporal Rodriguez."

She watched the young woman blush, her face turning visibly darker even in the light of the campfire.

Alexa beckoned around the glade, gesturing toward the various members of Rahanah's streak.

"I take it you got through to them. But...is this all that's left? There can't be more than what...thirty of you here," she said.

Rahanah nodded. "Thirty-six. All who remain."

"Why?" Becka's voice was hushed. "Who is hunting you?"

Rahanah didn't need to answer. Alexa had put the pieces of the puzzle together and replied on behalf of the tigress. "They have no idea," she said slowly. "That's why we're here...isn't it?"

Rahanah said nothing, simply put her food aside carefully. When she looked at Alexa, there was sadness in her eyes. She gestured around the camp.

"All we have is here. We are not rich. We have nothing to offer you." She could hear the quiet note of pleading in her own voice. "When you took Ashraff, you spared his life. You bested him in combat and delivered him alive. None of the others who were hunted were as fortunate.

"There is honor in you, Alexa Reynolds. It is to that honor which I appeal for your help. Please.

"Help me save my people."

| 30 |

BODY DOUBLE

— **Allyson Knightley** —
— *Tuesday — Nexus City, Iceland* —

Allyson kept her eyes fixed firmly on the body in front of her.

Her gaze never deviated

From this angle, Mercy looked serene beneath the glass canopy. You'd be forgiven for thinking she was merely sleeping. Her auburn hair lay still, its boundless waves resting across her shoulders. Her pale skin was blemish-free, enviously perfect until your eye-line wandered to her left cheek and neck. The illusion of peaceful slumber was snapped the moment you saw the burns and broken skin.

The ugly scars left by the explosion that killed her, all kept in perverse perfection by the stasis pod in which her corpse lay.

Mercy had been preserved for the purposes of the investigation, but apart from the injuries she sustained in the blast, her body was left untouched. Ally knew the FSE was pushing for permission to do an autopsy; she herself put in the request for it to be allowed. New Victus, however, had been resolute in their assertion Mercy remain untouched until they took over the responsibility of looking into the bombing.

Now that the investigation had been officially turned over to NVSec, it was only a matter of time before Mercy's body was handed over to them for scrutiny.

Lyssa was adamant she *had* to have Mercy back untouched.

Ally placed her hand gently atop the glass, pressing her fingertips against the cool surface.

"I'm so sorry," she whispered. "This never should have happened."

Though the sentiment was whispered to Mercy's pod, the words were also meant for the pod immediately to her right. The one at which she refused to look.

Because she knew if she did...it would break her.

The coffin-shaped glass cases in the room contained the bodies of the other attack victims. All waiting for the unsympathetic caress of a forensics pathologist.

Including her father.

The morgue was spotless. A cold room of clinical white tile and brushed metal surfaces. Every inch of stainless steel and ceramic scrubbed clean and disinfected thoroughly. All the tools of the coroner were laid out in rows so neat it would satisfy any obsessive-compulsive.

The smell of the cleansing fluids drifted into her nostrils, stinging them, making her eyes water, forming tears in the corners which started to run down her cheeks. She dabbed at them with a finger as she sniffed and swallowed hard.

Stop lying to yourself, Ally. It's not the chemicals, and you know it!

Barely unchecked emotions were rolling over her, a crashing wave of grief and sadness threatening to overwhelm her. It was met by a wall of remorse.

Fran had brought to her a message, weeks ago, about a bomb threat.

She'd even had *that* feeling at the time. The sort of 'uncanny Ally' feeling that something was off about the warning. A sense it meant more than the brush-offs everyone else seemed to be giving it...

"Likely another crank call," Fran had said almost dismissively. "We get dozens of them every Summit. Usually nothing."

And when she told her parents about it, her father had

said, "'Ah, I see. Wouldn't be the first. Should we be concerned?'"

"I don't think so, Ambassador," Fran had reassured him.

Yet *Ally* had been concerned.

So, why had she not pursued it? Why had she forgotten all about it?

Three people lost their lives in the explosion. The guilt of their deaths weighed heavily on her shoulders. She knew her father would be the first person to tell her not to bear such a responsibility. Lyssa, too. Though somewhat hypocritically, her lover also seemed intent on accepting the responsibility by blaming her lack of foresight into what she had always felt was a StormHall trap.

Allyson clenched her jaw tightly, screwing her fists into balls. Her fingers dug into her palms but couldn't generate the pain required to distract herself from the turmoil washing over her. Her fingernails were far too nibbled to cause any discomfort, so instead, she chewed on her lower lip so hard she almost drew blood.

It didn't help.

"Chief Knightley?"

The voice startled her, jerking her unceremoniously back into the moment.

"Yes," she croaked and then repeated after clearing her throat, "yes. I'm Allyson Knightley."

There were two of them. Standing inside the morgue with a trolley, upon which sat a stasis pod identical to the ones holding her father and Mercy. With her confirmation, the first of the newcomers sidled up to her. He was wearing the scrubs of an orderly at the FSE Nexus City Medical Centre—white pants and tunic with a diagonal turquoise arrow-like accent running from chest to right shoulder. The NCMC logo was prominent on the left breast. His companion, who remained in the doorway, her hands still grasping the handle of the trolley, was dressed similarly.

Allyson knew, however, these weren't staff who worked here at all.

The sallow color of the male's skin and the piercing blue

eyes of the female gave away their true identity to anyone observant enough to wonder who was pushing a new body into the morgue in the middle of the night. Imposters.

Vampyrii imposters.

On any other day, it would be Allyson's responsibility to arrest them, but today they were here on her invitation.

Okay, maybe invitation *is too strong a word...*

"You're Bobbi's people?"

The male nodded, then motioned toward the pod in front of which Allyson stood. "Is this the one?" he said with quiet professionalism.

Allyson nodded.

Without another word, the man gestured toward his partner who wheeled the trolley alongside them. Ally flicked her eyes toward the contents of their trolley and let out a small gasp of shock.

Mercy?

The stasis pod held a young woman. She had the same build and height, the same perfect skin, and the same cascading curls of auburn hair. As Ally's eyes wandered across the peaceful face of this unexpected doppelgänger, she noticed even the scarring down the face looked identical. Her mouth dropped open slightly as she leaned in to take a closer look.

"Will she pass muster?" the male orderly asked.

"Pass...muster?"

"Will she fool the coroner?" He rolled his eyes at her. "You didn't think we were just going to steal her corpse, did you? Best if, to all intents and purposes, your girl never actually goes missing at all."

Ally nodded in understanding. Bobbi had organized everything in isolation. All that had been required of Ally was open up access for Bobbi's people to do whatever they needed to do. As Security Chief, she could do that with no problem and no questions asked. They were right, however. She hadn't really thought the whole thing through, considered what would happen when Mercy's body turned up missing.

NVSec would know her code had been used to open up the

morgue, which would lead to many an uncomfortable question. And while Ally had an uncanny knack for telling truth from fiction, she wasn't great at lying herself.

Fortunately, it seemed like Bobbi had her covered in this respect.

Ally leaned over the body of the strange twin, taking a closer look. The likeness was eerie, but on closer scrutiny, even she, who had only met Mercy once, could tell this wasn't her.

"Who is...was this?" she whispered.

"No one of any importance," the male orderly said.

"Did you kill her?"

"No," he replied after a pause. Ally knew he was lying.

Do you really want to know the truth?

She stepped aside and let the two faux orderlies go about the task of switching the stasis pods. As they began to wheel Mercy out of the doorway, the male turned toward Ally and gestured at the body they had left in Mercy's stead.

"No one will be any the wiser..." He paused for a moment before nodding toward her father's pod. "Bobbi...she likes you. She wanted us to ask if you'd like a similar service for your own loss. Once NVSec takes over the investigation, they'll have access to everything. Is that something you want to avoid?"

He was right. The thought of a Vampyrii forensics technician, working for StormHall, laying their hands all over her father's body filled her with disgust.

He was a victim, not a piece of empirical evidence to be dissected and discussed.

No, it wouldn't happen.

There was no way she was going to let it, and if Allyson herself did not have the power to prevent it...her mother surely would. Or her uncle. Neither of them would allow *any-thing* to happen to Jaymes' body. Her father would be safe-guarded, of that she was sure.

Almost sure.

She resolved to talk to them about it as soon as possible.

And if they couldn't stop it...

"Maybe…" Ally said quietly. "But not tonight. I'll let Bobbi know if I decide action needs to be taken. But tell her…thanks. For the thought."

With a nod, the two Vampyrii left, and she was alone once more.

Just Allyson, her guilt, and some important decisions to make.

| 31 |

HOBBIES AND INTERESTS

— Michael Reynolds —
— Tuesday — London, England —

"Can we *please* take a break?" Gayle pleaded. "I don't think my brain can take any more."

Michael glanced up from the paper he was grading to see Gayle stretching and rubbing at her tired eyes. Not for the first time today, he debated the wisdom of setting the kids a ten-thousand-word history assignment on 'The Battle of the South China Sea,' their first deep dive into the war between Australasia and the Japanese Empire.

The submission deadline had been Friday, so he could grade them over the weekend. Gayle had looked at him like he was crazy when he proposed it, and she'd been right He *vastly* underestimated the time it would take to read through twelve huge essays. Monday passed by, and he'd found himself massively behind schedule. He had expected a deserved 'I told you so' from Gayle, so her volunteering to help instead was an unexpected, yet pleasant, surprise. She arranged for Lana and Amanda to cover their Tuesday classes so that the two of them could spend the day finishing up with the students' reports.

Arriving bright and early, they buckled down to scrutinize each essay, fact-checking and grading them. Now, the early evening sun was dipping low in the sky. Lunch had been skipped, and he realized the headache he had was probably a result of hunger combined with eyestrain.

He put the paper down and threw his pen onto the desk where Gayle had already discarded hers, regarding her from his seat as she stretched out, staring at the ceiling. He had seen her in casual clothes before, so the faded grey stone-washed jeans and black T-shirt she was wearing were no real surprise.

Her feet were up on his desk, knees bent, the fashionable holes in the thighs showing a little skin. Her T-shirt was another of those with a logo and slogan for which he didn't get the reference. The letters looked like a printed representation of red and yellow neon. He squinted slightly as he tried to read the print.

"Would you like me to flash you?"

His eyes flicked up to her amused face, and he realized he'd been staring at her chest. At least she was smiling about it.

"They *are* spectacular," she teased. "Totally worth the price of admission."

He ignored the comment and pointed to the logo. "What's *Flynn's Arcade*?"

"You've never seen *Tron*?" Gayle chuckled.

"What's a '*Tron*'?" he asked in confusion.

As Gayle's eyes widened, he suddenly found himself feeling a surge of surprise, too. Those eyes were not made up. In fact, he noticed for the first time in hours, Gayle was utterly 'au naturel' today. Her hair was scraped back into a neat ponytail, but there wasn't a hint of her usual cosmetic enhancements. Not that she usually wore much of it—she was naturally pretty anyway.

You're spending far too much time thinking about this, Michael!

"You were a kid on a Disney cruise ship, and you *never* stumbled over *Tron*?" Gayle laughed in disbelief.

"If it's a movie, then I only recall them having a library of mostly princess movies." He shrugged. "I liked the movie with the guy in the hat, though."

"The guy in the hat..." Gayle repeated, her eyebrow raised. "That doesn't give me a whole lot to go on..."

"Yeah, and the whip. I don't recall the name, but it was fun."

"Hat and whip…" Gayle considered. "Oh…*Indiana Jones*."

"Yeah, that's the guy."

"I *love* those movies."

"There was more than one?"

"Oh, Michael," Gayle laughed. "You poor, sheltered Texan. Yes, there was more than one movie. Three more, in fact. You never really watched movies as a kid?"

He shook his head. "We weren't kids for long. Everyone on the refugee ships had to work, to contribute to the community somehow. We grew up fast."

Gayle's face softened with a hint of embarrassment. "Fuck, I'm sorry," she apologized. "Here's me teasing you about your geek credentials when I had an embarrassingly cushy life growing up. My parents had money and status. I got a great education… I whine about being teased at school because of my hair color, but compared to what *you* went through… Yeah, now I feel like a spoilt bitch!"

Michael laughed. "Don't feel bad for me. It's history. Life may have *started* differently for us, but we ended up in the same place. My dad was always fond of saying, 'We wouldn't be the people we are today without the experiences of our past.'"

"Wise man," Gayle said quietly with a hint of sadness.

Shit! That was thoughtless, Mike!

Michael knew her thoughts were now on her father. He understood the grief of losing a parent, and despite her brave face, he knew she struggled with it. The not being able to say goodbye. Time would lessen the pain, but it would forever haunt her.

"So…*Tron*?" he said, gesturing toward her shirt again.

She glanced down at her chest and smiled. "*Tron*…is an old sci-fi flick about a guy called Flynn who gets sucked into a virtual world inside a computer. Shenanigans ensue. It's a certified early 80s classic."

"I can honestly say I've never heard of it," he confessed. "You like movies?"

Evidently, he had found the sweet spot for engaging her interests as her mood noticeably lifted.

"Fucking *love* them." She rolled her eyes upward in mock orgasmic pleasure as she said it.

Though he'd known her for a while now, he was suddenly aware that outside of one drunken night, they hadn't discussed anything like each other's hobbies and interests. As if reading his mind, Gayle smiled and continued talking.

"Everyone has to have a hobby, right? Fordith jokes I have too many," she laughed. "Cars, music, books, comic books... But the main one is a passion for old movies. Anything pre-Rising, especially science fiction. The big flashy special effects movies. Spaceships, aliens, superheroes, giant monsters...you name it, I'll watch it. Once the US became New Victus, those Hollywood blockbusters disappeared overnight."

"How did you get into them?"

"When I was about nine years old, Dad took a government job here in London. He'd come home to Ely most weekends, but sometimes we got to come visit him here instead. There was this cinema, in Leicester Square, which used to show old classic movies they managed to find or rescue. The first time Dad took me, it was...magical."

"I don't think I've ever seen a film at a theater," Michael said quietly. "Maybe I saw something with my folks before the Rising. If so, I don't remember it. There was a theater on the *Fantasy*, but it had been converted to a medical center, so...no films there."

"Dad told me there used to be TV channels that showed all kinds of movies all the time," Gayle said wistfully. "Or streaming off the old internet... I think he called it Webflicks or something..."

"Sounds like you'd *never* leave the house." Michael started laughing.

Gayle joined him. "That's not even a joke! I'd be a total couch potato if I had the choice!"

"What was the first film you saw?"

"With my dad?" Gayle asked, to which he nodded. "Star

Wars. Blew my teeny mind. To this day I *still* want a lightsaber."

"Star Wars…" Michael chuckled thoughtfully. "That's sounds familiar…"

If Gayle had been looking at him, she might have twigged the playful look on his face. But she wasn't. He was about to open his mouth to clarify his previous statement when Gayle abruptly pulled her feet off his desk and sat bolt upright. She had the look on her face of a woman with a plan.

"What?" he asked suspiciously.

She grinned. "Enough dreary essay marking for today. Get changed, Michael Reynolds, because we are leaving. We'll get takeaway food on the way."

"On the way?" he said confused. "Where are we going?"

"To a galaxy far, far away," she said cryptically with an enthusiastic smile.

| **32** |

THE WINDING PATH

— Alexa Reynolds —
— Tuesday — Independent State of Rio de Janeiro —

Nudging her sunglasses back up her slippery nose, a perspiring Alexa cursed under her breath at the absence of even a light breeze to take the edge off the unseasonal heat. Standing under the midday sun at the foot of *Diana's* loading ramp, she worked her way through her checklist, ensuring all the items she had requisitioned had been delivered as promised.

At least I'm not the one lugging the supply crates around!

Upon their return, about an hour ago, Becka had busied herself liaising with Braga's engineers about cutting short their overhaul, while Alexa had contacted the base stores with a very hastily composed list of the supplies they needed for their next trip. Food, water, toiletries, ammunition—she checked them off the list as they were carried aboard.

If anything was missing, they would simply have to wing it. She wanted them wheels up and away from Rio as soon as possible, before anyone caught wind of their new little secret. Least of all the base commander, who was now pulling up in his jeep. His driver kept the engine running as Marshal Braga hopped out.

"You're back a lot earlier than I expected." He raised an eyebrow as he approached her. "My staff haven't finished your overhaul yet. I thought you were planning to remain in

Rio for some RnR?"

"Something came up," Alexa answered as she counted the inventory in one of the supply crates. "But your staff did a great job on *Diana*'s engines, which was the main thing. The rest can wait till we swing back this way again."

Yes, I will be collecting on the rest of your debt at some point in the future.

Braga nodded vaguely as he watched a young woman, her long white hair tucked neatly beneath a grubby baseball cap, help Becka carry another supply case up the loading ramp into *Diana*'s cargo hold. His eyes narrowed slightly, and there was a crease in his brow as he observed them.

"Believe me, I'd rather be sunnin' myself on the Copacabana, but...needs must," Alexa said in an effort to draw his attention back to her. "Do you need me to sign anything for all this? The supplies, I mean?"

He looked at her blankly for a moment before shaking his head. "No, no," he said. "My quartermaster will sort it all out. Is there anything else you need?"

Alexa shook her head. "I think we have everything. Thank you."

"You earned it. You're sure the Harimau Jadian aren't going to be a problem anymore?" Marshal Braga asked slowly.

Alexa nodded firmly. "Absolutely. I guarantee you won't get any more trouble from them."

"How can you be so sure?"

She glanced at the white-haired woman who was now deep in conversation with Becka as they discussed the contents of the crate they had just stowed.

"They've been hunted too close to extinction in their native Malaysia, so they came here to start afresh. They didn't understand the position they were in at Bom Jardim or the local politics of the region. They've had issues with both the Coalition and Cartel smugglers and thought they'd be safer near you. We spoke to their leader and explained the situation. Suggested they would be out of harm's way if they moved their group further north, deeper into the ICSA. Find a place hidden in the rainforest."

It was the truth—just not the whole truth. The Independent Countries of South America offered ample opportunity for Rahanah's people to hide safely in the thick rainforests of Brazil away from those preying on them. The plan was indeed for them to make their way north and find an area where they could live peacefully.

"Their leader agreed to that?" Braga sounded skeptical.

He can sound as suspicious as he likes...

"I explained how the forests further north might be more conducive to their hunting while staying under the radar. They *really* did not want to trigger hostilities with you. They're already an endangered species, and they know if provoked, you could wipe them out. They understood the logic and agreed. They're movin' on."

The look on Marshal Braga's face didn't flicker. He still doubted her testimonial, but he had no evidence to suggest an alternative sequence of events. Finally, he relaxed his stance a little, seeming to accept the situation.

"Well then, sounds like a job well done," he said drawing himself to his full height. "Your fee has been transferred."

"Much appreciated, Marshal." Alexa nodded and stared for a moment at *Diana*.

The job was done, and the money was in the bank. She took a deep breath; it was time to end the bullshit.

What can he do now if I speak my mind? Demand a refund?

"I know how you thought of me after what happened in Sawtooth Forest..."

"Water under the bridge," Braga said with a shrug.

"What about Corporal Rodriguez?

She watched him bristle, his face displaying barely disguised disdain.

"What about her?"

"Will it be water under the bridge for her, too?" Alexa fixed him with a stare. "I saw what she had to deal with. There were over two hundred Harimau Jadian, all capable of becoming powerful, lethal, jungle cats. Tigers, Marshal. Her squad had no chance against them. I know, because I fought one of those things in Cuba and only just walked away with my life."

"She deserted her squad—"

Alexa shook her head. "—No, she survived. The Harimau Jadian are *exceedingly* proficient hunters, who expertly split Valentina's squad and disarmed them in *seconds*. She didn't know they meant no harm, so she escaped.

"She did what a soldier should. She got back here to warn you about a potential threat. You should be *acknowledging* that fact, not holding it against her. Or her squad mates. She's tougher than you give her credit for.

"As was I."

For a moment, she thought Braga was about to round angrily upon her. His face had started to turn an ominously darker shade of red. Yet, as rapidly as the moment seemed to be escalating, it faded just as quickly.

"Yes," he said. "Yes, you are. But you have to understand...Weres and Vamps were the enemy. When you came back changed—"

"I know," Alexa sighed. "Death before dishonor and all that. I get it. But I didn't *choose* to be turned."

"It didn't matter," Braga shrugged. "My opinion back then was you should have—"

"—Should have what?" Alexa interrupted. "Committed an honorable suicide?"

The Marshal said nothing.

"I'm *still* a Were. Nothin' has changed. I've simply learned to accept it. I'm a better hunter now. My senses are more sensitive. I'm faster. Stronger. I heal more rapidly. Without those things, I would *never* have caught that Harimau Jadian in Havana, and it was that experience which enabled me to solve your little predicament here."

It wasn't a lie.

But then, it wasn't the whole truth either.

"Corporal Rodriguez wasn't changed," Alexa continued. "She's still human. Give her the benefit of the doubt you never showed me."

She wasn't sure how Braga would respond to such forthrightness, but at this point, Alexa was beyond caring. These were sentiments she wished she had said in the aftermath of

Sawtooth.

Instead, I scurried away with my metaphorical tail between my legs.

Braga's face was inscrutable as he processed her words. As the seconds passed, Alexa braced herself for the inevitable backlash. But just as she thought the storm was about to rage over her, the Marshal put his hands on his hips and broke into a resigned smile.

"Maybe you're right," he sighed. "I can see now that I underestimated you back then. Maybe Corporal Rodriquez will surprise me the same way."

"That's all I ask, Marshal. Now, if you'll excuse me, I need to finish up our flight prep."

"You'll return soon?" Braga asked, gesturing at *Diana*. "To complete the overhaul?"

Alexa nodded. "We'll be back. Not sure exactly when, but soon."

"Then I wish you safe travels and good luck in your endeavors, Miss Reynolds."

"Thank you, Marshal."

She watched him walk back to his jeep and mutter an order to his driver. A moment later, the vehicle turned and quickly drove away. Alexa wondered where he was headed in such a hurry, but after a beat realized it was none of her business. She had more important things to concern herself with right now.

A glance at her checklist told her the last of the requisitioned items was aboard *Diana*. With a final look out at the Rio de Janeiro sunshine, she smiled and strode up into the cargo hold.

"Everything okay with Braga?" Becka asked as Alexa slapped the loading ramp retraction button.

She nodded. "Yeah. He may be less of an asshole than I thought he was. We ready to go?"

"*Diana* is prepped and ready to fly," Becka said. "All I need is for you to give me a destination."

Well, now that's the crux of the problem, ain't it?

Alexa turned to the newest member of her little crew. The

one with the white hair poking out from beneath the grubby baseball cap. "You sure you wanna do this?"

The eyes of the tigress flicked her way. Alexa could see the unmistakable fire burning within them.

"This is the start of the winding path," Rahanah growled softly.

"The winding path?"

"To the truth," the Tiger-Queen clarified. "While the truth is pure, it is often hidden behind trickery, lies, and deceit. To find it, you need to go over and around such falsehoods until you uncover that which they seek to conceal. You must follow—"

"—The winding path," Alexa nodded with understanding. "So, where to first?"

"You are the hunter," Rahanah shrugged. "You know this world better than I. This is why we chose you to help us. Where does the path begin?"

Alexa bit her lip and paused to think. "Nassau," she said finally. "The path starts in Nassau."

| 33 |

| QUIT

— **Allyson Knightley** —
— *Tuesday* — *London, England* —

Allyson gazed vacantly at the floor and nibbled on an already well-chewed thumbnail as she paced the corridor outside her uncle's office. It was eerily quiet, which didn't help her mood. The dark wood-paneled walls and the thick carpeting suppressed any noise she made as she traced and retraced her steps.

She knew he was in there.

His public calendar confirmed it. As did the quick call she made to his assistant, just to make doubly sure.

Her walk to the building had been determined. Pressing the elevator call button had elicited a flutter of nerves in her stomach. Now she was doubting everything she had been so sure about mere minutes previously.

This morning, standing in the morgue alongside the bodies of her father and Mercy, she realized she had some difficult decisions to make. A keen sense of focus on her career had taken her this far, and she *was* incredibly proud of the fact she had earned the job of Chief of Nexus Security at such a tender age. Her detractors had muttered about her youth and her connections, but Ally *knew* she deserved this job. She was very good at what she did.

Yet, over the past week, things had irrevocably changed.

Ally felt like the bomb that took the life of her father had also profoundly diverted the direction of her life.

She had questions.

Questions that desperately needed answers.

Answers she wasn't sure she was going to find while wearing this uniform and sitting behind a desk performing what had suddenly become a hollow role. The world she knew was spinning out of her control, and she needed to know whether it was her fault or not.

There must be something I missed. Something I could have done.

Those doubts had plagued her over the last few days. Second-guessing her choices regarding the plans she had put into action to keep the Summit delegates safe. The report Captain Reynolds had sent to her hadn't helped assuage her concerns either. There had been a few minor recommendations—which she duly implemented—but he had approved her approach and endorsed it wholeheartedly. Still, her confidence wandered wildly from moment to moment. One minute, sure she had done *everything* she could reasonably have done, while the next she was paranoid she had royally fucked something up.

She just didn't know what.

What she did know was she needed to do *something*. If her uncle wouldn't let her pursue the truth in an official capacity, then there was only one course of action open to her. Or at least, that was how she'd felt thirty minutes ago. Now, she was mentally debating whether she was doing the right thing, or whether this was a stupid knee-jerk reaction she would later horribly regret.

No. Stop arguing with yourself, Ally. You need to do this.

She took firm hold of the office doorknob, the metal feeling cool in her sweaty palm. Before she could change her mind again, she twisted and pushed, swinging the door silently into the office where General Norbel sat behind his desk, staring at her implacably.

"Allyson. I was wondering when you would cease wearing out the hallway carpet with your restless pacing." She thought she saw her uncle's left eyebrow twitch ever so slightly upward, and a subtle amused curl of his lips at the corners as she approached his desk, but it could have been a trick of the light. "It is good to see you this evening."

"I'm here in an official capacity, General."

"Oh?" Her uncle looked genuinely surprised. Then his eyes locked onto the pristine envelope Allyson was carefully gripping. "I hope that is not what I fear it is."

Allyson didn't hesitate. Too much time had already been spent dwelling on a decision she had made a dozen times over. Extending her arm, she offered him the crisp white envelope. When he made no move to accept it, she placed it gently down on his desk.

"I officially tender my resignation from the post of FSE Chief of Security for Nexus City. Effective immediately."

Norbel made no move to accept the envelope, let alone view its contents. Ally wished she could read his mind. His face had always had an element of inscrutability, but today he seemed particularly difficult to read. Had she disappointed him?

She waited, under his watchful gaze, trying to meet his eyes and failing. Instead, she flicked her line of sight past him to the curved window forming a single seamless wall across the back of his office.

Beyond it, the Goðafoss was floodlit, cascading the white waters of the Skjálfandafljót river into a natural basin of black-grey rock covered in lush green. Hundreds of thousands of gallons thundered into the illuminated turquoise lake below. It was breathtaking during the day, but in the darkness, like tonight, the lights made it a different type of spectacle.

Fuck, I'm going to miss this view.

Norbel cleared his throat, snapping her attention back into the room.

"I would implore you to please pick up the envelope, and retract your previous statement," he said quietly. "I understand your impulse—"

"It's not an impulse, General. I've thought about this carefully."

"Allyson, I was compelled, for political reasons, to turn the investigation over to New Victus Security. I had also been negligent in my responsibility to detach you from an investigation which was clearly a conflict of interests."

Allyson wasn't there to argue either of those points. She understood her uncle's actions and agreed with his reasoning. In the same position, she would have done *exactly* the same thing.

But she *wasn't* in his position.

"I know," she said softly. "But, while this is going on, I can't be here. Everywhere I look, in every aspect of my life here, I see my failure. A failure which cost me the life of my father..." She took a deep breath, her chest rising and falling as she struggled to suppress the tears brimming in her eyes, begging for release.

Norbel sat silently for what seemed like an eternity before, finally, reaching forward and accepting the envelope.

"I do not need to open this, Allyson," his voice was full of empathy, but his face was still serene. "I can hold the post open for you. Consider this a leave of abse—"

"No," Ally interrupted. "Give the job to Francesca Romano. She deserves it. I...I don't think I'll be coming back here. There are other things I need to do."

"You are certain about this?"

She nodded determinedly. "Absolutely. Yes."

Her uncle stood, straightening his uniform as he did so. He placed the still-sealed envelope back onto the desk before walking around to stand in front of her. What came next felt extremely out of character for the uncle she knew and loved.

Norbel hugged her.

She awkwardly reciprocated the surprising gesture. While doing so, she searched her memory, trying to recall if this had *ever* happened before, but came up empty.

After a few seconds, he released her, stepping back and putting his hands on her shoulders. He looked her in the eyes and smiled.

"Please, do not do anything inadvisable, Allyson. Your parents...your father would not want that. Yet, I know he would want you to follow your heart. Wherever it may lead you."

What the fuck is that *all about?*

"I...err...I'll be fine, Uncle. I know what I'm doing. I promise."

With a nod, he backed away from her and returned to the sumptuous leather chair behind his polished mahogany desk. He sat down slowly, turning back to face her with an emotionless sphinx-like expression. It was as if the last few seconds had never happened. His nimble fingers danced rapidly over the touch-sensitive keyboard inlaid into the desk's surface, and a flurry of documents flashed up on the glass screen too fast for Allyson to follow. When he stopped, the image on the screen flickered for a moment and then vanished.

"You have been discharged from your duties, effective immediately. I shall inform Miss Romano of your resignation and her change in status. All that remains for me to do now is to wish you good fortune in your future endeavors."

It felt very much like a dismissal, and so, after a muttered goodbye, she turned and left.

As she ambled through Nexus City, heading toward her mother's apartment, she couldn't help but dwell on the time in her uncle's office. How the mood had shifted, weirdly, from professional to personal. How out of character some of the beats of the meeting had been. Allyson had never considered the stress her uncle was under in his many bureaucratic roles. He was the face of the Fae in the Human world, the head of the Human Fae Alliance, the Principal of the HFA Academy, and most recently, had taken some administrational control in Nexus.

That was a lot to take on, even for someone like her uncle.

Yet, something about his behavior was triggering 'Uncanny Ally.' An uneasy sensation in her stomach that she couldn't explain.

Everything Norbel had said to her was truthful. He'd repeatedly given her the opportunity to back out of her decision, and when she hadn't, he gracefully accepted her choice. He had walked the fine line between being her superior and being her uncle.

Hadn't he?

Ally was still mulling it over as she placed her hand over the biometric entry scanner to her parent's apartment. The sliding door whispered aside. She walked in, pausing as she entered the lounge. Her eyes panned slowly around the large comfortable area, absorbing each detail as if this was the last time she was ever going to see this place. Absorbing every tiny memory. On the antique cabinet near the door sat a plethora of photographs, far too many to comfortably fit in the space, all framed in a litany of mismatched borders.

Her father's doing.

He had never taken a photograph of his wife or girls he didn't immediately love. Allyson's eye was drawn to a family portrait from a few years ago, taken during happier times. She picked it up and brushed her fingertips lightly over her father's vibrant image.

He looked so happy.

Serlia stood behind him, her arms around Carrie, wide grins on both their faces. Gayle was caught mid-laugh as she embraced Jaymes from one side while Allyson hugged him from the other. It was a particularly candid shot, one she remembered had been taken at the end of an official photoshoot for some magazine or other. Jaymes adored the shot, saying it encapsulated his family to a tee. He had asked the photographer for a copy to frame, a request which had been happily granted.

She chuckled sadly at the memory.

"Allyson?"

Ally glanced up and saw her mother looking at her, brow furrowed in a questioning look.

"Sorry, Mum. I didn't know you were here."

"Where else would I be?" Serlia said lightly with a smile. "With the Summit on hold, I have nowhere else to be until…"

She didn't say it, but Allyson knew she was referring to her father's funeral. It was already arranged, taking place at home in England as soon as his body was released from the investigation.

"Did I hear you laughing?" Serlia continued after a beat.

Ally nodded. "Yeah, a little. I was looking at this old photo and was thinking... If it was in black and white, you wouldn't be able to tell Gayle and I apart from each other. Are you positive we're not twins?"

"I would *certainly* remember if that were true."

"Well, I wish there were photos of me as a child to prove it," Ally sighed.

"I'm sorry, Allyson." Serlia shook her head. "We lost all those in—"

"—in the fire. Yeah, I know."

An inferno had taken their family home in Ely when she was five years old. She had a vague recollection but wasn't sure if it was a true memory. Or whether it was just that the details of the night had been spoken of so often over the years that it was a faux memory. Something tugged at the back of her mind, though, every time the disaster was talked about. Another example of her senses telling her there was more to the story than she had ever been told.

A few years back, she tried pressing her parents for details, but both had been deliberately vague on the facts and had actively collaborated to swerve the conversation away from discussing that night. Allyson had let the subject lie ever since, but the notion to find out what they were hiding still bubbled away in the back of her mind.

"Are you staying for dinner?" Serlia said, changing the topic again as if reading her thoughts.

"Mmmm," Ally murmured. "Mum, can I ask you something? It's about Uncle Norbel."

"Of course."

Ally followed her mother into the kitchen and sat at one of the tall stools next to the breakfast bar. Serlia pulled open the refrigerator and began to browse through its meager contents, searching for something the two of them could have for their evening meal. The refrigerator being bare was a telling anomaly. Food had always been plentiful in her parents' home. Foraging the kitchen for something to eat was more in keeping with an activity undertaken in Allyson's apartment, or Gayle's home. Never her parents'.

She was struck by how odd this tiny thing was. An indication of how even her usually unflappable mother had been tilted off her axis by the death of her husband. Serlia maintained she was okay, that Jaymes' death was all part of a grand design, and he was now 'one with the River.' But for those who knew her well, you could see she was hurting.

Grieving.

Ally reconsidered what she was about to ask her mother. "Never mind. It's likely nothing…"

Perhaps Uncle Norbel was just off-kilter the same way her mother was.

"He called before you arrived," Serlia said, as she slowly closed the refrigerator door, coming out empty-handed. "He told me what you did." She turned toward her daughter, a knowing smile on her lips. "I told him to allay his fears for you."

"You did?" Ally said, her eyebrows raised.

Serlia nodded. "You're planning to continue your investigation, aren't you?"

"I am."

"Good," her mother said. "I would like an answer to exactly who orchestrated this attack. I do *not* trust New Victus Security to provide me with that answer."

"I *really* thought you'd try and talk me out of it," Ally said with a wry smile.

"Your gift, Allyson, is for finding the truth. And this is something I very much want to know the truth about. Additionally, I get the impression there is more to this for you… This is about Lyssa, too, isn't it? You care for her."

Ally couldn't argue. "I know she and I haven't known each other long, but…there's a connection there. And I *know* she wasn't involved. She's as much a victim in this as we are."

"So, what will you do?" her mother asked.

Ally already had her answer.

She knew *exactly* what she was going to do next.

| **34** |

BAIT FOR THE TRAP

— **Sebastian StormHall** —
— *Tuesday* — *Nexus City, Iceland* —

"Welcome back to Nexus, Sir."

Sebastian barely acknowledged the greeting from his aide as he swept into his office. In truth, he hated coming here, and the view from the panoramic window reminded him why. Across the basin, he could see the lights of the Pack Nation and UFE sectors. Humans, Werewolves, and gods knew what else was less than a mile away. Too close for his comfort.

This was the *real* reason he never attended the Nexus Summit. Why would he *choose* to spend time in the company of inferior beings? Especially when that time would have to be spent putting on a façade of polite friendliness for the sake of political maneuvering. Staying here in the city was out of the question, hence for the current situation, he was only flying in when it was absolutely necessary.

Today was one of those days.

His position was a precarious one.

For a while now he had felt a groundswell of opposition toward him. While he still controlled the Night Quorum and, by extension, the Blood Council, the Earth Quorum had been steadily building its numbers over the last few years, an increase he knew was a result of the politicking of Lyssa Balthazaar. If she managed to build her support on the opposition to outnumber him, the Earth Quorum would take control of the Blood Council and, with it, New Victus.

Up until a week ago, she had been an untouchable opponent.

Her status as the leader of one of the four remaining Progenitor Houses had made her far too high profile to…remove from the equation. The bombing of the Nexus Summit had shifted the landscape very much in his favor.

Now Lyssa Balthazaar was a suspect in this prominent crime.

The fact that she had fled apprehension for questioning made her *look* guilty even if she wasn't.

In all honesty, Sebastian had been surprised when she took that course of action. He very much expected a woman of her standing to surrender to the investigation in order to clear her name and that of her family. He had, indeed, been preparing for a long and drawn-out inquiry where Lyssa's good name would be dragged through the mud.

He knew she wasn't guilty of the bombing, but this was an ideal opportunity to destroy her politically. The erstwhile leaders of the other Progenitor Houses were weak. They all knew, in terms of raw numbers, they couldn't match Storm-Hall's followers. It was only their religious importance that placed them in this pseudo stalemate. They were unwilling to rock the boat lest it capsize in these stormy waters.

But Lyssa Balthazaar was different.

She had fire in her belly.

Lyssa had already proven that where she led, the other Houses would follow. She was the reason why the original twelve Progenitor Houses hadn't supported him during The Rising three decades ago, a fact that rankled him.

He needed her to very publicly be blamed for this attack on Nexus. Even if the case fell apart later, and she was proven innocent, the damage would already be done.

Which was why he was here.

In order to maintain the pressure, he was being forced to assume control of the situation in person because, apparently, no one else here could.

Incompetence. I'm surrounded by utter incompetence.

"Averille," he addressed his aide as he lowered himself into the oversized leather chair behind his equally oversized mahogany desk. "Send Chief Vardan in immediately."

"Of course, Grand Chancellor," she said, turning quickly to exit the office, pulling the large double doors closed behind her.

A moment later the doors opened again, admitting the tall, wiry form of NVSec Chief Markeen Vardan. He carried himself with an air of professionalism. His face was like chiseled stone, but his pale green eyes betrayed him. StormHall saw no spark of intelligence behind them, just uncompromising obedience. Of course, that was *exactly* why Sebastian had given him the job.

There were times, however, when Sebastian wished he had promoted a minion with a modicum of initiative. Instead, he'd been forced to suffer through disappointing reports of Lyssa Balthazaar disappearing without a trace. After three days of incompetent futility, he decided he had no choice but to travel to Nexus and take control of the situation in person.

"Is there a good reason why you haven't yet apprehended Lyssa Balthazaar?" he asked menacingly, raising an eyebrow as he did so.

"I believe Ms. Balthazaar is no longer in Nexus City."

"Do you want to explain to me why you believe that?"

"My people have been unable to locate her anywhere within the boundaries of New Victus territory here, and our sources in the FSE haven't seen her there either. I very much doubt she could escape through Pack Nation territory."

"So, how are you of the opinion that she has fled the city?"

"I—" Markeen began, but StormHall cut him off.

"Because to leave Nexus City, you need to be aboard a flyer, private or commercial, or there is quite a rugged overland trip. Especially without a vehicle. Have any vehicles left the city?"

Markeen shook his head. "All factions closed their overland gates after the bombing. Flights have been restricted."

Sebastian shook his head in disappointment at the man's lack of intellect. There was no possible way Lyssa could have left the city, so ergo...

"She is still here..."

The Security Chief simply furrowed his brow in confusion. Sebastian was deep in thought, asking the very same question that eventually Markeen found the gumption to voice.

"Then...where is she? I assure you, Sir, we have left no stone unturned in our search—"

"What you don't know about this city *astonishes* me." StormHall shook his head in disappointment. "There is a healthy trade in black-market dealings happening right under your nose. Did you not consider Lyssa may have bargained for their services?"

"But... Your orders have always been to..."

Sebastian waved his hand dismissively. "I know what my orders were. The black-market trade often serves a purpose for me, hence I ordered you to leave it alone. That does not mean you can't...rattle a few cages, so to speak."

"Would you like me to start bringing in known black-marketeers?"

"No," StormHall said firmly. "It's too late for that. Lyssa is already underground. We need to draw her out..." He trailed off, deep in thought.

Markeen's limited thinking was correct in one regard—if she was determined not to face the music, then the best thing Lyssa could do was flee the city and head back to New Victus. Pack Nation and the FSE were off-limits to her, and without a flyer, she couldn't get anywhere else. Even if she did, where would she go? All her potential allies—the other Progenitor Houses—were in New Victus.

His spies were telling him House Balthazaar was already going underground, although no one had any idea where. Lyssa would inevitably want to join her family...

Family.

Inspiration suddenly hit him.

"She won't leave family behind..." he said slowly, turning to Markeen as he spoke. "Her niece, Mercy, is here still. Lyssa will want to have her niece's body to perform the Blood to Earth ritual. *That* is why she's still here.

"Have Mercy's body relocated to our morgue and keep a close eye on it. She'll come for her sooner or later."

"Did you want us to bring the other bodies, too?" Markeen asked, his voice low.

"Gods, no. If we try and move Ambassador Knightley's body, or that of their assistant, the backlash we would suffer from his widow would be...detrimental to my current standing with the FSE. No, leave them where they are.

"As for Sabadini, I'd rather not have his rotting corpse on our side of the border. Bring Mercy. She is our lead suspect after all, so it shouldn't raise any flags...especially not with FSE Security." He grinned smugly. "The only person who will care...will be Lyssa Balthazaar. Maybe it'll be enough to flush her into the open."

The intercom on the desk chimed softly. "Grand Chancellor, your daughter is here to see you."

"Send her in, Averille," Sebastian said with a smile before turning back to Markeen. "You may leave."

Promptly dismissed, the man turned to leave, looking uncomfortable and clearly worried about the repercussions of his failure to thus far carry out StormHall's orders. Sebastian, on the other hand, had never truly expected Markeen to be successful.

Lyssa Balthazaar was the thorn in his side. He was a firm believer in the adage 'know your enemy,' and as such, he had been compelled to learn as much as he could about her, her friends, and her family. He knew every friendship she had made, every alliance she had fostered. Of course, she wasn't stupid. Lyssa was a clever opponent, and she knew enough to keep certain things very discreet.

Her sister Vanessa's condition, for example.

That little nugget of information had reached him around the same time that his benefactor had 'requested' he deploy Thynan to the forests of Domaine Saint-Bernard to hunt down, turn, and capture Kareena St. Claire. He had taken the opportunity to give Thynan a side-mission of his own devising and then reveled in the pleasantly surprising carnage that

introducing his incubus to Lyssa's succubus sister had initiated.

Still, Lyssa was smart enough to keep some secrets away
from his detection. He knew, for example, she was prone to
disappearing for days at a time. His spies informed Sebastian
she was neither at her home in Albany, nor her offices in New
York. Where she was during those times was a mystery to him.

He also knew she had been diverting a significant proportion of her House wealth into a couple of personal and top-
secret projects. He tried many times over the years to place a
spy deep into Lyssa's organization but had thus far failed. She
kept her confidence only in close family members.

As did Sebastian himself.

"Daughter, welcome." Grinning widely, he walked forward
and embraced her in a warm hug. "Please, sit. Can I offer you
a drink?"

He gestured toward his drinks cabinet as the young
woman made herself comfortable on the blood-red leather
sofa. She shook her head. "No, thank you, Father. I can't stay
too long. While working with NVSec gives me a reasonable excuse to cross border control, there is currently too much scrutiny for me to be missing for too long. Especially in my new
position."

Of all of his children, his only daughter was the one of
which he was most proud. She had been subjected to a tough
upbringing, admittedly due to his own prejudices against
women. He had long viewed the opposite gender as being inferior. Weaker. More emotional. His daughter had, however,
engendered a slight shift in that view over the years.

She was beautiful, in a severe kind of way; a trait she inherited from her mother. She rarely smiled, her face often serious. The way her immaculate ebony locks were pulled back
in a harsh ponytail, making her face look older than she was,
certainly didn't help in that respect. However, she was also
very smart. She knew how to work people to her advantage
and maneuver herself politically to get into the right position.
Traits she inherited from him.

Yes, her brothers were perhaps faster and stronger than

she was, but as a mirror image of Sebastian himself, she was the *truer* reflection.

"Of course," Sebastian nodded as he moved to the sofa to sit down beside her. "Congratulations are in order. FSE Security Chief—I *knew* you could do it. I'm so very proud of you.

"So, tell me *everything* I need to know, Francesca."

| 35 |

I KNOW

— Gayle Knightley —
— Tuesday — London, England —

Gayle grinned as she lounged in her big comfortable chair, long legs crossed beneath her, supporting the mostly empty bowl of popcorn she had been slowly devouring over the last few hours.

The orchestral music swelled, and the end credits were rolling. She sighed, reveling in the bliss of having watched one of her all-time favorite movies and the anticipation of the next film on the list. She looked over at the sofa where Michael sat with his bowl of popcorn, an implacable look on his face.

"So?" she asked. "What did you think?"

"I don't get it," he said with a furrowed brow.

The response took Gayle aback a little, and her expression mirrored his as she responded. "Well, it's the middle episode of the trilogy, so granted, it does have a downer of a cliffhanger ending. And we haven't watched the third film yet...speaking of which..."

Placing the bowl on the coffee table, she hopped out of the chair. The vintage disc in her vintage BluRay player wasn't going to change itself. Dropping to her knees before the television unit, she prodded the button to release the disc-tray and waited while it whirred.

"No, I get that," Michael nodded.

Popping open the plastic box for the next film, she swiftly switched out the watched movie and inserted its sequel. As the new film started to load, she hunted for the case belonging to the one they had watched. She spun the silver disc on her finger as she scoured the cabinet with a frown.

I took it out of the box just two hours ago, how can I have lost it?

"So, is it the Vader-is-Luke's-father thing?" she asked.

Michael shook his head. "No, I get that, too... What I *don't* get is why doesn't he just tell her he loves her?"

"What?"

She found the box and stowed the disc away safely before tossing it onto the coffee table and re-acquainting herself with the half-empty bowl of popcorn. She plonked herself onto the sofa alongside Michael who was gesticulating with his hands as if something were coming down from the ceiling.

"The bit where they drop Han into the big machine pit thing. Leia tells him she loves him, which is quite the confession considering she was kissing Luke earlier in the movie..."

"Wait till the next movie for more on that!" Gayle chuckled.

"But all he says is 'I know,'" Michael finished. "Surely, if this is the last time they're going to see each other, he'd want to tell her he loves her, too?"

"He does. It's implied in the 'I know.'"

"But he could have said, 'I love you too.' This was possibly the last time they were ever going to converse. If it were me, I'd want to tell her how I feel."

"But it's not the last time they talk..." Gayle argued.

"Yeah, but *he* didn't know that. The character. They said they weren't sure he'd survive the...whatever-it-was process," Michael countered.

"No, he *knew*. That was in-character for him. The cocky smuggler. It was his way of acknowledging her love and telling her this *wasn't* over. He'd be back, and he'd tell her he loved her later. All encapsulated in two succinct words."

"But if that were you—if you were the princess—wouldn't

you be pissed? You fessed up and the only response you got back was 'I know?'"

Gayle mused on it for a moment before shaking her head. "No. Leia knows the heart of the man she loves. This was not a goodbye; this was a 'to be continued.' His answer conveyed faith that this was not the end for them. He was making a vow to come back to her and finish this piece of business, while at the same time his tone implies he loves her, too. She knows because he's proved it so many times, even if he never explicitly said it.

"Honestly, I thought it might have been the whole 'I am your father' deal that confused you."

"God, no. That bit's straightforward enough," Michael laughed.

The two of them sat for a moment, neither speaking.

"Thank you," she said quietly, breaking the silence.

"What for?" Michael furrowed his brow.

"This. Movie night..." she took a deep breath, "It's helped a lot...with my dad."

Michael nodded, his eyes full of sympathy as he spoke. "I was worried about you. I worried about you being in Nexus City where I couldn't be with you."

"Be with me?"

He smiled. "I think I was doing a pretty good job of being a good influence on you. I was concerned you'd slip back into your old ways without me around."

Gayle knew he was teasing, and there was a part of her that wanted to throw a little sass back Michael's way, but a larger part of her knew he was right. She recognized the changes in herself over the last couple of months and knew it was, at least in part, due to his influence.

"Don't worry—I'm *not* going to backslide. Took me a while to get a handle on how to process Valletta, but I'm doing okay now. Or at least getting there. I...am struggling a little, I'll admit. But I was trying not to have another moment like my breakdown the other day."

"You shouldn't be afraid to talk about it. I'm right here."

She smiled, wondering exactly what she'd done to deserve

such an understanding man in her life.

"I know," she said softly. "It's almost not so much that my dad is...gone. Not even the way it happened. What is going through my head over and over is how I never made amends with him before..." She couldn't go on.

"Everyone has arguments with their loved ones; it happens all the time. It doesn't mean that person doesn't *know* you love them. One argument doesn't undo a lifetime of love and affection."

"I was being so stupid..." Gayle shook her head.

"If *you* had died in the explosion, would you have wanted your father to think you didn't love him? That him interfering with your life and getting you back to this job here would have changed the way you felt about him?"

"No."

"Then accept he knew you loved him. That he went peacefully knowing he was loved by his daughters...all of them."

"It doesn't stop me wishing I'd been able to tell him one last time."

Michael beckoned toward the TV. "He didn't need you to say it. He knew. Just like—"

"—like Leia did," Gayle finished, shaking her head. "I see what you did there, Michael Reynolds. You can be a sneaky fucker sometimes."

"Guilty as charged," he said with a smile. "Which reminds me...there's something *else* I need to fess up to..."

"Okay... Is this something serious?"

"Depends on your definition of serious, and how badly you're going to take me telling a little white lie."

For a moment, Gayle felt a tiny pang of concern, but then twigged Michael's guilty grin. She had always prided herself on being able to join the dots. It was a gift. Her mind grabbed the facts and spun them through the cognitive part of her brain. Michael's willingness to indulge her science fiction passion. Using the details of this film as targeted therapy. The fact he'd lived on a former Disney cruise ship with access to a huge library of films including...

Her eyes widened. "Motherfu...you've seen *Empire* before,

haven't you?" she exclaimed.

"Again, guilty as charged," he laughed. "I've seen all seven films in the Star Wars saga...*multiple* times."

Gayle punched him in the arm playfully while laughing. Admittedly, rather than be angry, she kind of found the whole thing amusing. And more than a little endearing.

"Why the fuck didn't you say? We just sat through almost 4 hours of movies you've already seen, and you played dumb the whole time!"

"Honestly," Michael shrugged, "I love these movies. I was going to say something, but you seemed so content to be sharing something you'd done with your dad..."

Gayle's face flickered with a fleeting look of sadness at the mention of her father again. He looked into her eyes and moved his hand across to cover hers as it laid in her lap, gently squeezing it.

"Even before tonight, I knew what was at the root of your pain. On Sunday when you...when you cried in my arms, it was pretty clear. I didn't know how to fix it for you, but I wanted to try—"

"I'm not your responsibility, Michael," Gayle cut in as she turned her hand over and linked her fingers into his.

For a second, this simple gesture threw her for a loop. They had shared a few moments of intimacy previously—the post-tequila night kiss immediately jumped to mind—but this was something different. Something so innocuous.

Holding hands.

Michael smiled. "This is not about responsibility. It's about..."

Love. It's about love. Go on, say it! I dare you!

"...It's about caring."

Gayle was a little disappointed in his choice of words, but Michael didn't seem to notice.

"I remembered you said the last words you spoke to your father were..."

"'I know.' Fuck..." Gayle whispered, shaking her head.

Her eyes were locked with his. Neither spoke. She wished she could read his thoughts, to know what he was feeling right now. The moment started to feel a little awkward, so Gayle decided she needed to break the tension, quickly.

"Thank you," she whispered, extracting her hand and hopping off the sofa.

"Where are you—"

"Well, being as you've already seen Jedi, I think maybe we should watch something new," she interrupted. "New to you at least."

She skipped out of the room, leaving Michael to wonder where she was off to.

In her bedroom, she browsed through her movie collection and, with a grin, picked out the movie for which she was looking. As she headed back to the lounge, she caught sight of herself in the mirror and paused.

How do you want to play this, Gayle?

She considered maybe changing into something a little more provocative...but seduction seemed to be at odds with the general demeanor of their evening thus far. No, that was definitely the wrong direction to take. Instead, she grabbed a baggy sleep shirt and her pajama shorts, opting for comfort rather than sex appeal. Gayle quickly changed and loosened her ponytail, then regarded her reflection once more.

Her shorts fell loosely to just above her damaged knee, and with her ponytail like this, he could see the ugly scar running from her left ear to her throat. Doubt crept in, and she wondered whether she should change tack and maybe try to be a little more...appealing.

No.

If he doesn't love me at my most comfortable, he doesn't deserve me at my sexiest.

She took a deep breath and headed back into the lounge.

It took only a moment to exchange the disc in the player and retrieve her bowl of popcorn before heading to the sofa to sit beside him. To his apparent surprise, she snuggled closely into him, curling her legs up and leaning her head against his shoulder as she prodded buttons on the remote control to start the movie.

Michael glanced sideways at her, then shifted position

slightly to allow her into the crook of his left shoulder. She gladly accepted the invitation, leaning in closer as he put his arm gently around her. Gayle felt his fingers stroke the skin of her neck softly, caressing the slightly raised skin of her scar.

She didn't flinch.

It felt...nice.

"What are we watching?" he asked.

"Well, I figured we'd go with Tron," she chuckled. "I know you haven't seen *that*, since I caught you staring at my breasts."

"I wasn't staring at them."

"I'm teasing!" she grinned, holding her bowl out for him so they could share what was left of her popcorn. He took a handful and popped a kernel into his mouth.

"Now, relax and watch the movie magic unfold," she said as she pressed play.

He smiled, munched his popcorn, and did exactly that.

| 36 |

THE FENCE

— Damian Dane —
— Tuesday — Domaine Saint-Bernard, Pack Nation —

"By the gods, Damian. What have you done?"

Damian sighed and rubbed his temples as he watched General Wessex standing, hand on hips, shaking his head as he surveyed the scene at Domaine Saint-Bernard. There were dozens of Vampyrii milling to and fro, between the buildings and the trailers parked nearby.

"How many of them are here?" Wessex prompted.

"Around four hundred," Damian guessed.

"Do you realize the discontent that will rain down on you if the Pack Leaders find out about this?"

"Well, that's why I asked you to come. I'm going to need your help."

"Help?" Wessex said with a raised eyebrow. "You need more than *my* help with this situation. You're keeping too many secrets, Damian. Too many."

"Maybe not for much longer," Damian grunted.

The commander-in-chief of his military shook his head and smiled ruefully. "When you told me you were working on a solution to the StormHall problem, working with Lyssa Balthazaar of all people, I had my reservations...yet I accepted it. When you started sleeping with the Vampyrii, I bit my tongue and kept my silence. That was almost three years ago and, though you kept me in the loop on your plans, very little progress was seemingly made.

"You seemed content to sit on the fence, waiting for something to develop. Every day you waited, our position worsened. I pressed you for so long to make a decision. But this…" Wessex gestured toward the mass of Vampyrii toiling away under the dusk sky.

Damian had always known this would be an uphill battle. Persuading the Pack Leaders who formed the Moon Council to get onside with his clandestine plans to overthrow the StormHall regime in alliance with Lyssa Balthazaar—and any other allies they could muster—was never going to be easy. He had simply hoped he had more time.

"Our situation is no worse than it was a year ago, two years ago." Damian shrugged. "Even ten years ago. The status quo was established when the ceasefire was declared a decade ago. In fact, it could be said our position has improved somewhat considering StormHall's recent announcement."

Joseph Wessex was an old Wolf with at least a hundred years on Dane. He had fought Vampires for many of those years. His ledger bore the blood of a great many of them. In that sense, he was no different from any of the other Pack Leaders.

However, where most Pack Leaders were also resolutely old school, adhering closely to the adage that 'the only good Vampyrii is a dead Vampyrii,' Wessex was different.

Fortunately for Damian, the old Wolf was not only a superb warrior, an excellent strategist, and a distinguished field commander, he was also far more open-minded than most. Of all the members of the Pack Council, he had always been the one most likely to accept Damian's long-term plan and not blow a gasket about it. Indeed, since he had found out about the strategy to ally with House Balthazaar, he had been fervently pushing his king to *actually* put the whole plan into motion.

"I'm not sure that's true. I suspect much depends on what the NAA and the FSE decide to do," Wessex grunted. "Potentially, it leaves us in a very bad position."

Of course, Joseph Wessex knew the truth driving Damian's plan.

He knew the tightrope Damian had been walking for so long was a precarious one. Damian indicated for the general to follow him, and the two wandered away from the buildings, toward Lac Reynaud. The clouds were a hundred shades of vivid pink and auburn as the sun set beyond the horizon, casting colorful reflections across the placid lake surface.

When he was sure they were out of Vampyrii earshot, he stopped.

"Okay, talk me through this month's numbers, Joseph."

General Wessex paused for a moment, looking thoughtful.

In the early days of the War, immediately after The Rising, Damian held regular briefings with his senior military advisors, sometimes up to three times a day as the fluid nature of the War changed the theater of conflict at a brisk pace. When the Fae intervened, things began to stabilize, and the briefings became less frequent and less well-attended. Initially, moving to once a day, then weekly, and eventually monthly. Sometimes even that felt too many for Dane.

As the rest of the Pack Leaders stopped attending, arguing a status quo had been reached, General Wessex *insisted* they continue.

He was right, of course.

Complacency was the bedfellow of the unprepared. Regardless of how peaceful things had been lately, Pack Nation *was* still at war. Being unprepared was the real danger.

"As you said, there is little change," he begrudgingly admitted. "Our border stations are manned, but barely. Our total strength stands at a little over fourteen thousand soldiers spread exceedingly thinly across the frontline with New Victus.

"Fortunately, Intelligence has been reporting that Storm-Hall's troops are redeploying away from the border, though their whereabouts now is unknown. Our best guess is that they were being deployed in preparation for a potential NAA offensive push coming soon from the west or the Gulf of Mexico.

"If true, then it *would* be wise for them to bolster their defenses in those regions. Even so, their frontline forces on our border still outnumber ours by a considerable margin. Maybe...five-to-one. Better than it was previously, but still an untenable situation."

Some of the more gung-ho of his kin would declare one Wolf was worth fifty Vamps, but while Werewolves *were* stronger, hardier, and faster than their enemies across the border, that assertion was vastly untrue. While a numerical deficiency wasn't as bad as it might sound, the true ratio was far less. A factor of three or maybe four to one was closer to the right vicinity.

Still, being outnumbered along the border was *very* bad news.

This was the big secret Damian and his kin had kept for years.

For Werewolves, the bite was a sacred responsibility. In their culture, the tradition was deeply engrained into their way of life, and a Werewolf only turned someone if it was *absolutely* necessary or warranted. Rarely was anyone turned against their will except under very exceptional life and death circumstances. Much like Lonewolf had done for Alexa Reynolds in Sawtooth Forest.

While there *were* Vampyrii who treated their gifts with the same reverence, such as Lyssa and her House, StormHall and many of the younger houses cared little for tradition. Their eyes were focused on greed and the expansion of their power base. With that philosophy, they used their bite with wild abandon and turned tens of thousands of humans, especially any soldiers they could find, into Trampyrii. Unwilling slaves to the commands of their sire. An army of mindless drones who New Victus commanders viewed as disposable assets and outnumbered Damian's forces by a huge factor.

It meant the numbers they faced grew exponentially faster than their own. The pendulum swinging further in Vampyrii favor.

The Fae had intervened at a very opportune moment, as Damian's mother was facing the inevitability of losing their war against StormHall while he slowly seized numerical superiority.

Nobody outside the Pack Leaders knew how close they had come to defeat.

It was also a little-known fact that Werewolves had significantly shorter lifespans than their Vampyrii counterparts. Hence, in the years since the ceasefire had been ordered, many of the older generation had died. His mother, Danica, amongst them.

"I'd been hearing similar rumblings from Sabadini prior to the bombing," Damian admitted. "The NAA was being especially aggressive lately in negotiations with New Victus. All the signs were pointing toward a push to retake territory."

"Agreed," Wessex nodded sagely. "But the Grand Chancellor's announcement could change things considerably. If the NAA agrees to the proposal to cede the western states without bloodshed and signs a non-aggression or trade pact, the border between us contracts..."

Damian sighed and nodded, recognizing where General Wessex was going with all this talk. "New Victus would be free to redeploy its armies north along our now shortened frontline."

"Their numbers would be overwhelming," Wessex said bluntly. "We couldn't win a fight should they wish to invade."

"Yes, and that *can't* happen," Damian replied vehemently. "We have responsibilities."

"Yes. We do."

The two of them stood in silence. Damian could see his old friend wrestling with something internally and decided to give him the time he needed to sort out what he wanted to say.

He had known Wessex for many decades. The man had been a close friend and confidante to his mother and now continued in that capacity for Damian himself. He was the Alpha of the Wessex Pack, operating primarily out of Calgary to protect the treacherous part of the border spanning the Rocky Mountains. His Pack was grizzled, and battle-proven, just like their leader. This was why Damian had appointed Joseph

Wessex to the overall control of Pack Nation's defense.

"I have long supported you as our leader, Damian. Yet when you came to me a week ago and told me Lyssa Balthazaar's people were refugees and you were offering them safe haven here, I was... Well, I thought you'd lost your mind.

"But StormHall's speech changed *everything*. Whether he is behind the bombing or not is irrelevant. He's smart. He has used this to his advantage to back both us and his opposition within New Victus into a corner.

"You said Miss Balthazaar implied she has the support of the other Progenitor Houses?"

Damian nodded. "That's what she said, yes."

"Then, following this to its ultimate conclusion..." Wessex pursed his lips in thought. "StormHall won't *just* be gunning for House Balthazaar; he'll try and take out the other Progenitor Houses, too. He knows if they fight back, he has numerical superiority. If he can redeploy those forces, he can probably put together a main force of around a quarter of a million troops.

"I looked over the numbers that you sent me for Lyssa's projected strength. The remaining Houses of the still-living Progenitors have little over seventeen thousand. If—and it's a big if—she can bring the rest of the *other* Progenitor Houses into an alliance, they'll still barely top one hundred thousand.

"It's a fight he has the numbers to win and win fairly handily.

"Unless..."

"Unless what?" Damian asked.

"Unless, and I can't believe I'm advocating this," Wessex shook his head, "unless we ally ourselves to Lyssa Balthazaar's cause and assist her in removing StormHall from power. Our numbers won't balance the scales, but they will turn this into a less lopsided affair."

Damian looked back toward the buildings of Domaine Saint-Bernard. As the sun set further and dusk turned to darkness, the lights of the settlement started to come on. He could see Nykola exiting the side door of the trailer he now knew contained the hibernating form of her father. He hadn't told a soul about the secret hidden within. She walked from the truck and entered the Grand Saint-Bernard—the building where Eloise and her family had met their fate while under his supposed protection.

"I don't know, Joseph…" he said quietly. "We have a responsibility."

"A responsibility which we will surely fail if we do not take action, Damian," Wessex said forcefully. "It's time to get off the fence and choose to fight. *That* is how we will prevail."

| 37 |

THE MORNING AFTER

— Michael Reynolds —
— Wednesday — London, England —

Though Michael was wide awake, his arm remained soundly asleep.

He'd been up for a while now, his body clock habitually rousing him a handful of minutes before the soft bleating of the alarm on his phone. Michael swiftly silenced it before it disturbed his companion.

The morning sun was starting to creep around the edges of the curtains, providing enough ambient light to reveal the still-slumbering Gayle Knightley curled up in the crook of his shoulder. Her head lay on his upper arm. He smiled in mild amusement as he watched her.

Her hair was still in its ponytail, but the band had slipped down, leaving it much looser and a little disheveled. Her mouth was open, and a tiny line of drool hung out of the corner of her mouth as she gave another gentle snore.

Probably not the impression she wants to give, but godammit, she's cute like this.

He flexed the fingers on the arm pinned beneath Gayle, trying to work some blood back into regular circulation. The need to shift his position was growing, but he didn't want to wake her yet. They didn't have to be at the Academy for a couple of hours. He knew the last week or so had been difficult for her, and she deserved the rest.

The TV had turned itself off. Michael imagined that must have been when the film finished, yet he had no recollection of the finale. The last scene he remembered had the lead character—what was his name again?—playing some sort of game involving motorcycles that left colorful trails of light behind them.

In his defense, it had been late, and he'd been distracted observing the quietly snoozing form of his companion who succumbed to dreamland *long* before he had.

Barely eight weeks...

It seemed like they'd known each other so much longer, but in truth, less than two months had passed since Gayle stalked into his classroom, full of bitter anger. Having this level of emotional connection—this affection—for her seemed inconceivable back then when he'd expected every day to be a battle.

Yet, here they were now, comfortable spending the night in each other's arms in a purely innocent way.

Innocent? Don't kid yourself, Mike.

He *was* falling in love with her.

Truthfully...he already had.

It was the second time in the last three days they spent the night together. Of course, nothing had happened. It's not like they *slept* together in the biblical sense. They hadn't even kissed...

Really, Mike? Aren't you forgetting a couple of things?

Other than the night of the tequila-fest.

And the morning she injured herself running.

Those don't count...do they?

The latter had been mistakenly done in jest, while the former was the result of an overindulgence of alcohol. Both totally innocent, nothing to see here, please move along...

But...

On both of those occasions, Gayle was the one to initiate the contact. Yes, the 'my hero' thing had been a joke, but it *was* still her who leaned in first. And on tequila night, she admitted she faked her drunkenness. Not a drop of tequila had passed her lips, and yet the kiss she initiated was one filled with heat and *passion*.

A passion he, too, had felt.

He knew without a shadow of a doubt, they would have had sex that night if Gayle hadn't drawn away. He still didn't know why, but he didn't think it was about him. Or at least, not *just* him. She intimated as much with her parting words, and then further reinforced the sentiment during their heart-to-heart on Sunday evening.

He wondered what her secret was...

Gayle let out a gentle snore and shifted position slightly. Mercifully, her head fell sideways onto his chest allowing him to finally flex his arm. Michael groaned quietly, extending his elbow and stretching out the slightly numb appendage while wiggling his fingers to stave off the pins and needles.

Increasingly these days, a question kept popping into his brain. One for which he didn't have an answer.

What next?

Michael wasn't usually a passive passenger on life's great adventure. He preferred to seize control of his destiny. Had done so since he was a child. Growing up without parents forced him and Alexa to be independent from an early age. However, there was one particular area of his life where he admittedly sucked at being influential.

His love life.

When it came to matters of the heart, his judgment had traditionally been...flawed.

So much so that now that this opportunity presented itself, he felt like a deer caught in headlights. Unable to decide which way to jump. Gayle seemed far more assured, albeit a little confused. There were moments when she didn't seem to know exactly what she wanted, but at least she was making efforts to move the game in the right direction, while he had been...passive at best.

She had been the one to join him on his run in the park.

She had been the one to talk him into tequila night.

She had been the one to come to his doorstep when she got back from Nexus.

And she had been the one to initiate last night's movie-watching session.

And what have you done, Mike? Admit it. In Gayle's preferred vernacular, you've done fuck all!

He couldn't argue with Inner-Mike.

Taking a deep breath, he resolved to do something decisive. It was time to put his previous dating history firmly behind him and to stop being a passenger on this ride. Time to take the wheel.

Easier said than done.

There were some pretty epic disasters in his back catalog.

Gayle yawned and stretched. Pushing her legs out rigid, pointing her toes. Her eyes crept open slowly, and she looked up at him, dazed for a moment until realization dawned. At which point, a look of mild horror flickered across her features as she moved to wipe the drool from her chin with her hand.

"Mornin', sleepyhead."

"Fuck!" Gayle croaked, her voice was broken. "You're not supposed to see me like this...not again."

Michael smiled. "How am I s'posed to see you?"

"Well, not drooling all over myself for starters." Gayle grimaced.

"You still look beautiful," he replied without hesitation.

"So do you," Gayle blushed ever so slightly. "I mean, handsome. Really...handsome."

Outside the window, Michael could hear the dawn chorus sounding off. The twitter of birds signaling the arrival of a new day. Wednesday. He knew both of them needed to get off the sofa, clean themselves up, and head into the Academy for another day teaching the next generation of Hunters. But right now, he couldn't see any further than the face of the beautiful woman lying next to him.

The woman who was still comfortably nestled into his chest, which rose and fell in synchronicity to her own. He locked his eyes with hers as she looked up at him, an unspoken message passing between them and she tilted her head as he bent his toward her. His lips were millimeters from hers. He could feel her breath against his skin.

"Stop," she whispered huskily. "My teeth. I haven't brushed my teeth yet..."

"You really want to stop, right now, so you can go brush your teeth?"

Gayle groaned softly. "No..."

He made a decision and took charge of the moment. "Then kiss me. What's the worst that can happen? You'll taste like last night's popcorn...which, if I recall, was sweet."

"Fuck..." Gayle whispered.

He pressed his lips to hers.

| 38 |

THE PIPELINE

— **Alexa Reynolds** —
— *Wednesday* — *Nassau, Bahamas* —

Alexa sauntered into the Fort Nassau Detainment Centre and smiled at the man sitting behind the reception desk. He didn't reciprocate her affability, instead giving her a look suggesting more than a hint of irritation.

She didn't entirely blame him.

You could see what he was thinking. The hour had just ticked past three a.m. and the citizens of Nassau were sound asleep. This was the graveyard shift, and the Detainment Centre was on a skeleton staff. Its cells were mostly empty tonight. Business wouldn't start again for at least another five hours. He'd been looking forward to an uneventful evening; just him and a good book.

So, why was this stranger walking in at this obscene hour with such a sunny disposition?

"Can I help you?" His attitude was professional, if a little grumpy.

"I'm lookin' for a booking sergeant by the name of Anthony Rolle."

He very carefully placed his book down, still spread, cover upward. His eyes narrowed as he looked at her carefully. "Office is closed. We reopen at eight."

"I was hopin' to catch Sergeant Rolle while it was quiet."

Alexa met his stare. "So we could have some...one-on-one time."

"What's your business with Sergeant Rolle?"

So, we're going to carry on playing this game, are we?

"My business?" Alexa asked. "I want to know who you're working for. And I want to know what's happening to the prisoners who mysteriously vanish in the middle of the night when you're on duty here alone."

Beads of sweat started to appear on his brow. "I have no idea what you're talking about," he said carefully.

Sorry, Anthony. I call bullshit.

"Really? Exactly how *many* prisoners have you expedited the release of? Do you get paid a bulk rate? Or per prisoner?"

Sergeant Rolle was looking increasingly uncomfortable with Alexa's forceful line of questioning. His eyes began to flit from Alexa to the exits on his left and back.

"I told you, I don't know what you're talking about..." he repeated, this time a shade more nervously.

Alexa leaned forward onto the desk and tapped playfully on the surface with a fingernail. "I think you *do*, Anthony. What's more, I *strongly* suggest you're honest with me now. Because I *don't* think you'll like what comes next if you aren't."

His eyes flicked momentarily towards his firearm, sitting in its holster on the desk next to him. He was likely now wishing he hadn't taken it off to facilitate the comfort of his sitting position. Alexa shook her head slowly and made a show of unsnapping the safety strap on her own holster, leaving the *Freelancer* on her left hip ready to be drawn. Rolle noticed and instead began to push his seat slowly away from her. A subtle movement that—Alexa knew—he was hoping she wouldn't notice.

To be honest, though, this was what she had been expecting.

Here it comes...

He made his break for the exit, his chair sent clattering to the floor as it briefly tangled in his panicked feet. For a man of his heft, he was impressively nimble, and it took him only a handful of seconds to reach the door and flee.

Alexa casually scratched her nose. "Just like I said, they always—"

"—They always run." Becka sighed in her ear. "You really should get that printed on a T-shirt or something. Side door?"

"Side door," Alexa confirmed. "As anticipated. He's unarmed."

"Excellent. I'm unlocking reception for you now."

There was an audible click as Becka hacked the electromagnetic lock on the door allowing access behind the reception desk. Alexa ambled casually over and pushed it open.

There was no hurry. Everything was going according to plan.

Before walking into the Detainment Centre, they studied the blueprints of the building, and Alexa knew *exactly* where the door Rolle had escaped through led. Once she entered, Becka sealed the main door behind her with a few strategically placed zip ties around the pull handles outside. They'd already done likewise with all the other potential exits. The only people in here tonight—apart from the prisoners—were Sergeant Rolle, herself, and a certain third party who was about to formally introduce herself to poor Anthony.

Almost on cue, a terrified scream came from beyond the door through which he had fled.

Alexa followed the screams. While she couldn't see him, she *could* hear the thudding of his heavy footsteps as he continued his futile escape attempt by heading to the nearby stairwell. Alexa *did,* however, catch a glimpse of white fur disappearing up the stairs in pursuit.

"Is our Tiger-Queen enjoying herself?" Becka asked with a chuckle.

"It appears so," Alexa replied. "He opted to run upstairs..."

"Where does he think he's going?" Becka laughed. "The only exits up there are on the roof and from there it's a five-story drop. Maybe he's planning to smash out a window on the first floor?"

Alexa didn't think Rolle was that smart, but it was a possibility. "Keep an eye out just in case, but honestly, he didn't strike me as the sharpest knife in the drawer. Figure he's simply runnin' scared."

It made a nice change not to have to overly exert herself. Not that she had expected much of a pursuit. A well-trained dealer of death Rolle certainly wasn't.

But he *was* their only lead.

It had started simply.

They knew the date Ashraff had been picked up, so step one was to discover who was on duty that night. Finding that information had been relatively straightforward. Becka had headed into the Detainment Centre alone and then reappeared thirty minutes later with a name.

Sergeant Anthony Rolle.

The next step was to see if any video of what happened existed, which required another of Becka's many skills. Hacking. It took her a little while to crack the encryption on Fort Nassau's mainframe, but once she was in, she searched the archive for the digital security feed. Soon, they were watching the camera footage that showed Becka dropping off Ashraff and signing him over to the on-duty member of staff.

Rolling the video forward to the start of Rolle's night shift, however, they found the recording was mysteriously missing.

There were many possible explanations. Maybe the cameras had been down. Maybe something had gone wrong with the recording. Maybe the video was deleted for a totally innocent reason.

Alexa doubted all of the above.

Once they discovered it was Rolle on duty, they started to pull at that thread, trying to further unravel the mystery. His military service and medical records were...enlightening.

Injured in the line of duty eight years ago, Rolle had been assigned to light duties for the duration of his recovery. During this period, his food intake increased and his motivation for physical exercise waned. A year later, he failed his medical for active duty and was consigned to a cushy desk job. He'd been pushing paper in the Detainment Centre ever since.

Becka continued down the Sergeant Rolle rabbit hole and found it wasn't just his waistline getting fatter.

She was able to access NewNet through the Nassau relay

station and from there hacked into Rolle's bank records. An infiltration, she remarked, that was surprisingly easy. As she continued making snide comments about the bank's network security, Becka uncovered a pattern of sizable payments being made into the sergeant's bank account on a fairly regular basis.

Which was when they hit their first dead end.

The deposits were made in cash, meaning there was no transaction data to trace. The dates, though regular, also appeared to be random. On a hunch, Becka went back to the security footage for clues—specifically the timeline. Rolle deposited cash into his bank account two days after Ashraff had been wiped from the records. Using that as a marker, Becka attempted to obtain the security footage of the night shifts for the days leading up to each transaction.

All of them were missing or—more likely—deleted.

Fort Nassau wasn't an outpost run in a haphazard way with rules and regulations regularly flouted. It was a relatively modern FSE frontline base operated with the military efficacy for which the Federation was known. Everything was done by the book.

So, the fact the missing footage was only ever localized to the Detainment Centre—and *only* when a certain Sergeant Anthony Rolle was on night duty—was compelling evidence it *had* to be deliberate.

But with no video evidence, and no traceable bank details on the deposits, the trail ran cold. All the answers they sought were now locked up in Sergeant Rolle's brain, and Alexa knew he wouldn't be inclined to part with that information easily. However, maybe with the right 'incentives,' he could be persuaded.

Hence the late-night visitation.

Alexa jogged up the stairs as Becka gave her a running commentary on the haphazard escape plan of their mark. "Okay...so, target crossed the second floor to the eastern stairwell, our girl in pursuit. He ran up to the third, and now he's headed back toward you."

"Gotcha," Alexa answered, picking up her pace a little.

She was coming up the steps to the third-floor landing when the doors crashed open and a clearly terrified Sergeant Rolle stumbled through. He was evidently hoping he could throw Rahanah off the scent by returning to the ground floor but was stunned to find Alexa blocking his way—gun in hand.

"Anthony," she said, in a conciliatory tone, "honestly, we just want to talk to you—"

There was a crashing noise from the room beyond the doors through which he had come, followed by a deep guttural roar.

"Actually, it's *me* that wants to talk... I can't speak for my companion. I think she has a *very* different idea for the method she intends to use to extract the information we need from you."

Saying nothing, he grabbed hold of the stair rail and hauled himself toward the roof. Moments later, a blur of white and black came barreling out of the same doors, claws scrabbling on the concrete of the stairwell. Alexa pointed a finger upward in the direction Rolle had disappeared.

"This is what you wanted, yes?" the tiger growled as she paused.

"Perfect, Rahanah. Just perfect."

"I admit, this is...fun."

"Just don't have *too* much fun. We need him scared enough to talk, but not scared enough to leap off the roof!"

"Understood," Rahanah acknowledged before promptly heading up the stairs.

"She's *really* throwing herself into the part, isn't she?" Becka chuckled in Alexa's ear.

Alexa waited a beat before following Rahanah. "Maybe she'll consider a career change after this."

When she arrived upon the roof, she was greeted with quite the scene. Sergeant Rolle was standing near the northern edge, plainly terrified and brandishing some sort of antenna as if it were a fencing épée. It *appeared* as if he was holding Rahanah at bay with his makeshift weapon, but Alexa knew the truth.

The tigress was toying with him. Preparing him for Alexa's

more reasonable approach.

We should maybe patent the 'good cop, bad tiger' routine.

She ambled toward them as Rahanah roared and took a swipe at the antenna with one of her huge paws. Rolle screamed in a less than manly fashion and an embarrassing dark patch spread across his crotch. Alexa didn't entirely blame him—he *was* facing a tiger looking to tear him limb from limb. Seeing Rahanah like this brought back memories of fighting Ashraff in Havana which, admittedly, had not been a particularly enjoyable experience.

May not have been my finest hour, but at least I didn't piss myself!

"Look, Anthony, you can either have a pleasant conversation with me—telling me everything you know—or my friend here will extract the information she wants in a far less agreeable way. Your choice."

His eyes flicked between the two of them, weighing his options. Which, in itself, seemed...odd.

Why was he hesitating over a choice between a simple chat and being rent apart by an angry white tiger? Did whoever he was working for *really* have him more terrified of revealing the truth than he was of facing Rahanah?

"Eight weeks ago," Alexa said, "a bounty was delivered to you. A Harimau Jadian. He disappeared from your custody less than twenty-four hours later."

"I told you—I don't know anything about that!" he stammered in response.

"That's damn peculiar, Anthony, because a day later you dropped a pretty sizeable chunk of cash into your bank account."

"Unrelated," he said a little too quickly but did not deny the payment.

"I highly doubt that's true," Alexa sighed, "because we checked back through MercNet, and guess what we discovered?"

Now he was looking nervous for a decidedly different reason. Realization was dawning as to the extent of what they already knew. His eyes continued to dart back and forth, but his attention was starting to linger more on Alexa than on Rahanah. Something the tigress also noticed. She growled intimidatingly and gave another 'playful' swipe of her claws.

"What we found, Anthony," Alexa continued, "were a number of bounties who had been captured and delivered to this very detention center, only to then vanish without a trace. And *every* time it happened, there was no security footage, no paper trail, and weirdly, you were on duty when this mysterious chain of events occurred."

"You can't—" he started to object.

Alexa interrupted him. "—Now before you proclaim your innocence...again, I thought you should know we also checked your bank records. Every single time, you coincidentally deposited money into your bank account a day or two later. Now, you *are* right. That's not hard evidence, I guess, but my friend here isn't inclined to need any. You see, she's a Harimau Jadian herself, and it was *her* lover who went missing on your watch..." For a moment, she thought she heard Rahanah snort with surprise at the mention of Ashraff being her lover. Certainly, Becka was now pissing herself laughing over the comms channel.

"...and she is very keen to know where her life-mate has gone. Do you know much about Harimau Jadian, Anthony?"

He shook his head hesitantly. Obviously, his job description had not included swotting up on the people he was trading.

"Here's what you need to know," Alexa continued, making it up as she went along. "They mate for life. *Nothing* is more sacred to them than the mating bond. They will fight for their mate to the death. In their native Malaysia, they're known as being vicious and unrelenting killing machines. But they don't kill you fast. Oh, no...they slash you with those claws first. You see her razor-sharp claws, Anthony?"

Now that she had drawn his attention to Rahanah's huge paws with their knife-like talons, he couldn't take his eyes away from them. Which was a good thing, because Rahanah had tilted her head to stare at Alexa with a look of mild confusion on her feline features, obviously wondering exactly why she was telling such blatant falsehoods.

Becka, meanwhile, was giggling and feeding her more lies to tell. "Tell him her claws are filled with paralyzing poison..."

"Those claws are laced with a poison," Alexa relayed. "It won't kill you, but it'll paralyze you. Leaving you vulnerable..."

Becka wasn't finished. "Now tell him while he's paralyzed..."

"...and while you're lying there unable to move..." Alexa relayed.

"...she'll start to eat him alive..."

"...then my friend here will start to eat you...alive?"

Anthony didn't hear the questioning tone ending the sentence. Nor could he hear the guffawing coming across the comm channel. At this point, his terror had reached such a significantly high level, he broke.

"Okay, okay, I'll tell you anything," he babbled. "Just call her off. Please, call her off."

"Good decision, Anthony." Alexa nodded toward his trousers. "Now, tell us everything you know, and *maybe*...you'll get out of here with at least a little of your dignity intact."

| 39 |

ABOUT LAST NIGHT...

— Gayle Knightley —
— Wednesday — London, England —

Okay, so this is new...

Gayle strolled alongside Michael as they made their way to the Academy. The morning sun was low in the sky but shining brightly, not that it was making a noticeable difference to the temperature just yet. The frigid November air made her grateful for the long, red woolen coat wrapped tightly around her. She had toyed with wearing her CombatSkin today, for both comfort and warmth, but considering Michael was still wearing the clothes he had been in last night, she felt a need to dress down a little.

This was twice in three days they had spent the night together, however unintentionally. At least this morning they had both awoken in time to get themselves properly groomed without the mad scramble of Monday. Though that, in and of itself, had been an awkward experience.

To paraphrase the immortal words of Hot Chocolate...it started with a kiss.

A lingering, deep, passionate kiss. Definitely *not* an accidental pressing of the lips, and unquestionably mutual. The kind of kiss lovers shared. Which was where the crux of the confusion originated.

They weren't actually lovers.

Not in the biblical sense anyway.
We're not even in a relationship! Are we?

The initial kiss on the sofa turned into *more* kissing on the sofa. Which, in turn, became *considerably* more kissing on the sofa. Indeed the poor sofa had only been given a reprieve from such a compulsive display of affection by the eight a.m. beeping of Gayle's alarm, insisting it was time to shift her ass into gear and head to work. Thus, with some lack of enthusiasm, it must be said, they both came up for oxygen and the disappointing realization time had expired on their impromptu make-out session.

She graciously offered Michael first dibs on her shower, which he had even more graciously refused. This began a minute or so of them trying to 'out gracious' each other until eventually Michael reluctantly capitulated. She handed him a fluffy white bath towel—her favorite, by the way—and pointed him toward the bathroom.

The next ten minutes were *agony*.

As she heard the sounds of cascading water only feet away, she sat on her bed wrestling with her own flagging willpower. Vivid visions of his muscular six-foot-plus frame standing naked under the hot steaming rivers of water ran rampant and unchecked through her imagination, forcing her to squeeze her thighs together in an effort to stem the rising heat within her. Her feet bounced on the floor in frustration as she fought the urge to throw caution to the wind, strip naked, and join him beneath the torrid waters.

It *was* a big shower.

With plenty of room for both of them.

Oodles of space for them to clean themselves, run soap all over their bodies...over each other's bodies...to press slippery bodies against each other...her breasts against his chest...to feel Michael's fingers shampooing her hair...brushing her neck...

At which point she had fallen back onto the bed, grabbed the nearest pillow, and stuffed it over her face to stifle a frustrated scream.

Suffice to say, *her* shower had been of the cold variety.

Amanda was taking her first roll call this morning, before the kids' physical education class with Lana. Gayle and Michael weren't expected in till mid-morning. Thus, they had plenty of time to stroll to Buckingham Palace from her place in Clabon Mews.

They'd ambled up toward Cadogan Lane, heading for the Pont Street, where they turned right toward Chesham Place, their hands occasionally brushing each other as they maintained close proximity. In contrast to the practically inaudible footfalls of Michael's combat boots, her high heels made a clacking sound on the pavement, echoing around the quiet London streets. It amplified the silence between the two of them, which had started comfortably but was now feeling a little bit awkward.

It was becoming evident things were going unsaid between them, yet it seemed like neither wanted to make the first move.

Maybe it would be easier if I'd joined him in the shower and fucked his brains out? Maybe that would have dispersed this tension between us…

Possibly.

But knowing her own track record with such matters, if she had jumped his bones as he was showering, it likely would have made things worse. Whatever this was that was developing between them, she was terrified of screwing it up. Over the last decade or so, she'd had many sexual partners—too many, if truth be told—and her relationship experience was limited to the unmitigated natural disaster that had been Alastair Torbar.

Ugh!

Just thinking about it made her shudder. She forced herself to think about something different…

So, Michael Reynolds. Shower sex.

Was *that* the problem between them? Had Michael been *expecting* her to join him in a passionate bout of early morning copulation? Was he now walking alongside her, frustrated he had not gotten to sow his oats?

Gayle flicked her eyes sideways to glance at him.

No.

Michael Reynolds was not the type to think like that.

She considered their second meeting, the one where she had gone to his office to apologize for being such a royal bitch the day before, and ended up trying to use her pheromones to control him. To entice him sexually.

Fuck, that's embarrassing in hindsight!

Michael had easily—and actually, somewhat annoy-ingly—resisted her advances. Annoyance aside, it was some-thing she had been eternally thankful for ever since. She was ashamed to think about how close she had been to falling off the wagon that day. Michael's professionalism rescued her from ruining almost twelve months of hard work.

Of course, that *was* going to be a problem moving forward.

If they did move forward.

His hand brushed against hers again, sending a little shiver of goosebumps across her skin.

Is it wrong that I really want to hold his hand right now?

She took a deep breath, swallowed, and turned toward him.

"Mi—" Was all she managed to get out as he started talk-ing at *exactly* the same moment.

"I was think—" he said, and then stopped.

"Sorry," both said simultaneously.

They laughed together.

"You go," Michael said.

Gayle shook her head. "No, you."

"Okay, so I was thinkin'," he said slowly. "This thing we have…whatever this thing is. I'd like to let it develop. Grow. But it kinda feels like we've started off wrong somehow. I mean the kissing this morning—"

"Fuck, I'm sorry about that—"

"No, no," he said shaking his head. "Don't apologize, the kissing was great. It's just I was thinkin' maybe we make this more official…"

Gayle laughed. "You want me to sign something?"

"No. I mean, maybe we should…date," he said hesitantly. "Like, go on an actual date. Together. Dinner and a movie, that sorta thing."

"Well, we already did the movie part..."

"Dinner then?"

Dinner.

Such a simple little word. Yet one which sent a shiver of nerves down her spine as she realized this was a long way out of her comfort zone. The word implied romance. A slow getting to know each other over an intimate candlelit meal, with a pianist playing romantic music in the background while...

He's just asking you out for a meal, Gayle. Stop overthinking it!

"Dinner sounds...enchanting," she stammered.

Enchanting? Really? You went with enchanting?

A smile spread across Michael's lips, and the humor evident by the twinkle in his eyes made it clear he was having a similar thought. "Well, I'll try very hard to be *enchanting* company for you. How about we put a date in the calendar? How's next Friday?"

"That's over a week away..."

Michael nodded. "I'll need time to find a nice place to take you. I have to get some decent civilian clothes to wear. Plus, as we don't have classes to teach on Saturday, we don't have to cut our night short if we're enjoying ourselves."

Gayle raised her eyebrow and smiled. "Enjoying ourselves?"

"Well, you never know where the evening may lead..."

She was sure he wasn't talking about sex.

Okay, I'm fairly *sure he isn't talking about sex.*

If there was a singular thing she knew about Michael, it was that he had an innate sense of honor about him. Her father would have called him a gentleman. Which wasn't to say he *wouldn't* have sex with her on a first date—she was absolutely convinced he would if the mood was right—she just knew he wouldn't *expect* it.

So, all things being equal, how would he react under *those* circumstances if Gayle turned him down?

Not because she didn't *want* to have sex, because she really, *really* wanted to.

But while she had told him a great deal about her life and

her troubles, confiding in him secrets not many others knew, there was still one big secret she had yet to tell.

And the thought of telling him about it terrified her.

| 40 |

UNFINISHED BUSINESS

— Lyssa Balthazaar —
— Wednesday — Nexus City, Iceland —

She heard the gentle padding of Ally's feet on the carpet long before her disheveled lover came into view, stretching her arms above her head and yawning, her mouth so wide Lyssa thought she was about to dislocate her jaw. Her bright sapphire hair fell in a messy but sexy manner around her shoulders. Her black sleep shirt was oversized and fell to mid-thigh, with an asymmetric neck baring her left shoulder.

Gods, she looks adorable.

Lyssa smiled knowing Allyson would passionately disagree with that sentiment. Almost immediately a feeling of guilt spread through her, and her smile turned into a soft sigh.

Being with Allyson made her feel *good*, there was no denying it. Even in these trying times, when she was in Ally's presence, Lyssa felt the flutter of butterflies in her stomach. The kind of flutter she hadn't felt in a long time. An *exceptionally* long time. She was so far removed from this feeling that it felt almost fresh and new. Like she was falling for the very first time all over again.

It was also a feeling she'd never had with Damian. More reinforcement—not that it was needed—to the knowledge their sexual shenanigans had simply been a case of itch scratching, and never love. Affection, yes, but love...no.

Not like this...

Lyssa couldn't help but feel, however, like this was a case of *epically* bad timing. Their fledgling relationship was tainted by the stain of painful loss. Lyssa felt torn between two diametrically opposed emotions. On the one hand, there was a deep-rooted *need* to explore an exciting future with a woman to whom she already felt a developing connection. Yet she knew this could only clash with the profound responsibility she felt for her position and her people.

It was a clash that had been preying on her mind a lot lately.

According to Bobbi, NVSec was now working on the assumption Lyssa had somehow eluded them and fled back to New Victus. It was clear House Balthazaar had gone into hiding, so the theory was Lyssa had joined them.

Obviously, that wasn't the case.

While Bobbi was working on a plan to get her out of Nexus, her place was fully equipped with everything she needed to coordinate the Exodus Initiative from a position of relative safety. The last few days had been spent overseeing the movement of the people and equipment they would need for the fight ahead. But, the longer she spent 'lying low,' the more frustrated she became.

The more...unfocused.

Every moment her brain wasn't centered on matters of war and politics, her thoughts inevitably drifted back to Allyson and the knowledge she was only a few miles away across the sector boundary.

Thus, yesterday, when she determined the risk of detection was sufficiently low—and against Bobbi's advice—she decided to sneak through Bobbi's secret passage to the FSE sector. Her lover had been understandably surprised by Lyssa's reappearance and had, at first, argued vehemently that Lyssa was being foolish and should have stayed safely with Bobbi. The argument hadn't lasted long, but the 'makeup sex' afterward had. She enjoyed a few hours of simple, sweaty, and blissful ignorance to the world around her as she lay breathlessly in the arms of the woman with whom she was fast falling in love. When they finished, they lay naked in repose, talking in whispered voices about the inane and the trivial until Allyson eventually drifted to sleep. For a little while at least, Lyssa managed to push from her mind the fact she was the head of a Vampyrii house and a wanted fugitive.

As her companion snored gently in the moonlit bedroom, Lyssa's mind inexorably returned to matters of importance and the decisions she knew she had to make.

"Good morning," she said brightly as Allyson slumped bleary-eyed onto one of the stools that sat next to the kitchen counter.

"Mmmm," she grunted in return, yawning again. "Time'zit?"

"It's pretty early."

"How early?"

"Seven-thirty," Lyssa answered, and promptly heard Ally groan.

Allyson scratched her head for a moment, looking confused as she wrinkled her nose and sniffed. "Are you...cooking?" It was clearly a rhetorical question as the evidence of her efforts were in plain view right behind Lyssa.

"I couldn't sleep, so I thought I'd surprise you with my culinary expertise. Was it the smell of breakfast cooking that brought you out of your hibernation?" Lyssa laughed lightly as she picked up each of the frying pans in turn and started to deposit the freshly prepared contents onto the plates she had already warmed up.

"Nah," Ally said with yet another yawn. "There was just somethin' missin' from my bed."

Lyssa fettled the food on the plates, prodding it around with her fingertips to make sure the presentation was right before pushing one across the countertop toward Allyson, who looked at it in confusion.

"Who knew the head of House Balthazaar could make eggy-bread..." she said slowly.

"Eggy-bread?" Now it was Lyssa's turn to be confused.

Ally pointed to the plate as Lyssa handed her a knife and fork. "Eggy-bread."

"That's French toast," Lyssa said with a bemused smile.

"With bacon?"

"Well, back bacon anyway," Lyssa admitted with a shrug.

"*Back* bacon?" Ally looked at her like she was a little mad. "What the fuck is 'back bacon?' That's...well, that's just bacon."

"That's *not* bacon!"

"It is in these parts," Ally nodded. "What were *you* expecting?"

Lyssa gestured with her hands, trying to describe how the bacon she knew and loved looked. "Well, our bacon back home is about this long, thin, and it's crispy."

"That sounds...fucked up. Crispy bacon?" Ally shook her head and pointed to the kitchen cabinet behind Lyssa. "Pass me the ketchup, please?"

"Ketchup?" Lyssa shook her head. "Gods, no! *Maple syrup* is for French toast."

"Maple syrup? Do I even have maple syrup?"

Lyssa pushed a small jug across the counter toward Allyson.

"You do. I found that buried in the back of one of your cupboards."

Allyson peered into the small container with a frown. "Oh, I use that on my ice cream."

"Just trust me, okay?" Lyssa laughed.

Ally shrugged and poured a little onto the plate away from the food items. She carefully sliced a corner off the toast and, along with a chunk of the bacon, dipped it into the syrup before forking it into her mouth. Lyssa watched her face as she did so and witnessed Ally's expression change from one of suspicion to one of bliss.

"Fuck! Okay, color me a convert. *That* is good!"

"Told you so." Lyssa grinned triumphantly and poured a generous helping of syrup over her plate, smothering both toast and bacon thoroughly in the sweet, sticky substance. The minute she put the jug down, Ally snatched it up and likewise covered her food.

The two ate in silence, enjoying breakfast and the comfort

of each other's company. Allyson finished first and pushed her plate aside as she chewed the last morsel. With a tilt of her head, she looked at Lyssa.

"Y'know," she started, "I've been thinking a lot about the differences between you and me. I mean, this French toast thing…feels like a typical example of something much bigger. More complex. Everything I know about New Victus has been either secondhand info passed on by my parents or my sister, Gayle. Or it's been me speculating on what life is like over there by extrapolating from the things I've seen in old movies or TV shows.

"Did you travel much before the War?"

Lyssa nodded a little sadly. "When my father wasn't taking the Long Sleep, I used to globetrot frequently for business. Europe mostly."

"Favorite place?" Ally prompted.

"It's hard to remember. It's been so long now," Lyssa sighed.

"I guess thirty years is a pretty long haul to be stuck in one place. So, nowhere sticks in your memory at all?"

"Florence, in Italy. The memory has faded somewhat, but I do remember loving it there. I was pissed when Storm started the War because even if he had won, if Vampyrii had taken over the world, then he would have destroyed the cultures I have always found so fascinating."

"To be fair, he did destroy a lot of cultures. Africa will never be the same, for instance…"

"True." Lyssa looked down at the countertop sadly. "Unleashing the Adze and the Sasabonsam there has done untold damage… Damage I'll *never* be able to undo."

And there it was again. The accountability she couldn't escape.

Ally slipped her hand across Lyssa's, giving it a gentle squeeze. "Babe, it's not *your* responsibility to fix it. Storm broke the world, not you."

Lyssa knew Ally was right, but deep down, she still felt a certain amount of culpability for the state of world affairs. These days she was viewed as the strong-headed leader of

House Balthazaar and an activist for change. Back then, however, with her father in the infancy of his hibernation, she had been very new to the cut and thrust of Vampyrii politics. If she had known then what she knew about herself now, she wouldn't have hesitated to stand up to Storm and his regime much earlier, when she could have possibly prevented him from rising to power in the first place.

"Maybe," she said with a shrug. "Anyway, my wanderlust hadn't been satiated for a long time till I got to travel here to Nexus."

"So, am I simply a holiday romance to you?" Ally laughed, raising her eyebrow.

"Gods, no." Lyssa shook her head. "You, my love, are something unexpectedly wonderful. Something I would love to pursue..."

"There's a but coming," Ally said, astutely recognizing the pause in Lyssa's statement.

She was right. There was an issue, and it needed to be addressed. As much as she wanted to put off this conversation, there was no other time to have it. Time had, in fact, run out.

"Ally, I'm a Vampyrii. I can't travel anywhere in the world except back to New Victus. I can't stay here with you, and I can't come with you to the UK. I'm the head of House Balthazaar, and I have family who depends on and needs me.

"Furthermore, I have an impending coup to plan and alliances to forge to hopefully take back my country and clear my name." She stopped, exhaling heavily.

Ally looked at her with a furrowed brow. "Well, when you put it *that* way," she said with a chuckle.

Lyssa laughed, suddenly realizing there was yet another thing she adored about her new paramour. As she had been spewing all the reasons why a relationship between herself and Ally would be an issue, she could feel the tension in herself rising. She knew she had a habit of getting stressed, feeling like she was bearing the weight of the world on her shoulders. Her family position saw to it that having time to just be Lyssa was extremely hard to come by. Ally, though, seemed to have an easy, almost instinctual way to defuse her tension.

She made Lyssa feel like an individual, rather than the matriarch to a Vampyrii house.

In reality, though, that's exactly what Lyssa was, and it was a responsibility she could no longer ignore.

"I...I have to go back to New Victus. Or at least to join my House in Pack Nation. I have to take a more hands-on role in organizing the coming coup. If I want the other Progenitor Houses to side with us, I've got to be seen there. Not hiding in Nexus City.".

The bubble finally burst.

Lyssa knew that they were both suddenly recognizing that this might be the last day—and night—they ever spent together. Who knew where their lives would take them next?

Breakfast this morning wasn't just a way for her to keep busy. She realized now that it was a parting gift of sorts. One last small moment of normality before the weight of the world crushed their fledgling relationship with the reality of their lives.

"Come with me," Lyssa said impulsively.

"Come with you?" Allyson looked taken aback. "To Pack Nation?"

Lyssa nodded enthusiastically. "Why not? You quit your job, so you have no ties here anymore. And you won't need money or anything because I can provide everything you'll need..."

"I do have ties..." Ally said with a tinge of sadness in her tone.

Lyssa's heart sank. She knew what Allyson was referring to, and while she hadn't *expected* her to come to Pack Nation, she had hoped she might. But Ally quit her job for a reason.

If she was not allowed to chase justice through official channels, Lyssa knew Ally would pursue her investigation on her own terms. Every minute when the two of them weren't engaged in sexual activity or chatting amiably, she was consumed by the need to find the truth. The bio-chip they found in the World Council Chamber was never far from Ally's fingertips, and over the last day, Lyssa had caught her staring at it deep in thought.

"Yes..." Lyssa said eventually in what was almost a whisper. "I know you do."

"I have to find out what happened." Ally shrugged. "But know...if none of this had happened, I'd be coming with you in a heartbeat."

Lyssa smiled sadly and shook her head. "Allyson, if none of this had happened..." She took a deep breath before continuing. "Your father would still be alive, you'd still be the Chief of Security, and you and I would be nothing more than ships passing in the night. I couldn't stay here, and you would have a job and family.

"Maybe this was never meant to be."

"I don't believe that." Ally shook her head. "This feels too...real to not be anything more."

Lyssa said nothing. She understood the sentiment, but honestly, Lyssa couldn't see a clear path for them. Fleeting lovers seemed to be their destiny. A long-term relationship an impossible dream.

"So, what will you do next in your investigation?" she asked, changing the subject.

Ally took a deep breath. "I need to get some answers. So...I'm going back to London. I leave tomorrow..."

"Oh..." was all Lyssa could muster as a response as she felt disappointment swell within her.

"Yeah, I know," Ally said quietly. "I'm sorry...I should have told you earlier."

It was very possible Ally would return to London and stay there, maybe revisit her career as a police detective. If so, then it would be impossible for the two of them to be together. Her personal flyer, *Tawaic'iya*, was capable of short, stealthy trips to and from Pack Nation at low altitude, but it certainly didn't have the range to undertake an illicit trans-Atlantic rendezvous with a London-based girlfriend.

As for herself, it was likely she would not survive her planned coup. If Lyssa couldn't engineer allies to side with House Balthazaar and the other Progenitor Houses, then StormHall would have an overwhelming superiority in numbers. Defeat would be assured. And if StormHall won, then it was likely she would be executed as a traitor.

For the first time, the silence between them was uncomfortable. Each lost in thought about a future that seemed impossible to achieve.

| 41 |

NEXT STEPS

— **Alexa Reynolds** —
— *Wednesday* — *Nassau, Bahamas* —

"Well, that was a bust..." Alexa grumbled as she paced *Diana*'s cargo hold. There was more than a hint of annoyance evident in her voice.

Their approach of intimidate and interrogate had gone totally according to plan. The terrified Sergeant Rolle *had* spilled his guts, amongst other things, regarding everything he knew about arrangements for the prisoners. However, the results *hadn't* been entirely helpful.

When a job needed his attention he was contacted anonymously with an email stating the warrant number of the prisoner required. It was his responsibility to ensure that any records were deleted, the video security system was disabled, and access to the holding cells was provided.

A day or so later, a package would invariably arrive for his attention. The parcel would contain the pre-agreed remuneration for his services in cash, which he would duly pay into his bank account. He would then settle back into the day-to-day grind of his job, waiting for the next email to ping into his inbox.

The email address from which the instructions came was a dead end when Becka tried to trace it. As were the descriptions he provided for the men who came to remove the prisoners. Two men, around six feet tall, shaved heads, muscular, and wearing matching black jumpsuits, boots, and gloves. They never spoke, so he couldn't even give them an accent to narrow it down.

After leaving him to clean himself up—maybe change those soiled pants—and return to his job, they headed back to Diana, with a quick detour to Rolle's apartment en route. Letting themselves in, they gave his place a swift but thorough search for more clues, finding what they thought was the empty packet from his last money drop. Another dead end, as it had been posted locally.

Thus, after all that effort, they were no closer to finding the culprit than they had been a few hours ago.

Fuck.

While Alexa paced, Rahanah was sitting cross-legged atop one of the cargo containers. Becka sat at one of the computer stations, deep in thought and chewing the end of an already well-nibbled pen.

"Sometimes," Rahanah said with a shrug, "the winding path does not reveal where it leads on the first turn."

"That's mighty philosophical of you, considering these are *your* people we're trying to help out."

"We simply keep following the path." Rahanah smiled. "It led us to Rio, then to you, who brought us here. So, where do we go next?"

Alexa exhaled heavily. In truth, she had no idea. This had been her one shot to get a lead, and that shot missed its target. She was now dry of suggestions as to where to go next.

She slumped into the seat next to her partner. "I honestly don't know."

Becka, however, was looking at her with narrowed eyes, pursed lips, and an expression suggesting she had an idea.

Alexa raised her eyebrow. "Okay, spill it."

"How about..." Becka said slowly, "we don't go anywhere? Or rather, we go somewhere and then come back here."

Rahanah looked at them both blankly. "I do not understand..." the tigress said slowly.

"Don't worry, Rahanah," Alexa chuckled, "you're not the only one. Becka?"

Becka spun her chair around, her eyes twinkling with the embers of an idea she was keen to share.

"Okay, consider this… We *know* how the process works now. Job goes up on MercNet, then Rolle gets his 'work order' email. Freelancers, like us, pick up the bounty, drop it off here. Rolle informs his contact, etcetera, etcetera."

"Okay…" Alexa said slowly but was still confused.

"Well, I can clone Rolle's inbox…so his emails get sent to us, too. When we see one from his mystery contact, we take the job and make sure *we're* the team that grabs the bounty. Then we deliver it here, stake out the holding center, wait for the men-in-black to pick up the prisoner, and *then* follow them to the source."

"You think Rolle is going to keep doing this after the scare we put in him?" Alexa said.

Becka shrugged. "I've *seen* his bank records and the man has expensive tastes. Each one of these jobs earns him a cool 25k, but he wastes it. He's drawing the cash out in *big* chunks. I don't know whether it's women, gambling, alcohol, drugs…or all of the above, but the fact is he burns through the cash quickly. He needs constant injections of it to maintain this lifestyle. If another job comes up, he can't afford to pass on it."

"But it could be weeks until another job appears," Rahanah commented.

"I've been checking that, too. They're not quite regular as clockwork, but pretty close. He gets a job maybe once every three weeks…and if that holds true, then he's due one this week."

"You're sure?" Alexa asked slowly.

Becka leaned back in her chair and nodded confidently. "I've checked. If there isn't a job flagged up to him in the next few days, it'll be an outlier."

Alexa considered Becka's proposition. The plan had legs. As long as a job came in and as long as Sergeant Rolle was still willing to play his part, then it *was* probably the best shot they had at finding out who was behind all this. She could only see two problems…

"What about the drop-off?" she asked. "Let's say we intercept the job, catch the target, and bring him back here…Rolle knows our faces—"

"No," Becka interrupted with a firm shake of her head. "He knows *your* face. I've never met him."

"But if he decides to put two and two together, he'll look back and figure out who dropped off Ashraff and be ready for our names to pop up again. He'll see the trap coming."

Becka smiled slowly. "I thought of that, too. As I already have my Freelancer license, I did a quick name change on my MercNet record… Introducing Rebecca Danger. Freelance Peacekeeper extraordinaire!"

"Rebecca *Danger*?" Alexa chuckled.

"Well," Becka said with a grin, "actually Danger is…"

"Don't you *dare* say 'my middle name.'" Alexa shook her head in mock disgust. "That is *so* cliché."

Becka simply laughed, while Rahanah looked bemused.

"I will need to amend *Diana*'s ident-chip and create a new dropship record for me. I'm thinking Captain Rebecca Danger aboard her gallant dropship *Buzzkill*."

"*Buzzkill?*" Alexa said with a frown.

"Yup," Becka nodded. "Named after my troublesome first mate who's always raining on my parade."

Alexa shook her head and smiled. It was a crazy plan, but with a little tweak to *Diana*'s appearance—Becka's, too, for that matter—they *could* pull it off.

"Just so we're clear, though…" Becka said hesitantly, looking a shade nervous. "I'm only the pretty blonde-haired, brown-eyed face for this plan. You guys are actually *fighting* the monsters, right?"

"Monsters?" Rahanah looked across at Becka, a frown on her face. "Ashraff was no monster when you took him."

As realization dawned at her choice of description for their new crewmate, Becka's face went from smug amusement to horror at her unconscious prejudice.

"God, no… I didn't mean," she stumbled over her words.

"Rahanah, I'm sorry. Sometimes my mouth runs faster than my brain..."

Rahanah, for her part, gave a small smile and shrugged. Even in Human form, her face had a uniquely beautiful feline quality. Alexa had also noticed the tigress was a much more serene presence than you'd expect from someone who can transform into a huge predatory jungle cat at will. Where Alexa herself could be prone to dark moods, and where Becka could demonstrate an unfettered exuberance, Rahanah was always the calm center of the storm. Her reaction to Becka's faux pas was a case in point.

"I know you did not mean offense, Becka," she purred. "And you are right. There *are* monsters out there to be feared, so I understand. Though, I read your datafile on Harimau Jadian. It is somewhat...inaccurate. We are not magical or demonic; we are simply a peaceful people."

Alexa had to concede she had a point. Very rarely were people actually who they appeared to be. There were layers everywhere if you cared enough to pay close attention. The three of them sat in *Diana*'s cargo hold were as much an example of that as anything. Alexa felt like now was a good time to bail Becka out, before she put her foot any further into her mouth.

"Don't worry—Rebecca Danger will be our figurehead only. I'll do the huntin' when the time comes."

"I will help," Rahanah added, tilting her head quizzically. "Please, correct me if I misunderstand, these...MercNet jobs that you talk about... Anyone can take these jobs, correct?"

Both Becka and Alexa nodded, confirming her assertion.

"Then what is preventing someone else from completing the assignment before we do?"

Alexa shrugged. "Nothing," she said. "But we *do* have the advantage of knowing it's coming, so we can jump straight onto it. Then we just need to do a better job than our rivals."

"To be honest," Becka added, "even if someone else beats us to the mark, it doesn't matter. All we need to do is be here for when the handover is made, regardless of who turns in the target to claim the bounty."

"It would be nice to get paid for this, though..." Alexa commented with a wry smile. "I guess I'll pop out into town and see if I can rustle up something to disguise *Diana*..."

"What shall I do?" Rahanah asked.

"Sit back, relax...and watch the professionals at work," Becka laughed.

| **42** |

ONGOING INVESTIGATION

— **Allyson Knightley** —
— *Thursday* — *London, England* —

Home.

Ally had thought it might feel a little weird being back in London. But in real terms, she hadn't lived in Nexus for long. The two months she spent there hadn't been enough time to call it home. Her apartment there felt more like a hotel suite.

Here, in London, was where she had lived the longest. The property she'd purchased, decorated, and furnished to her tastes. While it was currently lacking the items of furniture she had shipped thousands of miles away to Nexus, it still felt infinitely more like where she belonged. There were memories here. Some of the more recent ones *weren't* the most pleasant Allyson had ever had, that much was for certain, but there were memories here nonetheless. Important memories.

Nexus had no such memorable moments.

Are you sure about that, Ally?

She smiled wryly to herself, realizing her apartment in Nexus *did* have a couple of memories this house didn't. The smile faded as she realized those recollections would remain overseas...and very far away.

She sighed, turning her attention back to the room in which she was standing.

Her former guestroom.

Ally had spent the last couple of hours removing all the furniture to make space. The bed was a particular challenge for her to dismantle and remove, but all that remained was a table and a chair, sitting centrally in the now empty room.

Vacant of furnishings at least.

Her tablet lay on the table, alongside several beer bottles and dozens of manilla folders haphazardly strewn across its surface. Both of them empty. While the alcohol had been consumed, the contents of the folders were now pinned up all over the walls. Photographs, crime lab reports, witness statements...copies of every document relating to the bombing of the World Council Chamber Allyson could lay her hands on prior to leaving Nexus City. Documents which, if anyone found out she had, would probably get her into serious hot water.

Meh, what's the worst that could happen? They fire someone who already quit!

She stood, arms folded, staring at the papers adorning the walls as she tapped her foot slowly. Her eyes flicked from picture to picture, report to report, seeking the common thread that would tie them all together. The single elusive truth which would reveal the complete picture of what had happened in the lead up to that devastating moment.

For the hundredth time, she tried to backtrack through the evidence.

It all started with the explosion and the four victims.

Four, as far as Allyson could tell, unrelated victims.

The bomb hadn't been particularly powerful, its blast radius relatively small. It was meant to kill the people in close vicinity. Which meant one of these victims had been targeted. This was an assassination attempt, not random terrorism.

But who was the target? And why?

She glanced at the four photographs pinned to the wall, her eyes inexorably drawn toward the one she knew the best.

Her father.

There was *no* way Jaymes Knightley was involved. Maybe it was bad detective work to rule out a suspect purely on an emotional connection, but she would not even consider a scenario in which her father was somehow complicit in the events leading to his death. It simply wasn't possible.

Nor was it possible, in her mind, for her mother to be involved.

No. The two of them were immediately crossed off her suspect list.

It was, of course, possible he had been the *target* of the attack...but for the life of her, Allyson couldn't piece together a credible motive.

Her gaze drifted to the next photo along, featuring her father's aide Narissa.

Narissa was a young Fae who had been attached to the diplomatic office for much of the past year. Ally pursed her lips and tilted her head as she stared, deep in thought. She had to admit, she hadn't known her very well. Not as well as she'd known Juliana, her parents' former assistant.

Juliana had worked with Jaymes and Serlia for almost a decade and had been a friend to the family before that. She wasn't sure exactly how, but Ally knew Juliana had been related to her mother on the Fae side of the family tree. Serlia's grief had been very real when Juliana was a casualty in the flyer accident which also claimed her uncle's husband, and almost Uncle Norbel himself.

Narissa was handpicked by Norbel as Juliana's replacement, and in the past ten months or so, while she hadn't felt like family, she seemed competent and professional. All Ally's dealings with her had been...pleasant.

Was Narissa involved? She *was* closer to the bomb than Jaymes. Had she been the target? But if so...why? Or was she simply an innocent victim?

Like Mercy.

Her attention shifted to the redheaded Vampyrii. She only met Mercy once, but Ally warmed to her easily. There had been an aura of wonder about her. An enthusiasm for simply *being* in Nexus that was as joyful as the bouncing waves in her long auburn hair. The photo pinned to the wall didn't do justice to the woman Ally met on the food court. She wished she had a better image of Mercy than this postmortem shot from the morgue.

I should have asked Lyssa for a better one…

Lyssa…

Ally doubted very much that Mercy had been the target of the attack. After all, she had only been there because she was filling in for Lyssa. If anything, she may simply have been collateral damage of a plot to kill the leader of House Balthazaar. This was, of course, Lyssa's own opinion on the attack…and Allyson had to admit, it was the most likely motive. Especially if StormHall was behind the plot. That everything had worked out perfectly for the Grand Chancellor was a fact that could *not* be ignored.

But of course, if he was involved, then he had kept his hands immaculately clean. The blame at this point was landing squarely on the shoulders of Lyssa's niece.

Lyssa vehemently assured her that Mercy was in no way involved with the bombing, but the cold hard fact was that Mercy *was* the one carrying the bomb. She was the one who handed the silver attaché case to Ambassador Sabadini, ready to shake his hand as the detonation occurred. If Mercy carried the case innocently, then the question shifted to who put that case in her hand?

A case that Lyssa confirmed she herself picked up from StormHall, and left securely in a safe in the World Conference Center that Allyson's own people kept a close watch on twenty-four-seven.

Is it possible that it could have been tampered with? Switched out somehow without anyone knowing about it?

Of course there was the other option. That despite Lyssa's confidence, Mercy *had* been the bomber. Was NVSec correct in treating her as the primary suspect? Had Sabadini been her target?

Which brought her to the Werewolf.

Ambassador Sabadini. Pack Nation's long-time Nexus ambassador. He had been there since the start, a mainstay of the community. Ally hadn't known him well but her parents had. That in and of itself wasn't unusual; Jaymes and Serlia were on good terms with many of the other diplomats stationed in Nexus.

But he *had* been the recipient of the case that was the origin of the explosion. There was no suggestion Sabadini was suicidal or was intent on making a political statement. Thus, there was little chance he was involved in his own death. He had neither motive nor opportunity. The silver case had never been in his possession till just before the explosion that killed him.

While the lack of a true suspect rankled her, the real thorn in her side was that fucking attaché case.

How the fuck did someone manage to smuggle an explosive device into the World Council Chamber?

Ally was wracking her brain trying to identify the loophole someone exploited in her security. She couldn't find it.

And *how* had the bomb been detonated?

She read the forensics report from cover to cover at least a dozen times, looking for any clue she could. There was no mention of a trigger device whatsoever. No timer. No radio receiver. No manual trigger mechanism...

Allyson looked at the little clear plastic bag sitting on the table containing the tiny piece of evidence she and Lyssa had illegally removed from the crime scene and not declared to the investigation team from NVSec.

That small piece of biological technology.

As much as she hated it, she knew what she had to do next.

| **43** |

ARMS RACE

— Sebastian StormHall —
— Thursday — Denver, New Victus —

Sebastian hadn't wanted to come here; something about hospitals and laboratories unsettled him. They were too white, too light, too clinical. He preferred things darker. Much like a ShadowWraith, he preferred to work in the darkness. He knew many of his detractors thought of him as being a façade of the traditional, but he knew the truth.

He didn't trust technology. He didn't like society's reliance on it. Humans. Fae. They were weaker races relying on their scientific advances to balance the scales. To equalize the superior physical abilities of the Vampyrii. And then there were the hated dogs to the north. Yes, they were perhaps stronger, but they certainly were *not* smarter.

They were all inferior.

All of them.

But brute force and cunning could only take you so far when you were outnumbered and outgunned. Tensions with Pack Nation and the NAA meant he was forced into a position to level the playing field through the very technology he despised. Standing in the laboratory of Doctor Shauston, his chief scientist, he knew for all his distrust in science, there *were* times when you had to embrace it.

This was one of those times.

"A war is coming, Doctor. I need weapons to fight that war, and recently I lost one of my best assets hunting down the girl in the forests of Pack Nation. I need a replacement. I need it soon."

Shauston sighed. "Thynan will *not* be easy to replace. Incubi are exceedingly rare, as you know. Even when created in a laboratory, like Thynan, they are difficult to craft. Lest I remind you, he was a failed experiment of sorts, too. We never could artificially foster the telepathy inherent in natural Incubi and Succubi—"

Sebastian waved his hand dismissively, cutting off the Doctor mid-sentence. "Telepathy was irrelevant to my needs. I wanted an able assassin. A killing machine I could point at my enemies, and in that respect, he spectacularly fulfilled the brief I gave you. Thus, the question becomes, can you do it again?"

Shauston looked at him and smiled confidently. "I believe, Grand Chancellor, I may be able to provide you with something much better."

StormHall raised an eyebrow.

Thynan had been quite the specimen. A former prisoner of war, one of several Werewolves taken during the conflict. Fodder for Dr. Shauston's experiments. Steroids increased his size and his speed. His memory had been wiped and reprogrammed, his conscience removed. He hadn't been the only one. There were fifty-seven 'volunteers' for Project Incubus. The aim was to create a killing machine that could manipulate the minds of their prey through pheromone and telepathic means.

Inspiration came from reading the reports that crossed his desk regarding two particular combat units regularly deployed to trouble-spots by the FSE. Two elite squads consisting of individuals he was convinced were an experiment in hybridization—the combined DNA of Human and Fae.

It disgusted him.

Sickened him.

The twisting of the purity of a bloodline. The mixing of two races was an abhorrent assault on the natural order of things.

Yet, if they were to fight back in the wars to come, they needed an edge of their own. They needed a Vampyrii combat unit that could hold its own against the likes of the FSE's hybrid units. So, he had tasked Dr. Shauston to create him one.

It had been a failure.

Except for Thynan.

"We learned lessons from Project Incubus. Valuable lessons. Between that, the bloodwork and DNA analysis from the girl, and the bio-tech knowledge we have obtained from our arrangement with TechMaster Takahashi …" Shauston paused and handed a manilla folder to Sebastian who flipped it open. "…I think we have come up with something…quite special."

As Sebastian flicked through the pages of the document, he began to smile. He didn't understand much of the scientific jargon, but Shauston had known him long enough to break down the important information into layman's terms and diagrams.

"How long?" he said finally as he looked up from the pages.

"I took the liberty of preparing the project already. However, to take it to the next level we'll need a…volunteer."

"Nathanial," Sebastian said without hesitation. "Use Nathanial."

| 44 |

THE FAVOR

— **Gayle Knightley** —
— *Friday — London, England* —

"Hey, Sis! I need a favor." Allyson's opening gambit was punctuated by a crack of lightning and the accompanying deep grumble as gunmetal thunderclouds blotted out the evening sky. Torrential rain ricocheted haphazardly off the streets forming tiny but violent rivers that chased down the gutters to the nearest drain.

Suffice to say, Allyson looked more than a little damp.

"Hi, Gayle," Gayle responded sarcastically. "May I please come in? How are you doing today? How have you been since coming back from Nexus?"

"Har har." Ally scowled. "Now let me in. It's raining in case you hadn't noticed!"

"I'm serious," Gayle laughed as she moved to allow her sister entry. "I open the door to my loving younger sister, whom I haven't seen in a week, and the first words out of her mouth are…'I need a favor.'"

"Fine!" Allyson said, running her fingers through her sodden hair as she strode into the hallway. "How are you today, sister dearest?"

"I am…very, very good."

"Really?" Allyson tilted her head curiously. "Color me intrigued…"

Gayle led them into the kitchen where she yanked open the dryer and rummaged through the contents before pulling out a freshly laundered towel. She threw it to Allyson, who shed her dripping coat and hung it over the back of one of the chairs at the dining table.

"Well, it's been a pretty good week, all things considered." Ally pulled out the chair where she had draped her coat and sat down, toweling her hair as she did so.

"Honestly," came the muffled voice from beneath the towel, "I was worried about your state of mind. I mean, losing your team spun you out of control, and you were only just on the bounce from that when... Well, let's just say I was afraid losing Dad would throw you back to square one. Especially when you fucked off back here to London!"

Gayle sighed, retrieving a pair of wine glasses from the cupboard and a random bottle from the rack. Her sister threw her an eyebrow. "Drinking?"

"I think I can cope with a glass of red." Gayle shrugged as she pulled out the chair next to her sister and sat down. "Truthfully, when I was in Nexus, I *was* worried a tailspin was imminent. There was a lot of pressure and... I didn't feel like I had any support system."

"Shit," Ally said with a frown. "The whole family was there. *I* was there!"

Gayle smiled sadly as she uncorked the bottle and poured them both a liberal helping of Spain's cheapest. Her intention hadn't been to insult her sister. The fact of the matter was Nexus wasn't her home—London was.

She took a deep breath and tried to better explain. "I know, but...Carrie and Mum were inseparable, and Mum herself was kind of weirdly zen about it all. And you had more important things to worry about than looking after your big sister, what with the investigation and all... I felt like I needed to come home."

"To seek comfort in the arms of a hunky American, no doubt!"

Don't deny it, Gayle. You know she's right.

Gayle simply smiled and took a deep drink from her glass.

She closed her eyes and savored the bitter yet fruity taste then sighed. It had been almost a year since alcohol of any description passed her lips. She had been so afraid of what getting drunk might do to her. But now the fear had faded. Gayle finally felt like she was in control.

"Ha, so you don't deny it!" Allyson chuckled at her sister's silence.

"I wanted to see him," Gayle shrugged. "And it helped. More than I expected it would. He's helped me cope with what happened to Dad. Especially with the fact we never really reconciled before...you know."

"I do," Ally said with a sad smile.

The next few minutes were spent with Gayle recounting the events of the week thus far. Telling Allyson about her breakdown on the first day back, her little jealousy fit at the Academy when Amanda arrived, and then about movie night and Michael's 'teaching moment.'

"Sneaky fucker!" Ally laughed. "But he's right, of course."

"He usually is. Anyway, why are *you* back here? In London, I mean."

"Quit my job," was Ally's succinct response.

A response Gayle had *not* been expecting. She recalled the moment Allyson had gotten the position; she'd been giddy with excitement and, of course, drunken shenanigans ensued in celebration. Gayle knew the job was stressful, even more so lately with what happened at the Summit, but quitting was something counter to her sister's nature.

Which means she must have a really good reason...

"Okay, so, I'm gonna ask...why?"

Ally sighed and placed down her wine glass. There was an expression on her face...a look Gayle knew well. Despite the couple of years between them, the two siblings looked so alike many people assumed they were twins. But that expression was one Gayle sometimes saw on her own face when she looked in the mirror.

Conflicting emotions were at play within her younger sister.

"It's a long story, Sis."

"Does it look like I'm in a rush to be anywhere or do anything?" Gayle said, giving Ally a reassuring smile.

Her sister said nothing while she continued to stare at the wine glass. Allyson had been stressed lately. The lead-up to the Nexus Summit put a lot of pressure on her. The result was a somewhat disheveled appearance and a tendency to drink a little more than she probably should, but Allyson always showed humor and a free spirit.

Now, this was a different Allyson Knightley sat here in her kitchen. One that Gayle had seen before, not so long ago. The last time she displayed this kind of demeanor was when she had been a detective here in London. When she was involved in her last difficult case. It consumed her and profoundly affected her emotionally.

The 'Holloway Horror,' as the media had snappily coined it.

The population of London might be significantly lower these days than in its heyday, but crime still happened. Murder still happened. Gruesome, horrible, affecting murder. It started with the horrific slaughter of an innocent family who should have felt safe in their home. Husband, wife, and their three daughters.

More victims followed.

Many more.

As pressure mounted on the police investigation, Allyson retreated into herself. She became driven to solve the case no matter the personal toll it took. She'd taken it personally, confiding in her siblings later that the vision of the dead children haunted her. The three daughters. Sisters much like Gayle, Allyson, and Carrie.

Speculation had been rife that somehow a monster got loose in London. The usual tabloid scaremongering, telling tales of a rogue Adze prowling the shadows of the streets.

Which Gayle knew was bullshit.

If there was *any* evidence of it being an Adze, her team would have been called in to flush it out and kill it. No, this killer was not supernatural, and Allyson knew it. He was a regular human. The only thing that made him different was his lack of empathy, a disregard for life, and his penchant for killing his targets in gruesome ways. He was smart, too, avoiding capture for three months as his kill count grew.

Ally never gave up, but the chase took its toll on her. She got her man, but that was the breaking point for her and the job.

"Okay," she said eventually, "so...you saw me in Nexus. I was pulling all the pieces of the puzzle together using the skills I learned in London. But suddenly, I was hitting roadblocks. First, StormHall declared Lyssa Balthazaar a traitor to New Victus..."

"I know, I was there," Gayle nodded.

"Of course, yeah," Ally said rubbing her temples. "But I *know* it's not her."

"Playing Devil's advocate for a moment, are you *sure* that's not just because you slept with her?"

Ally vehemently shook her head. "No. She said she didn't have anything to do with it, and I believe her."

"Okay." Gayle nodded. If Lyssa passed Ally's human lie detector test, then that was good enough for her.

Not that she had for a moment thought Lyssa Balthazaar was in any way a culprit in the crime. Gayle spoke at length with Mercy and enjoyed her company. She was convinced the Vampyrii had been nothing but honest with her.

"Of course, now I'm getting pressure to find and arrest her on sight," Ally continued, "all while I'm actually *hiding* her out in my quarters. Then Uncle Norbel relieves me from heading the investigation."

"Conflict of interest, I assume?" Gayle asked.

Ally nodded. "Yeah, but then rather than letting Fran take over the investigation, he hands it over to NVSec."

"Yeah, I heard that, too. Saw it on the news."

"Problem is," Ally sighed, "they've no interest in *actually* finding out who did it. They're in StormHall's pocket, and they've already pinned the blame on Lyssa and Mercy. A purely political move because now StormHall is using it as a rallying cry to garner support to oust the Progenitor Houses in New Victus. Which means no one is looking into what *really* happened. And I can't let that stand."

"Okay," Gayle said. "But quitting? You could have just taken a leave of absence."

Ally shook her head. "It's hard to explain, but... Lyssa is going to lead a coup. She's going to overthrow StormHall and...I want to help. But first, I need to find out who murdered Dad. I can't leave that mystery unsolved. I can't."

"Shit," was all Gayle could muster.

The two sat in silence for a minute or two as Gayle processed what Ally had told her. Continuing the search for the bomber, Gayle had expected. The running off to join in with a Vampyrii civil war, she had not. She looked across at her sister, a sense of worry settling into the pit of her stomach. It was Gayle's profession to fight monsters, including Vampyrii and their ilk. She was trained to an elite level in the art of war. When her powers were purring along at full strength, she was a match for pretty much anything you could throw at her.

Allyson was not.

In terms of raw power, her sister *should* be her equal. They had the same parentage, the same DNA. But the operative word was 'raw.' Her police training gave her proficiency in firearms, but her powers were an untapped resource.

"Are you sure about this?" Gayle asked. "The helping Lyssa thing?"

Ally nodded. "Yes. But investigation first."

"Okay, so, how can I help?"

"Well..." Ally reached into her pocket and pulled out a small, clear plastic bag with what looked like a broken piece of a circuit board in it. "I have one lead..."

"What is it?"

"Part of a bio-chip I found at the crime scene."

"What does it do?"

"Don't know," Ally admitted. "But I think I know a way to find out. It's why I need a favor from you..."

"What's the favor?"

Ally leaned across the counter and lowered her voice, as if afraid of being overheard. "Sis, I need you to do what you do best for a few minutes."

"Okay," Gayle whispered back. "What is it I do best? And why are we whispering?"

"Look, just know that what I'm about to ask you to do…" Ally paused. "It's going to help me catch the person who's framing Lyssa, and it's going to help me catch the person who killed Dad."

Teasing aside, Gayle knew Allyson wouldn't be here asking for a favor like this if it wasn't important. She knew that, unless it was something heinous—which her sister wouldn't ask her to do—then Gayle would find a way to oblige. That's what sisters did for each other. But even though she already planned to say yes to whatever the favor was, Ally's last comment sealed the deal.

Come hell or high water, Gayle wanted her father's killer brought to justice.

"I'm in," she said seriously. "What do you need?"

| 45 |

THE JOB

— Allyson Knightley —
— Friday — London, England —

"It's Ethan, isn't it?" Gayle purred, leaning seductively over the security desk.

"Yeah," Ethan replied hesitantly. "You're...Detective Knightley's sister, right?"

Gayle smiled warmly. "I am. How'd you know?"

"You kind of look like her." Ethan returned the smile.

"Kind of?" Gayle laughed. "Most people assume we're twins. With us, it usually boils down to if you prefer blue hair or pink. So, which do you prefer, Ethan?"

"Prefer... I..." The poor security guard stumbled over his words, not quite sure what the best answer was under these circumstances. Which was to be expected. Gayle Knightley had flicked the switch on her pheromone output, effectively scrambling the poor man's tiny male brain. Gayle gazed into Ethan's eyes and smiled.

"You don't have to answer," she whispered. "I'm just...teasing. But I *could* do with your help, Ethan. I really want you to jump me."

"Excuse me?" He sounded flustered and more than a little confused.

"Jump me," she repeated huskily. "Flat battery. I need a jump start. Do you have a car, Ethan?" Gayle leaned on the counter with her elbow and perched her chin on her hand.

"I... errr..." The young man couldn't disengage from the intensity of Gayle's stare as he stammered, "I don't. Have a car, I mean. Sorry."

"That's not a problem. I'm sure a big strong man like you could easily help me with a push. I need assistance starting my engine, Ethan," Gayle purred.

"I'm not supposed to leave the desk," he said looking genuinely pained. "I mean, I'd love to help you, but..."

"Ethan," Gayle interrupted, "it's two in the morning. Crime is sleeping soundly in its bed and a pretty girl is asking you for help. Are you absolutely *sure*...you can't spend two minutes helping me push-start my Mustang?"

"You have a Ford Mustang?"

"You like muscle cars?"

"Hell, yes!" Ethan exclaimed. "I love the American classics. You don't get to see many of them here in London these days."

Gayle looked genuinely bemused.

Allyson, hiding in the shadows outside eavesdropping on the earpiece she was wearing, almost blew her cover by snorting with laughter. This wasn't what they had expected at all. Ally knew Ethan from her frequent calls here to the Metropolitan Forensics Science Laboratory before working in Nexus. The two of them had a somewhat... uncomfortable past.

He had been young and new to the job. He seemed nice and so she'd always been sociable to him on her visits. Then, one fateful day, he mustered the courage to ask her out on a date, not realizing she was gay. Embarrassment followed, and subsequently the two barely exchanged awkward glances, let alone talked.

Tonight, though, Ethan was the gatekeeper for something Ally needed. And since she was no longer an FSE police detective—or Nexus Security Chief for that matter—she had no credentials that would legitimately get her into the building. Without them, she doubted Ethan would be pre-disposed to simply let her in. Which meant she needed a distraction to allow her a somewhat sneakier entrance. Hence the need for a favor from her sister; one Gayle was decidedly unhappy about.

Still, this was supposed to play into Gayle's unique skillset. Ally knew Ethan would find her sister attractive, and Gayle herself was no stranger to using her chemical advantage in the art of seduction. Thus, her sister had been doing her tempting best to entice Ethan away from his post, only to have her sexuality trumped by the young man's love of muscle cars.

"You must be losing your touch," Ally sniggered quietly over comms.

"Oh, screw you," Gayle whispered in return.

"Excuse me?" Ethan said with a frown.

"Oh, do you...want to come see it?" Gayle said innocently.

"Nice recovery," Ally giggled.

Ethan looked around the reception area, weighing the pros and cons of leaving his post for a few minutes.

"What type of Mustang?"

Gayle pulled her phone from her pocket and accessed the photo gallery on it. "2011 GT500. Here, look..."

Ethan whistled in appreciation as he peered at Gayle's phone. "It doesn't look its age. That's *really* a 34-year-old car?"

Gayle nodded and smiled. "Total restoration job. Not completely original, though...I had to make her a hybrid to sneak under the strict emissions rules..."

Clever girl.

Allyson shook her head in wonder, marveling at her sister's ability to fluidly adapt to the changing parameters of the mission, moving easily from seductress to fellow car enthusiast. She recalled how Lana had once said the key to the 137th Hunters reputation for improvisation was due to their pink-haired leader. The team took its cue from Gayle, and Allyson was now witnessing ample evidence of the truth of that statement.

She shivered a little. The moon was bright in the sky and the only clouds to be seen were the ones she was creating herself as she exhaled hot breath into cold air. Despite the insulation of the CombatSkin, a biting chill in the wind nipped at her cheeks and the tips of her ears, making her wish that this state-of-the-art battle suit had a hood. Or at least came with a matching hat. The more she wore it, though, the more she appreciated its comfort. Gayle had always said it was, to quote, "the most comfortable thing I've ever fucking worn."

She wasn't wrong. Even if it was tailored to her sister's parameters, the outfit was astonishingly snug. Then again, it wasn't just facially she looked identical to her sister; they also shared the same height, build, and weight.

Ally brushed a finger over the control panel integrated into the CombatSkin's left forearm and initiated 'stealth-mode.' The modest heels retracted, morphing into practical flats, while the soles softened in order to absorb sound. Gayle's default red and white color scheme darkened to a combination of black and grey that blended with the shadows of the London night, perfect for her final, hopefully unseen, approach and infiltration.

"In position," she whispered over comms as she reached the door.

On cue, Gayle tilted her phone and then clumsily dropped it behind the security desk.

"Shit!" she exclaimed as Ethan moved to retrieve it. "Sorry about that. Butter fingers!"

The moment Ethan bent out of view to gallantly retrieve the fallen device, Allyson grasped the handle of the front doors and pulled them open just enough for her to slip through and sprint across the reception area. She barely made it past the security desk before Ethan reappeared, phone in hand. Gayle's eyes glanced toward her. She nodded in response and crept through the internal doors and into the facility itself.

"I'm in," she whispered over comms.

"Be *fast*," came Gayle's equally hushed reply. "We're heading out to my car. I can maybe keep him busy for ten minutes. Fifteen tops."

"Copy that," Ally said, picking up her pace and running silently down the corridors.

While the MetFSL had not been her regular place of employment when she was a cop, she had been here often enough to know the building's layout pretty well. Especially this particular route. There was a time, not so long ago, when she made the trip down this very corridor fairly frequently. Like, two or three times a day frequently...maybe more on a good day.

Down the main corridor, take a left at the second junction, and carry on—past the canteen—toward the crime laboratory wing, through the double doors, and then the third office on the right.

As she jogged down the darkened halls, she marveled again at the borrowed CombatSkin. No matter how hard her feet came down on the ground, there was absolutely no sound. It was almost...eerie.

The corridors were dark—this was the night shift after all—and things were powered down to save electricity throughout the building. Though the building was pre-War, it had been retrofitted with the latest tech. 'Smart-lights' and 'eco-friendly' were the buzzwords the engineers used. That was the other reason Ally needed Gayle to distract security for the duration of her stay—she was going to need to turn on a few lights to see what she was doing, and she didn't want Ethan catching it on his security monitors.

Allyson reached her objective and crept into the crime lab. The laboratory had a number of diagnostic computers set up to run tests on electronics found at crime scenes. It was these machines she was here for, to plug in the bio-chip and run tests to find out exactly what it was used for. She wasn't a forensics tech, but she'd seen these machines operated enough to be confident she could get at least a rudimentary reading out of them.

As she pushed the door open gently to enter the room, she was surprised to find lights were already on. Not all of them, but a few of the desk lamps were already illuminated on the counters around the edge of the room.

Oh, shit!

Ally paused for a moment, an uneasy feeling in the pit of

her stomach. She *knew* the occupant of this room. She knew these specific counters and these desks. She knew them somewhat intimately.

Her plan, to come here at this late hour, had been specifically tailored to avoid any complications.

Maybe it was nothing. Maybe the lights had been left on by accident, simply an oversight or a glitch in the system that controlled the illumination. It wasn't unheard of. She stood very still and quietly listened for any sound that would give her a clue she wasn't alone, but all she could hear was her own nervous breathing and found herself terrified it would give away her presence. She chastised herself for her frankly foolish fear.

Calm the fuck down, Ally. It's not like you're about to be savaged by an Adze or something!

"Allyson?!" a soft feminine voice said from the doorway behind her.

She closed her eyes and exhaled heavily.

Fuck. No, not an Adze. Something much, much worse!

She turned, opening her eyes and trying to put on a happy face for her confrontation with the woman who had once broken her heart.

"Hi, Danni," she said sheepishly.

| 46 |

THE EX

— **Allyson Knightley** —
— *Friday* — *London, England* —

Dannielle Talbot.

Fuck!

Her initial greeting had been somewhat reflexive, but now Allyson was struck dumb. Other than saying 'hi,' she had no idea where to go next with the woman who had shattered her heart.

Ally took a deep breath and bit her lip gently.

Danni stood in the doorway, staring at her. Somewhat disappointingly, she remained as beautiful as when Ally had last seen her. Her skin was the same unblemished canvas of russet brown she remembered, and behind the horn-rimmed spectacles were the same hazel eyes. She carried a digital tablet in one hand while her other reached to push those glasses up on her wrinkled nose before tucking her braided hair back behind her ear in one smooth motion.

While Ally was taking in her first look at her ex-girlfriend in over nine months, Dannielle was returning the favor, evaluating Allyson with a confused frown.

"What are you doing here, Ally?"

It was an excellent question. One Allyson would probably have tried to answer if she hadn't been distracted by the one thing about Danni that *had* changed significantly. She wore the same long white lab coat she always did, but tonight it was unbuttoned. Ally's eyes focused on Dannielle's belly.

"Are you…" She already knew the answer but asked the question anyway. "Are you *pregnant?*"

Danni unconsciously stroked the flaring curve of her stomach. While her darker skin tone didn't reveal the tell-tale traces of blushing, Allyson knew Danni well enough to see the signs of her embarrassment. The subtle aversion of her eyes, the nervous licking of her lips.

"Yeah…" she said quietly. "About…five months now."

Ally did the calculations in her head.

They'd broken up not long past Valentine's Day, and it was now the middle of November. Five months pregnant meant conceiving around…mid-June.

Four months! She moved on and got pregnant in four months… Wait, what the fuck? Did she get pregnant?

"I know what you're thinking—" Danni started.

"You…got pregnant," Ally whispered.

"Yeah. Yeah, I did."

"But…you're gay."

"That doesn't mean I can't conceive…"

"But…you're *gay*," Ally repeated.

Dannielle shrugged and gave Allyson a somewhat apologetic expression. "Bisexual, actually."

"Why?" Allyson stammered.

"Why am I bisexual?" Danni looked confused.

"No… Fuck, no… I mean, why didn't you *tell* me? You never said anything…"

Dannielle walked into the room, making her way to the chair near her desk where she sat down and sighed. She put her tablet gently on the surface before looking Allyson in the eye.

"Was it relevant? I was with you. I was faithful…to you."

"Until you got bored of me."

"It wasn't like that, Ally, and you know it." Dannielle shook her head, a hint of annoyance creeping into her voice.

"Wasn't it?" Ally shot back angrily.

"No."

"So, you at no point said to me that you wanted to 'be with someone more normal'?" Ally said angrily.

"You're twisting my words, and I'm not going to rake over old ground with you again. Besides, judging by the way you're dressed," Danni gestured her hand towards Allyson's attire, "I don't think that's why you're here anyway. Is that a CombatSkin?"

Allyson cursed mentally at being distracted from the job at hand by the ghost of her past relationship and glanced down at her admittedly unusual appearance.

"It's errr... It's Gayle's," she stammered in response.

"That doesn't explain why you're creeping around the Metro Forensics Lab in the middle of the night dressed in one of your sister's spy outfits."

Danni was right, of course. Telling her who the outfit belonged to didn't clarify a damn thing. Ally glanced at the time readout on her forearm and saw she had wasted precious minutes. Gayle had estimated how long she could keep Ethan 'entertained' for, and that time was close to expiring. Thus far, Ally had achieved nothing. Maybe the whole gay-bisexual-pregnancy argument was something they could have at a later date. For now, Ally needed to focus.

She looked at Dannielle...maybe *she* could help.

"Danni, my dad—"

"Oh God, Ally. I'm so sorry," Dannielle interrupted with a mortified look suddenly on her face. "I forgot... Actually, I didn't forget. I... I mean you being here and... I meant to say I saw the news and... I am so sorry about your father, he was such a lovely man. So nice to me. I can't imagine how you're feeling right now...what you must be going through."

Allyson smiled sadly. "It's okay. I'm okay. But that's actually kind of why I'm here."

Dannielle returned to her confused expression, and rightly so. Allyson reached for her belt and extracted the remains of the bio-chip from one of the pouches, holding it up for her ex-girlfriend to see. Danni took it gently from Ally's hand and started to turn it over, inspecting it from all sides.

"Pretty sophisticated bio-chip, or at least what's left of

one. But I don't understand..."

"I pulled it out of the wall at the crime scene," Ally explained. "I think it was part of the bomb..."

Danni nodded with the dawning of insight. "So...you're looking to find out what it does?"

Ally nodded. "I figured I could maybe run it through your diagnostic computer thingummy and it might give me an answer."

Danni smiled. "My 'diagnostic computer thingummy'? You think you can do my job when you can't even remember what my equipment is called?"

"I watched you run diagnostics on electronics we brought in from crime scenes before." Ally shrugged. "I paid attention...kind of. But I have to admit, if *you* helped me, it would go a lot smoother. I'd be grateful for the help.

"For old time's sake."

Danni looked at the bio-chip, then back at Allyson. "Surely you have a crime lab in Nexus. Why aren't you running your tests up there instead of creeping around in the middle of the night in Lambeth?"

"Because they took me off the investigation."

"Ah," Danni nodded. "Conflict of interest?"

"Yeah, that bullshit," Ally confirmed. "Then they handed the whole kit and kaboodle over to NVSec, who don't know their arse from their elbows..."

"NVSec?"

"New Victus Security," Ally said by way of explanation. "But there is no way I'm leaving this in their incompetent fucking hands. So...I quit. I'll find the answers myself."

Danni stared at the bio-chip closely, her brow furrowed as she processed the information Allyson had shared. As the pieces of the puzzle started to slot together in her head, Ally could see the dawn of realization spread across her beautiful face. She nudged her spectacles back up her nose again, an unconscious motion Allyson had always found adorable.

"You stole evidence..." Danni muttered, "then came here in the middle of the night so you could *avoid* me..."

"I..." Ally hesitated.

Of course she had. Although her mind had been consumed with thoughts of Lyssa lately, there was still a level of pain associated with Dannielle. The goodbye she shared only yesterday with Lyssa had been one of sadness. A realization that it might be the last time they ever saw each other.

Her final words to Danielle nine months ago had been a very different, painful, and bitter experience.

"I know, I get it," Danni said quietly with a nod. "I've moved on with my life. I love Stephen, and I'm having his child. But this...seeing you here tonight... There's still a level of...discomfort."

"Yeah, there is." Allyson nodded and stared at her feet for a moment before taking a deep breath and looking back into those hazel eyes. "So, will you help me?"

Danni held up the bio-chip. "I think I'm going to have to," she said with a wry smile. "For starters, my diagnostic rig here isn't designed for bio-chips like this. We'll need to use the one up on the second floor. Also, the chip is broken. There's nothing to attach the diagnostic interface to, so I'll have to jerry-rig something to get it to connect. That'll take time."

"I don't *have* time."

"Can you leave it with me?"

Ally sighed. "It doesn't seem like I have a choice. How long do you need?"

Danni pursed her lips, calculating exactly what she needed to do and the time it would take. It was another expression with which Allyson was intimately familiar.

"I'll work on fixing it tonight for you. Then tomorrow night I'll see if I can run the interface on it and get you some answers. No guarantees, though. This thing looks pretty fucked up."

"You want me to come back tomorrow night?" Ally asked, hoping the answer would be a negative one.

"No," Danni said. "I can handle it. I'll courier the chip and my findings over to your home address when I'm done. Save us both the discomfort of...this again."

"Thank you, Danni," Allyson said sincerely.

"I *want* to help you find out who killed your father. I know it's important to you. I know you didn't intend to see me here tonight and... Well, I think you had the right idea..." Her voice trailed off, but the sentiment was clear. This was to be the last time the two of them saw each other.

Allyson couldn't disagree. There was nothing she wanted more right now than to run out of there and never look back.

She was trying to formulate her response when there was a gentle bleep and Gayle's voice came over the communications earpiece.

"Ally, you better be done soon because I don't think I can keep Ethan occupied much longer without shedding clothes...and it's fucking cold out here!" Gayle hissed quietly.

Ally reached up and tapped the earpiece to respond. "I'm on my way now. Two minutes," she said before turning back to Danni. "I gotta go. But thanks. Again."

"You're welcome."

With that she turned and made for the door, ready to dash for the exit before her sister had to return Ethan to his rightful place at the front desk. But before she headed into the corridor and broke into a run, she paused and looked back one last time at Dannielle and smiled. Genuinely.

"Good luck. With the baby and everything. Honestly, regardless of how things ended between us, I hope you find happiness with...Stephen."

Dannielle returned the smile. "You too, Ally. I hope you find someone too, and it all works out."

I hope so, too, Ally thought to herself as she fled into the corridor.

| 47 |

THE DEBRIEF

— Gayle Knightley —
— Sunday — London, England —

Gayle sat on the only chair in the room, her feet up on the table, staring at the walls of Allyson's former guest room.

"Holy motherfucking shit-balls..." she whispered.

"I thought you'd appreciate it," Allyson chuckled.

"You *have* been a busy little bunny." Gayle shook her head in amazement. "It literally looks like you have left no stone unturned...no ream of paper unopened, no ball of string unraveled, no sharpie uncapped...."

Every inch of every wall was covered with the totality of evidence her sister had diligently collected and collated. It looked like a scene out of every crime movie Gayle had ever watched brought to vivid life. A monstrous collage of paperwork, news clippings, reports, and photographs connected with crisscrossing lines of multicolored string. She'd been staring at it for five minutes and was *still* struggling to make sense of it all.

"Yeah, yeah, I get the point," Ally sighed. "But I'm still no closer to finding an answer."

Allyson looked exhausted. Her hair was tied in a loose, greasy ponytail, and there were dark bags under her eyes. Gayle got the impression this was all she had done since they returned from their infiltration of the crime lab. In fact, she suspected Ally had likely been obsessed with this room and her walls of evidence since she returned from Nexus.

Obsession was something Gayle recognized intimately.

After the death of her team, she became obsessive. Not in trying to understand it or find out who did it. She knew all of that. No, she had become consumed with trying to rectify every tiny flaw in her own persona that she felt had led to the Hunters' downfall. The drugs, the drinking, the sex...everything that steered her to the compromised state of mind she had been in that fateful day.

That infatuation faded somewhat since her return to the Academy. She wasn't fixed, not yet, but she did feel more relaxed now. Even after what happened in Nexus with her father.

Gayle was grieving, of course. There were tears. Frequent tears. There were nights when she couldn't sleep properly, waking in the dark and wishing she could turn back the clock to make amends with her dad. But this time around she recognized and accepted that she had a support system.

Her mother, her sisters, her friends, and, of course, Michael.

"Sis, have you slept since Friday night?"

Ally looked at her vacantly for a moment as if wondering what on earth the question was about. She frowned and shook her head slightly before turning back to the inspection of her evidence walls.

"The answer is up here somewhere, Gayle. I can *feel* it. There's a connection here. Something I'm missing that solves the puzzle..." She trailed off into thought.

"That didn't answer my question, Allyson."

"I'll sleep when I solve this."

Okay, so that's the way it's going to be. Big sister intervention time!

Gayle stood up and walked deliberately over to Allyson, the heels of her boots sounding a slow drum beat across the floor. She gently put her hands on her sister's shoulders and turned her around so the two of them were looking into each other's eyes.

"Allyson, I, as your loving elder sibling, am going to say something that *really* needs to be said. Look at me. I showered this morning. I shaved my legs. I washed my hair. I am wearing a rather sexy matching bra and knicker set—"

"I don't need to know that..." Ally interrupted looking more than a little bewildered.

"Shhh..." Gayle placed her finger on her sister's lips to shush her. "I have put make up on, for a change, and I am coordinating a stylish cream off-the-shoulder jumper with my favorite distressed jeans and a pair of black suede boots with killer heels—"

"Are you making a point?" Ally interrupted again, a hint of annoyance creeping into her tone.

"Yes. Yes, I am." Gayle nodded. "My point is that *you* are standing here smelling like a hobo that hasn't showered in days, barefoot in a pair of mismatched pajamas in the middle of the afternoon. Your hair is an unwashed mess that looks like it's been styled by a nesting squirrel. And your face bears more than a passing resemblance to a raccoon."

"This is my house. I can dress how I like!" Ally objected.

"And that is fine. Believe me, I have more than my fair share of slob-out days, too. But this... This is neglect. I get that you want to solve this case. I do, too. But...you need to look after yourself better than this.

"Since you got the Nexus job, you've been stressed to fuck. Learning a new job. Prepping for the Summit. Dealing with the bombing. This thing you're having with Lyssa Balthazaar... And now this..." Gayle gestured at the walls around them. "And to top it all off, you have a run-in with Danielle. Who's pregnant."

"And bisexual..." Ally muttered.

"And bisexual," Gayle repeated. "And don't think I haven't noticed the concerning uptick in your dinking habit lately either. It's too much. You remember a couple of months ago, you talked me down off the metaphorical ledge after my first day back at the Academy?"

"Yeah," Ally said, sighing and rolling her eyes.

"*You* helped me that day when I couldn't see the wood for

the trees. Now let *me* return the favor. You need to step back and take a breather. Just for a few hours. Please."

There was still a little fire in Allyson's eyes, a determination Gayle inherently recognized. But the slump of Ally's shoulders already told a different story. She was too drained to fight her big sister on this now. She knew Gayle was right.

"Do I *really* look like a greasy-haired hobo raccoon?"

Gayle nodded sagely. "If only Lyssa could see you now...she would be horrified."

Ally inhaled deeply and let out a heavy sigh, that turned into a prolonged yawn. "Okay. I guess you have a point."

"Too fucking right, I do." Gayle grinned. "So, here's what you're going to do. You're going to stop being a scruffy nerf-herder and take a *long* hot shower while I go put those disturbingly grubby pajamas in the laundry and make us some tea. Then you're going to dress nice—casual, but nice—and meet me downstairs where we will drink said tea, and then head out for a nice dinner at a restaurant of your choosing."

Ally's shoulders slumped further still, which Gayle honestly hadn't thought possible. Her sister was gearing up a small amount of stubborn resistance, which Gayle determined she needed to nip in the bud.

"Ugh, can't we please just get take-out?"

"Nope." Gayle shook her head. "We need to get you out of this house for more than just espionage. You *need* to decompress, Sis. Trust me. You can come at all this with a fresh head tomorrow."

The battle was won. Ally begrudgingly proceeded to the bathroom as Gayle headed downstairs. The sound of cascading water told Gayle the shower was on, and a moment later, the noise got slightly louder as the bathroom door opened briefly. A muted thump signaled the arrival of Ally's pajamas landing in a heap at the bottom of the stairs before the bathroom door closed again and the timbre of the shower changed subtly indicating her sister was now beneath its reinvigorating spray.

She was in there quite a while.

Gayle had time to put Allyson's pajamas—and a substantial pile of other dirty laundry—into the washing machine, boil the kettle three times, receive and sign for a package being delivered by courier, *and* tidy her sister's kitchen before she heard the water turn off. Footsteps upstairs told the story of Allyson's trip from bathroom to bedroom, and then five minutes later she descended the stairs while towel drying her hair. She was dressed in black jeans and a white t-shirt with a long, chunky-knit blue cardigan over the top.

"Did I hear the front door?" Ally asked from beneath the fluffy blue towel.

"Yeah." Gayle gestured to the package on the counter as she stirred milk and sweetener into the tea. "I assume it's from Dannielle."

Ally carefully tore open the packet and removed the contents. There was a document—maybe a dozen pages long—the bio-chip itself, and a handwritten note. Her sister read the note first, her face inscrutable. Gayle didn't pry, she figured that topic of conversation might come up over dinner later anyway.

Instead, she carried over the mugs of tea and set them down. Ally folded the note and slipped it into her pocket before reaching for the document, flipping through the pages one by one, skimming the content. Gayle snagged the little plastic bag with the chip in it, holding it up in the light close to her face so she could inspect it.

"Did she find out what it does?" she asked softly.

"Mmmhmm," Ally muttered. "It says here it's a bio-chemical receptor. It detects pheromones..." She tailed off, deep in thought.

"A pheromone detector?" Gayle was as confused as her sister.

"Yup. That's what Danni says..."

The two were quiet for a few minutes as they both considered this new information and what it could mean while they sipped on their tea. Gayle could see Ally being sucked back into the depths of the investigation again, the very thing she had been trying to get her sister away from. Worse still, Gayle could feel herself being drawn in, too.

Okay, snap out of it, Gayle! Step away *from the evidence!*

She reached over and slowly took the document away from Ally, who gave a little resistance but capitulated relatively passively.

"*This* is for tomorrow. Tonight, we relax. So, tell me, little sister, what did you want to do for dinner? Your choice, my treat."

Allyson said nothing for a moment as she carefully considered her options. Finally, she looked at Gayle and smiled. "You know anywhere that serves French toast?"

| 48 |

HELP WANTED

— **Serlia Knightley** —
— *Monday* — *Nexus City, Iceland* —

"Serlia, it is good to see you," Ambassador McAdams said with a polite bow of his head as he entered the room. "My sincere condolences on your loss. Jaymes was a well-liked and trusted colleague. He will be profoundly missed."

He was followed across the threshold by his long-time ambassadorial partner, Serena Peterson. The two had formed an exceedingly successful duo over the last few years, driving hard but fair negotiations on behalf of the North American Alliance.

Stephen McAdams had been a young American ambassador before The Rising, based in France if Serlia remembered correctly. His beard was white, his hair thin, and his complexion sallow. He could be a little old-school but was always fair of mind when it came to political matters.

Serena was his protégé, being groomed to take over from him as senior ambassador when he stepped down. A Canadian citizen before events had transpired to drive her from her home, her dark skin and braided hair made for a stark contrast to her older colleague. She had a smile that could charm even the most curmudgeonly of opponents and a mind sharp enough to cut easily through any diplomatic shenanigans thrown at her.

"Deeply missed by both of us," Serena added softly.

"Thank you. Jaymes thought very highly of you, too." Serlia smiled. "Thank you both for coming here tonight."

"To be honest, we were intrigued by your late-night invitation to what seems to be a very...clandestine meeting," Serena commented as she moved to sit on the sofa Serlia was gesturing toward.

McAdams sank slowly into one of the leather armchairs, nodding in agreement with his colleague. "I have to admit...your request that this meeting be 'off the record' has piqued the curiosity of this old man."

Serlia nervously smoothed her dress down over her hips. She had always conducted meetings like this with Jaymes, the two of them tackling every diplomatic problem that arose with a united front. Each bringing their own unique skills and talents to the situation. Tonight, her voice was the only one her guests would hear.

She glanced at the other armchair, which faced the windows of the apartment and gave a gorgeous view of the Goðafoss. It was Jaymes's favorite seat. Whenever they were faced with a tricky situation, this was the place where he would sit, drinking in the view and considering options and ideas before he was ready to share them with her.

Serlia could see him now, sitting there and smiling at her reassuringly.

"You have this, my love," he whispered supportively. *"You don't need me."*

She raised her eyebrow at him. A falsehood.

Right now, she needed him more than ever before. She was about to embark on a delicate diplomatic journey.

"I wanted to talk to you both about the problematic situation in New Victus," she began.

Both the NAA ambassadors displayed surprise, Serena with a raised eyebrow and Stephen with a wry chuckle.

"Well, that was *not* what we thought this would be about," he said.

"May I ask what you thought I'd invited you here for?" Serlia asked. "Just out of interest."

The two ambassadors exchanged a somewhat uncomfortable look, seemingly both wondering who should broach what appeared to be a thorny subject.

"Well, we thought you had perhaps heard the rumors…" Serena started.

"Rumors?"

"Scuttlebutt is that at least a few of the factions are considering a petition to have you…replaced as FSE Ambassador," Stephen finished.

"Replaced? Why?"

Another exchange of looks.

"Serlia…" Stephen continued gently, "Jaymes and yourself were perhaps the best of us. The axis on which the World Council spun. Of all of us, only you two held good relations with *all* factions.

"Yet the truth is some of the factions accepted you as a partnership because of Jaymes. He truly represented the Federated States of Europa because he was Human. You…are not."

"No, I'm Fae," Serlia nodded, finally understanding the issue.

She should have considered this eventuality. The FSE had now become, by default, a Human state represented by a Fae. This was a state of affairs that would not sit well with the factions that harbored a distrust of her people. She could already surmise her opposition. New Africa, the Independent States of South America, the Free Traders Association, and, of course, New Victus.

Not to mention that driving the last Fae presence out could conceivably see the return of Zǔguó and the Japanese Empire to the negotiating arena. Which, to be honest, might be a long-overdue positive.

"Not us, I hasten to add," Serena said reassuringly. "You have our unwavering support."

"Thank you, both. But it is perhaps time to step away and let new blood blaze a fresh trail for the FSE. Regardless, this is not why I asked you here tonight."

"Yes, you said this is about New Victus?" Stephen said.

Serlia took a deep breath. She would need to pick her

words carefully. "I know what Sebastian StormHall is offering you. A very tempting proposition indeed. A logical one, too. I assume you are very much considering accepting his terms?"

Serena nodded. "While we would like New Victus returned to us in its entirety, we are also realistic regarding our situation. Hawaii, Alaska, and the West Coast are crowded, but while we do need expansion room, we do not have the population to inhabit the entire country as before. After living for so long in exile and on ships, most of our people simply want *somewhere* to call home again."

"What if I told you we could achieve the same result *without* dealing with StormHall?" Serlia focused her look on Serena. "What if I told you we could also get back half of Canada, too?"

Serena and Stephen both gave the same frown.

"You'll have to explain how exactly that is possible."

"Lyssa Balthazaar is planning a coup. She intends to overthrow StormHall's regime."

"Lyssa Balthazaar, the fugitive wanted in connection to the bombing that killed *your* husband?" Serena's face wore a frown of disbelief.

"I have met Lyssa. I don't believe she is responsible. The events that transpired here to throw suspicion on her seem awfully convenient for Sebastian StormHall, don't you think?"

"You're saying the Grand Chancellor set her up to remove her as a threat?" Stephen asked.

Serlia nodded. "Yes. That is exactly what I'm saying."

"And she plans to uphold StormHall's proposal after overthrowing him?"

"Stephen, the proposal *was* Lyssa's idea. She has been advocating this within New Victus for years, using her position on the Earth Quorum opposite StormHall to garner support for it…"

"This doesn't explain the Canada part of the deal," Serena interjected.

"Lyssa is allied with Damian Dane."

"The Wolf King? And he's agreed to hand over half of Pack

Nation?"

Serlia looked Serena squarely in the eye and lied. "Yes."

Both of the NAA ambassadors sat quietly as they absorbed the information Serlia had divulged. Ambassador McAdams tapped his immaculately maintained nails on the arm of the chair before finally addressing her. The look in his old, yet wise eyes told Serlia he knew the answer to the question he was about to ask.

Yet he asked it anyway. "What do you require from us? Simply to turn down the Grand Chancellor's offer and wait?"

"No." Serlia shook her head. "I want you to commit your forces to fight alongside Lyssa and Pack Nation."

Stephen laughed and shook his head.

"You want us to shed blood to take back what is being freely offered without a need for loss of life?" Serena asked.

"Yes," Serlia nodded.

"I'm not sure I see the logic. As a Canadian, I want my country back...but the price we would pay in blood would be too high to justify." Serena shook her head. "I can't back this."

"I take it you have the FSE on board?" Stephen asked.

"Not yet, but I plan to soon," Serlia admitted. "I know you were preparing for an assault along both the San Andreas front and from the Gulf of Mexico. StormHall knows it, too, which is why he ceded to this proposal—"

"Good," Serena interrupted. "The threat of force achieved our goal without needing to lose lives."

"Lyssa is going to war with or without us. If we don't help, she's destined to lose, and if she does, then you'll have no choice but to deal with StormHall for the rest of his life...and Vampyrii live a long time. Plus, he'll likely control Pack Nation at that point, too, with all its resources. But if we help Lyssa Balthazaar win..."

"It doesn't matter, Serlia." Stephen shook his head sadly. "Lyssa Balthazaar may well *be* a better option than Grand Chancellor StormHall..."

"But she's still a Vampyrii."

And there it was, the real reason they wouldn't back this fight.

Pure, old-fashioned racial prejudice.

She closed her eyes briefly before glancing at Jaymes' chair seeking his spiritual support. She could see him, shrugging his shoulders sadly.

"It's hard to fight decades of inherent hatred," he said. *"Don't give up though, my love. This is but the opening salvo in a longer campaign. Patience is a virtue...you taught me that."*

He was right. There was nothing more that could be done right now.

She argued the case for a little while longer, running into the same roadblocks over and over. Eventually, she stopped, offered them drinks, and the three made pleasant small talk for a while before deciding the hour was late. She closed the door gently behind them as they left, leaving her alone in the quiet apartment. Leaning back against the door, she closed her eyes wearily.

"Well," she muttered, "I had hoped for better..."

"You did marvelously, my love," Jaymes' voice sounded in her head. *"This battle may have been lost, but the war has a long way to go. Backing Lyssa is the right thing to do...and speaking of the devil..."*

There was a gentle knock. If she hadn't been leaning against the door, she perhaps wouldn't have heard it, but as it was it startled her. Her eyes snapped open, the moment with Jaymes lost. She turned and opened the door again.

"I thought they'd never leave!" Lyssa said, an anxious look on her face. "Please, may I come in?"

"Of course," Serlia shepherded her quickly inside, then closed the door. "What are you doing here, Lyssa? Do you realize how dangerous this is?"

"Ambassador, I need a favor..."

| 49 |

NO TURNING BACK

— Lyssa Balthazaar —
— Monday — Nexus City, Iceland —

"Are you *absolutely* sure about this, Lys? Because if we start down that path, then there is no turning back. You understand?"

Lyssa nodded. Of course, she understood.

She understood *intimately*.

After all, this had been her idea.

Eight centuries ago, Vampyrii had been born into this world. The Progenitors. Twelve in number. Different from their descendants. They were stronger, faster, and had longer natural lifespans than their children.

Unlike their offspring, a period of hibernation would rejuvenate them. When they felt the grasp of Father Time begin to take hold, they would enter the Long Sleep. Balthazaar was currently undertaking that very process and would remain there for several more years. During this defenseless time, it became the sacred responsibility of the House to protect their Progenitor at all costs.

Because Progenitors, despite their physical superiority, *were* still mortal.

Still vulnerable.

Lyssa had her ideas regarding who was perpetrating the

clandestine murders of their forebears and why. After convincing the Houses of Jareb, Skarling, and Haggari to take extra precautions in the protection of their Progenitors, Lyssa instructed her family to excavate a secure vault deep beneath Hearst Tower where Balthazaar could sleep in safety. Only herself and a handful of intimately trusted others had access to it.

But that wasn't enough.

A contingency plan was needed in the event the worst happened and someone, somehow, got to Balthazaar.

Thus, Lyssa spoke to House Balthazaar's chief scientist, her younger sister Nykola. They spoke at length, juggling ideas and theories until, one day, they arrived at a solution.

Project: Lazarus.

"I understand completely, Nyk. Believe me."

Nykola looked at her from the monitor screen. Thousands of miles away on the other end of a video-conferencing link she may have been, but the image was crystal clear. She looked concerned.

"When we pulled out of New York, we took everything we could with us. We got father out, but...the rest we had to leave behind."

"Do you think you can get it?"

Nykola sighed and rubbed her forehead before shrugging. "I don't know. Maybe. I mean, I could go to New York with one of our Special Forces teams and try. If StormHall hasn't got to Hearst Tower yet, then maybe we can get in and out quickly. But...it's a lot of equipment. We'll need to use one of the trucks, which hampers us for both speed and stealth. And even if we do manage it, we'll only have what I'd got pre-prepared in my lab. And that's only enough for one shot at this, Lyssa.

"One. Shot."

Lyssa sighed. "I know, Nyk. I get it. But if we're going to win the upcoming war..."

"I know. I understand," Nykola nodded. "I'll get right on it. I just... I wanted to make sure you knew what you were doing. What it might cost."

She was well aware of the risk she was taking.

"When will you be back? We could do with you here to finalize our plans for this coup. *You're* the impetus behind this. Without you...I think Damian is wavering."

When they had been planning all this with the illusion of time, Damian had been supportive, yet reluctant. Not that she blamed him. There was a great deal at stake, and starting a war with Storm was not something to be taken lightly. Unfortunately, recent events had left her with no choice.

"I'll be there soon," Lyssa nodded. "But...I have something I need to do first."

| 50 |

THE TARGET

— **Alexa Reynolds** —
— *Monday — Nassau, Bahamas* —

"It is important to focus. *You* control the change. You control *when* you change and *how* you change. When you become the Wolf, *you* decide exactly how far you want to take the transformation—"

"Your English has gotten a whole lot better..." Alexa commented, interrupting Rahanah's tuition. The Tiger-Queen raised an eyebrow and sighed.

They were in *Diana*'s cargo hold with Rahanah sitting cross-legged atop one of the containers they had loaded in Rio de Janeiro. She was mid-shifted, her face more feline than Human, claws on the ends of her long fingers, and her long black and white striped tail curled up behind her. Alexa, meanwhile, was stood in the center of the hold, bouncing on her toes and shaking out her hands, like a boxer going through her warmup exercises.

"Focus, Alexa," she said. "Focus is key."

"Yeah, yeah, I know. I'm trying." It was Alexa's turn to sigh. "I've tried to learn this for a long time now and I can't. Damian attempted to teach me *repeatedly*."

"Damian?"

"Damian Dane, the leader of Pack Nation." Alexa abruptly stopped bouncing, having suddenly had a tiny epiphany.

"Goddamn it. I shoulda thought of this a *long* time ago. I bet he'd give your people safe haven up north. We should ask him."

Giving Rahanah a glimmer of hope for the safety of her people clearly distracted her from the task at hand. Her feline face lit up; her tail twitched excitedly.

"We have been at threat for so long now…it would be a dream for my people to live in peace. Do you really think he may be able to help?."

"I do. He's a good man."

"Then we shall ask him," Rahanah said decisively.

In their brief time together, there were two things about Rahanah that Alexa had noticed and begun to admire. When an opportunity presented, she seized it instinctually. Without hesitation. The way she had when Alexa found her in Rio. Secondly, when the decision had been made to take advantage of an opportunity, Rahanah lived with whatever the result was. There was no second-guessing or regret if things went wrong and no celebration when things went right. Simply zen-like calm. An acceptance that no matter what happened, she was on the path life had given her.

This winding path.

Alexa wished she could embrace that philosophy. It appeared a far less stressful way to pursue one's life.

The tigress had been patiently trying to teach Alexa the art of mid-shifting for the last hour. Despite Alexa getting increasingly angry and frustrated at herself, Rahanah demonstrated no impatience or negativity. She was serenely positive Alexa *would* master the art…in her own time.

"Focus and try once more," Rahanah said softly. "Focus on the form you wish to take. Not only the Wolf. You wish to be the Wolf *with* a voice. See yourself, in your mind's eye, the talking She-Wolf. Picture it. Focus on it. Then, when you are ready, *will* the change to occur."

Before leaving Pack Nation, she had asked Damian if he could rustle up a few of the transformation suits like the one Lonewolf had worn. The black neoprene-like material with white accents clung snug to her body, with a halter neck top and shorts that reached mid-thigh. The color scheme and the precise fit made Alexa wonder if these had been made especially for her. Perhaps back in the days when she and Damian had been an item.

She tugged at the leg, feeling a little self-conscious. The rubbery material was designed to stretch and contract with her transformation, which meant no more ruining clothes when turning to Wolf. More importantly, it also meant no more embarrassing nudity when changing back. But it did snag a bit at times.

Okay, concentrate, Alexa. You can do this. Tenth time is the charm!

Closing her eyes, she did exactly what Rahanah suggested.

She pictured herself. The snow-white Wolf, sleek and powerful. She focused on the details. The ice-blue eyes. The black streak which started on her nose and flowed up between her ears to fade out on the back of her neck. The black tip at the end of her tail. She thought carefully about her mouth, her fanged jaw. How she desired her human voice box and vocal cords.

The image coalesced in her imagination. A vision of herself, speaking from that toothy canine face. Repeating the phrase...

The badass white Wolf jumps over the lazy Vampyrii...

Alexa willed her transformation.

It took only a few seconds to shift. Since doing it for the first time in years in the forests of Montreal, she had been practicing on and off. The more she practiced, the easier and quicker the shifting became.

Alexa felt herself move to all fours, her body swiftly rearranging itself as the endorphin rush filled her with the familiar wave of ecstasy, numbing the pain of physical reconstruction. Her vision changed as color definition faded while peripheral increased. Her sense of smell ratcheted up several notches as her nose started detecting even the faintest scents.

She cleared her throat. "So, did it work?"

For a moment she wasn't sure if she was hearing her voice, or if it was in her head. It sounded...different. Deeper perhaps.

More...growly. The happy squeal of excitement, Rahanah's reaction, told her all she needed to know.

"You did it!" The tigress clapped her hands joyfully, her voice rising an octave. "I knew you could do it."

Alexa laughed, Rahanah's glee rubbing off on her, too. It sounded weird, not her usual laughter, but a kind of raspy giggle. It was an odd sound that made her laugh even harder, which in turn elicited more laughter from the She-Tiger. The two of them were lost in the throes of their mutual amusement so much Alexa almost missed Becka entering the cargo hold. Her fleeting look of confusion was quickly replaced by a smile as she realized what was going on.

"I guess congratulations are in order," she chuckled before turning to look at Rahanah. "I've been trying to get her to embrace her Lupine side for a while now, but she was adamant it wasn't what she wanted."

Rahanah looked back at Alexa, her face screwed up in bewilderment. "Why would you want to deny your true self?"

"This isn't my true self," Alexa growled. "I was turned, five years ago."

"Oh, I see..." Rahanah nodded. "Was it a gift?"

"A gift?"

"Yes. In our culture, the bite of the Harimau Jadian is given as the greatest, most honorable gift. When a Harimau Jadian falls in love, they must disclose their true self. Honesty with no secrets. An offer of the gift is extended as a proposal of unity. When the lovers are unified, the gift is bestowed that night to consummate the union."

"So, being turned is a wedding gift?" Becka said with an amused frown.

"Certainly," Rahanah nodded. "This is how we grow our family. Is this not the same for Wolves?"

"No. It wasn't really a gift," Alexa growled as she willed her transformation back to Human form.

She hadn't yet mastered the art of shifting back to a dignified standing position, so ended up on her hands and knees on the metal and rubber floor. After a moment, the buzz of the endorphin rush faded once more, and she stood to walk over to where her regular clothes were draped over another of the cargo crates. As she slid her legs into the baggy combat trousers, she continued her explanation of her turning.

"I was a soldier in the US Marines and became very badly wounded in combat. Mortally wounded. A former comrade in arms, Alex… was a Werewolf spy. He turned me to save my life."

"Ah, I see," Rahanah nodded. "Then, yes. It *was* a gift, given through love. He did not want you to die, so he gifted you life. That is an honorable motive."

Alexa shrugged as she pulled a black T-shirt over her head.

"Anyway," Becka interrupted, waving a digital tablet in the air, "I came bearing news. Target came through from our mystery collector. We're going to Venezuela, ladies."

"What's in Venezuela?" Alexa asked Becka as she padded barefoot over to lean against the cargo container on which Rahanah was sitting.

Becka placed the tablet down where they could all see it and swiped through a few screens before landing on a hand-drawn sketch of what appeared to be a woman in a white dress with long raven hair. The artist had scribbled in a pair of gnarled hands with long nails on spindly fingers. Her eyes were black pits in a face that wore a fearsome scowl and terrible curved fangs.

"A witch!" Rahanah whispered.

"A *Sayona*," corrected Becka.

"Sayona…" Alexa shook her head. "Doesn't sound familiar."

"Nor should it, they're as rare as fuck. Which is probably why our mystery collector wants one. The warrant hit MercNet about an hour ago. It was swiftly followed by an email to our friendly Sergeant Rolle who, as we expected, jumped at the chance for another payout.

"The job specifies a small city in Venezuela called Araure. At least it used to be a city. The population is about ten thousand these days. The job is a typical FSE warrant. Big bucks to bring the Sayona in alive, the payout is one hundred thousand credits. Dead…not so much."

Rahanah pointed at the image on the screen. "So, if she's not a witch...what is she?"

Her feline eyes were wide, her tail twitching. Becka lowered her voice conspiratorially and started to whisper, leaning into the rapt tigress. "Okay, so I looked it up. Took me a while because it's not in the 'paedia. But 'La Sayona' is, according to legend, the vengeful spirit of a woman who punishes men who have affairs outside of marriage. Her name refers to the long white dress she wears. It's said her face is just a skull with horrible teeth...

"There's a whole story about it once being a beautiful young woman called Casilda who discovered her husband was having an affair with her *mother*, so she brutally killed them both with a machete. Hacked. Them. To. Death."

"Oh, no..." Rahanah whispered putting her hand over her mouth.

"The other villagers could do nothing, only hear the terrified screams of her victims... With her final dying breath, her mouth filled with blood, her mother cursed her to walk the Earth for all eternity, avenging women by killing their unfaithful husbands..."

Rahanah's mouth was agape, her ears flattened against her head as she stared at Becka agog. "Such evil..." she said almost imperceptibly, "...a monster..."

Becka held her gaze for a moment, before suddenly smiling and turning to Alexa. "Other reports, however, tell of a creature who manifests to horny men working in the jungle. She appears assuming the visage of a beautiful woman, lures them into the forest, and then feeds off them, leaving behind their drained corpses..."

"Fuck." Alexa rolled her eyes. "So, another succubus?"

"Sounds like it."

"Since when did *I* become the go-to-girl for succubus hunting?"

"Some people are just lucky, and at least this one is working alone...*and* you've got help," Becka said, throwing a thumb in Rahanah's direction.

Alexa sighed. She'd have been happy if she never saw another succubus again, but Becka was right—the tigress would make for an excellent partner to back her up on this one, and she *was* now a pseudo-expert on the type. She straightened up.

"Are we...sorry, is *Rebecca Danger* the only applicant?"

"Yup." Becka grinned. "I jumped my alter-ego onto the job the second I saw the email to Rolle. It's an open contract, but we were the first applicant for the warrant, and we're close by, so should get the jump on any competition."

"Okay, get *Diana* airborne. Let's go snag us a succubus!"

Becka nodded, snatched up her tablet, and headed for *Diana*'s cockpit. Alexa turned to head back to her quarters; she needed to start getting ready as Venezuela wasn't far away. Hopefully, they could get this done quickly. As she left the cargo bay, she heard the quiet question of a confused tigress.

"What's a succubus?"

| 51 |

MEMORIES

— **Lyssa Balthazaar** —
— *Tuesday* — *London, England* —

She gazed up at the beautifully ornate clock face, observing the elongated black minute hand as it made its way inexorably toward the apex of the dial to join the shorter hour hand that was already stationed there awaiting its arrival.

It was *exactly* as she remembered it.

The sand-colored stonework, the gold detailing, and the intricate, exquisite architecture. The lethal-looking spires, the magnificent windows, and the gentle lead-colored slope of the roof. As she looked at the Palace of Westminster from her vantage point on the Westminster bridge, the picture-postcard scene before her brought back a flood of old memories.

The clock hands finally united, and atop the Elizabeth Tower, Big Ben started to toll midday. As the bell pealed its familiar chime, Lyssa closed her eyes to soak in the sound. A tear rolled gently down her cheek as she recalled the first time she heard it. She couldn't remember the year exactly, only that she'd been a youngster.

Or at least young by Vampyrii standards.

Around 1880 maybe? Back when it had been St. Stephen's Tower.

The exact year eluded her, but the image in her mind was

crystal clear. She and her father in an older version of the city. A Victorian London.

Opening her eyes, she looked around. It was an ordinary Tuesday afternoon, and the streets were busy, but there were certainly no prostitutes, pickpockets, or beggars. No horses clip-clopping down the gravel streets; only a few boats chugging down a sparkling river Thames. And the air...

She drew in a deep breath.

Clean. Fresh.

Very different from how it had been back then during the throes of the Industrial Revolution, with its steam-powered pollution and the stench of the sewers.

This London was the city it had always been destined to be. A place of old beauty and modern sensibility, finally coming together in harmony.

Together.

That was the keyword here, wasn't it?

Why she was here?

As the last chimes of Big Ben dissipated into the tranquility of the city, Lyssa began to walk. She had a destination to reach, a place she needed to be.

Her heart pounded in her chest. She tried to tell herself it was for a million different reasons, other than the truth. It was traveling outside of New Victus for the first time in all these years. It was being a tourist again at last. It was being in London and experiencing it afresh. It was the thrill of hearing Big Ben chime. It was the fear of being discovered, a Vampyrii illegally in the UK. The paranoia that someone would see past the hair dye and contact lenses and recognize her for who she truly was.

So many different reasons.

But Lyssa knew deep down the correct answer was 'none of the above.'

It was nerves, pure and simple.

She had traveled a long way incognito, via flyer and train, to reach here. Her final destination was now merely a few miles away on foot. Just a short walk through this beautiful city of her memories to reach an address scrawled on a scrap of paper that sat crumpled in her gloved hand as she clutched it like it was the most precious thing on this planet.

And maybe, just maybe, it was.

| **52** |

LIFE'S TOO SHORT

— **Allyson Knightley** —
— *Tuesday* — *London, England* —

Allyson yawned, carrying her mug of tea into her new 'investigation room' to stare at the wall again.

Dannielle's report was pinned to the center of the web of evidence that was organized all around it. So *much* evidence, but no proof. No answers. She had hoped the results of Danni's evaluation would be the final piece of the puzzle. The Rosetta stone that would unlock the mystery.

But it hadn't unlocked a damned thing.

Just more fucking questions.

To be honest, Ally hadn't known exactly what revelation to expect from the diagnostic. A remote trigger maybe? Something she could trace back to the individual who had detonated the bomb. Maybe even something that would shed light on how a bomb had been slipped through *her* security measures and ended up in the World Council Chamber.

What she had instead was a tangle of clues pointing in no specific direction, and the fulcrum on which this all balanced was a bio-organic pheromone detecting chip, built half a world away by a mysterious TechMaster nobody knew much about.

It was beyond frustrating.

As she sipped her tea, her brow furrowed in thought, she

thought she heard something...

Is that someone at my door?

She stood very still, being very quiet. Waiting.

A few seconds later there *was* a definite knocking, this time more assertive.

Still, she didn't move.

Who was rapping on her door at two in the afternoon on a Tuesday? Mum was still in Nexus, as was Carrie. Gayle would be at the Academy, so it was unlikely to be her. Besides, *she* had a key to let herself in.

Ally glanced down at herself and grimaced. She had stayed up late last night re-organizing the papers on the wall like you would the letters on a Scrabble board, hoping the answer she was looking for would coalesce out of the jumble. Her bed had beckoned around four a.m, and admitting defeat, she had slumped into it, wrapping the duvet tightly around herself and falling into a deep sleep.

Waking up late, she had felt a strong urge to slob out in her pajamas for the day, but Gayle's words about a greasy squirrel and a hobo raccoon haunted her. So, she took a shower and dressed in freshly cleaned pajamas, courtesy of the laundry Gayle had done for her a couple of days ago.

Still, she wasn't sure she was ready to answer the door to whoever was there, so she persevered with the tried and tested tradition of standing very still—despite the fact she couldn't be seen from the front door—and quietly hoping the visitor would simply leave.

There was another knock. Three of them. Solid, firm, and loud.

Fuck.

Whoever it was, they were not going away.

Fine. If I have to come down there and send you away so I can have some peace, then so be it...

Placing her tea down on the table with a sigh, she stalked out of the room and skipped down the stairs. Ally was just reaching for the door to open it when there was another forceful knock, which elevated her level of irritation. Grabbing the door latch, she twisted and yanked hard, ready to blast the person disturbing her afternoon with both barrels of her irritability.

It was a woman, in a long buttoned-up woolen coat falling to mid-calf. She was huddled with her arms wrapped around herself and a black beanie hat pulled down to her eyebrows. A tangle of curly blonde hair spilled out from beneath it. Despite the day being overcast, the woman was wearing dark sunglasses, which she started to remove when Ally answered the door.

Well, that's not at all who I expected...

As the sunglasses came off, a pair of hazel eyes greeted her. But despite the artificial change of color, Ally immediately recognized who was stood on her doorstep.

"*Lyssa?!*"

"May I come in?" Lyssa asked, looking around nervously.

"What the *fuck* are you doing?" Ally gabbled. "You can't be here! In London! Do you *know* how much *trouble* you could be in?"

"YES!" Lyssa hissed under her breath. "Which is why letting me in would be an advisable course of action right now!"

With the initial shock subsiding, Ally realized Lyssa was right. Pushing the door wide, she reached out, grabbed Lyssa by her coat, pulled her in through the door, then quickly closed it to the prying eyes of the world outside.

"Okay, so now would you mind telling me what the fumph—"

Ally's final words were muffled. Lost as Lyssa wrapped eager arms around her neck and pressed her cold lips firmly against Allyson's. The kiss was loaded with a thousand different emotions, and as Ally gave herself over to it, she experienced every single one of them.

The exhilaration of reunion.

The relief of acceptance.

The feeling of no longer being alone.

And more.

As the kiss lingered, the heat of passion begin to build.

The questions of how and why Lyssa was here suddenly seemed so trivial. She was lost in the pure joy of the moment.

Lyssa was here. Right here.

Here in my house...

The thought broke the spell. Gently pushing Lyssa back, she reluctantly broke from the kiss to catch her breath. They stood in silence, neither speaking, both just basking in the moment.

Ally knew it hadn't even been a week since they'd parted, so maybe it was silly that she was feeling this way. But she knew the two of them had been having the same thoughts when they said their goodbyes six days ago.

That this was over.

That there was no future for them.

The tears, the kisses, and the farewell wishes would be the last time they ever saw each other. Life would take them in different directions, leading them down paths that couldn't be reconciled.

And yet, here Lyssa was.

Risking her life to make sure their tale wasn't yet told. The book unclosed. Lyssa was showing Allyson that whatever this was, it was merely a bookmark, keeping their place in a story-line that she intended to pick up again at some point.

"How is this...possible?" she finally managed to say, shaking her head.

Lyssa smiled. "I was thinking about Mercy's visit, just before... I knew General Norbel had approved it, and I knew I couldn't come here as she had. But I did wonder if there was a way I *could* get here with a little help... So, I asked Serlia."

"My mother?"

Lyssa laughed. "That is your mother's name, yes."

"And she helped?"

"Well, obviously!"

Allyson shook her head again, the shock of all this was still fresh in her head. "I'm sorry, I'm... I mean... I can't believe you're here."

Ally took Lyssa's hand and pulled her into the lounge, directing her to sit on the sofa. She sat down next to her, resisting the impulse to kiss her again. Instead, she clutched at her soft hand, holding it in her own.

"I know," Lyssa said softly. "I assumed I'd never see you again. Concluding that our time together had run its course. But I couldn't let go of the memory of you, and the more I considered it, the more I rejected that narrative for us. This may not be a fairytale we're living in, but it is *our* story. We get a say in how it ends, and I for one wasn't ready to say goodbye. Were you?"

Allyson shook her head. "No, I wasn't. I came back here, and I buried myself in my work. Tried to distract myself." She closed her eyes and sighed. "Gayle called me a scruffy nerf-herder... I don't even know what that is..."

"It's a Star Wars reference," Lyssa chuckled.

"Figures. So, how did Mum get you here?"

Lyssa rummaged in the pocket of her coat and pulled out a small blue digi-card, which Ally immediately recognized as a UK e-passport. Lyssa pressed her thumb against the sensor on the small credit card-sized device and a tiny holographic image of the blonde woman sat on her sofa spun lazily in the air above it.

"Well, first Bobbi acquired a fake e-passport for me, with my new identity..."

Ally squinted at the name on the device. "Jennifer Haskins? So, should I call you Jenny from now on?" she laughed.

Lyssa rolled her eyes but carried on with her explanation. "It was your mother's idea. The name, the image. Serlia liked the idea of the blonde, but said that with the hair being straight, I still resembled me...hence the curls. She booked passage for Jennifer Haskins aboard an FSE diplomatic flight out of Nexus into the Gatwick SkyPort. I swear to the gods, Ally, I was nervous the whole flight, and walking through passport control when I got here was...terrifying. I thought for sure I was going to get caught."

"I feel like that every time anyway, even when I've got nothing to hide," Ally chuckled. "But why? Why did you risk so much to come here?"

"For you."

It was such a simple two-word answer.

"Lyssa, if they caught you... Fuck, I'm not worth that kind

of risk."

"Yes, you are," Lyssa said seriously. "I love you. And I think perhaps you love me, too. And maybe it's early in our relationship to say those three little words, but I'm two-hundred and forty-five years old, and I know how truly rare this feeling is…"

"I…" Allyson didn't quite know what to say. "Lyssa, we've only known each other for a month…"

"I love you," Lyssa said firmly. "I don't need you to say it back, but I needed to say it to you before I go to Pack Nation and start a war I may not survive. I'm under no illusions as to how dangerous the road I'm about to travel down is. I *will* fight for my family. If I have to, I'll die for my family.

"As long as my life has been so far, it's still too short to live with regrets. And I know for a fact that if I didn't tell you how I feel, I'd regret it. I have fallen in love with you, Allyson Knightley. I traveled here to tell you that."

"I…" Ally stumbled over the words.

Do I love Lyssa? This feels like love… But then, so did Danni.

She wasn't sure. She wished she was, but the truth was seeing Dannielle a few nights ago had rocked her certainty in how she perceived 'love' as something she felt. Danni had been the first and last person she uttered those three simple words to, and now, in hindsight, it was clear she had been mistaken as to what that relationship had been. While Danni had reciprocated the words, she betrayed the sentiment. Broken Allyson's heart while being seemingly untouched by the distress the breakup should cause.

Yet seeing her ex had not been as painful as Ally imagined. Genuinely, she felt more disturbed by the fact her former paramour lied to her about her sexuality. That Danni had been bisexual, and Ally was passed over for a guy had come as a real shock. Her heart still felt bruised, but not as broken as she once thought.

Maybe…this healing was due to Lyssa's influence.

Which prompts the question… Is this a rebound relationship?

"Allyson," Lyssa smiled at her, "I *don't* need you to say it back. I understand you may need more time than me to figure out how you feel. *What* you feel.

"It's strange. You'd think having a lifespan as long as we Vampyrii do, we'd take things slower. Play the long game, so to speak. But in fact, the lessons a long life teaches you are that you have to seize your moments when you have them, because such moments can be fleeting.

"This is one of those moments...so, I'm seizing."

Ally suddenly felt awful. She wanted to say those words but knew right now it could be a lie. There were certainly feelings there. Being around Lyssa gave her a feeling of joy and excitement. It made her forget the bad things that had happened, gave her a sense of support and direction.

Like being found when you had been feeling so lost.

She couldn't look Lyssa in the eye anymore. There was an overwhelming sense of failure surging through her, like she let her lover down by not being able to reciprocate the declaration.

"I'm sorry..." she started but couldn't finish.

Lyssa simply squeezed her hand reassuringly, and when Ally lifted her gaze to look at her lover's face again, there was no sadness in those eyes. Even behind the hazel-colored contact lenses, she could make out the twinkle of mischief.

"It's okay, really," Lyssa said. "But I *do* have one serious question..."

Ally didn't say anything, just tilted an eyebrow to prompt Lyssa to ask away.

"Why are you in your pajamas? Were you about to head to bed?"

Ally breathed a tiny sigh of relief and tried to put on her most seductive sexy smile. "No. But now you're here...that can most definitely be arranged."

| 53 |

NOSTALGIA

— **Amanda Forrester** —
— *Tuesday* — *London, England* —

Amanda saw Gayle ahead of her as she strolled across the Academy grounds toward the lights of the landing pad. She knew Gayle would be here, sitting on the steps nearby, and watching the buzz of activity around *Minerva* as she was prepped for flight. This was something she had done since they had lost Valerio on Operation: Radio Silence. Mission number ten for the 137th Hunters.

Amanda had once asked her why.

"Every flight from this pad is a mission into unknown dangers," Gayle had said. *"I'm either facing it myself, or I'm going to watch them depart...and wish them safe travels."*

It was as if Gayle took responsibility for ensuring good karma protected both her team and Torbar's. She watched *every* launch with her silent vigil.

"So...he finally asked you then?"

There had been a noticeable drop in temperature and the night was cold. Wisps of steam clouded the air as Amanda slowly exhaled the breath from her lungs through pursed lips. The wind whipped around her as she stood next to her friend, who hugged her knees to her chest and looked up at Amanda with a smile.

"Yes, he did." Gayle chuckled.

"Excited?"

"Nervous."

"Don't be," Amanda said, putting her hand on Gayle's shoulder. "If there's one thing I know…it's that Gayle Knightley *never* gives in to nerves."

"Normally," Gayle nodded, "but this is a whole different breed of nerves."

Amanda pulled her coat tighter around her body and sat herself down on the steps alongside Gayle. They remained in silence for a few minutes, both watching the ground crew as they finished fueling and arming the dropship.

A muscular man in a tight olive-green CombatSkin strode down *Minerva*'s rear loading ramp, his focus on the datapad he was carrying. Amanda recognized the dark-haired Asian immediately, though it had been a while since she had seen him. Dylan Blake, call sign 'Gambler.' He was the resident pilot for the 136th Terminators, and it was clear he was doing his final flight checks.

"Didn't you sleep with Dylan once?" Gayle said with a tilt of her head.

"More than once," Amanda nodded. "He was one of the only members of Torbar's merry band I could tolerate. I just loved the Welsh accent. Actually…that's not fair. Dylan's a nice guy. Do you miss it?"

"What? Sleeping with Dylan?" Gayle snorted. "I *never* slept with Dylan."

"No, I mean…shipping out on missions. I was always so nervous before a mission. I threw up *every* time."

"Is that why you were always the last one aboard *Artemis*?" Gayle laughed lightly.

Amanda shrugged. "Last thing I'd do before coming aboard was vomit in the bathroom. I *never* got used to it. So…do you? Miss it?"

Gayle was silent for a moment, deep in thought as she continued to remain focused on the activity a couple of dozen meters away.

"Yes…and no," Gayle finally answered quietly. "I really *thought* I did. When I first came back here, I believed I needed to be flying off on *Arty* and expressing my vengeance for fallen friends. But now... I've seen enough death, Amanda.

"I know that one day, probably with those kids in tow, I'm going to have to walk up that ramp, and Lana is going to fly us to God knows where to face God knows what. And hopefully, I'll have prepared these kids to be ready for it. Hopefully, *I'll* be ready for it.

"But...here, today... No, I don't miss it. I hope it's a *long* time before I have to take that ride. How about you?"

"I don't know," Amanda found herself saying truthfully.

Up until a few minutes ago, she would have given a definite, even vehement negative to that question. But standing here, watching *Minerva* getting ready to leave, gave her pause to change her mind.

What is it you miss, though, Amanda? Be honest.

"Before I came to the Academy, I was...nobody," she said quietly. "I wasn't smart in school, flunked everything..."

"Pffft." Gayle frowned. "That's got to be bullshit. You're one of the smartest people I know."

"Maybe, but I never applied it to academics. I was listless, lost. I was a hybrid but didn't have much in the way of power. The one thing I *did* have going for me was that I blossomed pretty early, so I identified as that. I was a troublemaker at sixteen, always getting into shenanigans with boys. Eventually, my parents had enough of my...promiscuity.

"They sent me to the Academy to try and instill some discipline into their wayward daughter."

The rest of the 136th Terminators were now walking out across the landing pad, all wearing CombatSkins matching the color and shade of Gambler's. One by one, they walked up the ramp into Minerva's troop compartment. Captain Alistair Torbar was the final team member aboard. He stopped at the top, engaged in a short conversation with the ground crew chief. Then with a nod, the chief exited the dropship, and Torbar hit the interior button to close and seal the hatch.

As the ramp slowly ascended, Amanda saw Torbar look over toward them, locking his eyes with Gayle's. She saluted to him, a quick flick of her hand near her temple. He returned the gesture as the ramp finished closing.

"Salvum itineribus," Gayle whispered.

"Safe travels," Amanda translated in the same hushed tone.

Minerva's engines started to cycle up, the familiar sound of her repulsorlifts thrumming in the cold night air. As they hit their peak note, the dropship rose from the ground while pivoting leisurely to starboard. Once the rotation was complete, the rear engines tilted to provide forward thrust and *Minerva* leaped skyward.

As she receded into the night, Gayle unfurled her legs to stand and smiled at her friend. "You didn't answer the question."

Amanda took a deep breath and stared up at the disappearing aircraft. Only its running lights could now be seen against the ebony sky, and soon those, too, would be lost amid the twinkling stars and passing clouds.

She nodded. "Yeah, I kinda miss it. As Zephyr, I made a mark. Found my calling, something I was good at. Since Valletta...since my surgery...I don't know who I am. This implant means I know I'll never see frontline duty. I'd never pass the physical.

"So, who am I if I can't be a Hunter?"

Gayle stood up, linking her arm through her friend's and gently urging her to walk beside her as they made their way back inside. Amanda didn't resist. It was too fucking cold out here to stay any longer.

"With my knee, I'm not sure I'd pass the physical, either. So, you're not alone. But that doesn't mean you're not a Hunter. We'll *always* be Hunters. Always. You, me, and Lana...the last of the 137th."

"At least until we train up these kids." Amanda shrugged.

There was something about that idea that niggled at her deep down. Maybe it was the feeling she was being replaced by a younger model. A younger model with an intact spinal column. Evidently, Gayle felt similarly conflicted.

"Actually," she said, "I've been thinking about that. Maybe the Hunters name needs to end with us, Amanda. The kids' *official* unit number is one-three-eight, so maybe we need a new name for them. What do you think?"

"What would you call them?" Amanda asked with a smile.

"I dunno. The 138th Teenagers?"

"The 138th Kiddiwinks!"

"The 138th Puberteers!"

The two of them giggled back to the warmth of the Officers Lounge, and Amanda had to admit... It *did* feel really good to be back.

| 54 |

NEW DOG; OLD TRICKS

— Rahanah —
— Tuesday — Araure, Venezuela —

Guilt.

There was no other word for it.

Rahanah had left her streak in the forests of Brazil for the perfectly valid reason of finding those responsible for persecuting her people. She *could* have sent Ashraff, but as Queen, she felt it her personal responsibility to undertake this task herself. It was her solemn *duty* to keep her family safe.

It was a path she was resolved to follow, no matter the dangers she would have to face. Rahanah had expected it to be an arduous journey. She anticipated it would take its toll on her in ways she couldn't fathom.

What she *hadn't* expected was for it to be...fun.

She experienced a perverse sense of pleasure terrifying the man responsible for 'trading' Ashraff in Nassau. Stalking him through the building reminded her of her days as a cub, playing with her brothers and sisters as they honed their hunting skills. She had even partaken in the same brand of familiar good-natured banter with them that she was now observing between Alexa and Becka.

Rahanah hadn't been sure what to expect from hunting with Alexa, but she was surprised to find it an enjoyable experience.

She wasn't sure *exactly* how she felt about that.

Guilt or glee?

Ultimately, she decided that it was okay to feel a little of both—as long she achieved her mission. And she was confident the best way to reach that goal was to follow Alexa's lead.

They had flown overnight into Venezuela and put *Diana*—or the *Buzzkill* as per its newly minted fake identification chip—down to the northwest of Araure near the local forests. Becka selected the location specifically after carefully analyzing the MercNet data-packet. She identified this as being the epicenter of the abduction reports.

Leaving Becka in the dropship, Alexa and Rahanah headed out to begin their hunt for the Sayona. They decided to stake out what seemed to be a relatively recently constructed extension of a lumberjacking operation not far from the forest. The settlement buildings here were all of a relatively simple, and ramshackle-looking, wooden construction.

Dusk arrived and the setting sun was slipping low in a burnt-sienna sky. Alexa lay patiently in the shadows of the treeline, surveying the activity at a shady-looking dive-bar on the outskirts of the village just across from where they were hidden. Rahanah lay behind her, in full tiger form, her tail twitching restlessly. They'd been here for hours, watching the locals wander into the bar, only to drunkenly stagger out again later on.

Rahanah was confused as to how this was assisting them in their current mission, a sentiment she eventually decided to voice to her companion. "How does sitting in bushes help us catch the witch?"

"We're sitting in this bush," Alexa whispered without looking up from her binoculars, "waiting for a *particular* customer."

That didn't answer Rahanah's question. "I still don't understand."

Alexa lowered the binoculars and twisted slightly to look at the Tiger-Queen. She smiled. "I guess this is different from the hunting you're used to."

"Harimau Jadian hunt for food. We don't hunt people."

"Okay. So, how do you hunt for food? Like the capybara we ate at your camp?" Alexa asked.

"If we're hunting for prey, such as capybara, we will find where they gather. A watering hole. Or source of food. Then we lie in wait until they present themselves, at which point we pounce."

"Well, this isn't *that* much different. We know our Sayona preys on men—"

"Unfaithful men," Rahanah interjected.

"I'm not sure that matters, to be fair. Disregarding the Sayona's mythical backstory, our girl sounds like a succubus. They prey on men, feeding off their sexual energy. *That* bar is the watering hole attracting her food source. I'm gambling she's here, hunting them—"

"Ah, as we are hunting her," Rahanah said, suddenly understanding.

"Yup." Alexa nodded, returning to her vigil.

Rahanah stood up slowly and stretched herself to work out the kinks in her feline spine. With a yawn, she padded over to the foliage in which Alexa was lying and pushed her head through to peer at the makeshift tavern herself. Without the benefit of field glasses, like Alexa's, she was having trouble making out the patrons in any detail.

She squinted. It didn't help.

"How do you know who we're looking for?" she whispered.

"I don't...but I'll know it when I see it," Alexa replied.

Rahanah settled back down, lying in the bush so she could still see out across the way. She sniffed the air but didn't detect anything she considered suspicious. Not surprising; tigers weren't generally renowned for their sense of smell. Tilting her head, she considered Alexa, wondering why she hadn't shifted to her lupine form to utilize the more perceptive senses she had available.

"Would the Wolf not be better for this?" she asked.

"Nope," Alexa said distractedly. "This is purely visual. I'm looking for something *very* specific...and...I think I just found it."

"What?" Rahanah shuffled to peer out of the bushes again.

"What are you seeing?"

"A very drunk man, staggering out of the bar with a woman on his arm..."

"But...what makes these two different to any of the others that have left?"

"Because this woman is *not* drunk," Alexa said slowly. "And she's leading her mark away from the town, rather than into it. *And*...she has long black hair and is wearing a white dress."

"Witch!" Rahanah growled.

Alexa put her binoculars down. "Time to go to work."

| 55 |

DÉJÀ VU

— **Alexa Reynolds** —
— *Tuesday — Araure, Venezuela* —

Why can I never get away from all the running?

Dashing down the dark and dusty streets, Alexa reflected on her final statement to Rahanah before beginning their pursuit of the Sayona through this modest shantytown.

"Let's try and make this quick and painless."

Famous last words.

An hour later, this particular pursuit had been anything *but.*

It turned out a Sayona was *not* simply a Venezuelan succubus. Their quarry appeared to be a crossbreed of sorts...

"Dammit..." Alexa muttered under her breath as she slid to a halt and played her torch beam down yet another dark alley.

Nothing. Fuck!

She tapped her earpiece, opening her comms channel. "Stripes, you found anything?"

After a short pause, Becka's voice responded. "I don't think Rahanah can use the comms while she's shifted, Zee."

"We need to figure that out, Becks. Especially if I'm going to be doing more of the Wolf shit moving forward."

"It's on my to-do list," Becka shot back. "I *am* tracking her signal. She's moving fast..."

"Where?"

"Two hundred meters west of your position. I think she may have found our Sayona."

"Shit…"

The trip to Rio de Janeiro was supposed to be a holiday. If she'd known *this* kind of adventure was in the cards, she'd have considered waiting until her bespoke CombatSkin was ready. The latest iteration incorporated a set of linked contact lenses providing a virtual head-up display. These CombatLenses—as they were branded—would have given her a live feed regarding Rahanah's current position, plus a whole host of other information and functionality.

Including night-vision, which would have been super helpful in these poorly lit conditions…especially as their target *appeared* to be part ShadowWraith.

Which had come as somewhat of a surprise.

"Guide me in toward Stripes," she panted. "And while you're at it, give me what you know on Wraiths."

"I don't have street maps of this shithole, Zee. Guiding you to Stripes is *not* going to be easy," Becka complained. "Try taking a half turn left—forty-five degrees—and then run straight ahead."

Alexa pivoted, exactly as Becka dictated. "Becks, there's a fucking shed…house…whatever this thing is, right in front of me!"

"I don't know what to tell you, Zee," came the response. "Improvisation is *your* thing, isn't it? But get a wriggle on; Stripes is moving *fast.*"

"Fuck!" Alexa grunted.

The rickety-looking abode was a one-story affair with a low roofline. She glanced around. The other buildings on the street were pretty much the same—some sort of primitive pre-fabrication. Makeshift homes that had become more or less permanent over the intervening years. Four rotten wooden walls roofed with rusty corrugated steel.

Improvisation…fine. Let's improvise then!

She leaped upward, caught hold of the guttering, and pulled herself up. Hooking her leg, she climbed onto the wobbly corrugated steel covering. Not only did it feel insecure, but it was slick from the rain they'd had earlier that evening. Before she could change her mind, Alexa turned back to the direction Becka had indicated and pushed off. As she started to run, she could feel the metal roof clatter and shake under her with each footfall.

So much for being discreet...

Anyone peacefully sleeping in these ramshackle homes tonight would be abruptly awoken by her racing across their rooftops. Stealth was now a forgotten concept.

Not that she had a choice.

She had never faced a ShadowWraith directly, but by all accounts, they were a dangerous foe, and not one Alexa was inclined to let Rahanah face alone.

"Becks! ShadowWraiths! Anything you can give us," she prodded her partner.

With the channel open, even if Rahanah couldn't answer, she would hear Becka relay the details on how to possibly defeat these things.

"Not much detail on them, and what we do know about them doesn't track with what our girl is doing. Not totally. Some speculation that ShadowWraiths are a crossbreed of Vampyrii and Adze. Primary killing tools are their long fingertip claws. They get their name due to their obsidian skin color and ability to blend seamlessly with shadows."

The description didn't line up with what they had seen of the Sayona thus far. Their target looked like an attractive, if pale, human woman in her mid-twenties. Alexa and Rahanah had tracked her as she walked with her victim from the bar, and when she revealed her intention to feed off the poor inebriated soul, they stepped in to prevent it.

Alexa hoped a show of force—like walking out with a fucking great white tiger —might persuade the Sayona to surrender without a skirmish. Thus, they had both flanked their target with the express goal of preventing her from fleeing into the forest.

Things hadn't *quite* gone according to plan.

Come on, Alexa! You know *they always run!*

She hadn't even had time to do her spiel about being an

FSE-sanctioned Peacekeeping Agent before the Sayona had unceremoniously dropped her prey and hightailed it back toward the town they'd just left.

It immediately became obvious their quarry was no ordinary succubus.

For starters, she was fast.

Really fucking fast.

Alexa considered herself to be quick. Her athletic build, in addition to her Werewolf-enhanced physique, meant she could cover ground at a pretty rapid pace, even in Human form. The Sayona, however, was in a different speed class altogether. As they gave immediate pursuit, it was clear only Rahanah in her tiger form could keep up.

But it was when she reached the shadows of the town that the bigger surprise was revealed.

The moment the Sayona entered the first darkened alleyway between the wooden domiciles, she disappeared from view.

Not simply hiding.

Vanished.

Though she hadn't faced a ShadowWraith thus far in her career, she *was* well aware of their reputation. They were a different type of shapeshifter, more chameleon than therianthrope. They didn't shift form, but could alter their skin color, tone, and pattern to blend in seamlessly with any background, the darker the better.

This Sayona *definitely* had ShadowWraith traits.

When Alexa caught up with a puzzled Rahanah, all they had found were the tattered remains of their target's white dress in the shadows of an alleyway. She was still there somewhere, naked and camouflaged. Alexa could smell her scent.

"She's here. She's moving. I can hear her," Rahanah had growled as her ears twitched atop her huge feline head. But, evidently, she couldn't get a bearing on their mark either.

Their problems were further compounded by the fact that this makeshift town was an unmapped warren of cheap do-it-yourself buildings, built close to each other and providing a myriad of dark passages down which the Sayona could disappear.

It was at that point Alexa had decided that to increase their odds of finding their prey in this hell-hole, they would need to split up. She ordered Becka to deploy *Diana*'s seeker drones to assist in the sweep. It was one of these that had found the Sayona near Rahanah's location, and the tigress was now in pursuit. Alexa was playing catch-up.

She approached the edge of the roof and, pacing out her footsteps just right, launched herself across the eight-foot gap to the shack next door. Her plan—use the rooves like stepping stones to get to her location more directly. As she landed, her feet slipped awkwardly on the ridged metal. She grimaced at the hyperextension of her knee but pushed onward.

"Okay, here's something..." Becka said in her ear. "ShadowWraiths play in the shadows because their camouflage ability is iffy under normal light conditions. An unverified entry here talks about them having a skin pigmentation that glows under UV light."

"Ultra-violet? Like a blacklight?"

"Yup," Becka confirmed.

"Becks, do I seem like the kind of girl who routinely carries a blacklight around with her?" Alexa grumbled as she leaped another gap, this one onto a rotten wooden roof that she was almost positive was likely to collapse under her weight as she crossed it.

"Keep ya knickers on, Boss," Becka shot back. "Our drones have UV searchlights. I'll deploy them over your location."

"Great," Alexa replied. "It would make life a whole lot easier to take her down if we could *see* her."

"Working on it. Now slow up. Rahanah is right there...you're pretty much on top of her..." Becka's last words were almost prophetic.

Alexa cleared another gap onto another roof. Rainwater and a generous growth of some form of moss combined to reduce the friction co-efficient to something in the region of a banana skin. This time she wasn't so lucky as her boot skidded on the slippery surface upon landing. Her legs flew out from under her in a particularly ungraceful manner, and she fell on her derriere with a thump.

Which was the moment she discovered this particular roof *wasn't* made from wood or metal like its predecessors; it was made from old plastic which had become brittle over the years. There was no way it could support the weight of a falling Alexa. It shattered into large shards and plunged into the building it was meant to be protecting from the elements.

Alexa following suit a split second later.

"*Fuuuuuuck!*"

She braced herself for a rough landing on her ass, but fortunately, her fall was somewhat broken by a large mass of white fur with black stripes.

"*Sohai!*" Rahanah rumbled under her breath as the wind was driven from her.

Alexa groaned as she rolled off her new partner and onto the wooden floor. She lay there for a second, trying to catch her breath.

"Maybe it's time you became the Wolf?" Rahanah growled, shaking her head as if to clear it, her bright blue eyes glinting in dim light.

"I didn't wear my morph suit, and I'll be damned if I'm going to leave my guns lying around to be looted, *or* be naked in the middle of this fucking shanty town if I need to change back. Come on!"

She pushed herself to her feet and surveyed their position. This was a longer structure than the others, some sort of large storage building. It was maybe sixty feet square and filled with freestanding shelving carrying all manner of supplies and equipment. She moved to take a step forward, but Rahanah placed one of her oversized paws against her leg.

"Wait," Rahanah growled. "The witch is in here..."

"You're sure?"

The huge feline head nodded. "I saw it enter and followed it. It is still here. I can hear it..." Her big ears twitched atop Rahanah's head. Searching.

Alexa dropped her voice to a whisper. "Guard the door. Do *not* let her out."

She unsnapped the straps holding her *Freelancers* and drew the one on her left hip. Her thumb slid across the biometric safety sensor, eliciting the soft beep that indicated the weapon was ready to fire. With her free hand, she switched on the petite but powerful flashlight built into the firearm, then moved to snag a stasis-grenade from her utility belt. The tiny glass disc-like device was the same as the one she had used to put Ashraff 'on ice' a couple of months ago. It was designed to be thrown, breaking on impact and releasing a chemical reaction that instantly and harmlessly paralyzed its target.

While the interior of the shed was quiet, she could already hear the people of the settlement starting to gather outside, wondering what was going on in the middle of the night.

We need to get this finished quickly!

Alexa began a slow advance, the plastic shards of the roof material splintering under her boots.

"Becka, I *really* need one of those drones at my location..." she muttered.

Becka's reply was immediate and professional. "Inbound. Sixty seconds."

It was too dark in here for Alexa's liking. There were far too many places for the Sayona to secret herself in the shadows. She stalked forward, brandishing her *Freelancer* before her, finger poised on the trigger. The warrant specified 'alive' as being the preference, but this situation was now feeling so perilous that Alexa wasn't prepared to take chances. If possible, she would fire to wound, but if it became a matter of self-preservation, she wouldn't hesitate to put the Sayona down.

At the first set of shelves, she swiftly panned left and right, checking the aisles.

Nothing.

She inhaled deeply. Her nose may not be the equal of what it was in Wolf form, but it was still far more sensitive than a regular Human's. Rahanah was right—the Sayona *was* here somewhere, perfectly camouflaged. Alexa peered carefully into the gloom, following the powerful beam of her gun-light and wishing it had a UV setting. She hoped she might be able to detect *something* that would tip her off. A weird curvature of the light, a ripple of movement, anything. But there was no sign of the Sayona in the area her shaft played over.

Panning the illumination back to the central aisle, she slowly slid her foot forward, moving carefully toward the next row of shelves. Alexa methodically repeated her previous sweep pattern, quickly scanning left and then right, her light tracing a tight figure-eight motion to cover as much area as possible.

Another dead end.

Or so she thought.

As Alexa started to move on…all hell broke loose.

It started as one of the drones controlled by Becka descended through the ruined roof into the building and bathed the room in the gentle purple glow of UV. The Sayona was abruptly exposed. Flushed from her hiding place…

…In the row Alexa had swept only a moment ago.

With a surprised hiss, the Sayona moved to escape, shoving Alexa aside hard and causing her to stumble backward between the shelves opposite. The Sayona took immediate advantage and headed for the doorway Rahanah guarded. In her haste, she pushed off against the nearest shelf, toppling it and beginning a domino effect as each of the freestanding units cascaded into the one immediately next to it.

Alexa threw her arms up to protect herself from falling supplies and equipment as she attempted to dive back toward the central aisle. She didn't make it. Within seconds her legs were trapped beneath the avalanche of random items from the broken shelves. Her Freelancer, knocked from her hand, skittered across the floor out of her reach.

The Sayona had now reached Rahanah and the two of them were facing off. Under any other circumstance, Alexa probably would have put all her chips on the tigress winning this particular fight, but the falling debris had also damaged the drone. It too was trapped, and its UV searchlight was flickering wildly. It created a strobe effect, causing the Sayona to strobe in and out of view intermittently.

"Zee!" Becka called urgent over comms. "I've lost the drone feed! What the fuck is happening in there?"

Alexa ignored her and continued to push at the shelves that trapped her legs. A deep guttural growl drew her attention back to Rahanah. The tigress took a blind swipe at her erratically reappearing foe.

She missed. By a wide margin.

Alexa was no expert on the visual acuity of tigers, but it seemed clear that Rahanah was effectively blinded.

"Becka, we need help in here! Now!"

"I'm on my way, Zee," came the taut reply.

The Sayona extended her claws and fangs and was advancing menacingly toward the flailing Rahanah. Alexa needed to do something.

Fast.

Trapped as she was, there was only one avenue of attack open to her...the stasis-grenade she was still clutching in her right hand. A bout of frantic shuffling got her into a half-sitting position allowing her room to swing her arm. She prodded the activation button, took aim...and threw the tiny disc-shaped object at the Sayona.

It arced through the air and the fragile glass smashed on impact.

She watched as the soft ice-blue effect spread rapidly...

...across the black and white fur of Rahanah.

"Shit!" she cursed under her breath.

This is why you don't throw right-handed!

Rahanah half-turned to look at Alexa as the grenade took effect, her bright blue eyes widening in shock.

With both her opponents out of action, the Sayona sensed victory. Her black eyes moved from Alexa, who was now desperately trying to extricate herself from her trappings, to the newly frozen tigress. With a hiss, she ignored Alexa and started to move toward what she evaluated as the more powerful threat, looking to neutralize the incapacitated jungle cat while she had the chance.

Alexa's mind raced.

One Freelancer was lying uselessly out of reach. The other

was stuck in her holster buried beneath the supplies piled atop her. She kicked frantically with her legs, trying to worm herself free of the shelves...

Shelves!

Her head snapped toward the storage units she had already walked past when she started searching for the Sayona. Still standing and *perfectly* positioned.

Alexa reached out and grabbed the leg of the unit closest to her and yanked. Hard. It skewed a little and then began to slowly topple. As it fell, gravity gave a helping hand. It picked up speed before crashing into the one immediately preceding it, twisted and toppling that shelf, too. Directly at the Sayona.

The cacophony drew the target's attention back toward Alexa again, but it was far too late. Physics was playing out its inevitable course. Alexa had simply been hoping for a distraction that would allow her to free her trapped legs in time to save her partner, but her fortunes appeared to have changed. The corner of the falling unit struck the surprised Sayona on the temple.

She collapsed to the floor in a heap, the contents of the shelves scattering all over her.

Alexa watched for movement —to ensure their quarry was disabled—but there was none. Finally, she slumped to the dirt floor and exhaled heavily in relief.

Seconds later, the door to the storage shed burst open and Becka dashed inside, UV flashlight in one hand and her firearm in the other. Behind her, Alexa could see the inhabitants of the little town milling around, trying to peer through the door to see what the hell was going on. It didn't take long for Becka to flit her eyes from the Sayona to Rahanah, and then to Alexa.

"What the *fuck* happened here?" she asked with a hint of amusement.

"Can you help me out of here, please?" Alexa growled from the floor.

Becka shut off her flashlight and holstered her weapon. Her right eyebrow twitched into an amused arch as she nodded toward Rahanah.

"Did you...*ice* our Tiger-Queen?"

"It was *not* my finest hour, I'll grant you that," Alexa sighed.

Before moving to help her partner out, Becka stooped to check the pulse of their target. A moment later, she pulled a pair of zip-ties from her belt-pouch and trussed the Sayona at the wrists and ankles. As Alexa lay there watching, she was actually kind of impressed by her protégé's professionalism.

Alexa glanced at the unconscious Sayona, lying peacefully on the floor.

It may not have been my finest hour, but I gotcha!

Phase two of their plan was complete.

| 56 |

INTIMATE ASSURANCE

— **Lyssa Balthazaar** —
— *Wednesday* — *London, England* —

Ally sat with her feet up on the table, reclining lazily on her wooden chair as she munched leisurely on the bowl of porridge and strawberries cradled against her chest. It was an odd dichotomy of the sexy and the mundane. Her ankles were casually crossed, and the brevity of her midnight-blue nightdress was showing off her long lean legs which, Lyssa had to admit, were *almost* distracting her from the fear that precariously balancing the chair on its rear legs was going to end in potentially hilarious disaster. She was one slip away from being sprawled on her back covered in her own breakfast.

Not that her lover seemed concerned, continuing to confidently rock back and forth with practiced ease.

Lyssa was also finding a compelling distraction in the evidence walls Ally had assembled. She moved deliberately around the room following the crimson threads from paper to paper, photograph to photograph, tracing the story of what the media were now referring to as the 'Nexus Terror Attack' in meticulous detail.

"Did you do this with all your cases when you were a detective?"

Ally gestured toward the wall with her empty spoon. "Pretty much," she shrugged. "When we had a big case like this, they'd assign a team and an incident room to it. I'd delegate much of this shit to my squad, and we'd put it on these mobile boards that could be wheeled around. I like to be able to...visualize things like this."

She stirred the remaining contents of her bowl and then spooned another mouthful.

Lyssa could see what Ally meant about *visualizing* the crime. Laying out the events, with the evidence all clearly placed out along the timeline, *did* make it clear where the missing links were. She padded barefoot around the room, her finger trailing lightly along each scarlet string until she reached the dead-ends, of which there were many.

When she got to one specific piece of evidence, she tapped it with her fingernail. "Is this the report on what that fragment of bio-chip does?"

A vaguely distracted "Hmmm?" was all Lyssa got as a response.

She turned to find Allyson very slowly chewing on her food and staring distractedly at Lyssa's legs. The borrowed baggy, off-the-shoulder shirt with the cute cartoon cat on the front didn't seem to have dulled Ally's interest one bit judging by the vaguely lascivious gaze. Lyssa chuckled to herself, catching Ally in the act of being distracted by the very same feature she had been admiring about her lover only minutes before.

"Hey!" she laughed. "Eyes up here!"

"Sorry." Allyson blushed. "I was... I was just thinking about something...." She shook her head subtly as if to clear her thoughts. "Okay, sorry. So, what do you want to know?"

"The bio-chip?"

"Ah, yes. So, my...friend analyzed it. It is, apparently, a pheromone detector." She paused briefly, before continuing. "Lys, can I ask you a question?"

"Of course."

A moment ago, Lyssa thought her lover had been admiring her with lust in her thoughts, but Allyson's demeanor now seemed very different. She looked...anxious. Lyssa pushed her thoughts of the evidence wall aside to focus on what was suddenly concerning Ally, who placed her now empty bowl back on the table.

"Back in Nexus, when we went to see Bobbi...she told me you were bi-sexual. Is that true?"

So, that's what this is all about.

"And earlier," Ally continued, "she also said something about you 'not being finished with the Wolf King.' Are you and Damian Dane in a relationship?"

For a brief second, Lyssa considered a tiny white lie to allay her lover's fears. But then she remembered that Ally would instantly sense any dishonesty. "Would it put your mind at ease if I told you that while Damian and I had...sexual relations, it never parlayed into anything more? I care about Damian. He's been there for me in so many ways over the past few years. I love him...but I'm not *in* love with him. That's the truth. I promise."

"But you just said you slept with him..."

Lyssa sighed. "It's complicated..."

"I was under the impression you were gay, but... I mean, sleeping with Damian, I guess, *does* make you bisexual. Is that... I mean, do you identify as bi?"

This was beginning to feel like a tricky situation. How could she reassure Allyson her bisexuality wasn't going to be an issue while simultaneously trying to understand what had triggered this insecurity in the first place?

"Okay," she started slowly, "cards on the table. Yes, Bobbi was right. I do identify as bisexual, But I also skew *heavily* to a female preference. Like how you're attracted to women, but may have a preference for blonde, brunette, or redhead—"

"Brunette," Allyson interjected.

"Exactly. It's the same principle. I'm attracted to both men *and* women...but I *prefer* women. I've lived a long life, Ally. When I was born, it was during a time when being gay just wasn't a thing that was accepted. Especially in the US. It was okay to have 'female friendships,' or to have what was known as a 'Boston Marriage,' but to openly be in love with a woman... Fuck, no. Hence, in order to fit in back then, I tended to simply date guys. It was less complicated.

"These days, it's my position as Balthazaar's daughter that

limits my options. Many of the Vampyrii Houses are *not* progressive, especially those of Storm and his band of bigots. When they came to power, diversity became a dirty word. I haven't dated seriously since he was voted in."

"Shit!" Ally exclaimed. "So, that's what? Thirty years?"

"Give or take," Lyssa said with a shrug.

"That's *quite* the dry spell..."

Lyssa sighed. "You lose track after a while. It just became...business as usual."

"Till Damian?" Allyson asked, her voice subdued.

Lyssa shook her head. "No. Till you. As long as you consider *this* to be dating..."

She was rewarded with a small smile as Ally tucked an errant strand of blue behind her ear. She didn't answer, but the subtle nod she gave was enough for Lyssa to breathe a tiny sigh of relief.

"Does my being bisexual *bother* you?"

Ally said nothing, just bit her lower lip and stared past Lyssa deep in thought. Lyssa followed her gaze, finding it directed toward the tiny bio-chip pinned to the evidence wall in its clear plastic bag.

"The bio-chip?" Her voice hinted at her confusion.

Ally shook her head slowly. "The 'friend' who ran the analysis on the chip...was my ex."

"Dannielle?"

Ally nodded. "Turns out she's also five months pregnant, so..."

As Allyson's shoulders slumped, realization dawned for Lyssa.

The former girlfriend by whom Ally had been dumped turned out to not be as gay as previously advertised. The fact her new Vampyrii girlfriend was *also* bisexual had, therefore, now taken on a new significance.

"Oh," Lyssa sighed. She carefully considered what to say next. She had already used the three little words that conveyed her complete devotion, so what else could she possibly say to assure Allyson her feelings were immutable?

Maybe I don't have to say anything...

Maybe this particular situation required a more demonstrative act of commitment, rather than an easily dismissed verbal declaration. She took a deep breath, hoping she wasn't about to make a horribly misjudged mistake.

Lyssa spun slowly, lifting her heels to stand on her toes, fully aware standing like this would accentuate the curve of her calves and thus draw her lover's attention. She sashayed deliberately over to where Ally was seated, exaggerating the sway of her hips as she did so. Allyson's tongue moistened dry lips, and Lyssa saw her swallow as her eyes lazily traveled up Lyssa's shapely legs, from the tips of those toes to the hem of the sleepshirt sitting midthigh.

Right where I want them...

Lyssa crossed her arms in front of her, each hand grasping the opposite side of the hemline with which Ally was transfixed. She started, very slowly, to lift it upward.

Seductively.

As Ally took her legs off the table, Lyssa could see the rapid rise and fall of her breasts beneath her silken nightdress. She moved to stand, but Lyssa shook her head.

No. Stay right *where you are...*

Ally obeyed, sitting back and watching as Lyssa's shirt resumed its upward trajectory. Her hands balled into fists and moved to her lap. As the shirt crept upward, Lyssa became aware that her own state of arousal was building in direct proportion to how much flesh she was showing.

Gods, I'm so fucking hot...

Lyssa had never felt *quite* like this before; like she was going to burn up. All she could think about was Allyson and the heat now raging within her. She knew, even without touching herself, she was ready. She could feel it, damp on her inner thighs as she stood and squirmed. With half-closed eyes, she watched the face of her lover. Ally's gaze was singularly focused on the rising line of cotton, her breathing suddenly as labored as Lyssa's.

And then she was revealed. As the material slid over Lyssa's hips, she could feel the intensity of Allyson's eyes as they stared, entranced by the sweet spot between Lyssa's soft thighs.

It was a look full of hunger. Desire was etched all over Allyson's features. A craving Lyssa *knew* her own face mirrored. She started to tremble.

What is *this I'm feeling?*

Her mind felt delirious, like she was having some form of out-of-body experience. She'd never felt so...alive. Never had she felt such a wanton desire as she was feeling right *now*. Every molecule of her being seemed to be aflame.

Lyssa pushed onward, almost as if on autopilot, pulling the shirt up across her stomach, sucking it in as she did so. She continued toward her breasts, acutely aware of how her nipples had hardened to aching diamonds, reveling in the erotic sensation of the soft fabric dragging slowly across them. With a final flourish, she pulled the garment up and over her head, feeling the cool air of the room on her body. Her impromptu striptease now complete.

Dropping the shirt to the floor, she shook out her long, now blonde, hair, and stood naked and vulnerable before her hybrid lover.

No apparel.

No jewelry.

Just Lyssa, as naked as the day she had been born.

She sucked in her tummy, pushing her breasts forward as she felt the weight of a sexual tension that seemed to have ratcheted up a thousandfold. Ally didn't move, save for the slow rhythmic motion of her thighs squirming and rubbing against each other. It seemed Lyssa's sexual disrobing had manifested the desired effect in her paramour, shoving aside the doubts, and stoking the fires of passion within her.

It was a raging inferno to which Lyssa found she was not immune. The heat between her own legs was becoming unbearable. She throbbed physically and intimately, feeling an impulsive need to be touched.

Reaching forward, she put her hands confidently on Allyson's shoulders while using her foot to nudge her ankles apart. Ally immediately obliged, parting her legs as she stayed seated. Lyssa looked into her lover's beautiful blue eyes, her dilated pupils beneath eyelids heavy with lust.

She gradually lowered herself, deliberately straddling Allyson's left leg. A tiny moan and a shudder rolled through her as her crotch made contact with silken thigh. She pushed down a little, pressing against it. Her hands gripped the delicate straps of lover's nightdress, wrapping them desperately in her fingers, almost as if those flimsy strands were a lifeline, the only things preventing her from drifting away into the blissful abyss.

Her body burned. She *knew* what she wanted. Leaning in, Lyssa pressed her lips firmly and hungrily against Allyson's. The kiss was all things at once. Soft, yet urgent. Playful, yet full of meaning. She felt Ally's tongue flit mischievously across the sharp points of her fangs, a subtle acknowledgment of who Lyssa was and her acceptance of that undeniable fact.

Allyson arched her back, pushing forward into Lyssa. As their upper bodies pressed against each other, Lyssa could feel the thin material of Ally's nightdress against her breasts, a mix of silk and lace, rubbing against her wildly sensitive nipples. As she squirmed, she realized Allyson was experiencing much the same sensation from her own hardened buds.

Now fully embracing Lyssa, Ally's hands tangled in her hair behind her back, pulling on it slightly. Lyssa couldn't help herself. Her body arched, taking on a mind of its own as she started to grind her hips in a deliberate back and forth motion, attempting to salve her erotic torment against Allyson's willing thigh. Her tempo increased gradually as her pleasure intensified.

Eyes closed, she pulled back from their kiss for a moment, yet stayed mere millimeters away from touching. She could feel Ally's hot breath on her lips.

"Can you feel that?" Lyssa heard herself whispering huskily. "How hot I am for you?"

Ally nodded, her breathing ragged as she squirmed on the wooden seat.

"I want you..." she panted. "Fuuuuck... I *want* you... You make me...want to touch you...want to feel you..."

"Touch me…" Ally whispered.

The offered invitation was gratefully accepted. Lyssa quickly slipped her right hand down between Allyson's thighs, feeling them part a little wider to allow her complete access. She opened her eyes a crack to find Ally's now closed as she gave a long guttural moan when searching fingers found her sensitive spot. With delicate strokes, Lyssa began to manipulate the slippery, sensitive nub of flesh, turning the moans of desire to a low mewling of wanton need.

"Please…" Allyson whispered. "Fuck… Please!"

Lyssa knew what Ally was pleading for. "Together," she growled, starting to grind harder onto her lover's leg.

The reciprocal motion was pulsing tiny ripples of pleasure up her spine in waves, and Lyssa could feel her orgasm building urgently. She mirrored the tempo of her thrusting hips with the movements of her fingers on Allyson's sex. A firm but gentle rubbing back and forth. It wasn't long before she felt Allyson's body start to tense and shudder. Her soft whimpers rapidly moving from lustful to needy.

They crested the peak.

Together.

"Oh, god…" Allyson moaned under her breath as her body began to convulse.

"Fuck…" Lyssa hissed as uncontrollable quakes ran rampant through her, too.

Her body was now a runaway train, any control she may have previously had was now a distant memory. The tempo of her hips took on a mind of their own, pushing harder, moving faster. Lyssa squeezed her eyes closed as the pleasure crested and her body stiffened, back arching. She withdrew her trembling fingers and wrapped her arms desperately around Ally, drawing her body in tightly against her own. The two of them clutched each other. She felt Allyson's fingernails digging gently into the soft flesh of her back as they both endured the rolling waves of pleasure in each other's grip. Her own fingers reciprocated the desperate grasping embrace.

Lips met once more. Tongues desperately seeking a shared intimacy as they moaned into each other's throats.

And then it was over.

Lyssa slumped forward, placing her head on her lover's shoulder. Exhausted. Allyson embraced her tightly as they each let their pounding hearts and ragged breathing slowly return to normal. She had no idea how long she remained like that. Time seemed to have lost all meaning.

She wished she could stay this way forever.

"Ow..." Ally groaned softly.

Ow?

Lyssa pulled away a little to look at her lover. She was horrified to see a trace of blood running from Allyson's lower lip. Her tongue flicked out to taste it. "Did you... Did you *bite* me?"

Oh, gods!!!

Lyssa's tongue flicked across her own teeth, finding her fangs extended, their razor-sharp points dangerously prominent.

"I...I am *so* sorry," she stammered. "I swear that's never happened before... I..."

"Shhh!" Ally smiled, breathing heavily from her exertion. "I'm fine. It's just a scratch, and probably my fault if I'm totally honest..."

Lyssa attempted to stand on wobbly legs. Then decided that was a bad idea and instead lowered herself to sit on the floor next to where Ally was still slumped in the chair looking slightly dazed. Her hand moved to her mouth, fingers running over her now retracted fangs.

What just happened? How did I lose control like that?

She leaned against Allyson's legs, resting her head on the thigh on which she'd had possibly the best orgasm of her life.

"I'm so sorry..." Ally said, sounding a little sheepish.

"Fuck... What the fuck are you apologizing for? That was..." Lyssa found there were no words other than... "wow! But...it's me who should apologize..."

She reached up to touch Ally's split lip, but her lover's hand intercepted hers en route and squeezed it tightly. Reassuringly.

"I told you. I think that was my fault you lost control. Sometimes... Well, sometimes I can't control my pheromone output, and it can…have unforeseen side effects.”

“*That's* what that was? *That* was your pheromones?” Lyssa exclaimed.

“Yeah. On occasion, I get so into the moment I can’t stop them. I’m told they enhance the sexual experience for my partner…”

“Oh, my gods, so *much* enhancement…”

Ally laughed lightly; a sound that made Lyssa smile happily. “You enjoyed it?”

“Fuck, yes. Don’t *ever* apologize for that! Holy crap…” Lyssa exhaled heavily, still returning to earth after her impromptu trip to the stars.

“As hybrids, we’re *always* unconsciously producing our unique pheromones to some degree. But I really try not to use them deliberately on people. It doesn’t seem…right. If you know what I mean. I hate to feel like I’ve manipulated someone to experience an emotion they otherwise might not.”

“Oh, don’t worry about that with me,” Lyssa giggled. “I have absolutely no objections to you doing that again.”

“Fine,” Ally laughed and slumped exhausted in her chair. “As long as you promise *me*…that if I *ever* bring the bisexual thing up again…you’ll also do that again. *Please*”

Suddenly a bolt of inspiration shot through Lyssa’s brain. “Pheromones… The bio-chip!” she squeaked. “Fuck!”

“What about it?” Ally said, her voice expressing her curiosity.

“It was the bomb trigger!”

Ally shook her head. “No, I’ve considered that already. The only Fae in the room were my mum and Narissa. Even if the bomb was set to trigger when it detected either of their pheromones, then it would have gone off much sooner. If you watch the video footage, Mercy brings the case in at the start of the conference and walks past both of them. No bang.

“The device was specifically triggered at the moment the case was handed to Sabadini by Mercy. Deliberately. If that chip was the trigger, then that means Mum or Narissa detonated it. There’s no way Mum would do that to Dad…and Narissa never struck me as a suicide bomber.”

"Okay, but..." Lyssa sat up straight. "You said pheromones are unique. Like a fingerprint."

"Yeah, so?"

"So, did the report say whether it was a generic detector, or was it looking for something specific? Can we determine the fingerprint that the chip was set to detect?"

"It didn't... But I still don't see how that helps us?"

"Because then we can link the chip to a specific person..." Lyssa sighed, and scratched her head. "I dunno. I just thought maybe..."

She glanced at Ally, expecting to see a dismissive look on her face, but instead she was staring intensely at the wall in front of her, focused on the bio-chip while nibbling on her thumbnail. The cogs were visibly whirring away behind her furrowed brow.

"Hold on..." she said slowly, "maybe you're on to something. I'm hitting a dead end on every avenue I go down, so this is definitely worth looking into. The only problem is..."

"It'll mean talking to your ex again?"

"Yeah, which will be awkward. We kind of agreed that maybe seeing each other was not a good idea."

"Maybe...send her an email this time?" Lyssa laughed.

| 57 |

DELIVERY

— **Becka Dawkins** —
— *Wednesday* — *Nassau, Bahamas* —

Nerves.

I haven't felt like this since my first time with...

She shoved the thought to the back of her mind. She didn't want to think about it. It was a bad memory, one that she had tried to forget over the years.

Becka took a deep breath, tugged a little at the snug leather catsuit she'd borrowed off Alexa, and closed her eyes for a moment to focus.

You are Rebecca Danger. Rebecca Danger. Danger is your name...

She mentally repeated the mantra for a few seconds before opening her eyes and pushing through the double doors to a familiar location. The reception area of the Fort Nassau Detainment Centre.

Striding toward the reception desk, while trying to promote a swagger she didn't truly feel, Becka smiled warmly as she approached Sergeant Anthony Rolle. He didn't know her face. They'd never met. Someone else had been manning the desk a couple of months earlier when they dropped off Ashraff. Still, there was a hint of paranoia within Becka that he would somehow see through her ruse.

He regarded her with suspicion. This wasn't the first time

a strange leather-clad woman had visited him in the middle of the night. The memory of just over a week ago was still pretty fresh in his mind. To be fair, being chased through a building by a tiger and pissing your pants on the roof wasn't something anyone was likely to forget anytime soon.

Still, Becka was now beginning to regret wearing one of Alexa's old combat catsuits as it was perhaps a little *too* familiar.

Just go with it, Becka. Can't change it now. Try and distinguish yourself somehow...

"Hey, handsome," she said with a flirtatious smile. "Is this the right place to be handing in my MercNet contract? Your guys have unloaded my bounty and taken her away, but I have to confess, I'm a virgin at this...and I'm not sure what to do next."

Despite her flirting and evident naivety, Rolle wasn't totally buying her act.

Not yet.

"Do you have your contract number?" he asked.

"I have the paperwork they gave me," Becka said placing the contract sheet and receipt paper on the desk in front of him.

He stared for a moment, before reaching slowly for them. She knew why. Ordinarily, this stuff was all done electronically, but while she was fairly confident her fake alter-ego would stand up to digital scrutiny, she was *less* sure about the rest of the details of her hastily constructed cover. With no history on her MercNet record, they had decided her best option was to act like a rookie who didn't understand the proper protocol yet.

"You don't have the *digital* transfer number?"

"It's not on there?" Becka asked, feigning innocence.

"No. This is the contract paperwork. You should have been sent the digital transfer number from MercNet when you accepted the case." Rolle sighed.

She could see his suspicion being slightly displaced by a sense of exasperation as he came to the realization her lack of apparent experience was going to lead to an increase in his workload. He flicked through the paperwork and tapped her MercNet identification number into his computer. A moment later he looked up at her with a frown.

"Danger? Rebecca *Danger*?"

Okay, so now I wish I'd gone with a more ordinary name...

Hearing her alter ego spoken out loud by the Sergeant made Becka visibly cringe.

Fuck it! Roll with it, Becka!

"Yeah, I know," she said, averting her eyes from his. "It's *not* my real name. I chose it for my MercNet name because I thought it would sound cool. But now that I hear it out loud..."

To her amazement, Rolle smiled at her. "Well, it does sound *pretty* bad-ass," he laughed. "I'll give you that."

"So, you don't think I should change it?" she grinned back at him.

He shrugged. "Maybe you could make a reputation for yourself under this name. It's certainly a name you're not likely to forget in a hurry."

What had been an ill-conceived joke was turning out to be the chisel to chip through his defenses. Slowly, his suspicions were fading away, and he was now actively reciprocating her flirtation.

Excellent. I can use that to my advantage.

"Do you have your FSE receipt slip?" Rolle asked her, referring to the documentation she had been given by the ground crew when they had unloaded the Sayona off *Diana* and taken her to the holding cells.

"Is this what you're looking for?" Becka asked as she handed over the paperwork she knew full well he wanted.

He nodded as he received it.

A flicker of something passed over his features as he noticed which contract she had delivered. If their positions were reversed, Becka would have seen a late-night visit from a stranger passing an *obvious* alter-ego while serving up *exactly* the bounty he was waiting for as a reason to be even more suspicious...

Evidently, all Sergeant Rolle saw was a pretty young girl and a boatload of cash.

Thank God for simple and shallow men!

"Yes, this is it. So, you bagged a Sayona. Can't say we've seen one of these here before."

"They're pretty rare," Becka nodded. "That's what drew me to it. Plus, I figured it wouldn't be too hard for my first time out. Boy, was I *wrong* about that!"

Rolle chuckled as he tapped the touchscreen computer, probably inputting the details of Becka's claim, though she couldn't see the screen to know for sure.

"Tough hunt?"

"Yeah, not my finest performance."

"How so?"

Becka leaned across the desk toward him, lowering her voice to a conspiratorial whisper. "You promise you won't say a word to anyone...Sergeant Rolle?"

"Call me Anthony, please." His voice dropped in tone as he answered. "I promise your secret is safe."

She beckoned for him to lean closer, putting her hand on his shoulder as he leaned in. As he closed the gap between them, she could smell the faint, but unsurprising, aroma of alcohol on his breath.

"Well, Anthony, I decided to stake out a local bar, see if I could spot her picking up a local to feed on. That part of the plan worked like a charm. But when I confronted her, she ran. Jeez, she's fast! Faster than me, anyhow."

"How'd you catch it?"

Becka shrugged. "By accident."

She gestured up to the shoulder of her borrowed catsuit. This was the one Alexa had worn to chase Ashraff through the streets of Havana, the one she had torn through the shoulders of when jumping through a glass window. It had been stitched back together but the damage was still evident.

"She was running through this rundown lumberjacking village northwest of the town. Loads of blind alleys to hide in. I couldn't keep up, so I figured I'd climb onto the rooftops and run more directly, jumping from roof to roof..."

"Smart..." he said, smiling and backing away from her a little so he could carry on filling in the electronic forms on the computer. "Do you have the account details for your payment transfer?"

"Yeah, of course. I can enter them if it's quicker?"

"Sure," he said and spun the screen around for her to punch in the details.

With a few deft strokes of her fingertips, she entered the credentials for her and Alexa's MercNet account and, before the Sergeant could see, hit the transfer button.

"Whoops," she said, feigning innocence. "I don't think I should have hit that button…"

Rolle smiled and shrugged. "That's okay. I'd already put in the amount. As long as you're sure that was your account—"

"I'm sure."

"—then no harm done. If you'd accidentally sent it to the wrong account…well, then we'd have a problem."

"No, I'm sure that was the right one." Becka nodded.

"So, how'd you get it? The Sayona. You said it was an accident?"

Becka laughed. "Yeah, so, I'm running and jumping from roof to roof, trying to keep up with her. Then suddenly I land on a roof and it collapses! The rusty tin slices my shoulder, and I'm a bloody and bruised heap on the floor of this hut.

"But, as luck would have it, it's the same shed the Sayona is hiding in. And I've fallen on top of her, knocking her out cold!"

Rolle laughed and shook his head. "What are the chances?"

"I know, right?" Becka chuckled, shaking her head. "Anyway, I trussed her up, dragged her to my ship, and brought her here as it said to on the warrant."

Rolle tapped a few more keys, finishing the transfer before looking up and smiling at her. "There. All done." He paused for a moment before carrying on. "I don't know if you're sticking around in Nassau for a while, but I get off shift in a couple of hours, and…"

Becka feigned her best 'disappointed face' and tried to adopt an apologetic tone. "I'm sorry, Anthony. I have to get back to my ship and head home."

"Where's home?"

"Can't you guess by the accent?" Becka smiled.

"You're a Brit?"

Becka nodded. "I wouldn't normally have ventured this far, but that Sayona *really* intrigued me."

"Ah," Rolle said, disappointedly.

"Hey, you never know. I might be back again. Never say never, right?" She watched his face brighten a little. "Maybe we could do something next time I'm in town?"

"Yeah, I'd like that."

"Then, Sergeant Anthony Rolle, I'll see you next time!"

He nodded, and then laughed again. "Till next time, Miss Danger!"

She was outside the building, the doors swinging closed behind her as she headed out into the night when she heard Alexa's voice over comms in her ear. "That...was fucking awesome! Good job, Becks!"

"Thanks. The bug is planted and live, too," she replied quietly. "Now...we wait."

She strolled back toward *Diana* with a smile on her face and a spring in her step.

I knew I could do this! Fuck you, Gayle Knightley!

| **58** |

CRAZY FOR YOU

— **Michael Reynolds** —
— *Friday* — *London, England* —

"You look...real pretty." He stumbled over the compliment a little.

His declaration had been intended to defuse the tension, but from the look on Gayle's face, it may have had the converse effect. It wasn't that he didn't mean it, quite the contrary. It was simply that being here—in this formal restaurant setting—had dragged both of them far outside their comfort zones. Since placing their orders with the waitress, an awkwardness had settled upon them.

"I... Thanks," she said nervously. "I wasn't sure if I should... I mean...it's been a *long* time since I've..."

"Been on a date?" he asked, confident those were the words she was searching for.

At least he seemed to have chosen the ideal restaurant.

It was quiet in here; just themselves and another couple sitting a few tables over. There was music playing softly, an ambient soundtrack of old love songs. Nothing Michael explicitly recognized. Tunes from the 80s or 90s if he were to hazard a guess.

"Yeah. A date," Gayle leaned in, whispering. "I mean, it *feels* like a date."

Michael mimicked her action and hushed tone. "That's be-cause...this *is* a date."

Gayle rolled her eyes. "I know, but... We've already been doing this dance for weeks, so I wasn't sure if I should dress up... Or down."

She had paired a long black turtle-neck sweater over snow-colored jeans with boot-fit bottoms. A pair of white high-heeled boots that boosted her height close to his com-pleted the outfit. The monochrome nature of the ensemble was the ideal juxtaposition to her candy-floss hair that was unfettered tonight, falling loosely across her shoulders.

Dunno why she's frettin'.

"You look perfect to me," he said, this time without hesi-tation.

She smiled bashfully as she tucked a loose strand of hair behind her ear, biting her lip in a manner Michael found ador-able.

"Really? I'm thinking maybe I should have gone with the former..."

Michael shook his head. "I think we're well past trying to impress each other. Don't you?"

"Then why did *you* come suited and booted?" she replied with an upward tilt of her eyebrow.

Michael shrugged. "I figured you'd like to see me out of my fatigues."

Gayle burst out laughing causing Michael to replay his last statement in his head, joining her laughter as he realized what he'd said. As the amusement faded, the awkwardness returned. He could see she was mentally wrestling with some-thing.

After a moment, she spoke softly. "I'm sorry about 'the dance'—"

"Don't be," he interrupted. "It's not your fault. You've had a rough time lately."

"No," she disagreed. "It's more...*fundamental* than that. Dating is... I mean... I don't know how to do the dating thing. It's a skill I never learned. Fucking, yes. Dating...no." She blushed and went quiet, avoiding eye contact while staring at the glass of water in her hand.

He knew what she was thinking. *'Why did I just refer to fucking as a learned skill? On a first date!'* Michael decided to try and defuse the moment with a little humor.

"Funny, I didn't catch that talent listed when I was browsing your file..."

Gayle closed her eyes and shook her head. There *was* a smile on her lips, though. "Can we change the subject *away* from my sexual CV, please? Before I start to ask *you* about yours!"

Their food arrived, putting a brief pin in their conversation. Gayle poured herself another glass of water from the decanter and took a sip. As the waitress left, Gayle tilted her head and looked at him.

"So, how about you? Dated much?"

"No. Not for a while." He paused to cut a sliver off his steak, placing it into his mouth and savoring the taste before continuing. "There wasn't much time for romance in the Marines, so all this..." he gestured with his now empty fork, "is pretty new to me, too."

"Really?" Gayle looked thoughtful for a moment. "Well, *this* is an excellent start. I thought I knew all the best restaurants in London, but I've never been here. How'd *you* find this place?"

"I had help," he admitted.

Gayle was sampling her fish, which seemed to agree with her. She was chewing her second mouthful as she mumbled her question. "Lana?"

"And Amanda." Michael nodded as he inserted more steak into his mouth.

"Wow," Gayle grinned. "You pulled out *all* the stops for this one. I'm honored."

"No," he corrected her. "You're *teasing*."

"A little." She narrowed her eyes at him. "Are you telling me you don't like a little teasing?"

Is she flirting with me?

"I can stand a little teasing."

"Good to know."

Gayle popped another fork of fish into her mouth as Michael took the knife to his steak again. She chewed thoughtfully for a moment before tilting her head and pointing her knife at him. "So, playful banter aside, I want to ask you something…"

"Anything."

"Are you sure? Because the last time I asked this specific question, you dodged it and said it was a story for another time…"

"Ah, the 'Have I ever been in love?' question?"

Gayle nodded.

He shrugged. "Well, I thought etiquette on dates was to not talk about former relationships?"

"Normally true," she agreed. "But I've been thinking about it since tequila night. What could have been *so* traumatic that you refuse to talk about it?"

"It's a long story…"

"Do I look like I'm in a rush for tonight to end? I haven't finished my fish yet," she laughed. "And fair warning—I'm expecting a *spectacular* dessert course."

"And here I was hoping you were a cheap date."

"Hey," Gayle said in mock protest. "Think of the money I'm saving you by just drinking water!"

"I noticed." His quick reply caused Gayle to glance down at her plate sheepishly, her fork playing with the last portion of her fish. The memory of her well-intentioned deceit on tequila night *had* been put behind them, yet it was still too recent to be totally forgotten.

Do something, Michael, you idiot! Fix this!

The real reason he didn't want to tell this story was that it didn't show him in a particularly good light. Gayle previously voiced her aspirations to live up to his example and that misguided sentiment seemed to be working for her. Maybe, it was time to balance the scales a little.

"So…" he began, "I was reluctant to share because… I'm not proud of what I did. I wasn't ready for you to think badly of me."

"Oh, Michael Reynolds." Gayle frowned. "Did you *really*

think I believed you were perfect?"

"Yeah, I kinda did."

"I'm twenty-eight, not eight," Gayle laughed. "I understand *nobody* is perfect. You've had a peek under my hood, so to speak, and you know the mess that awaits. I'm flawed as fuck, but you still like me enough to bring me to a fancy restaurant to get into my knickers."

"That's not why—"

Gayle burst into more laughter and cut him off with a wave of the hand. "I'm kidding! Listen, we *all* have things in our past we're not proud of. Everyone. Life happens, and in those moments, we all handle our shit as best we can. Sometimes we do things other people might disagree with or view unkindly. You show me someone who hasn't got some form of fucked up relationship in their past and I'll show you a bloody liar."

She had a point.

He took a deep breath. "Seven years ago, I got injured on the San Andreas front. A Vampyrii soldier slashed my leg, slicing ligaments. I spent nine months in a Honolulu hospital getting it surgically repaired and rehabbed. It was a...frustrating experience."

"I can empathize," Gayle murmured.

"As I started to get more mobile, one of the rehab nurses suggested I run on the beaches. Without tourism, they were pretty quiet, so I took her advice. The sea, the sand, and the fresh air. It was a good idea. I'd been doing it for a week or so when I spotted her."

"Who? The nurse?"

Michael nodded. "Yeah. I didn't recognize her initially. She was coming out of the sea. Long brown hair, perfect sun-kissed skin, little black bikini—"

"Okay, I'm not sure I want to hear this story of unblemished scantily-clad beauties emerging sexily from the ocean waves..." Gayle raised an eyebrow. "It's making my pale-skinned, scarred ass feel decidedly inferior."

She was joking, of course, but he could sense the undercurrent of insecurity contained within her reply.

"You *more* than hold your own. Trust me," he said, which brought a blush to her cheeks. "Plus...all was not as it seemed."

"Ah, a *mystery* woman! Fair enough, tell me more."

He chuckled. "I will if you'll let me finish! Anyhow, I ran on, telling myself she was just another pretty girl on a beach. But I *couldn't* get her outta my head. Next day, she was there again. Same exact place."

"Did you stop this time?"

Michael shook his head. "Nope. Ran past again. But every morning she'd be there, smiling at me as I jogged past."

"How long before you got the hint?"

"Two weeks...that's when I finally recognized her. When I thought she was a pretty stranger, there was no way I was going to stop. I was pretty inexperienced with women back then and had no idea how to approach one. Let alone one that looked like Mililani."

"Beautiful name. Don't Hawaiian names have meanings?"

Michael nodded, feeling his face warm subtly. "I looked it up on NewNet once. Translated to 'heavenly caress' or something along those lines..."

Suddenly Gayle dropped her fork onto her plate with a clatter and stared wide-eyed at Michael. "Holeeeey *fuck*!" she whispered. "Heavenly caress... She was your 'first,' wasn't she? Mililani *deflowered* the great and noble, Michael Reynolds."

She laughed lightly, and he knew she was teasing him. He also knew that she would be expecting him to join her in the amusement, but he couldn't. It struck too close to home for him to find it funny.

She noticed his neutral expression and as her chuckles faded, her eyes widened even further. Her hand flew to her mouth, and a fleeting look of mortification crossed her features. "Oh, shit... Oh, fuck. This story is about *that* moment, isn't it? This is the thing you're ashamed of?" Gayle seemed to have an uncanny instinct for making absurdly accurate leaps of cognitive reasoning.

"We'd been dating for maybe three months, and I'd been

extremely...gentlemanly."

"Three months?!" Gayle squeaked. "Without shagging?"

"Are you going to let me finish?"

"Oh, God, I'm sorry." Gayle winced. "I honestly didn't mean to make light of it. It's just... I mean, you're so..."

He wasn't entirely sure what she was getting at, and as she stumbled over her words her skin flushed slightly.

"I'm sorry," she said after a moment. "Please...continue."

Michael took a deep breath and did just that. "So, eventually I realized there was no dodging the fact that sooner or later...we were going to have to have...relations. It's not like I was saving myself or anything. But I'd never been with a woman before. I was nervous. I figured a woman like *her* would have had strings of partners before little ol' me."

Now Gayle was beginning to look uncomfortable as she forked the last of her fish into her mouth. She chewed for a moment.

"Would that be a problem?" she muttered after swallowing.

Interesting...

She spoke in a future tense, rather than a past one. Would...not was. Referring to herself maybe?

"No. Not now," he shrugged. "But back then I was intimidated by her. The longer I put it off, the worse it got. I didn't want to be a disappointment."

"Was it disappointing?"

"No. It was amazing."

"You rocked her world?"

"You could say that."

"So, what's the problem?" Gayle said, her brow furrowed in confusion. Sounds like you lost your virginity like a champ... But this story isn't about your first time, is it?"

Michael shook his head. "No. It's about what came next."

He paused to organize his thoughts and looked across the table at his date. Gayle's eyes met his as she nodded very slightly, encouraging him to carry on with his tale.

"Whatever it is," she said softly. "You can tell me."

"Living in the NAA is *not* like living in Europa," he sighed.

"We're a displaced population. Xenophobia seeped into the core of our culture. If it was different. It was the enemy."

"You don't strike me as a raging xenophobe." Gayle frowned. "I'm half-Fae and you're sitting here having dinner with me. You're teaching a class full of mixed heritage kids."

"Alexa and I were raised by liberal parents to be tolerant of people. When we were kids, we didn't care about things like race, gender, sexuality... But after years without their influence and surrounded by that kind of vitriol, it rubs off on you without you even noticing. I'm different now," he said with a heavy sigh. "But back then...I was an asshole."

"I'm not sure that's even possible," Gayle smiled kindly.

"Oh, believe me, it's possible, and it manifested itself in a mighty ugly way when I found out Mililani wasn't human."

"What was she?"

"She lived in this small house off the beach. White with a turquoise roof. It was in the perfect spot to see the sunrise and catch the waves for some early morning surfing. One morning I decided to pay her a surprise visit. I knocked on the door, but there was no answer. I knew Mililani could be a bit of a bed jockey, so I let myself in, calling her name as I headed toward the bedroom."

He paused, his throat dry as the memory conjured vivid images of that morning in his mind. He took a sip of his light beer and licked his lips to wet them before continuing.

"When I entered, all I saw was this huge lizard. Scaly, black, like a Komodo dragon. I'm not sure who was more shocked, me or Mililani."

"She was there?"

"She was the *lizard*."

"Oh, shit..." he watched the cogs turn in Gayle's head as she figured it out. "She was a Mo'o?"

He nodded.

"Fuck me." She sat back in her chair looking shocked. "I always wanted to see one. I remember studying them at the Academy. Water spirits; shapeshifters. Oh...folklore said they often took the form of a female seductress."

"Yup. I fell in love with a Hawaiian water deity."

"What did you do?"

"I tried to shoot her."

"*Shoot* her?"

"In my defense, I thought my girlfriend had been eaten by a giant black lizard. I drew my gun and took a shot. Fortunately, I missed, allowing her to shift back to her human form."

He paused as the waitress cleared the main course away and delivered their pre-ordered desserts. A thick wedge of New York-style cheesecake for Gayle and a slab of apple crumble with ice cream for him. As they started to tuck into the food, Gayle prompted him to continue his tale.

"Doesn't sound all bad so far. At least you didn't kill her."

"No, I did something worse. I broke her heart. I couldn't accept the fact that she was...different. I tried, but whenever I was with her, all I could see was the lizard. Was she the beast or woman? How could I love someone when I didn't know what they were? Their true nature.

"It was a week before Mililani confronted me about it. She said I *knew* her. She was the woman I fell in love with. What did it matter *what* she was when I knew her heart?

"She was right, of course, but I was too blind to see it. I broke it off and walked away. I could hear her sobbing, begging me to turn around and come back, to give us a chance. But I carried on walking. Never looking back.

"As I said... Asshole. Stupid, prejudiced asshole."

"Okay, maybe not your finest hour," Gayle admitted between forks of cheesecake. "But you were young, and the situation was...well, how is anyone supposed to react to that? And, as I said, none of that dovetails with the man I know today. The man sitting across from me."

"I'm different now. Changed. I understand what Mililani was feeling. Even back then I felt...conflicted. Like I was railing against my upbringing. But I wasn't a big enough man to push past my pride and go and see her again. To make amends and reconcile. Then orders came through for Operation: Homeland. Before I knew it, I was off fightin' to re-take the West Coast from the Vampyrii. I never set foot on Hawaii again."

Gayle slid her hand across the table to cover his. "You know...after the buildup, I was expecting worse." Gayle smiled warmly and took another mouthful of dessert. She looked thoughtful for a moment as she chewed slowly on the cheesecake.

"You ever wonder?" she asked. "What happened to her?"

"I used to. I haven't for a while. Honestly, I don't like to. It feels..." He trailed off, not wanting to complete that particular line of thought. "She was the *first* woman I ever fell in love with and, when push came to shove, I couldn't accept her for who she truly was. My folks would have been so disappointed in me. *I* was disappointed in me."

"We all make mistakes, Michael," Gayle said softly as she squeezed his hand. "I should know. I've made more than most. Don't beat yourself up over something that happened so long ago."

Both of them ate in silence for a minute or two, each buried in their thoughts. Michael glanced across at Gayle who was staring at her cheesecake. Her demeanor had shifted a little, and he could tell that something was on her mind.

What's she thinking about? Dammit, I knew telling that story was a bad idea!

"Are you okay?" he asked, reaching across the table to cover her hand.

Her eyes flicked up toward him. "Yeah, I'm good," she lied.

"Did my...confession change your view of me?" he asked.

Gayle blinked at him, her eyes suddenly wide. "Fuck, no! No. Not at all. I... I'm glad you opened up to me. Really."

"So, why the distracted look?"

Now it was her turn to search for a way to convey what was bugging her. Michael recognized the signs of a person looking for a good way to bring up a tricky subject. Her fork was playing with the last piece of cheesecake on her plate, pushing it around distractedly.

"Okay..." she eventually said. "So, you said Mililani was your first, but you *have* been with other women since, right?"

Michael laughed. "A few."

Gayle pursed her lips. "Define a few."

"You seriously wanna compare numbers?"

She nodded. "How many people have you slept with?"

"Six," he answered immediately. "How many *people* have you slept with?"

"Women or men?" Gayle said matter-of-factly.

"You have *both* on your list?"

Gayle shrugged and nodded.

"I'm sorry I assumed you were...you know...straight."

"Oh, I am." Gayle smiled nervously. "Men do it for me...if you know what I mean. The women were really just...a means to an end."

"I'm not sure I want to know what that means."

"I wouldn't think about it too hard."

"So, how many then?"

Gayle paused for a moment and her eyes flickered upward while she mentally did the calculations necessary to answer his question. Finally, she grimaced slightly as she looked at him.

"Men... maybe in the mid-thirties." She paused to gauge the look on his face. "Women, definitely only seven."

"Shit!" was all Michael could say as he slumped back in his seat.

"Okay, now I thought you might react like that, but Michael... I need you to understand the context of all that sex." Gayle scratched her head and bit her lip, evidently wondering how to explain away her promiscuity.

He watched as she spooned the last mouthful of her cheesecake into her mouth, her tongue flicking out quickly to catch the errant drop of cream on her top lip. All at once, she was a million miles away from the Gayle he had met two months ago. He hadn't known if he could work with that woman, but the one sat across from him now was someone he *wanted* to be close to.

He closed his eyes, taking a deep breath. The air was filled with the scents of food and her sweet fragrance of honey. The music in the restaurant had a slow rhythm.

"Dance with me."

"Here?" she laughed. "In the restaurant?"

He nodded. "Why not?"

"Because...it's a *restaurant*."

"And?"

She looked at him with a furrowed brow of confusion as if to ask why he needed a second reason. "And..." She paused for a moment. "Because I don't dance."

Michael wasn't taking no for an answer. He rose from his seat, offering her his hand. Gayle looked around at the other diners, hesitating.

"Fuck, no," she said eventually with a nervous laugh.

"Are you scared?"

She threw him a look that implied he was crazy for stating such an absurdity before taking his hand firmly. She stood, pulling him to the small, clear area near the table, and placed her arms around his neck.

"Do I look scared *now*?"

Michael shook his head as they began to sway slowly in time to the tempo of the music. Gayle rested her head against his chest as if she were listening to the rhythm of his rapidly beating heart. The words to the song drifted to his ears...

Coming from Gayle.

Her voice joined the singers in perfect, beautiful harmony. She tilted her head up to look at him, continuing to quietly sing. The restaurant faded into a fuzzy grey background, and all Michael could focus on was the vivid green of her eyes and the vibrant pink of her hair. It was like a blanket of fog had filled the room and all he could see was her.

For the briefest moment, he wondered whether this was her doing. She had promised she would never use her phero-mones on him again, but as her lips moved to the words of the song and she pressed herself closer against him, he started to feel something he hadn't felt before. Her right arm slowly re-tracted, her fingertips drifting across the skin of his neck, stroking his cheek tenderly. At that moment he realized the influence she was wielding on him was free of her chemical persuasion.

It was simply the zenith of a journey they started two

months ago.

He felt her breath hot on his lips as she gently urged his head down toward her. He instinctively recognized where all this was leading and trusted his heart knew what it was doing. All he knew was that, in this moment, her touch was electric. He wanted her more than he had ever wanted anyone before. A sensation he couldn't explain with words.

But there *were* other ways to communicate exactly how he felt.

He leaned in.

Their lips touched.

This time it was no accident. Everything he wanted her to know about how he felt was there in his kiss.

| 59 |

NAKED

— Gayle Knightley —
— Friday — London, England —

Promiscuous.

That was the term.

Gayle had lost count of the number of times she had engaged in sex with a willing partner. For that matter, she had also lost count of the number of willing partners she had engaged in sex *with*. The number she'd given Michael was nothing more than a guesstimate. Not that it mattered. Her vast experience had, mistakenly, led her to the conclusion that when it came to sex, there was nothing left for her to learn. Every position had been tried, every kink explored.

I couldn't be more wrong.

Gayle Knightley had never, *ever*, felt like this before.

The fantasies started the day of her accident in the park. She wasn't a woman who needed rescuing, but rarely had she been so vulnerable as she was that day. Michael had been her white knight. Since then, her thoughts as she lay alone in her bed were filled with visions of erotic intimacy with him. Visions that led to many a breathless conclusion as her own hands played out his imagined actions.

Yet they were *nothing* compared to reality.

In the twilight of her bedroom, he slowly drew her sweater

over her head, exposing her neck and chest. Where his fingertips led, his lips followed. The gentlest of touches and soft lips laying a trail of red-hot markers. A nuzzling kiss that started behind her earlobe left her breathless and tingling before moving leisurely down her impatient neck.

She could hear the low growl in her throat as her suppressed need took hold. His eager mouth reached heaving breasts and she squirmed deliciously. A heat built deep within her which intensified as his mouth moved further south, laying hot kisses on the smooth flesh of her tummy, heading toward the waistband of her jeans.

How is he doing this? How can I be so close to losing my fucking mind so early in the game?

Except...this wasn't a game, was it?

This wasn't sex for recreation. This wasn't a means to an end.

This was something else entirely.

A shiny new experience.

His mouth teased the top button of her jeans open as his hands lay flat on the flesh of her stomach. She started trembling uncontrollably as they slid sedately upward beneath her bra, pushing it up and over her tender breasts. She arched, pressing herself against his hands, reveling in the sensation of her sensitive nipples against his palms.

Her legs felt weak. Her mind was spinning. How could she be in this state? His hands were on her heaving bosom and his hot breath on her tummy, inches from the raging inferno between her thighs.

They were about to cross a line, one that would change everything. She felt more vulnerable now than she had that day in the park.

He stood slowly, his fingers nimbly unclipping the front of her bra and letting it open, leaving her exposed to his eyes. She felt out of control, and a flutter of fear spread through her. What was left of her rational mind tried to calm her. This wasn't like before. This wasn't addiction; this was something purer.

She could feel it.

His hand wrapped itself in her hair, as hers grasped at his neck. He urged her face toward his. She pulled him toward her, groaning with a need to feel his lips on hers. They met halfway and devoured each other fervently. The kiss was tender yet also so raw and passionate. She responded in kind, her tongue probing his mouth as her trembling hands pulled at his shirt, clumsily unbuttoning it. Finally, she pressed her naked skin against his. Melting into him, losing herself to the sensation of his chest hair against her sensitive peaks.

There were no words; neither wanted to come up for air long enough to speak. Her body was on fire, sweat beading across her skin despite the coolness of the autumn night. His hand moved to tug at the button-fly of her jeans, popping enough buttons to allow them to slide easily over her hips. Their mouths parted as he crouched to push the denim down over her thighs. For a second, she cringed as they passed beyond her surgically repaired knee and its scars, but her fear evaporated as she felt his lips tenderly lay a trail of torrid kisses across the joint before moving upward to her trembling naked thighs.

She felt his hot breath on the crotch of her knickers. Heard him inhale deeply and plant the gentlest of kisses onto the perfect point of the delicate silken fabric. She gasped in pleasure, her mind lost as it whirled with the possibilities of feeling his mouth on her most intimate spot when that final barrier was finally removed.

Her hands were on his head, pulling him into her as he toyed gently with her. He kissed her repeatedly on her mound as she sighed and gyrated slowly. His hands slid up her hips and beneath the side of her knickers, pushing them upward.

Wrong way!

But then she felt what he was doing and sensation kidnapped any remaining rational thoughts. As he gently but firmly applied pressure, the crotch started to pull upward insistently between her legs. Parting her. Pressing into her in the most erotic way imaginable. She couldn't restrain herself from bucking and writhing as a mini-orgasm shuddered through her, a precursor for what was to come.

She started to feel her mind slip further away into the moment, struggling to register anything but his hands, his lips, his touch, his breath... It felt like her body had been transformed into one enormous erogenous zone, sensations flooding her from all directions. Diamond-hard nipples, sensitive breasts, and the throbbing between her thighs...every *inch* of her body seemingly programmed to drive her upward to ever higher planes of pleasure.

How is this possible?

The world tilted, and she realized Michael was easing her backward onto the bed, gently laying her on the cotton sheets. He pulled at that final piece of clothing, leisurely sliding them down her thighs, far slower than Gayle would have preferred in her impatience, but perfect in the moment. As soon as they were near her ankles, she urgently kicked them off herself, along with her jeans and her boots, and spread herself apart for him, exposing her naked desire and inviting him to explore her.

As he stood and slowly removed his remaining clothes, Gayle played her right hand between her legs as her left caressed the skin of her breasts, teasing herself with feather-light touches. She arched and moaned, biting her lip as her lust burned hotter, aided by the sight of Michael, naked and ready in front of her. She wanted...no, she *needed* him inside her.

Right fucking now!

He, however, was in no rush and had other wicked ideas. He knelt on the bed between her legs, smiling as his face descended toward her crotch.

Oh. My. God!

His lips met hers again, and his tongue tenderly drew casual patterns of desire on her most sensitive flesh, making her bow in sheer unadulterated pleasure. She felt his probing fingers, and his tongue pushing inside her, tasting her. She whimpered unintelligibly as every muscle in her body spasmed uncontrollably through a series of leg-trembling, back-arching orgasms that engulfed her. She lost count of how many times pleasure took away her rational thought.

Her ardor now had a mind of its own. She could feel it. Her body wanted more...craving that last intimate connection. She *needed* to feel him inside her, connected to her. But first, she wanted to do something for him, to repay in kind the pleasure he had just given her. She would be damned if she was going to be a passive partner in all this. She pushed him gently away and sat up quickly, grabbing him and urging him to lie on the bed beside her. With the touch of his mouth and his hands, he had made her body tremble and gifted her at least a half dozen orgasms already.

With just a touch!

She straddled his naked body, feeling her crotch press against his thigh. Closing her eyes, she forced herself not to grind on him for her gratification. Her lips kissed his chest, hot and wet, leaving a trail of passion as she progressed lower. Across his stomach, moving toward her ultimate destination.

It was time to return the favor.

Her tongue flicked out delicately, tasting him. She parted her lips and moved her head, taking him into her mouth and slowly sliding him deeper. She heard him growl, and she smiled. This was something she was *very* good at, and she knew it. His hands tangled in her hair, and his breathing became ragged as she rhythmically fucked him with her throat. She used her tongue to circle his head with each thrust, caressing him on every leisurely stroke. He twitched inside her mouth as he approached the inevitable conclusion to her ministrations. She could already taste it. He tried to gently pull her off of him before that moment came, but she held on. No *way* she was letting go.

She tilted her head up at him, her green eyes signaling to him her permission. He had tasted her, now she wanted to savor him. She had surrendered her body to him, now she wanted to feel that same moment of release. This wasn't a game or a power trip. This was something she had never experienced before, something on which she couldn't put her finger in her current state of mind.

His body stiffened. He cursed and gave a long low groan. She felt him tighten in her mouth as she milked him for every last drop. She watched his face contort with pleasure, his eyes rolling back, and she grinned to herself. When he was finished, she finally let him slip from her mouth and coyly flicked her tongue over her lips to catch any love that had escaped her.

Now, it was time.

It didn't take long to get him ready again. She slid her body up against his, lying next to him, her legs straddling and grinding against his thigh as her hand worked gently but diligently to urge him back to attention. Their lips met passionately. This time she could taste herself on him. Could he taste himself on her? The thought made her even hornier.

Finally, he was ready, rigid once more in her hand.

"I want you...inside me," she whispered breathily between kisses.

Michael simply nodded.

She slid across his body, positioning herself to accept him. She closed her eyes as she felt him. So close. A hesitation...then she committed herself. Pushing back as she felt him slide deeply into her. Gayle didn't move, holding position. Her body trembled uncontrollably. Something was wrong.

Sex didn't feel like this.

Sex *never* felt like this.

The Fae in her blood had driven her to treat procreation as a hobby. A tool. She'd fucked and been fucked more times than she could count. She'd fucked friends, enemies, and strangers. She'd fucked sober and drunk. She thought she'd experienced every type of fucking there could possibly be. But this... This was new.

She felt tears on her cheeks.

Nothing prepared her for how this would feel.

The edges of the world faded to black. She could feel him inside her, keeping so still, not rushing her or forcing himself on her. Her breathing quickened, her lips trembled, and her eyes widened as she felt the panic rise from deep within her. What *was* this? It had been almost a year. Was this simply pent-up lust? Or was this the return of something she had been striving to give up?

Is this what an alcoholic feels like when they fall off the wagon?

Her eyes met his. Those kind eyes in that handsome face with those beautiful lips. He smiled.

"It's okay," he said softly. "It's okay."

She nodded and started to move, grinding her hips in a tempo he reciprocated. They both picked up the pace, each stroke coming faster and faster.

"Fuck me," she growled.

He flipped her over onto her back, and now he was in control. Between her legs, he fucked her faster, harder. Her orgasm was building. No, not just building. This was coming at her like a runaway train. Exhilarating and scary at the same time. There was no way to stop it, and she truly didn't want to. She wrapped her legs around him tightly, urging him deeper, faster. Her nails clawed at the skin of his back, and she buried her face in his shoulder as she whimpered and moaned, thanking God for what she was receiving.

Nothing else mattered. She felt nothing but his flesh on hers, inside hers.

Nothing.

Not even the sheets of the bed. It was like she was flying.

And then it hit her. An orgasm like none she had ever had in her life. She came hard and out of control. Her body thrashed and writhed as they arrived together with perfect timing. She was floating on a cloud of pure ecstasy. Her mind was white light, pure pleasure, and consumed by two pertinent questions.

Is this what love feels like?

And why am I bumping my head on the light fitting?

| 60 |

WHAT THE FUCK!?

— **Allyson Knightley** —
— *Saturday* — *London, England* —

First, it was the doorbell, which she duly ignored.

Then there was the knocking, which started out subtle, but progressively became louder and more urgent the longer Allyson ignored that, too.

Finally, her cellphone vibrated merrily on the bedside table, insistent to gain her attention.

Reluctantly, she dragged herself away from what she was doing and picked it up. Squinting in the semi-darkness at the bright screen, she made out her sister's image just as the call rang off.

Her first thought was mildly curious.

What does Gayle want at this time of night?

The distinctive sound of keys rattling in the front door triggered her second, more panicked, thought.

Oh, fuck!

She heard her door open, close, and then the rapid approach of her sister's footsteps up the stairs.

Ally was in the process of jumping up off the bed when the bedroom door burst open to admit her frantic sibling.

"Ally-I-need-to-talk-to-you!" Gayle's mouth was moving so fast her sentence sounded like one confusing compound word. "Where's the fucking light switch...?"

"Gayle, no, don't..." Allyson started to protest but was too late to prevent the room from being brightly illuminated by the flick of a switch.

The next words were all said in unison.

"What the fuck!" exclaimed Gayle in shock.

"What the fuck!" exclaimed a naked Allyson in anger.

"Hi," said Lyssa in a small voice from where she was lying handcuffed nude to the headboard, squinting and desperately trying to pull her knees up to cover her modesty.

The next few seconds seemed to stretch into eternity for Allyson as the three of them regarded each other. Gayle's eyes flicked between Allyson and her Vampyrii lover. Evidently, words failed her as the only thing she seemed capable of was mouthing was 'What the fuck?' again, only much more slowly as her eyes gradually widened.

Ally abruptly realized her current nakedness and grabbed for her robe which was lying haphazardly across the back of the chair at her dresser. As she pulled it on hurriedly, tying the sash around her waist, she glared at her sister. By now the anger was dissipating and being replaced with an acute sense of mortification at being discovered in such a compromising position.

"Err, Ally..." came the hesitant voice from the bed. "Much as I'd like to meet your sister, do you think we could...you know...naked here."

Lyssa was squinting, her sensitive eyes watering, as she tried to protect herself from the glare of the bulb while gesturing urgently toward the discarded sheets with her cuffed hands. Ally quickly moved to grab the covers and throw them over Lyssa to hide her nudity.

"Gayle!" she exclaimed as she did it. "What the *fuck* is so important you had to break in?"

"I didn't break in," Gayle protested. "You gave me a key, remember?"

"Yeah, for emergencies," Ally shot back. "But when I'm home you don't just bust in, regardless of whether you have a key!"

"Talking about keys..." Lyssa said waving her cuffed hands.

"You didn't answer the door. I knocked, *and* I called," Gayle argued. "What was I supposed to do?"

"Take the fucking *hint*!" Ally snapped as she searched for the keys to her handcuffs.

"You could have been lying dead in here!"

"How likely is that?" Ally mocked.

"In my mind, more likely than what I *actually* found," Gayle deadpanned. "I didn't need to see this... This is going to scar me for life. I'm going to need a *double*-length session with Dr. Griffin for this..."

Allyson's heart was pounding in her chest, the aftereffect of adrenaline pumping through her system from the sex, the surprise, and the embarrassment. She tried to calm it a little as the situation began to settle. Finding the keys, she bent over the bed to locate the tiny receptacle in the cuffs to free Lyssa.

"...and, of course, for what happened tonight," Gayle finished.

That piqued Ally's interest and distracted her from the mortification of the situation. As Allyson unlocked the cuffs, she reiterated her earlier question. "So, what happened that's got you in such a tizzy you had to storm round here at..." she glanced at the clock on her bedside table, "...two in the morning?"

"I fucked Michael," Gayle said in a subdued tone.

Ally dropped the key down the back of the bed in surprise, bringing forth a small sigh of exasperation from Lyssa. Allyson slowly straightened and looked back at her sister, only now recognizing the disheveled and flushed state her sibling was in. Gayle looked genuinely *terrified* at the prospect of what she had done, and suddenly Allyson realized the monumental importance of the moment.

"Oh, my God," she whispered.

"Mazel tov?" Lyssa chimed in from under her sheet.

"We're not Jewish," Gayle said with a smile and a shrug.

"It was the first thing that popped into my head," Lyssa shrugged. "I wasn't sure what the appropriate response was supposed to be..."

"Oh, my God," Allyson muttered again. "We need Carrie for this."

"Who?" Lyssa asked.

"Our other sister," Gayle helpfully filled in the blanks. "Gayle Knightley, by the way."

"Lyssa Balthazaar," Lyssa responded with a smile. "I'd shake your hand, but…"

Allyson stepped in to take control of a situation that was rapidly spiraling into some form of weird nightmare. She pointed to the door and gestured for Gayle to leave.

"Go downstairs and make tea. I'll be down shortly."

Gayle needed no further hints. She left the room and Ally heard her footsteps drum a staccato rhythm as she jogged down the stairs. Dropping to her hands and knees, she searched under the bed for the key to the remaining cuff, and swiftly released her captive who rubbed her wrists and smiled mischievously at Ally.

"Well, that was not exactly how I saw tonight ending," Lyssa chuckled.

"I'm *so* sorry," Ally apologized. "You don't know how…truly ground-breaking this is. I'll try and wrap it up quickly, okay?"

"No rush," Lyssa said softly, pulling Ally closer so she could place a tender kiss on her soft lips. "I'll come down, grab a drink, and then leave you sisters to your privacy."

"Thank you," Ally said gratefully.

She gave Lyssa one of her spare robes, and once the two of them were decent, they headed downstairs. The kettle was already spewing steam, indicating its readiness to be introduced to the teabags Gayle had already put in the mismatched mugs on the work surface. She was currently hunting through a cupboard, evidently looking for sugar, which she wouldn't find. Ally tugged open a different cupboard door and grabbed the sugar jar, placing it next to the mugs. Gayle smiled gratefully.

"Don't mind me." Lyssa smiled. "I'll be out of your hair as soon as I grab a coffee." The Vampyrii hesitated for a moment, her grin fading. "Captain Knightley, I just—" was as far as

Lyssa got before Gayle interrupted her with a dismissive wave of her hand.

"After the trauma you and my sister just put me through," she laughed, "I think we can dispense with the formalities, don't you? Please, call me Gayle."

"Gayle... I wanted to extend my deepest condolences on your father's death. I had resolved to tell you as soon as I saw you next, but...circumstances a moment ago didn't seem appropriate to show my sincerity."

"It's okay." Gayle nodded and smiled warmly. "Likewise. Please accept my sympathies about Mercy. I only spent a day with her, but she made a *huge* impression. Life-changing in many ways. She spoke extremely highly of you. Any friend of hers..."

She didn't finish the statement; it really didn't need it. Gayle had previously commented on how Mercy's death had impacted her despite the short span of their fledgling friendship. But, until now, Allyson hadn't really absorbed it. Now Allyson understood exactly how far her sister had grown as a person. This thing with Lyssa was very new, and she had to admit she had been reluctant to disclose too much to Gayle regarding it because of her sister's history fighting Lyssa's people.

She hadn't worried about Carrie. As a journalist, her younger sibling lived a life of inclusion where all races fascinated her in equal measure. But her assumption that Gayle would have been vehemently against such a union seemed to have been very wrong indeed.

"Thank you," Lyssa was answering Gayle. "She spoke highly of you, too. I cannot tell you how *excited* she was to come visit London and meet the infamous Captain Knightley. When she wasn't obsessing over 'The Black Katana,' she was *always* talking about you and your team—"

"The Black Katana?" Gayle furrowed her brow.

"It's what she christened this mystery assassin who was hitting targets in New Victus over the last few years. One of the only witnesses to survive an early encounter gave details of a ninja with a katana of black steel."

"I can see how that would have piqued her interest," Gayle chuckled.

"Indeed. So much so that she got a katana of her own and took up swordplay. Got pretty proficient at it, too." Lyssa smiled. "Anyway, upon her return home, she was even more enthusiastic to tell me about the woman you *actually* are. She enjoyed your company immensely."

"We had...a rough start," Gayle admitted.

"To be expected, considering the status of our races as long-time enemies," Lyssa shrugged. "But Mercy told me how flexible of mind you are. That you accepted her as a friend means the world to her."

Ally observed her sister, perched on a stool in her kitchen in the middle of the night, talking openly with a woman who, until recently, would have been considered a bitter foe. Not because of *who* she was, but because of *what* she was. Gayle had liberated herself from such prejudices, and Allyson was incredibly proud of her sister for managing it.

"Don't thank me," Gayle laughed gently. "It takes no effort to be open-minded to change."

Lyssa shook her head, smiling. "I've lived for over two centuries and I can personally vouch for how rare it is to find people willing to make that small amount of effort."

"Two centuries," Gayle whistled. "Then you can *definitely* stay for the next part of the conversation. I may need the advice of someone with two hundred years under their belt."

Allyson poured the freshly boiled water into a trio of mismatched mugs, two with teabags while the third had instant coffee in it. She pushed one of the teas along the counter to her sister and the coffee went to her lover. For a few seconds, she watched as both of them spooned two helpings of sugar into the respective beverages, added milk, and then picked up their mugs at the same time. Both then used an identical motion to blow on the hot drinks and then tentatively sip. It was almost like they had choreographed the whole routine, but both were completely oblivious to their mirrored actions, much to Allyson's amusement.

Okay, enough of this pussyfooting around...

"So, spill it. Tell us what happened."

Gayle sighed, then launched into a monologue of the evening's events. First, she skimmed over the dinner date with Michael. More information began to creep into the story as she went over the walk home and the inevitable kissing. The details got even more salacious as she finally got into the nitty-gritty of the two of them sleeping together. Inevitably, Ally had to intervene and plead with her sister to spare the more disturbing details, which solicited a roll of the eyes from Gayle. Clearly what she had witnessed earlier entitled her to payback.

So far, so relatively ordinary. But it was when she got to the end of her tale that she started to look uncomfortably disturbed by whatever had happened next. She paused to take a deep breath before continuing.

"So, we're fucking and he's on top. I've got my legs wrapped around him and I orgasm...hard..."

"*Too* much information..." Allyson muttered with a grimace.

"No, it's important, because as I come, I arch my back and open my eyes..."

"Please stop..." Ally shook her head.

"...and suddenly, I'm staring at the fucking light fixture!" She stopped talking as if that explained everything. Ally saw Lyssa's eyes flick toward hers with a look of confusion, and then back to Gayle.

The Vampyrii woman addressed her sister in a soothing tone.

"I get bored during unfulfilling sex, too. Sometimes I end up staring at the ceiling, counting the details on the lights or—"

"No," Gayle interrupted, shaking her head vehemently. "That's not it. You don't understand. I was in *heaven*. Seriously. Best. Sex. Ever. My mind...*bliss*. I feel like I'm floating, light and fluffy as a cloud. When I say I was *looking* at the light fitting, I was looking right at the light fitting. Like, it was here next to my head. That's when I realized we weren't on the bed anymore; we're floating up on the ceiling."

"What?" Lyssa said confused as Ally started to laugh.

"Seriously," Gayle nodded. "Michael bumps his head, and I'm thrashing in my throes of orgasm, while my sex-addled mind is wondering what the fuck is happening. Then we both plummet back to earth... Oh, fuck. I think I might owe him a new bed..." She trailed off, distracted by the thought of the unwitting destruction she wrought to Michael's furniture.

Allyson, meanwhile, continued to chuckle as she fished her cell phone from her pocket and swiftly texted their younger sister. She, of course, knew what had happened to Gayle, but wasn't going to divulge the secret just yet. Carrie *needed* to be in on this. No sooner had she texted than the phone rang almost immediately. Allyson answered. "You're on speakerphone, Carrie,"

"So, what warrants a 'Code Red' text at two-thirty in the morning?" came the sleepy voice of the youngest Knightley sister through the tiny speaker.

"Tell her," Ally said to Gayle, gesturing to the phone.

With a sigh, Gayle launched into repeating the same series of events she had relayed to her audience in the kitchen. It took a few minutes, but her retelling was swifter and more animated this time, even though Carrie couldn't see it. She got up off the stool and started to pace around the kitchen. Her tone was a mixture of bemusement and irritation by the time she finished. Which only got worse as Carrie began to giggle down the line. It was clear Gayle was now at a point where she simply wanted to know what Carrie and Allyson knew about her current predicament that she didn't.

Lyssa, for her part, still looked bemused.

"Do you want to tell her or should I?" Carrie eventually said with a chuckle.

"Tell me *what*?" Gayle looked from the phone to Allyson in confusion.

"Gayle Knightley," Allyson said over-dramatically. "You might want to sit down for this... You, my dear sister, are in love."

"With Michael?" Gayle spluttered. "It was one date..."

"Doesn't matter," Carrie interjected. "Biology never lies."

"I don't understand," Lyssa said quietly, voicing the same thoughts Gayle was apparently having.

"What she said," Gayle nodded toward Lyssa.

"Show her," Carrie's voice echoed around the kitchen.

Allyson stood and moved to the center of the kitchen, away from the work surfaces. She closed her eyes in concentration. Focused on a memory. It was not as powerful as it had once been, but it was still there, though now tainted by the sting of heartbreak. She and Danielle as they had been early in their relationship; after the giddy glee of infatuation had come the *real* love. She tried to push aside the memory of how it had all gone so wrong, how she had been torn apart by her ex-girl-friend's hard words.

It was enough. Barely.

She slowly opened her eyes to see Gayle and Lyssa both staring in stunned amazement. Trying not to break her concentration, she gradually looked toward her feet to confirm she was indeed hovering about two feet off the ground. Albeit a rather shaky hover. As she tried to correct her wobble, she glanced at Lyssa who was looking at her, mouth agog. She was gorgeous, with her disheveled hair falling across her face, and... Almost immediately Ally's focus shifted. The moment was lost. She landed back on the kitchen floor with a less than graceful stumble.

Her point had, however, been demonstrated.

"What...the fuck...did you just do?" Gayle finally managed to splutter.

"Human-Fae hybrids have five powers, not four, contrary to popular knowledge." Ally smiled and started counting them off on her fingers. "Earth, Air, Fire, Water, and..."

"Flight," Carrie finished over the phone.

"Flight?" Gayle said slowly.

"Flight," Allyson confirmed. "Technically, we assume it's an extension of the Air ability, but...you *only* unlock it when you fall in love because it takes a potent positive emotion to be able to harness it. That's the best I can do by using my memories of Danni..." She looked hesitantly across at Lyssa, the woman she had been sleeping with only a handful of minutes earlier. There was something inherently awkward about talking about an ex while your current lover is standing right there. To Lyssa's credit, she gave no reaction to the situation other than curiosity.

"So, how is this not general knowledge?" Lyssa asked inquisitively.

"Exactly," Gayle nodded enthusiastically. "How the fuck do I *not* know about this, but both my sisters do?"

Allyson wasn't sure how to respond diplomatically to this question, and she was searching for an answer when Carrie rescued her.

"Well, to be fair, it's never happened for me," she said almost regretfully. "For Ally, it happened about a year or so ago... When you were—"

"—in therapy," Gayle finished, suddenly understanding.

"And then Danielle and I broke up," Allyson found herself saying a little more forcefully than she'd intended, realizing her firm emphasis was for Lyssa's benefit. "It didn't seem right to talk to you about it back then because of your...issues."

"What issues?" Lyssa said once again showing an innate curiosity that this time probably crossed personal boundaries. She realized what she said the moment the words left her lips and scrabbled to take it back while a mortified look crossed her face. "Oh, gods, I'm sorry. I didn't mean to... "

Gayle, to her credit, simply shrugged. "It's okay. It's not something I talk about," she said quietly. "But then it's not something I'm ashamed of either. Not really. I'm being treated for...an addiction. Of sorts."

For a moment, Lyssa looked confused as she cycled through the possibilities in her head. Drugs, alcohol...then finally it dawned on her when she pieced together the other satellite parts of tonight's conversation and the look of panic on Gayle's face when she had first walked into the bedroom.

"Ah, of course..." she said softly. "You, err...fell off the wagon tonight, I guess."

"Flew off it, apparently," Gayle muttered ruefully.

"This is *not* the same, Sis," Carrie's voice came over the

phone speaker gently. "What you did tonight was *not* what you were doing eighteen months ago."

Her younger sister couldn't see it, but Allyson clocked the mischievous look that flitted across Gayle's features as she grinned slightly,

"Well, some of it was *very* similar..." she murmured.

"That's *not* what I mean," Carrie chided, but there was humor in her tone.

"I feel like I'm missing an important piece of the puzzle..." Lyssa said slowly.

It was Gayle who, after exhaling heavily, answered the question. She actually seemed relieved and emboldened by the fact her secret was now out. Like talking about this was lifting a proverbial weight from her shoulders, one that had been weighing on them for far too long.

"Fae-Human hybrids harness our abilities through the use of emotion," she explained to Lyssa. "Anger, fear, grief on the negative. Love, affection, excitement on the positive. A few years back we, the Hunters, found that we could temporarily...amplify our powers through sexual pleasure. Riding the dopamine dump, so to speak. You know, the pleasure chemical that orgasm floods you with when you..."

"We all know what you're talking about, Gayle," Ally interrupted.

"Fine! So, anyway, at first..." Gayle paused for a moment as she realized, even emboldened as she was, the topic she was about to broach could be considered an embarrassing subject. "At first, masturbation was enough to suffice. But then we discovered that actual sex was better. You know how they say athletes shouldn't have sex before a big game? Well, for us it was the exact opposite. We called it 'supercharging.'"

Lyssa gave a sly glance sideways at Ally, "I get that. Sex with the right partner can give you a glow for hours after..."

Allyson found her skin burning and knew if she could look in a mirror right now, she would likely be crimson.

"...but why is that a problem?" Lyssa finished.

"Because you start chasing the high," Gayle answered quietly. "It's not the sex...it's the fact that after the sex, your power feels...incredible. Like you can *literally* do anything."

She paused searching for an analogy. Ally got there first. "You told me you like cars, right?" she asked Lyssa who nodded. "Well, imagine you spend your time driving around in a Ford, and then one day you're given a Ferrari to test drive—"

"—But to *keep* driving the Ferrari and not be sent back to your Ford, you have to have sex," Gayle finished.

"Then I'd probably be having an awful lot of sex," Lyssa laughed.

"And now you're an addict," Gayle shrugged. "But it's *not* the sex you're addicted to. That's just your gateway drug. It's the car. For me, it was the feeling of power. It's...intoxicating."

"But," Lyssa interjected, "your sisters are right. You're not sleeping with Michael because you're chasing the high this time. You're doing it because you want to. Because you're in love with him. Which is, admittedly, in itself an intoxicating feeling."

Allyson saw her sister slump down onto the stool again, a look of slight shock on her face.

"I am, aren't I?" she finally said. "I mean, I knew...I had feelings for him. But love? Fuck, you guys were right. Torbar was definitely not love."

"*Now* she listens to us," Carrie laughed.

Allyson reached for her sister's hand. "Okay, so does this put your mind at ease now, Gayle? What you're experiencing is a perfectly normal reaction to being in love."

"I'm not sure 'normal' covers it..." Gayle muttered.

"All I'm saying is it's almost three in the morning...and I'd like to get back to my *own* night of passion..."

Gayle grimaced. "Shit, I'm so sorry. I'll get out of your hair."

"Yeah, I gotta go, too," Carrie yawned. "I have an early morning schedule to keep, so need my beauty sleep. I'll catch up with you all later. It was nice to meet you, Lyssa. Night all."

There was a chorus of reciprocating goodbyes from everyone in the room, and then Carrie disconnected as Gayle snagged her coat and shrugged it on.

"How long are you here for, Lyssa?" she said as she fastened the buttons. "How much of your time did I steal?"

"I fly out of the Gatwick SkyPort first thing Monday morning," Lyssa sighed. "Your mother organized discreet travel arrangements for me."

"Really?" Gayle looked taken aback.

Lyssa laughed. "Your mother is a…surprising woman."

"You're not wrong," Gayle admitted as she fished in her coat pockets for gloves. "If you need a lift to the SkyPort, I'd be happy to take you. Make up a little for tonight's rude interruption…"

Allyson was suddenly aware of both Lyssa and her sister looking at her. "What?"

"Unless you want to do the honors?" Gayle said slowly, then grinned. "Teary fare-thee-wells at the departure gate and all that."

"I think I'll say my goodbyes in private before she leaves," Ally said rolling her eyes, then looked at Lyssa. "Unless…"

"That's fine, honestly." Lyssa smiled. "I hate protracted goodbyes."

"Then it's settled. As Allyson doesn't have a car—" Gayle started.

"—and my sister wants to avoid Michael for as long as possible…" Allyson interjected, which brought on a scowl from Gayle.

"—then I'll pick you up on Monday morning. Get Ally to text me the time."

"That would be helpful, thank you," Lyssa said gratefully.

"Least I can do." Gayle smiled as she headed for the front door.

Ally followed her down the hallway with Lyssa in tow. After she unlatched the door to let herself out, Gayle turned to face Allyson, embracing her tightly.

"Thank you," she whispered.

"Don't thank me," Ally said in reply, returning the hug in kind. "We're sisters. This is what we do. Just…talk to Michael as soon as you can. Tomorrow, preferably. *Don't* leave him hanging, okay?"

She heard Gayle groan into her ear. "He's probably wondering what the fuck happened tonight. I have an awful lot of explaining to do..."

"Well, at least you have answers now."

They hugged it out for a few seconds more before Gayle released her and headed out through the front door into the cold Knightsbridge air. She looked back briefly and winked.

"You kids have fun tonight. See you Monday, Lyssa."

On that note, she jogged off in the direction of her own place as Allyson closed the door to the frigid night. After locking it, she turned and was met by Lyssa's lips, which pressed themselves firmly to hers. The initial surprise turned into a lingering pleasure as Ally reciprocated, starting to feel her lust rising again. After passionately devouring each other for what seemed like forever, they came up for air.

"So, back to bed?" Allyson panted.

"Fuck, yes," Lyssa whispered huskily. "Now that I know it's possible, I want to see if we can make you fly!"

She grabbed Ally by the hand and pulled her toward the stairs. Allyson had to admit...she was more than willing to participate in this particular experiment.

| 61 |

GOODBYES

— **Lyssa Balthazaar** —
— *Monday — London, England* —

"I didn't think you had cars like this in the UK."

"We did get the Mustang over here, but they're hard to find now. I had to restore this one from a very sorry state," Gayle answered over the rumble of the engine. "*Sally* is one of a kind."

Lyssa laughed and reached out to stroke her hand across the dashboard. "Mustang *Sally*. From the song, right?"

Gayle shook her head. "The movie."

"Movie?"

"The Commitments. I used to watch it with my dad when I was younger."

Lyssa smiled. "The song predates the movie by a *long* way, you know."

"Really?"

"I forget the original artist," Lyssa nodded, "but the Wilson Pickett version in '66 was very popular."

"That was fifty years before I was born!" Gayle laughed.

"So, you're saying I'm old?"

"Let's go with...experienced."

"I'm not sure that's any better!" Lyssa laughed. "So, this is what...a 2012 model?"

"2011 actually. GT500, but with some...tweaks."

"Tweaks?"

"Inner London is a zero-emissions zone these days. Electric cars only, so I refitted *Sally* to be hybrid. V8 when I stretch her legs on the motorway, electric when I enter the city."

"Hybrid, that's...very fitting," Lyssa nodded in appreciation. "You fixed her up yourself?"

Gayle nodded. "Yup. Everyone has to have a hobby. You are giving off a definite petrol-head vibe..."

"I have a Dodge Charger. The 2014 RT in blood red."

"Blood red...also very fitting," Gayle commented with a smile.

"Had her since new. Unlike you, however, I'm useless mechanically. I pay people back home good money to keep her in tip-top shape."

"Talking of back home..." Gayle glanced across at her from the driver's seat. "What's the plan? I mean, your false credentials will get you into Nexus, but where to from there?"

Lyssa looked out of the window to her left, watching the English countryside fly past. The motorway was practically empty at this time in the morning; just a few other cars and trucks on the road. She flicked her eyes over to the speedometer, backlit in a red glow. The needle was a shade over eighty-five. The speed didn't bother her; she'd been faster in her Charger.

"Montreal. It's trickier to get there, though. Coming here was easy. Contacts and hair dye make me pass for human, but if I tried that on a flight into Pack Nation, they'd sniff me out in a heartbeat. So, Damian Dane has arranged to smuggle me aboard the personal flyer of one of his trusted generals..."

Gayle noticed the tone in her voice. "You sound nervous about that."

"I wish it was Damian coming to get me. I don't know this General Wessex. But I have no real choice but to trust him. Anyway, once I'm in Montreal, I'll join up with the rest of my House, and..." She paused, thinking about what would happen next.

Gayle glanced sideways at her and helpfully filled in the

blank. "...and get on with the overthrow of the StormHall re-gime."

Lyssa nodded. "That's the hope."

Silence descended on the car, leaving only the sound of the engine and the low volume of the stereo playing a tune Lyssa didn't recognize but quite liked. She wasn't sure *what* to say if she were brutally honest. The plan had always been to go home and free her people from the reign of Storm, but lately, she didn't feel hopeful that plan would work.

She was a fugitive. Her family and the Houses of her allies were branded blood-traitors. Damian was hesitant about committing to war, and she failed to gain allies in the form of the NAA and the FSE. Storm had the numbers, and Lyssa had no idea how to overcome that particular advantage.

It all seemed so...hopeless.

Especially as she was now leaving behind the woman to whom she had declared her love.

"Y'know..." Gayle broke the conversational lull, "when I met Mercy, I was *very* skeptical about her motives at first. I don't have my sister's uncanny sense for when someone is lying to me. I have to try and figure it out the old-fashioned way. Experience told me a Vampyrii couldn't be trusted. Every combat-honed instinct told me to be wary of the wolf in sheep's clothing, as it were.

"But we walked through London, took in the sights, ate and drank together, and she talked. Boy, did she talk."

"Mercy does tend towards being somewhat of a motor-mouth," Lyssa smiled.

"She won me over. Quickly, I might add. She fangirled a lot about me, which I found *really* uncomfortable, and a lot about her hatred of the StormHall regime. But what really won me over...was when she talked about you."

"Me?" Lyssa exclaimed.

"Mmmhmm." Gayle smiled but kept her eyes on the road. "She spoke of you in a way I recognized. The same way I talk about Allyson or Carrie. Abject pride for her aunt and what *you* were doing.

"You can't fake that sort of devotion and love. I found my-self wanting to meet the woman who she firmly believed would overthrow Sebastian StormHall and bring some sense of normality back to this world. I thought she was bonkers, but she was *absolutely* adamant you were the one to do it. As the evening went on, I can't say I *believed*...but I did start to wonder." Gayle paused, indicating and smoothly moving to overtake a slower car in their lane.

Lyssa said nothing, doubting her driver was finished with her monologue.

Sure enough, as Gayle eased the Mustang back into the center lane, she continued. "I started to wonder if this larger-than-life figure, Lyssa Balthazaar, could live up to the hype. Could she *really* do all those things Mercy was so confident she could? She made you sound like some sort of Wonder Woman. An eight-foot-tall Amazonian gladiator with the brain of a supercomputer..." Gayle glanced sideways at Lyssa with an amused grin. "And then I met the legend. Naked and handcuffed to my sister's bed."

Lyssa felt herself blushing with embarrassment at the memory. "Oh, Gods, please don't remind me!"

"No, but you see it was the *perfect* introduction," Gayle chuckled.

"Are you joking with me?" Lyssa asked incredulously.

"I'm serious!" Gayle shot back. "Could we have met in a more dignified fashion? Yes. But in that one moment, I saw the true Lyssa Balthazaar. Not the sworn enemy of tyranny. I saw a strong, independent woman who had traveled thou-sands of miles at great personal risk to make a declaration of love to my little sister before returning home to start a civil war against overwhelming odds to try and make the world a better place.

"I saw the kind of woman who inspires loyalty and respect. I saw the Lyssa that Mercy was trying to tell me about."

"I... I don't know what to say..." Lyssa said quietly.

"You don't have to say anything. I just thought you should know," Gayle shrugged. "You *can* do this, Lyssa. Mercy told me you could, and I trust my friend."

"Thank you. She'll be happy you said that."

"I mean it. She made a huge impact on my life in such a short space of time. Forcing me to reevaluate how I see the world. I *needed* a new perspective and for that, I will be forever grateful. I was truly looking forward to seeing her again someday…"

Lyssa didn't reply, simply turned to look back out of the passenger window. In the glass, she could see her reflection. Or at least this woman who bore a passing facial resemblance to her. She smiled. Gayle's words had given her a gift.

Confidence.

No matter the odds, I will *succeed!*

For all those who had lost their lives because of Storm. He had far too much blood on his hands to be allowed to stay in power. There *would* be a reckoning.

Lyssa turned back to look at her unlikely cheerleader. "Thank you."

"What for?" Gayle chuckled.

"The pep talk. I needed it."

"I led a team for almost a decade. I'm pretty good at knowing the right time for an inspirational speech."

Time to return the favor.

"In return, may I offer a little advice?"

Gayle flicked the indicator lever on the steering column, signaling their departure from the motorway. Gatwick SkyPort was close now, their journey almost at an end.

"This is about Michael, isn't it?"

Lyssa nodded. "It's clear you're in love with him. It's also clear you understand the fragility of life. You've walked with death; you know how fickle he can be. I came here to declare my love to your sister because I don't know what my future holds.

"I will fight Storm with all I am, tooth and claw, until either I defeat him, or I am dead. I didn't want to leave anything unsaid. It doesn't matter to me that Allyson couldn't reciprocate those words. I never expected her to. Hoped, maybe. Expected, no. I was more afraid of heading back to fight for New

Victus having *not* told Ally how I feel than I was of her not saying it back. Life is made of a series of moments...and you have to take advantage of each one because they are fleeting.

"You love Michael, so put your fear aside and tell him. I think you'll be surprised by how much better you'll feel about all this when you do. Regardless of what he says to you in return."

Gayle eased the car to a halt at a set of traffic lights that were glowing red. As the engine burbled, she turned slightly to face Lyssa. "You're probably right. If I can find a way over the embarrassment of the flying incident, then maybe I will tell him." She paused for a moment, then turned to look back out of the windscreen and at the still red traffic signals.

"A part of me," Gayle continued after a beat, "wishes I was coming with you. To help fight the good fight. But..."

"You have your responsibilities here, I know. This is not your fight—"

"But I think it is," Gayle interrupted. "I'm going to see if I can talk to Mum, my uncle, and any contacts I have in the FSE and the NAA to see if I can get us involved. To help. But in the meantime, if there's anything I can do, please, just ask. I'll do anything in my power to assist.

"You have an ally in me."

| 62 |

IN ENEMY WATERS

— **Alexa Reynolds** —
— *Monday* —*AustralAsian Airspace* — *Pacific Ocean* —

"Where the bloody hell are we going?" Becka's muttered question echoed the thoughts that had been running through Alexa's mind for the last twenty minutes.

After delivering the Sayona, they carefully monitored Sergeant Rolle's cloned email account. Within an hour of 'Rebecca Danger' exiting the Fort Nassau Detainment Centre, Rolle had fired off a not-so-cryptic message to the address from which he'd been receiving the jobs. Four days later, a flyer arrived to pick up the target.

Becka ran the flyer's ID through the FSE database. Once she blew through the shallow smokescreen of forged identities that didn't stand up to careful inspection, they found the flyer didn't officially exist. Not a terribly shocking turn of events.

What *was* surprising, however, was the direction the flyer headed post departure. It made a speedy beeline southwest. It was a smaller, older model flyer, but had unquestionably been adapted for speed. *Diana* was heavily modified herself, with an advanced sensor suite and uprated engines. Even so, Becka was having a hard time keeping up with their mystery guests while trying to stay at a discreet distance *and* flying low enough not to be detected.

A job that became even more challenging when they entered Free Traders Association territory, swooping low across Costa Rica.

For the past few hours, they had been skimming the waves of the Pacific, not an easy task in the black of the night.

Rahanah sat cross-legged on the floor to the rear of the cockpit. "What lies in this direction?"

Alexa leaned forward, brushing her fingertips across nav-computer's screen, zooming out the view. The blinking cursor indicated the position and direction of *Diana*. She drifted her finger across the glass, following the direction the cursor was pointing.

"Looks like...we're on a more or less direct line to New Zealand..."

"AustralAsian Alliance territory," Becka nodded from the pilot's seat. "But why? It doesn't make any sense... Hold on, they're slowing down."

She eased off the throttle, slowing *Diana* in sync with the flyer they were shadowing. Rahanah stood and leaned forward between them to squint through the windscreen and out into the darkness.

"What is that?" she whispered.

Alexa followed her stare. At first, she saw nothing but blackness and sea spray running up across the glass, but after a moment, she glimpsed what had caught Rahanah's eye.

Lights.

"A boat..." the tigress murmured .

"A *big* boat," Becka said in the same quiet tone.

Without warning, the ocean was illuminated as the 'boat' in question suddenly made its presence distinctly overt.

"No," Alexa corrected. "That's a fucking aircraft carrier!"

Becka immediately brought *Diana* to a halt, hovering just meters above the waves. All their running lights were off, and the dropship was operating in as close to stealth mode as she could. Still, a vessel like that would have all manner of sensors at its disposal to detect unidentified aircraft.

It would also have ample means to *deal* with such threats.

"Can they see us?" Alexa hissed at her pilot.

"Honestly?" Becka hesitated. "I have no idea. But the DH426 Dragonfly was already mostly radar invisible anyway, and our mods have made *Diana* stealthier than standard. So...maybe not. But... Alexa, you do see the flag flying on the control tower, right?"

She did.

A golden rectangle with a red circle emblazoned in the center.

"Japanese Empire..." she muttered.

"Yeah, all the way out here in AustralAsian Alliance waters and running silent," Becka hissed. "But that's not all. Look at the flag below."

Alexa flitted her gaze to the other flag, just as the lights went out. The flyer had landed, and the carrier was back to running dark.

"A crimson flag with black symbols..." she shrugged. "You know that flag, Becka?"

"Not specifically. But I know what it means," Becka said, her face serious. "Alexa, that's a *TechMaster* carrier."

"Fuck! Becka, get us the hell out of here. *Now!*"

Even as Alexa gave the order, Becka was already spinning *Diana* on her axis and powering up the engines. With a surge of acceleration that pushed them firmly back into their seats, and sent Rahanah stumbling backward before she caught herself, they sped away from the Japanese carrier.

"Why are we running away? That is where the path has led us." Confusion was evident in Rahanah's voice.

"Because your path has led us to the door of a very technologically advanced warship with a fuck-ton of weaponry that can blow us out of the sky if it spots us and chooses to do so."

Rahanah didn't look placated by Alexa's answer, however. On the contrary, she looked even more confused. "But you said Japanese Empire ship, yes?"

"Yes. So?" Now Becka sounded puzzled.

"Because Malaysia—my home—is inside the Japanese Empire."

Satisfied they were now out of range of the carrier, Becka eased off the throttle and *Diana* slowed, her engine noise abating. She turned to face Rahanah and Alexa. "What are you saying?"

"I'm saying," Rahanah continued, "the Japanese Empire is honorable. They protect all inside their borders. Including Harimau Jadian. They have fought against Zǔguó many times to protect Malaysia during the Dragon War."

Alexa sat back in the worn leather co-pilot seat. It creaked slightly.

She didn't know where this 'winding path' Rahanah insisted they were on was taking them. But it was certainly turning out to be quite the little adventure.

The question was…where was the path leading them next?

| **63** |

WALK OF SHAME

— **Gayle Knightley** —
— *Monday — London, England* —

Please don't be here, please don't be here, please don't...

The silent plea cycled repeatedly in her head as she turned off *Sally*'s engine, silencing the V8 rumble and using the electric motor to sneak the car into an empty parking spot outside the Academy building.

Thank God for hybrids!

Normally, parking in the courtyard was frowned upon, but with the 136th off on deployment, the Academy had been fairly quiet, so spaces were available. The security guard had waved her through with little enthusiasm, not in the least bit interested in why she was arriving so late for her working day.

Dropping Lyssa to the SkyPort *had* been a cunning excuse to avoid the inevitable morning staff lounge meeting and a face-to-face with Michael. Deep down, she knew she should have spoken to him yesterday, but Gayle was beginning to realize that in emotional matters such as this, she was an abject coward. To be fair, she knew she wasn't entirely mentally or emotionally prepared to see Michael after what happened on Friday evening despite the roughly ten thousand times she rehearsed what she was going to say.

Yawning, she stepped out of the car and started dragging

her feet unhurriedly toward Buckingham Palace and the sanctuary of her office. Her thoughts kept being inexorably drawn back to Friday night, and she groaned with self-loathing. Dinner had been delicious, dancing had been fun, sex had been *amazing*...and then she'd blown it all by freaking out.

Not her finest hour.

After falling—literally—back to Earth following her close encounter with the light fixture, Gayle *had* panicked. Michael was barely able to get a word in as she babbled about a wonderful night and that they should do it again sometime soon. Within seconds, she hastily dressed and fled the scene of the crime.

Why, Gayle? Why are you such an emotionally stunted fuckwit?

Yup. That bitch Inner-Gayle hadn't shut up since Michael's door slammed shut behind her.

She pulled on the handle to the Academy's doors only to find they were locked. Patting her pockets down, she realized she'd left her keycard at home.

"Fuck. Fuck, fuckity fuck!" she hissed under her voice.

Staring at the building, she tried to reason where her most likely point of entry might be without having to stumble back to the gatehouse and ask security to let her in, but lack of sleep had dulled her brain's usually sharp edge. She rubbed at her temples, trying to fend off the headache creeping up on her.

Okay, so I go around back and in from the landing field. Easy.

Decision made, she began to turn away when she heard the magnetic lock release before the door swung open.

Gayle closed her eyes.

Bollocks.

She knew who would be stood there for a very good reason. Karma.

Yup, life definitely *wants to kick me in the proverbial nuts for my previous act of cowardice.*

She took a deep breath, her nose confirming her hypothesis. The faint aroma of his cologne greeted her, making her heart skip a little faster. A mixture of nerves and perhaps a little something else.

"Hi, Gayle," Michael said as she slowly rotated toward him.

"Hey." The sheepishly said word was all Gayle could summon as a response.

"When I didn't hear from you yesterday," he continued, "I *figured* you might skip out on this morning's meeting..."

The protestations started to spew forth from her mouth before her brain was properly in gear. Inner-Gayle was shaking her head in shame at such a continued display of emotional cowardice. "Actually, honestly, in truth, I had to take Lys..." She stopped herself short of saying Lyssa's name completely, suddenly aware her presence in London was supposed to be a secret. "...Al-*lys*-son to the SkyPort this morning..."

"She goin' somewhere?"

"No..." Gayle hesitated, caught in the lie. "...She was...picking up lost luggage. Fucking airlines."

"Don't they usually courier lost luggage directly to your home?"

Gayle nodded slowly and then started shaking her head. "Yes, they do...do that...usually. But in this instance...they couldn't because...of...reasons."

Stop lying, Gayle. You're just digging a deeper hole for yourself. Show some guts!

"I see," Michael nodded. "That sounds reasonable, of course. But I'm guessin' the *truth* might be a tad more believable."

"Fuck," Gayle muttered, to which Michael laughed.

He reached out, taking her hand in his. A small gesture that made her tummy flutter. Squeezing it gently, he led her away from the door and out into the car park. It appeared counter-intuitive, but being out in the center of the courtyard, away from the palace itself, actually gave them more privacy.

"Listen, Gayle. I get it, okay?" he said softly. "The whole levitating sex thing freaked me the fuck out, too. I *was* gonna ask if that was normal for you after it happened, but by the way you jack-rabbited, I'm guessin' it ain't."

"Not even on my *best* day..." Gayle shook her head.

He chuckled. "The sex *was* pretty good, though, wasn't it?"

Gayle grinned, feeling her cheeks warm as the rush of blood colored them a similar shade to her hair. This wasn't how she had rehearsed this yesterday.

She took a deep breath and was about to answer when a sudden, high-pitched wail interrupted. The distinctive screech of an extremely rapidly approaching Banshee, the same type of aircraft that had whisked her to Nexus only a few weeks ago.

They both cast their eyes skyward, momentarily distracted by the low-flying aircraft that screamed overhead and pivoted to a hover above Buckingham Palace. As the engine note dropped, Gayle realized there was another sound growing in volume as the origin of it got closer.

It was one she recognized—the drone of repulsorlifts, like the ones that powered *Artemis*—but there was something that didn't sound quite right. Like the engines were cutting in and out, a stutter in what should be a uniform note.

Gayle pivoted in the direction of its approach and her mouth fell open. "Fuck…"

For a sickening moment, she thought it was *Artemis*, but after a beat she recognized it as being her sistership, *Minerva*. Just a few days ago, Gayle and Amanda watched the 136th Terminators head out on a mission. She didn't know where they were going or what the assignment was. At the time, she had been emotionally distracted, and after the event, she hadn't been interested in finding out.

But when that dropship headed into the starry sky, it had been in pristine condition.

That was absolutely *not* the case anymore.

Minerva was listing horribly to port, an intermittent stream of black smoke coughing from the portside engine. There was a huge tear in her left flank and the cockpit glass was spiderwebbed with cracks. Her flight path was erratic, dipping and rising, looking like she was going to plummet from the sky at any moment. As *Minerva* passed overhead, Gayle tracked it with her eyeline, noticing only two of the three landing wheels were deployed.

Michael noticed it, too. "It's gonna crash..."
Gayle broke into a run.
Michael was right behind her.

| 64 |

MINERVA DOWN

— Michael Reynolds —
— Monday — London, England —

Gayle was sprinting, her long legs covering the ground at an impressively rapid pace. Michael was running as fast as he could but was struggling to keep up.

Which was surprising.

For the first time since they'd met, Gayle was acting more like the woman he had read about in the mission reports. The second she spotted *Minerva*, she reached the same conclusion he had—the dropship was coming down hard. Even as he was voicing that end result out loud, she was already in motion, brushing the control panel on her CombatSkin to retract the heels and taking off at speed.

If her knee was still bothering her at all, she wasn't showing it in the slightest.

They were following the pathway that led them to the landing zone in Palace Gardens when the earth shook beneath them as *Minerva* kissed the ground hard. The sound of tearing metal and a series of explosions followed a split second later.

If anything, this just made Gayle increase her pace.

Rounding the corner, the extent of the horrific crash became clear.

Minerva had missed the landing pads, plowing a deep furrow into the previously immaculate lawns of the garden itself.

There was smoldering wreckage scattered everywhere, and what was left of the dropship was burning. Michael could see several gaping holes in the main fuselage that hadn't been there before, no doubt as a result of munitions exploding on impact. His mind turned to those trapped inside.

They would need help.

Quickly.

He heard sirens in the distance. Fire and rescue crews on their way, but gauging by the intensity of the flames, they would likely arrive too late. The Academy ground crew was on the scene already, but their extinguishers were utterly inadequate against such an inferno. Michael knew the protocol for an emergency landing like this should have seen the pilot take the dropship to one of the major Skyports around the city. He wondered why *Minerva* had been brought back here in such a state, rather than to an airfield equipped to cope with this kind of emergency.

As they approached, he slowed down to consider what course of action they should take.

Gayle never missed a beat.

Shedding her overcoat and dumping it unceremoniously on the ground, she charged in toward the wreckage, skidding to a stop on the ruined grass only a few meters short. Not wasting a moment to think, Gayle threw her hands up in front of her and gestured with a twisting motion toward the downed dropship. Her face was a study in concentration as both her hands swirled independent of one another, like she was conducting an orchestra.

Michael stopped further back as he felt the wind pick up considerably, twisting and buffeting him. He braced himself, planting his feet firmly against the rising air pressure of the gale being created by the woman with the same name. A swirling funnel of air manifested above her, carrying leaves and debris, sucking the oxygen out of the vicinity of the wreck. He gasped for air, suddenly finding it in limited supply and an understanding of what Gayle was attempting dawned.

She was starving the fire of one of its primary fuel sources.

Abruptly, his access to plentiful oxygen was restored, and

panting heavily, he turned to see the arrival of Amanda and Lana along with a gaggle of curious students. The latter was taking charge of the kids, ordering them to keep away from the crash site, while Amanda was making her own gestures similar to Gayle's.

"I may not have her raw power," Amanda shouted over the sound of rushing air, "but if I can't control a little bit of wind, I don't deserve the call sign Zephyr."

Despite the bravado of her words, Michael could see even neutralizing Gayle's powers to the extent that they could breathe and talk was a huge effort for Amanda. Her face was red, her jaw clenched as she concentrated.

Students dealt with, Lana joined them. "What the hell happened?"

Michael shook his head. "I have no idea."

A heavy deluge of rain began to pour out of the heavens, localized only over the dropship. As the water streamed down, the twister eased. The whole exercise took less than a minute, but as Michael watched, the fires flickered and then went out. Gayle dropped her hands, the rain subsided, and the wind returned to normal. She glanced across at Michael, Lana, and finally at Amanda.

"Help me!" she shouted as she started to approach *Minerva*.

Without hesitation, he tried to follow her but was thwarted by the superheated steam caused by rainwater evaporating off hot metal. Gayle, on the other hand, was already picking her way up the partially open, but severely buckled, loading ramp. She ducked under and around the twisted metal, disappearing from view.

How the hell did she do that?

The heat coming off the dropship was intense, and the closer Michael got, the worse it became. He faltered as he approached the hatch, but watched Amanda swiftly dodge past him to follow Gayle into the wreckage.

"Back it up, Rogue," Lana advised sharply, "Let them do their thing."

It sounded peculiar, hearing Lana using his call sign, but it made sense. Gayle, Lana, and Amanda were the last three of the 137th Hunters, and this was them immediately snapping back into a practiced routine they'd spent almost a decade performing.

"I can help..." he started, but Lana shook her head.

"Knightingale and Zephyr are wearing insulated CombatSkins. We're not," she said by way of explanation.

Of course. Heat resistant.

"We've got to do something..."

"Our chance will come when they recover the survivors," Lana replied. "Be patient."

As if on cue, a figure coalesced out of the smoky shadows. The form of Zephyr backing slowly out, pulling what looked like a body, materialized. Shielding his face from the heat, Michael ran toward her. As soon as she was close enough, he grabbed the shoulders of the body and lifted. Amanda moved to the feet, and between the two of them, they carried the limp and unconscious form of Alastair Torbar.

The once distant sirens were now much louder, and seconds later, a fire engine and a pair of ambulances came tearing in on the access road to their left. They bounced across the lawn before sliding to a halt on the wet grass. In moments, the paramedics were attending to Torbar and his many injuries.

Michael was no medical professional, but he had undertaken some rudimentary military training in battlefield triage. He could see evidence of burns and a possible broken left arm. Most concerning, however, was Captain Torbar's sallow complexion and the numerous lacerations he had suffered. Michael doubted very much *they* were a result of the crash. His CombatSkin was sliced open in multiple places and heavily stained with what he assumed was Torbar's blood.

With the captain in safe hands, Michael turned back to Amanda who was doubled over and breathing heavily.

"Are you okay?" Lana asked her.

She nodded and stood up straight, bending over backward a little as if stretching out her back.

"Yeah," she wheezed slightly. "I just...since the surgery I've not exerted myself like that..."

Her face was bright red. Michael couldn't tell if it was a result of her physical exertion or if she was suffering slight burns from the residual heat in the recently flaming wreckage. His thoughts turned to Gayle, who still hadn't reappeared from the dropship's interior.

"Dammit! Gayle's still in there!"

"She'll be *fine*," Amanda coughed. "Trust me."

"How can you say that?" Michael rebutted. "Look at the state *you're* in!"

"I'll try not to be offended by that, but in all honesty... Michael, you saw her just now, right? Without thinking, she used her abilities. Instinctually. That's something she hasn't done since she got back from Valletta." She finished with a cough, bending double again and sucking in fresh air in huge gulps.

He looked between Amanda and the *Minerva*, realizing she was right. It was the first time he had seen her use her abilities to that degree, and it *had* seemed utterly natural to her.

"*This* is what she is trained to do," Lana continued where Amanda left off. "Right now, she's not thinking about her hang-ups or personal demons. This is muscle memory in action. Conditions in there are bad but nothing she can't handle."

As Lana finished, the slender figure of Gayle emerged from *Minerva*. She ducked out of the ruined hatch and strode toward them, her face implacable. She flicked her eyes briefly toward Torbar and the paramedics, confirming he was being properly attended to, and then stopped next to Amanda, hands on her hips, and exhaled heavily.

"Where's the others?" Lana asked.

Gayle simply shook her head. "No one else in there. I searched everywhere. Ship's empty."

"What the fuck happened?" Amanda wheezed and coughed.

Michael looked around the small group. No one said anything. Only one man knew the truth behind what had happened to the 136th Terminators, and he was lying injured on the Academy lawn, fighting for his life.

| 65 |

LIBERATION IS TO SOME...

— **Lyssa Balthazaar** —
— *Tuesday* — *Domaine Saint-Bernard, Pack Nation* —

Lyssa stretched her arms over her head and yawned till her jaw ached.

"Maybe you should get some sleep. We can run this through later."

She looked at Nykola and shook her head a little more wearily than she had intended.

"No," she sighed. "The clock is ticking, and I lost a couple of days traveling to London as it was. We need to go through this now, *then* I'll sleep while you get things underway."

Times like this she wished Vampyrii were more like the stories made them out to be. For instance, being tireless undead monsters with unbeating hearts. Alas, Vampyrii had internal biology almost identical to humans, including the muscle which pumped crimson blood around their very much *not* undead bodies. As a result, they suffered from fatigue as much as the next supernatural entity.

When was *the last proper sleep I got?*

Her sleep-deprived mind started to backtrack to answer the question her subconscious had posed. There had been the three-hour drive to Domaine Saint-Bernard from Montreal, for which she had been behind the wheel. Before that, the six-hour flight from Nexus City, on which she had been far too nervous to sleep. Her brief layover in Nexus had been a frantic couple of hours making sure she dodged NVSec before General Wessex slipped her aboard the flight to Pack Nation. That was after waiting three hours for her delayed flight at Gatwick SkyPort, upon which she spent a further five on the trip to Nexus City. An hour in the car with Gayle, and before that...

Well, let's just say that there wasn't much in the way of sleep last weekend.

"I haven't seen you smile like that for a while. Do I *need* to ask who you're thinking about?" Nykola commented.

Lyssa glanced at her younger sister and her cheeks warmed.

"I think you should concentrate on our planning session rather than thinking about my love life," Lyssa admonished, making Nykola laugh. "Okay, so, bring me up to speed."

They were stood over the planning table in the makeshift command center Nykola had set up in the Wheeler Pavilion. There were maps of New Victus spread all over the table, mostly of the East Coast states concentrated around New York. Nykola spun one of the larger maps around so they could both see it, then jabbed at it with her pencil.

"We managed to evacuate most of our family out of New Victus and across the border. Damian found safe havens for our civilians a little further into Pack Nation, but our military is camped out in the forests near the border. They're spread pretty evenly from Kingston to Cornwall and not far from the banks of the St. Lawrence River. As you know, we're very much outnumbered."

"What about the other Houses?"

"Well, Haggari and Skarling have sent word. They'll follow our lead. Since StormHall seems primed to be moving against the surviving Progenitors who threaten his powerbase, they want him overthrown as much as we do. Which would bring our standing army to around thirteen thousand soldiers."

"Okay..." Lyssa bit her lip thoughtfully, "what about Jareb?"

Nykola shook her head. "Don't know, didn't ask. But you've got to assume they'll back StormHall."

"Most likely," Lyssa sighed. "And the rest?"

"The Houses that don't have an immediate vested interest are a little more on the fence...officially at least. Waiting, I assume, to see what happens next. It's Jareb that's the problem."

"Yeah, I thought they might be."

Storm held the political high ground at the moment, and hence, most of the power. In Vampyrii society, however, there was a trump card. Progenitor status. There was not much even Storm's political muscle could do about it.

Unless, of course, he could *discredit* them somehow.

There were four surviving Progenitors and placing the blame for the Nexus bombing on Lyssa had gone a long way toward removing one of them from the equation. That left Haggari, Skarling, and Jareb, the first two of which would be next on his hit list.

Jareb was the wild card.

It was the domino that Lyssa had no idea which way it would fall.

Would the House of Jareb come out on Lyssa's side and ally with them to overthrow the regime of Storm? Or would it ally itself to Sebastian Storm, the man formerly known as Sebastian Jareb? Alas, the latter was more likely, and that was Storm's ace in the hole.

Discredit—or preferably kill—the other three Progenitors, and then his mother was the last one standing. He would be able to claim the backing of the last surviving Progenitor, and his stranglehold on Vampyrii society would be unbreakable.

"Okay, so, first things first...we need to get Haggari and Skarling to safety."

Nykola nodded. "Plans are underway to extract them, but we're being careful so as not to alert StormHall of our intentions. As Haggari is sleeping in Chicago, Skarling will be taken there and then we'll get them out by boat across Lake Michigan."

"By boat? How many people are we talking about?"

"Just the Progenitors and their escorts at first," Nykola sighed.

Lyssa nodded. "What about the Haggari and Skarling forces?"

"Also rendezvousing in Chicago. But we don't have enough boats to get them all across at once, so we'll need to ferry them. We'll evacuate the civilians first. It'll take a while."

Lyssa looked at the map carefully, tapping her pencil on it in thought. "No," she said eventually. "Contact them and tell them to send their forces east…"

"What are you thinking?" Nykola leaned over the map, her brow furrowed.

"There's no point in bringing them over the border only to send them back again when we launch our offensive. We don't have the numbers to fight along an extended front, and I want us to have a foothold on the east coast…"

"It'll be dangerous," Nykola considered. "StormHall's forces have been spotted gathering in Ohio and the Virginias. He looks to be heading east, too…"

"No doubt coming for us," Lyssa muttered.

"He'll be sorely disappointed when he doesn't find us."

"Oh, he'll be *pissed*. We're going to take back New York and the East coast, but to keep it, we'll need to establish a line. The shortest line for us to establish runs from Cleveland to Pittsburgh, and then to Baltimore. We'll merge our forces on the front and hold it."

"Hold it for how long?" Nykola sighed. "Lys, StormHall is pushing a half-million troops. We can't match that, even if we get Damian's help. And I have to say…he seems really on the fence right now about getting involved so soon. I think he thought he'd have more time to get his people onside."

Lyssa sighed. "I know. I'll talk to him about it."

"Even if he *does* move to help us, he is stretched thin as it is. I've been looking at his numbers. *Maybe* he can spare us a couple of thousand soldiers, but it's not going to make much of a dent in StormHall's advantage. So, what are we holding out for?"

"For help to come."

"You really think it's going to? That the FSE or the NAA is going to come riding in to help us?" Nykola said, looking at

Lyssa as if she was deluded.

Lyssa locked eyes with her younger sister. "I'm working on it."

| **66** |

...AS INVASION IS TO OTHERS

— Sebastian StormHall —
— Tuesday — Denver, New Victus —

Sebastian had never been fond of heights, so setting up his headquarters in Denver, the 'Mile High City,' was somewhat ironic in hindsight.

While his residence had been constructed out in the White River National Forest, he never wanted to use it for official business. He *knew* he was destined for greatness even before his mysterious benefactor sought him out. Head of the Blood Council was something he had always strived for, but he was still keen to keep his private life distinctly separate from his professional one.

Because with that power came unimaginable stress.

His home was his refuge. A place to isolate and surround himself with the peace and quiet of nature.

Still, the business of being Grand Chancellor needed to be attended to, hence trips into Denver were a regular occurrence. The city offered a variety of high-rise options for his headquarters. Tall buildings of steel and glass reaching skyward. Like Hearst Tower, the building Lyssa Balthazaar had chosen in New York City.

He'd always hated that city.

Back before The War, it had been an overcrowded cesspool of Humanity.

Denver was no better, but it was the closest city to his home. He had spent days searching for the right building that met his criteria until finally, he settled on the Brown Palace Hotel. It was an Italian Renaissance revival-style building built back in 1892, thirty years before he was born.

He appreciated the style, with its dramatic wedge shape and the red-brown coloring. When he ventured within, he had been taken by the glorious balconied atrium and the magnificent stained-glass ceiling. The historic staircase and its intricate carving.

This was the place.

Once cleaned up and converted, it became the StormHall Building and home to most of the central government facilities for New Victus. Including a fully functional, state-of-the-art war room in which he was stood right now, with his assembled generals and advisors

A group of people with which he was especially displeased at the moment.

"Why?" he said in a menacingly quiet voice. "Why can *none* of you perform the *simplest* tasks I ask of you?"

His question was met with silence. Sebastian wasn't unduly surprised that no one wanted to go first. He cast his eyes around the group before settling his glare on the leader of his armies.

"Grand Chancellor, we..." General Gilgar paused, trying to pick his words carefully while looking nervously at the other officials in the room. "Until we get an official acceptance of your offer from the NAA, we feel it's prudent to leave our forces where they are to adequately defend the San Andreas Front and the southern coast."

"I understand that, General," StormHall sighed. "But our Intelligence Service is telling me the military forces of Houses Balthazaar, Skarling, and Haggari are pulling *out* from their defensive responsibilities."

"We're well aware of that, Grand Chancellor," Gilgar said. "Rest assured we have more than enough manpower to defend our borders."

Sebastian closed his eyes, slowly shaking his head.

Incompetence. I'm surrounded by incompetence.

In some ways, he had only himself to blame.

He was self-aware enough to realize that over the years he had pursued a policy of overlooking the most qualified people for particular positions in favor of putting in place someone he could trust implicitly. Everyone in this room was loyal to him, of that he had no doubt, yet when it came to intelligence and aptitude for their roles, they were sadly lacking.

It was a situation that had been acceptable in peacetime, but with war on the horizon, this situation had become...untenable.

Case in point was his military leader's blindness to their current situation.

"I expect the NAA to sign the treaty soon enough, General. What concerns me more is that this defection of the Progenitor Houses, along with the fact that Lyssa Balthazaar has not been found, is a precursor to civil war."

"Even if that were true, Sir, the forces they can mobilize are tiny compared to those we can bring to bear..."

"Do you honestly think Lyssa Balthazaar does not *know* that, General?" Sebastian retorted. "That she hasn't made plans and contingencies for that?"

"What could she possibly do?"

Sebastian gritted his teeth. "*That* is what you are all supposed to tell *me*. Why is it my most senior staff seem to be stumbling around in the dark? *Where* is my intelligence?"

Around the room, his top commanders shared the same nervous look, all of them ending up looking to Director Shakani, the head of the New Victus Intelligence Agency, who appeared to be the designated bearer of this particular bad news.

"Grand Chancellor," she said tentatively, "as you are no doubt aware, the Council of Blood reduced our operating budget over the last few years, and as such, our intelligence gathering capability has been...compromised. To be cost-effective, the NVIA sub-contracted House Balthazaar as our primary source of information gathering regarding the military movements of the NAA, FSE, and Cartel activity south of the border.

"For obvious reasons, their office in New York is now...offline. We are trying to plug this deficit in our capabilities, but as you can imagine, cultivating intelligence pipelines takes time and expertise we no longer have access to."

Anger continued to build within Sebastian. He took a deep breath and tried to relax his clenched jaw before he damaged his teeth. He glared accusingly across the table at Director Shakani.

"Director," he said calmly, though with anger in his tone, "you and I had a meeting over two months ago where I advised you to start gathering information regarding House Balthazaar.

"It was *clear* she had been lobbying for political support to overthrow my majority on the Council of Blood. To swing the power to the Earth Quorum. Something I told you I could *not* allow. I wanted evidence on Lyssa Balthazaar's dirty little secrets. You brought me information regarding the condition of her sister, Vanessa. You discovered a secret project called Project: Lazarus, which I then instructed you to find out about.

"Yet, despite the fact that it was clear I was looking to have her reputation and that of her House ground into the dust...you continued to use their services for *military* intelligence?"

Shakani opened her mouth to respond, but Sebastian lifted his hand to stop her in her tracks.

"I don't care for more excuses, Director Shakani. I want you to find Lyssa Balthazaar. I want you to get me intelligence on what she is planning to do. I don't care what it takes. Just do it." He turned to address General Gilgun. "And I want a proportion of our forces redeployed east. I *want* New York City in our grip. I want Hearst Tower.

"I want Balthazaar."

| 67 |

TRAVEL ARRANGEMENTS

— Carrie-Anne Knightley —
— Tuesday — Nexus City, Iceland —

It rose into the sky, a jagged peak of gunmetal grey granite with patches of mossy green where the native vegetation had taken root over the years. She knew it had been constructed, but it truly looked like it belonged, blending perfectly with the Icelandic backdrop. The early morning sunlight refracted off the natural windows of perma-ice that granted rainbow-infused light to the mountain's interior.

The NordScania Embassy was as majestic as it had been on Carrie's previous visit.

This time, however, the experience was bittersweet. Gone was the sense of joy and wonder she felt the first time she witnessed this spectacular building. Those emotions had been a shared experience with her father. The last beautiful memory she had of him.

She remembered the confused ecstasy she felt when given access to move beyond the Clypeus Mountains. The visa Al-zim had granted her was dated, 19th January 2046, a little under three months from her visit. Her eagerness to prepare could barely be contained. She'd waited a week before departing Nexus City to head to NordScania, and during that time she buried herself into her research. She'd barely spent any time with her parents apart from a family dinner with them,

Allyson, and Uncle Norbel.

If she would have known what was about to happen, she would have spent more time with them. Made more precious memories to cherish.

With a deep breath, Carrie strolled up the gently sloping pathway toward the huge granite doors and their carved runes. Old Norse, her father had told her, though he didn't know the translation. The doors were open wide enough for her to walk through into the lobby of the embassy.

Alone.

Ambassador Yetu was standing ready to greet her, his image reflected perfectly in the floor of polished ice, the scale of the stone chamber dwarfing even him. Carrie felt her mood soften and mused upon whether it was a side effect of the gentle hues of blue and grey that dappled the room from the crystal windows.

"Welcome, Knightley-daughter friend," Yetu said softly. "Sorrow I must express for loss. His song is ended. I wish it were not so."

"Thank you, Ambassador," she said, forcing a smile.

He approached and, without warning, folded her into an embrace. The hug, while unexpected, was warm and gentle. Carrie wasn't sure how to respond or what she was supposed to do, but a moment later Yetu began to sing in a low tone.

There was no discernable tune. It almost sounded random, but it was hauntingly beautiful, encouraging Carrie to feel weirdly mournful yet uplifted at the same time. She felt his voice reverberating through her, like the purring of a cat. Soothing her. Closing her eyes, she focused on the sensation and on the song itself. She couldn't make out the words, wasn't even sure if there were any.

After the initial bout of awkwardness, she found herself feeling comforted. Physically and spiritually. Time lost meaning, and Carrie wasn't sure how long he held her, but finally, he finished his song and released her. She blinked back tears and stumbled a little.

"Wow..." she whispered.

Everything was...different.

Her heart felt lighter, and the sadness of a moment ago was somehow...altered. The grief was still there, but now there was also a sense of acceptance.

It wasn't just her mood that was changed; it was her senses, too. She could smell the moss growing bright green on the slate grey rock. The veins of copper, silver, and gold that ran like tiny vertical streams across the walls shimmered and gleamed, and the embedded diamonds and rubies that littered the lobby were vivid flashes of sunlit white and crimson.

"Apologies for my perhaps overstep, Carrie-Anne friend." Yetu bowed slightly. "Hope is that uncomfortable you are not."

She smiled, genuinely, up at his large face, with his bulbous nose and his soulful eyes. "No. God, no!" She exhaled heavily. "What...what was that?"

"In NordScania, when grief is stricken upon a friend, clan embrace, attune to the Song of The Winds. For Troll, it helps. Acceptance that missed is at one with The River. Does Carrie-Anne friend feel...improved?"

"Yes, thank you, Ambassador Yetu. I feel...very much improved."

Yetu laughed delightfully. Deep, loud, and infectious. As he did so, his belly and his bulging nose jiggled amusingly, making Carrie giggle along with him. "No need title," he snorted. "Yetu only. Just name, yes? We friends, like Yetu and Knightley friend."

"Okay," Carrie agreed. "Just Yetu then. No titles."

Yetu turned and began to walk away, gesturing for her to follow.

He ambled, allowing her to easily keep pace with him despite his lengthier stride. They traversed the same bio-luminescent lit corridor with the high-arched roof, and followed the same downward spiral as before. The same tiny central stream of water traced the path splitting off again under the rune-etched door to the chamber of Ambassador Alzim.

The Ice Giant.

The last time they met, he had been seated on a majestic throne of glacial ice, looking almost regal. Today, he stood in the center of the chamber, towering above her at least fifteen feet tall. Alzim turned his head when she entered. Though he had the appearance of living ice, his motion was fluid, like water. With a simple nod of the head, Yetu was promptly dismissed, closing the door behind him as he went.

Leaving her alone with Ambassador Alzim.

"Carrie-Anne Knightley." The voice was lighter than last time they had met, almost feminine, though still smooth like audio velvet. "Welcome. My sincere condolences on your father's passing. Please, be consoled by the fact that he is now at one with The River." He bowed his head slightly as he finished.

Carrie was a little taken aback.

Alzim had been kind of aloof when they last conversed. Impassive almost. Cold even—no pun intended. Today there was a softer, more caring undertone in that rich voice. As she looked at his face, she could have sworn there was a smile there.

"You're not mistaken, Carrie-Anne," Alzim said softly. "I *am* different. Ice is water, and water is fluid. As is our gender. Ice Giants are both genders simultaneously. We shift fluidly between male and female at our whim.

"My male persona can be a little...callous. Though that may be a harsh word. For today's consultation and in light of your recent loss, I considered you would perhaps prefer the more compassionate female Alzim.

"And yes, this is a smile."

Carrie realized that her mouth was hanging open. She wondered how many other people knew the nature of Ice Giants as she now did. *Nothing* like this had turned up in her research, and her father had never mentioned it.

"I... Thank you," she stuttered. "Are you...telepathic, too?"

"No, Carrie-Anne." Alzim sounded amused at the thought. "My race is empathic, and I simply understand how my two aspects differ, and the confusion it can cause."

This visit was turning out to be revelatory in many ways. Carrie felt honored to be learning so much about the two races of NordScania that few other people knew. Her mind boggled once again as to how they'd managed to keep their existence a secret for so long. It also felt a little strange that the individual she had been considering male for so long was now female.

Or maybe that was entirely the wrong way to view Ice Giants. Were they effectively genderless?

Focus, Carrie. That's a question for another time!

"You're perchance wondering why I asked you to meet today?" Alzim said as she walked back toward her throne.

"I thought it might be to amend the visa documents. In light of what happened at the Nexus Summit."

Alzim shook her head. "There is no change."

"But...Mercy balthazaar was killed in the attack...and Lyssa Balthazaar is a fugitive. I'm not sure why they were on the visa in the first place—"

"Balent sent word that they should be," Alzim interrupted.

"Regardless, surely—"

"Please, Carrie-Anne, there is *no* need to worry. The documents remain unchanged."

"But," Carrie pushed, "they must be mistaken..."

"Balent listens to the Song of The Winds," Alzim explained. "The Song knows all."

She said it as if it explained everything, but Carrie was still confused. How could the Song be insisting a dead woman would be in the party?

"Maybe Balent has mistranslated," she suggested.

Alzim laughed lightly. "The Dragon-King is never wrong, Carrie-Anne. Have faith."

"So, what *have* you called me here for?"

Ambassador Alzim sat on her throne and gestured at the ice floor in front of her. The ice flowed upward to form an identical throne in a smaller size. Carrie's size. As the chair solidified, Alzim beckoned for Carrie to be seated.

"Please, be comfortable, Carrie-Anne. There is much for me to tell you before you venture beyond. Much for you to learn..."

| 68 |

BEDSIDE MANNERS

— **Michael Reynolds** —
— *Wednesday* — *London, England* —

It had been two days since *Minerva* carved an ugly furrow in the previously well-manicured lawns of Buckingham Palace, and Alastair Torbar had been whisked to London Bridge Hospital for emergency medical care.

Two days during which Gayle had not left his side.

Which, Michael had to reluctantly admit, bugged him.

He knew the two had a long and complicated history, but Gayle rarely, if ever, mentioned him in passing conversation. He assumed they had once been intimate, but if that were true, Gayle never spoke of it, seemingly content to let that particular memory wither and die.

Hence, it seemed strange that not only had she *insisted* on riding in the ambulance that ferried him from the Academy, but she had remained at the hospital ever since. When he expressed his thoughts to Lana, she greeted his concerns with a knowing smile.

"Alastair has always been the closest thing Gayle has to a peer," she had said. "Actually, no...more like a rival. From day one, the two of them competed, driving each other crazy. But they also *pushed* each other to excel. Gayle Knightley would not be Gayle Knightley if it weren't for Alastair Torbar. Theirs is a...complex relationship, but it's not a relationship *you* should find threatening, Michael. Trust me."

He did trust Lana, and her comments *had* somewhat put his mind at ease.

Though he showed no sign of waking up, Torbar's injuries were treated and the doctors declared him stable. Yet Gayle continued her vigil. Michael decided forty-eight hours was enough space for now.

He quietly approached the private room and glanced through the small glass window. Gayle was curled up in a cozy-looking armchair, pulled close to the bed, with what looked like a crossword book in her hand. She appeared deep in thought, tapping the end of the pen she was holding idly against her chin. Her eyes flicked toward him, and she smiled, beckoning for him to enter.

"Sorry," he whispered as he entered. "I didn't want to interrupt. Just wanted to see if you're okay."

Her face lit up, giving him a warm feeling and quelling his paranoia.

"I'm good," she whispered, then raised an eyebrow. "But I know why you're *really* here. Pull up a chair."

Michael glanced around the room, spotting a couple of cheap-looking plastic chairs, very different from the considerably more comfortable chair in which Gayle was ensconced. As he picked one up and carried it over to where she was sat, she shifted position and addressed the difference.

"A porter brought it in from one of the lounges. Being as I was objecting to leaving, they at least decided to make me comfortable."

Putting the chair close beside hers, Michael sat down. Gayle shifted her position to lean sideways and reached for his hand to pull him slightly closer before resting her head on his forearm. It was a tiny gesture, but it brought a smile to Michael's face.

They sat quietly. He was surprised by just how comfortable their silence was, despite the still unanswered questions about what had happened on date night. After the sex, and the fact that she had fled from the aftermath, Michael had been feeling understandably anxious about what the future held for them. While he knew it really couldn't be anything to do with him, the spontaneous post-coital levitation still left him with a sense of paranoia that he had done something...wrong. Performed badly.

With the simple gesture of seeking comforting contact, Gayle had gone a long way to restoring his confidence. Now he felt quietly assured that, in time, they would have their conversation regarding that night, clearing the air in a manner that would allow them to pursue their fledgling relationship. He stroked her hair tenderly, tucking the pink waves behind her ear as his fingertips brushed against the skin of her neck.

"How is he?"

"Out of the woods," Gayle murmured. "He's been medically induced to help him heal. He won't wake up for a while."

"Did the doctors say what injuries he sustained?"

"Spiral fracture in his arm that needed reconstructive surgery. A bunch of lacerations and burns. Most will heal without any complications. But...a few of them were close to the spine, probably causing nerve damage. They won't know how bad those are till he comes out of the coma. But..." Gayle paused for a moment, taking a deep breath, but she didn't move. She seemed content to stay curled in her little ball with her head being stroked like a kitten. Finally, she continued. "...The injuries are similar to Amanda's. Worse, though."

"They fixed her. They'll fix Captain Torbar," he tried to reassure her.

"I don't know, Michael. Amanda's spine was hit once. A clean strike and then...well, she was medically evacuated and got *almost* immediate treatment. But Alastair... He somehow got back to *Minerva*, got her in the air, hit the autopilot to get her back here, then suffered the crash and the burns.

"His injuries are *so* much worse. I don't know if they can heal this."

Michael regarded the heavily bandaged figure lying peacefully in the hospital bed. The only sounds in the room were the rhythmic hisses of the ventilator providing him with fresh oxygen, and the gentle bleating of the monitors he was hooked up to. He didn't know Captain Torbar well; the two had only conversed a handful of fleeting times as they met walking the Academy corridors going about their own separate business. Hence, it seemed a little strange sitting here on a watching vigil for the man.

He reminded himself that he was really here for Gayle.

"So, do you want to tell me why you're still camped out at his bedside?"

"It's complicated," she whispered.

"It always is, but I'd like to hear about it. We got time."

She didn't move, just lay quietly on his arm for a moment, seemingly gathering her thoughts. He didn't push or prod, leaving her to talk in her own time.

"Did you know Alastair is like me?" she eventually said.

"Like you how?"

"His father is a Human admiral in the FSE Navy, but his mother is Fae. They're married like my parents are...were. Alastair was conceived in love, just like I was. Of all the students here at the Academy, he is the only one who can match me in terms of power level. My equal. Some things I was better at, some things he had the edge, but overall...we balanced out pretty evenly.

"It was only natural we became rivals. We were both driven to be the best by the chips on our shoulders. It only got worse when we were both promoted to squad leaders. The competition spilled over to become my Hunters versus his Terminators. Most people thought they would have the advantage and we were considered the 'B' team.

"Torbar and his team were previously Army, Air Force, and Navy. They had *all* been through military training of some sort before being selected for service in the HFA. They were disciplined, knew military protocol, and trained in things like how to strip a weapon, or what to do when stranded in a desert somewhere. We were coming in raw.

"Early on, I decided *that* was our advantage. My Hunters were diamonds in the rough—not colored or conditioned by preconceptions of any previous service. It enabled us to look at things differently, less rigidly. Think outside the box.

"Alastair...didn't agree.

"He was convinced that military discipline was the key to being successful. And thus, our rivalry was born. Both of us trying to outdo the other while dragging our teams along for the ride."

"But you and he..." Michael interjected. "Y'all had a relationship once."

He felt Gayle's head bobble a little as she chuckled. "You know what happens when you put two alpha dogs in a room together? They both try to assert dominance, and inevitably, that ends in a fight. Believe me when I say Alastair and I fought *a lot*. Real fights, too. Not just arguments. We have *physically* come to blows more than once.

"There was this one night in Barnun, both teams were there, drinking and fronting up to each other...nothing unusual in the early days. But this was after the Farallon Islands mission..."

He knew the mission she was talking about; they'd mentioned it in passing on their tequila night. Her Hunters had been responsible for taking down the monitoring stations on the islands to allow the liberation forces the element of surprise.

"While we had been doing the crucial behind-the-scenes stuff, the Terminators were front and center with the invasion force. Tip of the spear. It was during the first part of that sequence, Operation: Radio Silence, where we lost Valerio."

Michael stayed silent. He knew from the unit records that she was referring to Valerio Nazario, call sign 'Bear.' The first and, up until Valletta, only casualty the Hunters ever endured.

"We were grieving, but Torbar's guys were celebrating. It was a recipe for disaster."

"What happened?" Michael asked.

"Alastair and I faced off. He said he wouldn't hit a girl. So, this girl punched him in his arrogant face, initiating a pretty sizable inter-team brawl."

"Who won?"

"You really need to ask?" Gayle chided gently. "Actually, no one. Police were called, and we all got a bollocking by Norbel.

We were denied recreation time for a month."

"I can imagine…"

"But…it was also the first night we slept together."

"Oh. I got the impression y'all's relationship was more recent than that."

"The relationship, yes. But we slept together a few times before we made our disastrous run at a commitment. That was years later…" Gayle stopped and tilted her head to look up at him, her brow crumpled. "Sorry, I…didn't think. Does talking about this bother you?"

"No, not at all." Michael shook his head. "Everyone has a relationship history."

"Yeah, but me being here is *not* about our personal relationship. Not really."

"What is it about?"

Her hand reached up to interlink her fingers with his, squeezing gently. It was a gesture, he realized, more for herself than for him. Like she was trying to reassure herself he was there.

"I've been sitting here, thinking…wondering."

"Wondering what?"

"Wondering about the similarities between what happened to me and what happened to Alastair. I'm intimately familiar with those injuries. Those are Adze wounds. I know that for a *fact*."

Abruptly, Gayle sat up and turned slightly to look at him.

"A week ago, the 136th Terminators flew off on *Minerva* to parts unknown…top-secret mission. Twelve months ago, give or take, the 137th Hunters flew off on *Artemis* on a top-secret mission to Malta…"

Michael nodded. Suddenly the pieces of the puzzle dropped neatly into place. This was all about two things—professional empathy between team leaders, and the mystery of what happened to Captain Torbar's team…and maybe by extension, her own.

"When he comes out of his coma," she said, nodding toward the bed, "I know how he's going to feel. I know the anger that will simmer inside him. The thirst for vengeance against those that did this. Because that's what drove me. I was *so* angry at my uncle, and then at my father for keeping me off active duty."

"Because you wanted vengeance?" Michael asked.

Gayle shook her head. "No. Because I was...scared. Afraid I was broken. Not only physically, but mentally. My dreams were nightmares, filled with visions of gleaming fangs and razor-sharp claws. The death of my friends played out in my mind over and over and over. I'd wake up every single morning drenched in sweat...shaking.

"I was *thankful* that I was being held back. I didn't want to face Adze again. But my terror was also my shame. What kind of leader was I that I was *grateful* I wasn't being put back on the frontline? What kind of a coward?

"I *hated* myself for feeling like that. For letting my team down. The day I met you, I walked into the Academy full of anger at myself. I was hoping, *praying*, Norbel would return me to active duty, forcing me to face my fear. A fear I couldn't conquer on my own. But instead, Norbel held me back here. Pushed me into a role as a teacher. A safe, cushy job as far away from facing my fears as I could get.

"I was furious. Boxed into a position where all I could do was live with my cowardice. But in hindsight—which is a fucking wonderful thing—it was *exactly* what I needed to do. Where I needed to be. When Alastair wakes up, he's going to need someone to help guide him through the minefield of emotion he'll have to negotiate."

For a moment, she stared at the hospital bed. Michael watched her face harden, her jaw clenching. A look of determination flashed in her emerald eyes as she turned back to him.

"Valletta was an ambush," she said with a hint of anger. "We knew it at the time. Someone set a trap designed *specifically* for us.

"And I think Alastair unwittingly led the Terminators into a similarly constructed trap. If that's true...I want to know all about it. I want to find out who the fuck is behind all this, and once I do…" Her voice trailed off when it hit a note of grim determination. She didn't need to finish the sentiment. Michael knew exactly what she was implying, and the thought sent a cold chill down his spine.

| 69 |

OLIVE BRANCH

— **Gayle Knightley** —
— *Wednesday* — *London, England* —

She stretched her tired limbs and raked her hand back through her tangled pink hair. Michael had headed back to the Academy a few hours earlier leaving her once more alone with her thoughts as she continued her vigil. With a yawn, she regarded Alastair Torbar.

He was a man who always filled her mind with conflicting emotions. There had been a time when she *thought* she loved him. There were more times when she *knew* she hated him. He had been her toughest rival, her staunchest critic. He was the one who inspired her to the heights of her profession, yet he was also the one who had dragged her to the depths of her depravity.

Today she saw him in a new light. With empathy and understanding.

His eyes fluttered for a moment as he struggled to open them, and he made a small coughing sound as if trying to clear his throat. Leaning forward in her seat, Gayle rested her hand gently upon his.

"Take it easy, Alastair," she said softly.

"..." Torbar parted his lips to speak, but no words came out.

The doctors had removed the ventilator not long after Michael left, and Gayle recognized the sore dryness of the throat that took away Alastair's speech; she experienced the same thing when she awoke in hospital twelve months earlier. Picking up the plastic cup from the bedside table, she carefully angled the straw and held it to Torbar's lips. He took it, gratefully sipping on the cold water.

"Thank you," he croaked when he was done.

"You're welcome." Gayle smiled.

The two sat in silence for a few minutes. She watched as her one-time rival and lover wrestled with his thoughts and emotions. Reconciling what happened would be difficult for him; nobody understood better than Gayle. He needed time, so she decided to sit and wait. He would talk when he was good and ready.

It wasn't long.

"So..." he started, his voice still gravelly, "this is about the time you say, 'I told you so.'"

Gayle shook her head.

"You really think I'd be that petty, Alastair?" she said. "I've been where you are right now. I lost my team, too, remember. Can you tell me what happened?"

"Valletta..." he said quietly.

"What?" Gayle was momentarily taken aback, wondering why he was referring to her darkest hour. Then she realized what he truly meant. "They deployed *you* to Valletta?"

Torbar nodded slowly, his eyelids heavy.

When he responded, his speech was labored. "Norbel said...request came from FSE Naval...Headquarters. After your mission...Navy shelled the island...soft bombardment..."

Gayle had read the reports of what happened post Operation: Malta. Once she'd been evacuated, the FSE 3rd Fleet moved into range and subjected the island to a prolonged bombardment of gas-shells. They were non-explosive, designed to limit the destruction of property, but on impact would release a biological agent that would eliminate anything living in the fallout radius.

While there were rules against biological warfare, Adze were considered monsters. Their chemical extermination was considered similar to pest control. They treated the threat the same as they would an infestation of cockroaches.

"But why?" she said, confused. "There's nothing there...."

Torbar continued as best he could. "A month ago...scouts started to report sightings... Adze...back on the island. Norbel said...routine bug hunt. Find the nest. Kill the Alpha." He paused, staring at the ceiling. There was a haunted look on his face, one Gayle recognized intimately. His memory was replaying the events that led up to the death of his team.

"Gambler...brought *Minerva* down low..." His breathing was labored as he tried to relay the story. "There was...nobody to rescue...I decided on...direct approach. I ordered Gambler...put *Minerva* down near the city gate...at Triton Fountain.

"Team disembarked. No sign of the Adze. It was daylight...we thought we were safe. Gambler and Hammer stayed...rest moved out...toward Fort St. Elmo. Intelligence said...Adze would be there...that was our target.

"We got to...St. George's square...heard an explosion behind us. Gambler was babbling on comms...about a trap. The Adze hit *Minerva*. Hammer was already dead...ship crippled." He hesitated. His face was hard as stone, but there was a tear running down his cheek.

"I ordered retreat...it was too late. I heard Gambler...scream on comms...then he was gone. The Adze came...out of buildings...all around us. So many of them..." His voice trailed off as he lost himself in the memory.

"But you said it was daylight?" Gayle muttered, confused. "Adze don't come out during the day."

Torbar's eyes flicked toward her. "They didn't care...dozens...hundreds of them. Suicidal...ignoring their own pain. DeeDee and Landslide were...dragged off into the shadows...I heard their screams...

"We tried...to make it back to *Minerva*...even crippled she might fly. But in the narrow streets...they came at us from everywhere. Every storefront...every house...every building we passed...another ambush. Claws and fangs...dragging us away...darkness...one by one."

Torbar coughed. His body shook. Gayle offered him more

water, which he gratefully accepted.

"I saw *Minerva*...right in front of me. Alone...team gone...all of them...just gone. She was leaning slightly...bomb damage. Starboard landing gear was broken...damage to the engine on that side, too. Bomb damage..."

"Adze using munitions?" Gayle shook her head. So much of this made no sense. "They're highly evolved killing machines...they don't need to use weapons."

Alastair shrugged. "I got onboard...they were waiting...two in the shadows of the troop compartment. I got them, but...they got me, too."

Gayle didn't need him to elaborate. She'd seen the medical charts and spoken to the doctors. His injuries were horrific; far worse than hers had been. More akin to those suffered by Amanda; however, Alastair's prognosis wasn't nearly as optimistic. He had suffered nerve damage to his right arm, his spine, and his left leg at the hands—or claws—of the Adze. There was also a vicious cut running down the left-hand side of his face from ear to throat, which would leave a scar almost identical to Gayle's own Valletta souvenir. His injuries would need surgery, and possibly implants like Amanda's to carry the nerve signals properly, but he would never be the same.

His days in the field were over.

For the first time since she had come back from Valletta, Gayle actually said a silent prayer of thanks that her injuries had been largely superficial. Her knee would heal, given some time, and she would be pretty much back to normal. For Torbar, that was now a fantasy.

"You and me...we're the same," Torbar said, closing his eyes. "Driven...to be the best. That's why *we*...were the leaders of our teams. We were confident...strong...powerful... no one could take that away from us.

"But now...they're all dead, Gayle...Bloodhound, Gambler, Baron..." He paused for a moment to swallow the obvious lump in his throat. "...DeeDee, Hammer...Charger, Hitman, Omen...Mojo and Landslide...all dead. There was nothing...I could do...nothing."

"I lost my team, too..."

"Zephyr survived," he said. "You saved her... I tried...tried to do what you did. But..."

"Alastair, I have no idea how I did what Amanda said I did. I have no recollection of it whatsoever."

"Doesn't change...fact you did it."

Gayle sat back in her chair and rubbed at the bridge of her nose. She wasn't sure what to say next. What more could she say? What advice could she offer to move past this tragedy? She may understand what he was going through, but she herself was still haunted by it a year later. Still letting it affect her life.

There *was* a difference between them, though.

Over the course of their careers, Norbar's Terminators had lost people before. Gayle's Hunters had gone almost a decade without loss. She looked up at him, lying in the hospital bed.

"Can I ask you something, Alastair? About you and the Terminators?"

"Sure," he replied quietly.

She paused, trying to consider how best to phrase her question. "I don't mean to sound insensitive when I ask you this," she said hesitantly, "but you've lost people before. I used to think that the fact the Hunters hadn't suffered the death toll your team had was a matter of pride..."

"You should." Alastair smiled. "You're a good leader... Don't doubt that."

"But since losing Valerio so early, I never had to deal with that kind of loss. I've been struggling to adjust to this. Struggling to figure out how to move on..."

"You're asking...how I did it?" he asked.

Gayle nodded.

Torbar took a deep breath and thought about it for a moment. "A decision...very early on," he said. "I learned...from what happened...when you lost Bear. You took your team...off active duty...while you found a replacement for him..."

"Losing Valerio really hurt us as a team," Gayle admitted. "I felt we needed to lick our wounds, get our heads straight..."

"...which I...disagreed with," Torbar wheezed. "Losing a team member...like falling off a horse. You have to get...straight back in the saddle...conquer the fear. The Terminators *never* feared death...never worried about loss. Think maybe...you saw us as...too gung-ho. We saw your Hunters...too reserved."

His last comment stung Gayle's ego. She had prided herself on the fact that her team was adaptable to any situation, often thinking outside the box in order to achieve a mission objective. Torbar was looking directly at her and saw the flicker of anger wash across her features.

"Nothing wrong...with that," he said slowly. "You kept your team...alive...intact for a long...time. The Terminators had...eight deaths. You were the scalpel...we were the hammer... We knew...accepted it.

"But after our first loss...losing Aztec...on that rescue mission...in Tunis, I decided...we...needed to face loss...head on. There was an NAA recon team discovered on the wrong...side of the Straits of Gibraltar...cut off. Surrounded by Adze..."

"I remember," Gayle nodded. "In Tangier. You volunteered to go in and get them out. I recall arguing with you at the time, that it was too soon."

"I wanted my team...to face their fear and overcome it. Quickly as possible. As the scalpel, your team...always honing their skills...finding that edge. As the hammer...we needed to make ourselves harder. Like tempering steel. Heat...quench...repeat. Over and over. No matter the loss...Terminators would *never* break.

"Your Hunters, though..." he sighed. "Scalpels can be brittle...snap under pressure..."

Gayle had to admit, Torbar had a point. She had often used the 'precision instrument- blunt force' analogy herself when talking about the difference between the two units, but she never took that comparison any further.

But now, as she sat here looking at Captain Alastair Torbar lying in his hospital bed gravely wounded, there was no acrimony. Those twenty-four hybrid soldiers had been paired down to a mere three. Herself, Amanda, and the man she was talking to.

So much loss...

Alastair's eyes drifted closed while she sat quietly contemplating what he told her. It took only moments for her to detect the change in his breathing, indicating he had drifted back to sleep.

Gayle smiled sadly and gently pulled the sheets up a little to make sure he wasn't cold. She reached out and very lightly traced the wound on the side of his neck and face with her fingertips. She couldn't remember the last time they had spoken like this—open, honest, and without any undercurrent of mind games.

It's sad it took something like this for us to actually talk. Maybe if we could have been like this when we were together, we could have made something real of our relationship.

That ship had long since sailed, though, and Gayle wasn't regretful about it. In truth, she and Alastair were never truly well suited. She and Michael, on the other hand, fit together perfectly.

Like they were meant to be.

Leaning in close to Alastair, she kissed him gently on the forehead.

"Rest well, Captain," she whispered.

She walked out of his room, leaving the hospital wing deep in contemplation. So many thoughts were running through her head. From Michael to the memories of Valletta and to how her conversation with Alastair changed her view about her current condition.

Gayle wasn't sure what to do next.

But she knew she *needed* to do something.

| 70 |

FORK IN THE ROAD

— **Michael Reynolds** —
— *Wednesday* — *London, England* —

Déjà vu.

Gayle was sitting peacefully on the exact same wall near the landing pad where he had found her a little over a month ago. On that occasion, she had been in her gym clothes, hugging her knees close while nibbling nervously on her thumbnail.

This was *not* the woman he found here tonight.

There were no nerves or sadness in her demeanor. She simply looked calm, almost resolved, as she sat on the wall dressed in her CombatSkin, watching the ground-crew as they fussed over *Minerva*. Michael ambled over, trying to look nonchalant as he sat down quietly next to her. For a few minutes, neither said a word, until eventually it was Gayle who broke the silence.

"I'm okay. You don't need to worry."

"Do I look worried?"

Silence descended again. He looked out at the *Minerva*, evaluating the damage. The drop ship was still listing noticeably to port, shockingly so when compared to the pristine *Artemis* sat alongside her, fresh back from its refurbishment.

"I *know* what you're doing," Gayle said.

"I'm not doing anything."

She turned to look at him with a raised eyebrow. "You're doing that 'silent sentinel' thing. Hoping I'll eventually break and talk to you."

"Is it working?" He smiled at her.

"Nope."

She turned back to stare at landing pad three where an FSE Banshee sat. Michael recognized it as the fighter that had escorted *Minerva* in. Bathed in the glow of the landing lights, it looked menacing even sat there unattended.

"He remembers what happened," Gayle said softly. "Every single detail. Every tiny moment."

"Captain Torbar?"

She nodded. "I don't know what's worse." She turned slightly to look at him. "I thought *not* being able to remember was bad. Valletta haunts me; not because I remember what happened, but because I don't. I have no recollection of how my friends died; only the words of Amanda's report. But Alastair remembers every screaming moment of pain his team suffered, every gruesome death.

"But, somehow, he's not the mental mess I am. He maintains the deaths his team historically experienced prepared him for something like this. Tempered him. But...what if I can't do what he's done? How do I move past what happened to me?"

Michael shrugged. "Exactly how you *have* been dealing with it. One day at a time."

"Have I? Have I *really* been dealing with it?"

He slid his hand over hers. Was this her self-doubt manifesting itself again? An emotion that had been eating at her since they first met.

No. I was right earlier. This is something different...

Her posture was upright, shoulders square. The tone of her voice was stronger, more determined. There was a steely look in her eye, one he'd only seen before when she was consumed by rage. But tonight, he didn't sense any anger. She seemed calm. Considered.

"Look how far you've come since I've known you," he said softly.

"Not quite far enough," Gayle muttered.

"What does that mean?"

It was clear that talking to Captain Torbar had triggered something within Gayle.

But was it something good?

Or something bad?

He had seen her hit low moments. He had seen her span a wide range of negative emotions that ran counter to her reputation. Tonight, though, there was a sense of this being the Knightingale he had read about in the combat logs and reports.

"My life, for the past year, has been consumed by fear," she said softly. "A fear I didn't recognize. One I couldn't identify the source of. I came back from Valletta physically broken, afraid I'd never be the same again. But...I'm healing.

"Despite frequent nightmares about the Adze, I sucked it up and taught that class to the kids. I dodged a relationship with you because I was afraid of where it would lead, what I would do if I let it go too far. But now we've dated, kissed, and... and more.

"So, what *was* my fear?

"My most recent theory was it was my powers. They're all kinds of fucked up. I proved *that* on the shooting range. Was I afraid *I* was broken? That I'd never be the same again? Was I afraid of what it would do to me if I used them?

"Amanda said I needed to face my fears head on. That we'd do it *together*, the Hunters way. 'Stronger together.' She was half right. Talking to Alastair...it was like having an epiphany. Clarity, finally. I *know* what I'm afraid of now. I know what's broken and how to fix it."

Michael wasn't sure if he was doing her any good being here. Did she need a friend tonight? A lover? Or maybe just a little space...

"Whatever it is, I'd like to help," he said softly.

She didn't answer him, just turned back to stare at the landing pad. She looked...distracted.

"What do you need?" he prodded gently.

"What do I need?" she said distantly. "Like Amanda said, I

need to face my fear head on.
    "And I need to do it alone."

| 71 |

THE OATH

— Damian Dane —
— *Wednesday — Montreal, Pack Nation —*

Dane tapped his foot nervously as he waited, staring into the sky, its brilliant blue broken only by a few tiny wisps of cloud.

Perfect weather again. This must be her doing, surely?

To be honest, it wasn't even a question worth asking. Of course it was her doing. When you had her abilities, why would you *not* give yourself clear sunny skies? Even the temperature seemed unusually warm for this time of year.

As if on cue, he saw the tiny but rapidly expanding dot of a modest personal flyer as it approached the Montréal-Mirabel Skyport out of that idyllic sky. It was eerily quiet, its engines a mere whisper carried on the breeze. The beetle-shaped aircraft descended in a speedy yet perfectly controlled manner, slowing abruptly before gently kissing the asphalt.

The hatch on the side of the flyer cycled open as a ramp unfurled downward, like a techno-organic tongue. Indeed, the aircraft as a whole gave the impression it had been grown rather than constructed. There were no seams, no welds. The transparent windows of the cockpit blended directly into the main body, making it impossible to tell where the fuselage ended and crystal clear glass began.

Fae-tech was always impressive when you saw it up close.

She appeared at the hatch, stepping elegantly out of the

flyer's interior and looking exactly as she had the day they'd first met twenty-five years ago.

Damian remembered the time *vividly*, like it had been only yesterday.

To be honest, it was always destined to be a day he would never forget.

He had been holding his mother's hand as she peacefully slipped away from life. Danica had never truly healed from the wounds that had been inflicted on her during The War. At her age, there was only so much the Wolf could do to cure what ailed her. It was simply her time to go.

Danica Dane had always been a realist.

The Wolf-Queen had never feared death, rather embracing it as an inevitability. As long as she had lived her life honorably and upheld The Oath to the best of her ability, then she had no regrets.

The woman stepping gracefully down the ramp, dressed in an elegant, yet practical, black jumpsuit had come that day to pay her respects, assure Danica that her duty was fulfilled, and take the ritual of The Oath Swearing with her son.

"Damian. You look well."

He bowed his head in a show of deference. "It is very good to see you again, Serlia."

Serlia Knightley smiled as she approached, lifting her arms to embrace him in a warm hug. He grinned as he returned the gesture in kind.

"It's been too long..." he said with a sigh.

"Over a year, I know. I apologize for being such an inattentive godmother to you and your sisters," Serlia said softly as she withdrew from the embrace.

"No need for apologies. I think we've both had plenty to keep us occupied as of late. My condolences on Jaymes. I... I wanted to come to Nexus to see you, express my sorrow earlier, but..." He gestured back toward SkyPort.

Serlia's eyes followed his hand. Her flyer had landed near the terminal, but everywhere they looked military dropships were being fettled ready for combat. She raised an eyebrow as she turned her gaze back toward him.

"It seems that preparations are well underway," she commented. "May I ask what it is you are preparing *for*?"

Damian smiled wryly at Serlia and shook his head. "You've been talking to Joseph Wessex," he said, putting his hands on his hips. "Is that why you're here?"

"One of the items on my agenda," Serlia admitted. "War *is* coming, Damian. You knew after the bombing that this was inevitable...so why are you sitting on the fence about committing to it?"

"I am committing to it," he argued. "These troops are bound for the Pack Nation border. To shore up our defenses in case—"

"*That* is not committing to the war, Damian," Serlia interrupted. "That is preparing for Lyssa Balthazaar to fail."

"Serlia, I don't think you fully understand the position I'm in. Lyssa and I were making plans to overthrow StormHall, but we weren't ready yet..."

Serlia laughed lightly. "To quote Chaucer, 'Time and tide wait for no man.' Destiny does not wait until *you* are ready, Damian. The River runs its course with little regard to our whims."

"Regardless," Damian sighed, "there are too many issues preventing our involvement. The plan had been to get the support of the NAA and the FSE before we committed to triggering a war. I understand Lyssa's hand has been somewhat forced by the current events, but without support, there is little chance of victory."

"Damian, the day your mother died, you took The Oath. The promise Danica upheld for over a century. On *that* day, the responsibility fell to you—"

"And I have continued to hold true to that oath, Serlia," Damian interjected firmly. "The vow the Fae swore us to was to protect humanity. My ancestors took on that promise, my mother upheld it, and I have done everything in my power to carry on her legacy. Even after The Rising. We offered Humans haven here in Pack Nation. Protected them to the best of our ability.

"The oath I swore does not include protecting Vampyrii."

Serlia smiled and gestured broadly northwest with her hand. "Out there is a Vampyrii who never made the promise you did. Yet, she is working to make this world a better place for *everyone*. She doesn't care whether the people she is fighting for are Vampyrii, Werewolf, Human, or Fae. Lyssa is simply driven to correct what she perceives as a wrong.

"You have no idea how...surprising that is."

Damian shook his head. "She has no choice—"

"Everyone has a choice," Serlia interrupted. "She could have sat back and chosen to live life under StormHall's rule. It would have been easier for her in many ways, instead of putting herself and her family at risk. But Lyssa chooses to fight. To seek alliances with races that consider her a mortal enemy to try and do what is right.

"And all that...*without* swearing The Oath."

Damian closed his eyes and tilted his head back. He exhaled heavily. He knew Serlia was right, but he still felt that the risk was simply too high.

"I understand that," he said quietly, "but if we do this and fail, I won't be able to protect the Humans we have sheltered here. What of my oath then?"

Serlia simply smiled. "Trust me and have faith, godson. Do what you feel in your heart is right. Now, talking of Lyssa, did she arrive safely?"

Damian nodded. "She's in Domaine Saint-Bernard, camped out in the command center they set up in the Pavilion, working flat-out. She rarely leaves."

"Has she spoken to you? About...Allyson."

"Your daughter? No, why would she...?"

"Ah." Serlia smiled sadly. "It's not my place to say anything. You should talk to her, though. Sooner rather than later."

He returned her smile and held out his arm for her to take. The two walked slowly, side-by-side, toward the terminal building and the waiting transport that would take them to his home.

"Of course," he said. "Just promise me you and I can have dinner and a proper catch-up that's not related to politics or impending war."

"Well," Serlia said with a sly smile, "before we take those topics off the table altogether, I do have an idea I want to run past you..."

| **72** |

WHAT'S NEXT?

— **Alexa Reynolds** —
— *Wednesday* — *New Africa Airspace* —

Nothing but blue skies.

If you could ignore the constant drone of *Diana*'s engines, then there was no more peaceful place to be than cruising at forty thousand feet with open sky above and wisps of cotton-wool clouds below. Alexa sat in the pilot's seat with her feet up on the console, staring out at the horizon. The cockpit windscreen was a single curved piece of plexiglass, giving a stunning one-hundred-and-eighty-degree panoramic view of the horizon.

The vista was...breathtaking.

Above her, the sky faded from brilliant azure to deep indigo with the tease of a star-filled night sky. Ahead of her *Diana* chased the setting sun toward the gentle curvature of the Earth as they headed west. Below the clouds, the anarchic lands of Africa passed by beneath them as the autopilot counted down to their north turn toward the FSE.

London was calling.

But after that, what the fuck do we do next?

Becka was sleeping soundly in her quarters, and Rahanah was using Alexa's bunk to similarly rest while Alexa kept an eye on the flight deck. She enjoyed her alone time up here. It was where she did some of her best thinking.

Tonight, though, her idea pool was dry.

She was heading to London simply because she had no idea where else to go. Alexa figured maybe talking this through with Mikey might help. Perhaps he could see a path she couldn't.

It wasn't like the trail was cold.

They had been led directly to the door of the next mystery.

An aircraft carrier flying the flags of the Japanese Empire and one of the legendary TechMasters. Metaphorically, it was a door made of steel, encased in diamond, and placed behind a level five forcefield without an apparent keyhole.

Yet, all doors can be opened if you know how.

Alexa had been thinking about this conundrum for a while now, and she had no answers.

The next logical step would be to find out which Japanese TechMaster they were dealing with, why they would be collecting a variety of supernatural creatures, and what they were doing with them once they had taken receipt. The first question should be relatively easily answered. *Diana* had cameras that were constantly running, recording everything that happened. They had video footage of the carrier and sensor readings. If they could find someone with intelligence about the TechMasters, they should be able to identify who they were dealing with.

Alexa thought she knew who they could talk to on that front.

The other issues were far more difficult to find a route around.

Even if they found the name they were looking for, it was unlikely that they could waltz up to the TechMaster in question and start asking questions. The Japanese Empire had closed its borders a decade ago, and they'd kept their affairs private ever since. If the Empire in general was secretive, then the TechMasters were worse.

Apart from their names and a few items of technology that appeared occasionally on the black market, almost nothing was known about them.

That was their dead end.

Yet, Alexa felt a need to try and find a way.

So...the best plan she had at the moment was to head to the UK to collect their CombatSkins and talk to Michael. From there, it was a short hop to Nexus City to see a woman about a ship.

| 73 |

FACING HER FEARS

— **Lana Fordham** —
— *Thursday* — *London, England* —

Lana ran.

She had to find help. Fast.

What the fuck is she thinking?

Barreling through the Academy's main doors, she made a beeline for the Officers Lounge, praying Michael and Amanda were lunching there. Reaching the lounge, she yanked the door open and burst in, breathlessly coming to a halt.

Thank fuck!

The very two people she was hoping to find looked up from the tablets they were holding, surprised by the sudden interruption. Before either could speak, Lana blurted out the news, a little louder than she had intended.

"Gayle's gone."

"What do you mean gone?" Michael said, looking confused.

"She's stolen a flyer...and fucking *gone*."

Amanda stood up so fast her chair toppled over. "She's *what*?"

"Gayle's taken the Banshee that escorted *Minerva* in," Lana spat out between labored breaths. "I don't know why, or where she thinks she's going, but understandably FSE Air Command is *pissed*. She took it without authorization."

"Where...the fuck...is she going?" Amanda muttered as she started pacing.

"I told you, I don't know." Lana shrugged. "She didn't say a word to me..."

"I haven't seen her today, but I spoke to her yesterday evening," Michael offered. "She didn't say anything about this."

Lana turned to stare at him. Amanda did likewise. Michael's eyes flicked between the two of them, his features betraying a confusion Lana was sure was mirrored on her own face. But while he may not have answers, maybe he *could* help them figure out exactly what was going on.

"Where? What *did* she say?" Lana pried.

"She was out on the landing pad... Fuck." He whispered the curse, and Lana realized it might be the first time she'd ever heard him use profanity.

"What?" she prodded.

"She was watching the ground crews repairing *Minerva*, then she started staring at the Banshee. I tried to get her to open up about what she was thinking, and after a minute she started talking about how she'd visited Captain Torbar. How she felt she hadn't been dealing with what happened in Valletta...stuff like that."

Amanda stopped her pacing and stared at Michael. She held up her hand and made a circular motion with it. "Hold on. Rewind," she said. "Tell me *exactly* what she said."

Michael nodded and thought for a moment before talking. "She said Captain Torbar remembered everything that happened to him and his team..." he paused to think again for a beat. "She said she felt like she hadn't dealt with her emotions about Valletta. And something he'd said about being tempered—"

"Tempered?" Lana interrupted, confused.

"Yeah," Amanda nodded. "I remember Gambler once telling me that the reason the 136th always went straight back out after a loss, even if short-handed, was because Torbar felt it 'tempered' them. Allowed them to cope with inevitable loss. He said they thought of themselves as the hammer to our—"

"—our scalpel," Lana finished, nodding. "Yeah, they used that analogy a lot."

Amanda turned to Michael. "Gambler was Dylan Blake, *Minerva*'s pilot."

Michael nodded. "Yeah, I'm familiar with the roster. Okay, so then she started telling me how she'd been talking to you, Amanda, on the gun range. That you'd told her she had to face her fears head-on...and that she'd finally figured out what that fear was."

"Figured out her fear..." Amanda's voice trailed off as she started pacing again, deep in thought.

Lana slumped down into one of the comfortable chairs in the lounge, desperately trying to figure out where Gayle needed to go badly enough that she would risk her career by stealing a Banshee. She started running the calculations in her head, whispering them out loud as she did so.

"She's not going to Nexus—a commercial flight could have got her there without risking her career. Likewise, the rest of Europa..."

"So," Michael contributed to her quiet rationalizing, "she's heading somewhere she can't get to under normal circumstances. But why the Banshee? Her family has a personal flyer, don't they?"

"Yeah, it's hangered at Duxford," Lana confirmed. "She could have got to it in a little over an hour."

"But she chose not to. Why not?" Michael pondered.

"Range," Lana suggested. "It's a de Havilland F144 Banshee, one of the fastest attack flyers in the FSE Air Force, but it also has a roundtrip range of 2500 miles...almost twice that of her family's flyer."

"Okay, so 2500 miles..." Michael was pacing now, too. "Well, that's too short for a trip to the west, so not to New Victus. Not sure why she'd go there anyway—"

"You said she talked about facing her fear?" Amanda interjected quietly.

Michael nodded his confirmation.

"Then, shit," she said, closing her eyes. "I know where she's going."

| 74 |

BACK TO WHERE IT ALL BEGAN

— **Michael Reynolds** —
— *Thursday* — *En-route* — *Valletta, Malta* —

Artemis's engines reverberated through the troop compartment as Amanda sat with her foot agitatedly bobbing.

"What the *hell* was she thinking?" she whispered angrily.

Sitting across from her, Michael had to admit he was contemplating exactly that. What *had* possessed Gayle to appropriate an FSE Banshee and abscond back to the very place that had caused her so much distress?

"Amanda...I need to know what happened on the Valletta mission."

She glanced at him and shrugged. "You know what happened," she said quietly. "You've read the—"

"—Yeah," he interrupted. "I read the words. But I need to *hear* it from you. I'm sorry, but I need to *understand* what happened there. I need all the details that you couldn't put in an official report. Okay?"

After a beat, Amanda reluctantly nodded and took a deep breath.

Her eyes glazed over with the unfocused stare of someone reliving a memory. He could see the fear in her face, her tense body language. Michael didn't blame her. Knowing the extent of the injuries she had sustained, he would have been more surprised if she *hadn't* been terrified of returning to Valletta.

"Did you ever fight on the African front?" she began quietly.

Michael shook his head. While he knew the Navy operated over here, the NAA Army had never fought in Africa. This was predominantly an FSE conflict.

"The African front is a seething cauldron of feuding nests populated by the various vampire breeds, each slightly different from the other. The Obayifo, the Tikoloshe, the Asanbosam... There are *many*... Where the Vampyrii are civilized by nature, many of the other breeds can be more...Darwinian."

"Survival of the fittest." Michael nodded his understanding.

"The Adze are the worst," Amanda continued. "Nobody knows where they came from, but they are—by far—the most fucking terrifying of all the vampire breeds. Almost a force of nature. The most...inhuman. They don't talk. They don't use technology or machines.

"They form nests...or broods with each individual a part of a kind of hive mind. And they spread like a virus. Or maybe a plague. One Adze bites a Human, infecting them. That person bites another, then their victim bites another, and another, and so on. And the turn is...fast. Get *bitten* by an Adze and you have minutes to put a bullet in your brain before you're in the thrall of the Alpha.

"Each brood is ruled by a king or a queen, or whatever title they bestow on themselves. We refer to them as Alphas for simplicity. They are always the strongest of their clan, but rarely the smartest. They rise to power through sheer brutality.

"Once you're part of the hive mind, you're lost. The complete genetic transformation takes a couple of days, but what made you an individual—a person—is already long gone. You're just a drone. If you happen to be bigger and stronger than the Alpha, then maybe you can challenge them. Take over. But you're *still* Adze. Still part of the single consciousness."

She paused for a second, swallowing hard at the memories

of the monsters who had left her at the edge of death. After a moment, her eyes locked with his again.

"During 'The Rising,' these other breeds of Vampyrii swept across Africa with frightening speed, carving out huge swathes of territory for their groups. Once they'd taken the continent and had nowhere else to go...the infighting started.

"Back then, the FSE didn't care; they had bigger fish to fry. But then, out of the blue about a year ago, the squabbling stopped and they started getting...coordinated. Strategically organized. Intelligence said they were being guided by something—or someone—they referred to as Tok. We don't know if Tok is a he, a she, or a they, and we have no idea of their motivations. All we knew is suddenly the Vampires of Africa were united and looking to push into Europa.

"FSE forces had a foothold territory in Morocco and Algeria, but a surprise Obayifo offensive drove them back into Spain. Which presented a problem. The Straits of Gibraltar became a battleground, and the battle was preventing the FSE and NAA Naval Fleets from entering the Mediterranean...or those that were already there from leaving. Tunisia was *already* in enemy hands. Sardinia and Corsica were under constant assault. Worse still, they now also held the ports of Tripoli. The strategy seemed pretty clear...Malta was the next step for them, their stepping stone into Italy.

"A potential staging ground for a push deep into the FSE.

"Unfortunately for us, the bulk of the FSE forces were fighting in the Straits of Gibraltar. By the time those forces were diverted toward Malta, it was too late. The island was already under siege.

"The Sixth US Fleet was stationed in the Tyrrhenian Sea, but the Tikoloshe owned the waters of the Mediterranean due to the fleet they had operating out of Tunis. Not a huge fleet, but enough to hold its own against the Sixth and to get a small Adze force onto the island of Malta itself..."

She trailed off for a moment. All this was a matter of record. He'd been a US Marine in Alaska at the time, but he'd been well aware of how the war was progressing on all fronts.

"Malta had huge strategic importance," she continued

eventually. "The FSE used it as a forward outpost to observe and report on movements in the Mediterranean. Since we lost global satellite surveillance, having listening stations was *key* to our security. There weren't many civilians left on the island; most had been killed during 'The Purification' and many more had evacuated. But there *were* still some manning the listening station at Fort St. Elmo in the capital at the north end of the island. Valletta." She smiled briefly and a little sadly.

"So...the HFA sends in its infamous 137th Hunters to evacuate them. The plan called for *Artemis* to drop us off a couple of kilometers outside the city. From there, we'd head up to Fort St. Elmo, sweeping the city to clear out any Adze we found while getting civilians back to the fort ready for extraction.

"We had a three-hour window before *Artemis* and a fleet of troopships from the *USS Ronald Reagan* would swoop in to pick up us and any survivors from the roof of the fort. Then the FSE would begin a soft naval bombardment to 'cleanse' the island before landing troops to retake and secure it.

"Intelligence estimated there were less than fifty Adze on the island. A small advance force sent to establish a beachhead before a larger force of Asanbosam troops arrived.

"Intelligence was *wrong*.

"As we headed deeper into Valletta, it became clear the Adze had infiltrated the island *much* earlier than we'd thought, and in greater numbers. They had already turned many of the FSE troops based there."

"So, what happened then?" Michael asked.

She looked up at him, her eyes heavy with tears that threatened to run down her cheeks at any moment.

"We fucked up," she said quietly.

| 75 |

OPERATION MALTA—PART 1

— **Amanda Forrester** — **Call sign 'Zephyr'** —
— *1 Year Earlier* — *Valletta, Malta* —

"Admiral, the island is compromised. Your intelligence—if you can call it that—was incorrect. We're estimating one thousand plus Adze here. We need air support and ground reinforcements."

"What is your current position, Captain?"

Gayle looked around for identifying features. "We're in a car park off Triq Nazzjonali, near a structure like a pair of arches—"

"Bieb il-Bombi," Gabe interjected.

"Bieb il Bombi," Gayle repeated. "We're about to enter the city, but are detecting a heavily embedded enemy presence. Exceeding the level intelligence suggested."

There was a prolonged silence from the other end of the radio call. Amanda watched Gayle cast her eye at Gabriel who shrugged back at her.

"Fleet, this is Captain Knightley...can you please give me an answer on the reinforcement request?"

"Captain Knightley, this is Admiral Matthews. You're ordered to withdraw to the Marsa Horse Racing Track for immediate extraction. The *Artemis* is en route. What is your estimated ETA?"

Amanda looked at Ghost. Maggie's face was ashen.

"Begging your pardon, sir," Gayle replied, "but we came here to extract the FSE outpost staff and their families. The job's not done yet."

There was not even a moment of hesitation on the radio before the message came back. "New intelligence concurs with your assessment of the current situation. A main force of Adze *is* already in the city. The area is considered too hot to get drop-ships in for evacuation or reinforcement. We have deemed the odds of a successful evacuation as being too low to attempt. The fleet will arrive in three hours to begin a soft bombardment. With all due respect, Captain, this job is too big for your team. Let us handle it."

That last comment elicited a palpable response around the group. Hackles were raised at the mere mention that this was a matter above their capabilities. Amanda looked around to see ten other determined faces staring back at Gayle as she prepared her response to the clearly misinformed commanding officer of the FSE Sixth Fleet. Only Ghost kept her eyes averted, staring at the ground.

Nobody else seemed to have noticed, but it concerned Amanda to see *that* look on her friend's face.

She knew what it meant.

"With all due respect, Admiral," Gayle shot back defiantly, "you have *no* idea what my team is capable of."

"That's an order, Captain. We're pulling you out."

Amanda checked the magazines on her *Firestorms*, knowing what was coming next. Locked and loaded and ready to go. The other members of the team, while unarmed conventionally, still had their own ways of preparing for the combat to come. The decision to carry out their mission whatever the cost had been determined the minute they stepped off *Artemis* and watched Lana depart. Regardless of Admiralty orders, the 137th *were* going in.

She wasn't afraid; quite the opposite. Confidence ran high for the 'Hunters.' The unit had a track record of achieving the impossible, and this was simply shaping up to be another one of those times. Veterans of three hundred and seventy-five missions and counting, with only a single casualty back in their early days. Not a single mission failure scarred their track record. Quitting this one before it had even really begun was not a palatable option. Especially knowing the hundreds of innocent people who would perish in a hail of friendly fire if they bugged out now.

"Technically, Admiral, I take my orders from HFA Command...not the FSE Admiralty. We're staying," Gayle said firmly. It was a technical loophole at best, one Amanda wasn't sure would stand up in a court-martial hearing. "So, I suggest you get your precious little boats over here and rendezvous at the Fort as per the original plan. Knightingale out."

She tossed the radio down in disgust before he could respond and turned to face Amanda and Gabriel, sighing heavily.

"Are you two with me?" she asked.

Rio looked back at her with an expression that queried her sanity. The handsome Brazilian raised his eyebrows and flashed his wide smile of perfect teeth. "You really feel the need to ask, Captain?"

"Zephyr?" Gayle prompted.

Technically Amanda was third in command, so if Gayle and Gabe agreed on a course of action, she couldn't overrule them. But Gayle liked to get multiple inputs on her decision-making and always took Amanda's opinion as seriously as Rio's, which Amanda greatly appreciated. There may have been a growing sense of tension and disharmony lately in the group when they weren't on active duty, but in the field, they didn't miss a beat.

"You know that order likely came from Norbel, right?" Amanda commented.

"Yeah, and there will likely be hell to pay when I get back. But I'm *not* leaving defenseless civilians to be wiped out by our own guns or get turned by Adze. If I can use our presence here to force Admiral Matthews' hand...then I'll fucking do it."

"Then I'm in, no question...but," Amanda hesitated.

"What?" Gayle asked.

Amanda took a deep breath and flicked her eyes toward Ghost. Gayle followed her gaze. "Shit..." she muttered. "Shit."

"She's never wrong," Amanda said quietly.

"I know. Fuck!" Gayle exhaled heavily. "But it doesn't change the equation. I'm supposed to choose one of us over hundreds of defenseless civilians?"

"No, I'm not saying that at all." Amanda shook her head. "I'm in. We all are. I just…"

"Maybe she's wrong this time," Gabe said softly.

"You heard Amanda," Gayle sighed. "Ghost is *never* wrong."

"Your call, Captain," he said, subtly fingering his crucifix.

Gayle composed herself for a moment, then raised her voice to address her team. "Okay then, Hunters. I want to be in Fort Elmo before sundown and in plenty of time before the fleet arrives." Gayle turned her attention to Chloé Barbier, their navigation specialist. "Misty, give us three flanking routes up to the Fort. Rio, you take your team southeast, Zephyr to the northwest. My team goes straight up the middle. This territory still has a heavy enemy presence, so no stupid mistakes. I want everyone to be extra vigilant. Stay sharp. Cover each other and don't take chances. You find Adze, you clear them out if it's safe to do so. Don't take unnecessary risks. Am I clear?"

The team nodded and grunted their acceptance of her instructions.

"Any civilians you find, you escort safely to the Fort for extraction. We rendezvous in one hour. Do *not* be late. Right, you've got your orders…jump to it!"

There was no need for a chorus of 'Yes, sirs' or 'Affirmatives', they all knew what to do.

| 76 |

TOTAL RECALL

— Gayle Knightley —
— Thursday — Valletta, Malta —

She left the Banshee powered down and secured at the Marsa Horse Racing Track, in almost the same spot *Artemis* had dropped off the team a year earlier. From there she made her way northeast, re-treading the path the 137th had taken toward Valletta.

This much she remembered.

Gayle walked with measured purpose until she arrived at the familiar sight of the Porte des Bombes about thirty minutes later. She paused beneath the decorative arches where Triq Nazzjonali became Triq Sant' Anna, her hand softly brushing the stone.

They had passed through here.

This…is where it had all started to go wrong. She looked toward the spot where Maggie had stopped, the memory coming back to her like a specter of the past manifesting to tell her the story she couldn't remember…

- - 1 Year Earlier - -

Three clicks.

Bollocks!

Gayle heard the signal she had been dreading since Amanda drew her attention to Ghost's distress earlier. She prayed that maybe the feeling would pass. A forlorn hope. Zephyr was right—Maggie's feeling was never wrong. Maggie signaling to get Gayle's attention now could only mean one thing... The feeling was getting worse.

Gayle motioned for her team to hunker down quietly and keep their eyes peeled for trouble while she attended to Maggie. Her face was pale and drawn. Though she knew what was wrong, Gayle asked anyway. Trying to keep it casual.

"You okay, Ghost?"

"Something..." Maggie's voice trembled as she spoke.

Fuck.

"Like Valerio?" Gayle asked quietly.

Maggie nodded.

Fuck!!

She hated to ask the next question, but she needed to know. "Any idea...who?"

A shake of the head. "Gayle...this is like Valerio multiplied tenfold. Something is very, *very* wrong here... We have to leave. We have to leave *now*."

She knew what Maggie's feelings meant. It was a premonition. The Reaper was stalking them, hiding in the shadows waiting to claim one of them.

Whenever Mags felt like this, death *always* followed.

"We can't go back now. We need to get to the rendezvous, link up with Rio and Zephyr's teams, and call in Fordith. She can drop *Artemis* right down into the Fort and we're out of here. Okay?"

Maggie nodded, but the look on her face was one of resignation.

Someone was dying today...no matter what they did.

- - Now - -

Gayle vividly remembered the feeling of dread in the pit of her stomach after she spoke with Ghost. The knowledge that she or one of her team would not make it out of this mission alive was sobering. Her only option at that point had been to try to keep the mission on track and find some way to make any inevitable loss worth it.

Not for a second, at the time, had she considered the scope of the disaster that awaited them.

She retraced her steps, walking the deserted streets. Strolling down Triq Sant' Anna, each building she passed encouraged a new sliver of recovered memory. When her team had walked this route, they checked through many of these structures, searching for survivors who may have taken refuge from the Adze infestation.

They had found none.

It didn't stop them from searching.

Turning left onto Triq Sarria, she curved around past the domed roof of the Sarria Church. Gayle paused for a moment, admiring the architectural beauty of the building. Something she hadn't been able to do on the mission. She'd had neither the time nor the inclination.

They had checked inside here for survivors, hoping *this* might be somewhere the scared and vulnerable would gather. But it was empty bar a few Adze hiding in the shadows, waiting for sunset to arrive. Her team quickly dispatched the monsters, leaving this former place of worship feeling eerily more like a tomb.

All the Sarria Church had done was move the needle on Gayle's suspicions. There was no one alive in Valletta, not anymore. It was a hypothesis reinforced further when they moved down the street to the St. Publius Parish Church.

She walked beneath the trees of Triq Sarria until she reached the open cobbled ground in front of St. Publius and stopped. She peered up at the twin bell towers, closing her eyes for a moment and taking a deep breath before opening them again. *Everything* was identical to how it had been that evening one year ago. The smell of the air, the eerie silence, the dappled golden shadows of sunset splashed across the ground.

The gates and the doorway to the church were still open.

Just the way they had left them...

- - 1 Year Earlier - -

"Misty!" Gayle whispered urgently.

Her team was crouched behind a couple of rusted cars, likely abandoned in the street decades earlier during The Rising. Gayle prided herself on her vehicle knowledge, but even she had no clue what make and model these had once been. Today, though, they were simply cover.

"Oui, boss," Chloé Barbier whispered as she approached Gayle.

"Razor and I are going to check out the church. I need you to keep an eye on Ghost."

"I don't think that's a good idea." Chloé frowned. "You should not enter short-handed."

"I'm fairly sure Razor would take offense at that." She deadpanned before nodding toward Ghost. "Besides, I don't think we have a choice. Mag's is getting worse by the minute. Keep her safe out here, okay? Razor and I can handle a quick sweep"

Chloé didn't look sold on the plan, glancing at Ghost before turning back with a sigh. "We all know what Ghost's feelings mean," she said, but stopped short of actually saying it. "This may not be a good time to split up. We don't know who is...at risk."

Gayle could see a mixture of doubt and fear in her eyes, and she had to admit, Chloé had a point. But with each minute that passed, Maggie was looking less and less able to protect herself, let alone assist them in a search exercise. Would Ghost be the victim of her own prophecy?

Seven years ago, they hadn't understood what Ghost's 'feelings' signified. Now they did. But did being forewarned mean they could prevent catastrophe? Or was someone's death an inevitability?

Valerio had been but the first. Maggie had also predicted the loss of members of Torbar's squad, in addition to close family members of the Hunters. Her distress unfailingly predicted bereavement.

"Noted," Gayle growled. "Just keep her, *and* yourself, safe."

Chloé nodded her acceptance of the task. Gayle signaled

for her to return to Ghost while she kept low behind the car and crept up to where Riku Shi—Razor—was keeping an eye on the church, tapping her on the shoulder when she arrived. Hand signals communicated her intent.

I'm on point. Stay close. Be ready.

Riku nodded.

Gayle counted them in with her fingers. *Three...two...one...*

She broke cover, sprinting across the open ground. The metal gates were already twisted and broken, giving them access to large wooden doors that appeared firmly closed. Barricaded from the inside perhaps. Gayle didn't stop to check; simply hit them with a concentrated blast of wind, focused like a battering ram. The doors flew violently open, wood splintering off the locks as the hinges bent under the force.

- - Now - -

The door sat askew, hanging awkwardly. Her fingers brushed lightly over the wood as she entered. Claw strikes marred the smooth surface with ugly splintered scars where Adze had tried, and failed, to gain access.

Yet, despite the doors thwarting their efforts, they *had* found a way in.

Gayle walked down the aisle, her footsteps echoing in the ominous tranquility. She stopped when she reached the center of the church's cruciform layout and looked up at the rich red walls with their ornate gold detailing.

She hoped it might spark something that would reconnect her broken memories.

Spotting what looked like an information pamphlet amongst the dust and debris strewn across the colored stone floor, Gayle crouched to pick it up. She leafed through its tattered pages, pausing to read a section that detailed the paintings decorating the ceiling. It said they depicted the tragedy of Saint Paul's shipwreck and his resultant stay in Malta. Her eyes flicked from the murals to a statue of Christ, and then to the many bloodstains that tarnished the religious chamber.

The bodies of the victims were long gone.

The memories flooded back.

So *many* victims.

She and Riku had breached the church ready for a fight, expecting to rescue the civilians sheltering within. They were too late. Very much too late. All they had found in the church was a tragedy about which no one would ever paint murals.

Gayle didn't know where those bodies were now. The church was empty. Did Adze devour their victims? Perhaps hungry stray animals had feasted on the corpses. Either way, they were gone. The train of thought brought dark musings about what might have happened to her teammates. Closing her eyes, she tried to remember the details...but that memory wouldn't come.

Maybe because she hadn't arrived at that part of her journey just yet.

The pamphlet fluttered back to the floor as she turned and headed back out to the street.

- - 1 Year Earlier - -

The bloodbath they found in the church brought a dark cloud upon them.

With Gayle acting as rearguard, her team moved across St. Publius Square, heading for the Phoenicia Malta Hotel. An ashen Maggie was in bad shape ahead of her, being physically supported by Chloé as they staggered across the open ground. She'd *never* seen Ghost this debilitated before. The further they pressed northeast toward the Fort, the worse she seemed to get.

Gayle was now actively questioning the wisdom of this course of action.

The specter of Death was close; even she could feel it.

There was no one left to rescue here but themselves, and whether they could pull that trick off was becoming increasingly open to debate. She considered breaking radio silence to talk to Rio and Zephyr. To get their opinions on what to do next.

No. Stick to the plan.

If she broke protocol and called them now, she could expose them. They were staying dark to facilitate their stealth through the city. Yet, it was increasingly evident to Gayle that stealth was now irrelevant. The Adze *knew* they were here.

The Hunters had become the hunted.

And time was now very much of the essence.

Passing the hotel, Gayle glanced at the readout on her wrist monitor looking for distance and time. Turning back was out of the question. They had long passed the halfway point. The Fort was now the closer destination for them to reach. Their best hope for getting out of this mess was to get there and pray the evacuation dropships arrived in time.

- - Now - -

Her journey was almost complete.

She stood at the bottom of the steps that would take her onto the roof of the Fort, where the final stand of the 137th Hunters had happened twelve months ago.

The rest of her journey had been a trip down memory lane; this was where she entered unknown territory. Those memories had been a salve on her emotions. It felt like her team was with her again, following her through the darkening streets and now standing beside her as she paused before taking her final steps.

But this was something she was going to have to do alone.

These steps were her last vague memory; everything afterward was a fiction made real in her head through the words of others.

To truly heal the rift in her soul, she needed to reconcile with the ghosts of her history, then leave them where they belonged. In the past. That was why she had come. It was a pilgrimage of sorts.

Amanda had told her to 'face her fear.'

She realized now that was exactly what this was about.

Fear.

She had made excuses. Dozens of them.

Broken. Washed up. Unloved. Unlovable. Addicted. Angry.

Out of control...

Therapy had helped. Having her friends around her again had helped even more.

And then...there was Michael.

She closed her eyes and thought about him for a moment. The man she had fallen in love with, though she was too scared to voice it out loud. Their blossoming relationship had become a lifeline, saving her from sinking. She had grasped it with both hands.

Yet something held her back from committing fully.

It was a good relationship, exactly what she needed both professionally and personally.

But was she *using* him as a crutch to prop herself up?

It was a question that hadn't occurred to her until she spoke to Alastair. Their relationship had been toxic in the extreme, a fact she historically blamed on *him*. But during their conversation, she realized she was just as complicit. She had hated *him* for a situation for which they had been equally culpable.

This was when the epiphany hit her.

It was all about balance.

She needed to let go of the things that were out of her control. What happened to Alastair *proved* they'd been set up from the start. Targeted.

And Lana and Amanda were right. She *had* made the decisions, but with the way she led the 137th, anyone *could* have questioned her. Yet nobody had. All of them had been cocky, arrogant in their untouchability, and it led to their ultimate downfall.

Yet, she couldn't divorce herself from all the blame.

Gayle had to accept some responsibility for her situation. Her actions *had* helped lead her to this dark place. Should she have seen the ambush coming? Maybe.

The Hunters had been a thorn in the side of their enemies for a long time. Perhaps it had only been a matter of time before they conspired to take them down.

And she *had* been the one making the final decisions, even if her peers hadn't challenged her.

She needed to be here today. Needed to face this moment of her past if she wanted to move past it.

With emotion surging within her, she slowly lifted her foot, taking that first step toward accepting the past.

And who she was going to be moving forward.

| 77 |

OPERATION MALTA—PART 2

— Amanda Forrester — Call sign 'Zephyr' —
— 1 Year Earlier — Valletta, Malta —

Amanda led her team down Triq Sarria, sticking to the shadows of the buildings as the sun continued its leisurely arc toward the horizon. Jaylen took point, her body covered in a thin layer of the protective stone. Behind her, Mae was laying down a protective blanket of localized fog, while Ralf, the team's foremost hand-to-hand combat specialist, acted as rearguard. Their call signs suited them well—Tank, Vapor, and Scrapper.

She knew it wasn't a coincidence they were assigned to her. In terms of raw power, she was one of the weaker members of the unit, thus her team consisted of some of the most potent. Vapor's ability masked their presence as they advanced. Tank and Scrapper acted as Amanda's protective detail. They moved with practiced speed and stealth.

Ghost's portentous feelings had persuaded Amanda to take no chances. She wanted to get her team to Fort St. Elmo intact and as soon as possible. Maybe Gayle would be pissed that they hadn't diligently scoured every nook and cranny of Valletta as they slipped silently through it, but Amanda didn't give a fuck.

She had a very bad feeling about this place.

Thirty minutes later, the sun was setting, and Zephyr was

crouched in the orange-hued shadows of a building across from the entrance to Fort St. Elmo. For decades, the building had been a museum dedicated to the history of Malta as a prominent site in warfare. Today, though, with its strategic position on the tip of the peninsular, it had been pressed back into service as a fortress containing the FSE listening post.

Amanda cradled her right arm and glanced down at the bloodstains on her CombatSkin. They didn't show too badly due to the darkened color of the stealth-suit. She cursed herself for being careless during the brief skirmish with a few Adze they ran into en route. Razor-sharp talons had made short work of the Kevlar-layered fabric and cut deep into her flesh. The outfit repaired itself and sealed up her wounds, but could do little about what she suspected was a broken, or at the very least fractured, forearm.

They were the first team to arrive, but within minutes, Gayle's team filtered in through the doorway. Misty, Razor, Ghost, and then Knightingale herself.

"Jesus, Zephyr, what happened?" Gayle whispered, her voice filled with concern as she noticed Amanda's injury.

"We ran into a little resistance, and I was a shade too slow. It could have been worse," she said reassuringly with a smile. "I'm a better shot with my left hand anyway."

"Stay close to your team, hear me?"

"Yes, boss," Amanda replied with a nod. "Did you find any civilians out there?"

Gayle shook her head. "None."

"I got a bad feeling about this, Gayle," Amanda warned, her voice low.

"You and me both. I feel like the other shoe is yet to drop. And it's not just that..." Gayle nodded back toward an ashen Ghost.

"Fuck," Amanda muttered. "This looks worse than usual..."

"I've *never* seen her this bad," Gayle said, concern heavy in her tone. "We've got to get the fuck off this rock."

"Agreed," Amanda nodded. "There's no civilians here. They're all dead or turned, and we will be, too, if we don't leave *now*."

As if on cue, Rio and his team arrived. "We need to go," he said succinctly. "The mission's a bust. The sun will be down soon, and you *know* what that means."

"Way ahead of you," Gayle agreed. "We were discussing the same thing." She beckoned for Ghost to bring her the communications pack. "Don't worry Ghost—we're getting out of here," she said as Maggie passed her the pack.

"It's too late..." Maggie muttered distantly.

Amanda felt like a shard of ice pierced her heart at Maggie's quiet proclamation. She checked the wrist panel of her CombatSkin, verifying the time. The final few seconds ticked over the three-hour mark. The Sixth Fleet would be in the vicinity by now.

"Fleetcom, Knightingale. Copy," Gayle spoke quietly into the microphone.

The answer was immediate. "Knightingale, Fleetcom. Go ahead."

"1-3-7 on site at Fort Elmo. Minimal enemy contact thus far. No...repeat *no* survivors found. Request *Artemis* inbound for *immediate* extraction, over."

This time there was a pause before the response. Gayle had expected Admiral Matthews to come on the line to give her a dressing down for disobeying the order for evacuation, but instead, she heard a woman's voice. "Knightingale, this is Captain Ramsey of the USS—" Ramsey got off just eight words before a squeal of static disrupted the transmission.

"Someone is jamming communications..." Ghost said after a brief check. "There's nothing I can do..."

Amanda took a deep breath. *We're in trouble...*

Moments later, she heard the ominous thunder-like rumble of big guns being fired repeatedly, warships facing off in the distance.

Big trouble.

| 78 |

VALLETTA

— Amanda Forrester — Call sign 'Zephyr' —
— 1 Year Earlier — Valletta, Malta —

From the moment she met Gayle Knightley, waves of confidence rolled off the young woman like an inexorable tide. She never let the 137th believe they were the 'B' Team. Never indulged the myth they were inferior to 136th.

The Hunters had been recruited nine years ago because they were kids with raw talent. Untrained, but with potential. Amanda knew the reason they reached that potential was because of Gayle's determination. She demanded a high set of standards from herself which raised the bar for everyone around her. And everyone was happy to follow her lead because of her charisma and natural leadership qualities. When you were at the edge of quitting and thought you couldn't push any harder, she was there to run through that brick wall with you.

They were an experienced team, and they all instinctively knew what that squeal of static meant for them. Even so, Amanda was shocked to see a fleeting look of despair on the face of their captain. She was the source of their courage, their optimism...but right now, even Gayle recognized this was a no-win scenario.

Yet in a flash, the look was gone. Gayle's eyes started darting around, surveying their location as her brain searched for a way out. Something—anything—that would allow them to survive whatever was about to engulf them.

"High ground," she muttered. "We need high ground..." Her eyes flicked to the upper level of the Fort. Decision made. "Move like you got a purpose 1-3-7," she barked. "I want us all on that roof. Stat."

With practiced efficiency, they moved, quickly finding the stone stairs that led toward the rooftop. They were atop the Fort in seconds. Gayle immediately started barking orders at them.

"Rio, Misty, Vapor—take the northeast side near the sea. Tank, back them up. If you can use the sea to your advantage, then do it," Gayle ordered. "Zephyr, I want you in that guard tower to the east. Get on the radio, go old-school, and punch through that jamming. Get a message to *Artemis*. Tell Fordith to get her lazy ass over here for extraction. Razor, Scrapper, you're her protection detail. Once the call is made, Zephyr, use the shelter of the tower and lay down suppressing fire. Cover Scrapper and Razor while they protect you. Everyone else, spread out along the roofline and keep your eyes peeled."

Each member of the team promptly set about their assigned duties. Amanda hurried up the long ramp leading to the guard tower, lugging the radio pack with her good arm, Scrapper and Razor following closely.

While she hated being the one on radio duty, she *could* see the logic. For starters, she was injured. Additionally, her powers were subtle and all about ranged support. The guard tower would allow her to strike from range with some semblance of protection while Scrapper and Razor—both close combat specialists—could protect her from any enemy who got too near. As she clumsily unpacked the radio, she observed the other Hunters fan out across the roof in a tight semi-circle so their fields of fire overlapped.

Ghost, Celeste, Monsoon, and Bulldog stood along the edges of the roof facing inland toward the city. Any assault would likely come from that direction rather than from the sea. With the high ground established, they could hold off an attacking force with numerical superiority.

Theoretically, at least. This was Battle Tactics 101.

Knightingale prowled behind them, at the center of the formation, her face etched with concentration and concern.

"Oh, my God…"

The night was so quiet that Amanda could hear Ghost's quiet exclamation clear from the other side of the roof. Shock and despair were evident in her tone, but she didn't hesitate in taking action on what she saw. Fire poured forth from her hands, supercharged by her air powers. A devastating pair of biological flame throwers strafing back and forth into the darkness.

Moments after Ghost's initial onslaught, other members of the team opened up with their abilities. The dancing light of golden flames lit the stone of the fort as the earth trembled beneath her feet. Winds began to whistle and swirl violently around her as the sea crashed against the shore, sending waves high into the air. It was a symphony of elemental powers being used to devastating effect by eleven powerful hybrids.

Just like that, the tranquility of the night was shattered by the cacophony of battle.

From her vantage point, Amanda had no visual on what her teammates were attacking. Not that it mattered. She knew exactly what creatures were crawling out of the shadows. She was itching to get out there and help, but that wasn't the job she had been assigned to do.

She snatched up the communications pack.

They'd been burnt by jammed comms before, and Knightingale liked to be prepared. Sometimes modern problems required vintage solutions. Jaylen, who doubled as their tech expert, had used the designs of an old-school radio transmitter to add a non-standard alternative option to their comms pack. It added an element of heft to the previous lightweight equipment, so they took turns lugging it around, but it had saved their collective asses on more than one occasion. Amanda fired it up and started transmitting the emergency code Fordith monitored via a custom receiver aboard *Artemis*. She waited for the light to turn green, giving a tiny yelp of joy

when it did.
    Link established.
    Help was coming. All they had to do was hold on.

| 79 |

HISTORY LESSON

— Michael Reynolds —
— Thursday — En-Route — Valletta, Malta —

He listened with rapt attention as Amanda told the tale of the last battle of the Hunters.

And he watched.

Watched her face change as she relived the details of the events of over a year ago. It was obviously distressing for her, and Michael began to worry about what she was experiencing. As she paused in her narrative, he reached out, putting his hand on hers.

"I'm sorry. I shouldn't have asked you to talk about it."

She looked at him with unfocused eyes for a moment, as if coming out of a dream. Finally, she gave a small wry smile and nodded. "It's fine. I haven't spoken about it in a while. I had extensive counseling while I was in hospital, but even so, it's just...well...it's hard, y'know?"

He nodded his understanding.

"Back at the Academy," she continued, "before we graduated, we talked about the Fae a lot. The pure Fae. The ones who taught us how to manipulate our powers and embrace our emotions to enhance them. All of us had the ability to some degree..."

She held up her right hand and, as Michael watched, a tiny flame spontaneously ignited. As he watched, it morphed to form a tiny dancing woman that writhed seductively in her palm.

"See, I can do this without any real thought. I can generate and manipulate the flame... At the same time, I can also..." She held up her left hand where, on its palm, she generated a miniature tornado, maybe three inches in height and rotating counterclockwise. It spun for a moment before changing form to become a tiny ethereal male figure that danced to the same rhythm as the incendiary girl on the other hand.

Her eyes narrowed, and she took a deep breath.

Almost instantly, the two miniatures on each palm grew a few inches in height and levitated, drifting toward each other in front of her. The diminutive performers linked tiny elemental hands and started to pirouette together. Fire and air whirling hypnotically in mid-air.

"Wow... That's...impressive. Beautiful," he said. "But I thought..."

"That I was a 'one-trick-pony?'" Amanda smiled. "Yeah, I am...kind of. I can manipulate fire and air, but I don't have the *raw* power of the others. This is about my limit. At the Academy, I could propel tiny marble-sized fireballs on currents of air, but never quite figured out how to make them...bigger. We had a teacher called Lyvonna; she told me not to worry about that, to just try and use the power I had. She said my level of control was...unprecedented."

"Unprecedented?" Michael asked.

"Yeah, the dancers... None of the others could do that. Only me. Lyvonna taught me that there was more to using our powers than simple brute force. Which was why I started trying to use my more delicate touch with conventional weapons. Guiding bullets became my specialty. But my control and the others' raw power was small potatoes against what a full Fae could do. We saw tasters of it in class when they were teaching, but we never saw them cut loose.

"We used to talk all the time about what it would be like to see it. To see a full Fae go nuts and unleash all the power at their disposal. Just think about it...being able to throw a flaming boulder surrounded by a cloud of superheated steam with unerring accuracy? Or more than that...how about a full-scale tornado of fire circulating a maelstrom of jagged rocks and stones? Just mix and match any four elements, then throw in exquisite control and your imagination."

"Holy shit..." Michael muttered.

"Exactly. We always wondered what that might look like, but the Fae have never entered into battle. Always behind the lines...never on them.

"But that night. That night at Fort St. Elmo in Valletta...I witnessed the closest thing I think I'll ever see to that."

Michael cocked his head and looked at her curiously. "What did you see?" he asked her.

The tiny dancing apparitions vanished into the ether from which they came as Zephyr shut off her powers and looked at him seriously. "I saw...an evolution happen before my eyes. I saw..." Amanda paused for a second, her eyes glazing over as she remembered a moment in time almost a year ago. "No, I *heard*... Knightingale sing."

| **80** |

BLOODY VALLETTA

— Amanda Forrester — Call sign 'Zephyr' —
— 1 Year Earlier — Valletta, Malta —

The shadows writhed.

Adze.

Ghost screamed as she disappeared under a seething mass of black as they poured over the walls, an irresistible wave of gleaming fangs and claws.

Those eyes. Hundreds of horrific, unblinking eyes.

So many of them.

Too many of them.

This is it... This is where it ends.

They were so fast, all around them. Zephyr lost track of Rio, Vapor, and the others. Vanished almost immediately from view by the Adze, like some macabre magic trick. Now you see them...now you don't! Scrapper and Razor closed ranks, moving back-to-back as they tried to shield their wounded teammate from the advancing horde, bracing themselves for the onslaught to come. Amanda dropped the radio and snatched up her *Firestorm*, aiming it at the closest of the Adze.

She fired.

Over and over and over.

Every bullet struck its target with unerring accuracy. Headshot after headshot, killing the monsters by the dozen. It wasn't close to being enough. For every one she dropped, two seemed to take its place.

Scrapper pirouetted elegantly, pursuing his own unique form of deadly martial arts, slashing out at the Adze with blades of sharpened stone conjured from his hands. Razor, likewise, took care of her lethal business. With fists covered in an impenetrable layer of jagged rock, her own perfectly choreographed punches and kicks were air-assisted, knocking Adze flying with every defensive move. Both were lethal fighting machines in their own right; together and acting in unison, they were practically unstoppable.

Yet against these numbers...they had no chance.

The *Firestorm*'s first magazine ran dry. Amanda desperately tried to clumsily reload it, but her broken arm did her no favors. Years of practice meant she would typically have achieved this feat in less than a second, dropping one magazine out and seamlessly snapping the next one in place. Doing it one-handed took significantly longer.

Too long.

By the time she resumed fire, Razor and Scrapper were overwhelmed, falling to the ground beneath the irresistible black tide. She heard Riku scream as she melted into a writhing mound of tooth and claw. The realization there was nothing she could do about it hit her like a sledgehammer. Tears streamed down her face as she watched Ralph, likewise, vanish from view.

She knew beyond a doubt that both her friends were dead.

The Adze advanced on her now, so close she didn't even need her abilities to hit them. A good thing as she couldn't concentrate anymore, smothered as she was in a suffocating blanket of fear. She couldn't breathe. Her hand shook almost uncontrollably as the second magazine ran empty. She dropped the gun and fumbled the other *Firestorm* out of its holster, firing it randomly into the crowd as they finally breached the door to the guard tower.

It didn't stop them.

As the last of her rounds fell spent to the floor, bouncing haphazardly off the concrete with an unheard clink, the Adze closed in. She twisted around looking frantically for an escape route, her eyes locking onto the window. A forlorn final desperate impulse. Protecting her face with her good arm, she leaped, smashing the glass and feeling its jagged shards tear at her as she passed through. She was mid-jump when she heard the sound of the razor-sharp talons cleanly cutting through the tough armor of her CombatSkin. It might as well have been made of tissue-paper for all the protection it offered her in that moment.

A split second later she felt overwhelming pain lance across her back as a million pain receptors triggered all at once. It took her that tiny moment to process the brain-shocking agony of her skin being ripped, her flesh being torn into, and then the horrific sensation of talon meeting bone as she was cut clean to her spine.

She didn't even hear her own scream as she crashed hard onto the concrete on the other side and slumped sideways to the floor. Through the pain, she tried to get up, but her legs wouldn't respond to her commands. Digging her nails into the concrete, she tried to pull herself along using her one good arm. To escape from the death blow she knew would come soon.

But her body was a dead weight, immovable, and all she could think about was the large, dark pool of ruby blood forming around her face as it pressed against the floor, and how sticky it felt on her hands as she clawed at the ground trying to drag her mortally wounded body away from danger. She was already growing cold, which made for an odd sensation as she felt the warm blood of her own body between numbing fingers.

Death did not come for her, though.

As her eyes fluttered and a cloud of darkness crept in around her peripheral vision, she witnessed something so profoundly astonishing that she would never, *ever* forget it.

Thunder clouds were rapidly rolling in, and with them came the most torrential rain Amanda could recall experiencing. Her prone body was abruptly battered by raindrops the size of golf balls. The wind picked up, too, swirling faster and faster as a dozen tiny tornadoes sprang up out of nowhere.

An almighty crack signaled the arrival of lightning, followed by the deep rumble of thunder overhead. Flashes of jagged light filled her vision, illuminating the darkness and showing her exactly *who* was responsible for this natural show of force.

A bloodied and broken Gayle Knightley hovered about twelve feet above the fort, her face contorted in grief and rage, her long pink hair flying in the tempestuous winds, and her eyes glowing bright crimson. Fury washed off her in waves. Amanda was no empath, but she could *feel* the raw unfettered emotion crashing over her.

A Hunter's power was fed by feeling, and Knightingale's pain was giving it ample fuel.

She was screaming.

Through the cacophony of noise and discord, Amanda heard it, clear as crystal.

A mournful song of despair.

Amanda had fought Adze any number of times, and they had always been the stuff of nightmares, but for the first time, she saw a terror in *their* eyes. For while they were monsters, right now they were facing something akin to a goddess out for vengeance. Intent on repaying in kind every single drop of Hunter blood spilled this night.

Nothing less would sate her appetite.

The wind rose and the fiery tornadoes roamed the rooftop, seeking out every Adze they could find and shredding them to pieces in a hail of flaming rock, literally torn apart before Zephyr's eyes.

So much blood.

Everywhere she looked, the floor was stained crimson as the blood of the slaughtered Adze mixed with the driving rain. Above it all, Knightingale hovered in the sky like an avenging angel of death, enveloped by the swirling elements she commanded to rend her enemies.

As her eyes began to close for what she expected would be the last time, Amanda didn't know if what she was feeling was awe...or fear.

Her hands grasped weakly, reaching out for her friend, her

captain, one last time before everything faded to black.

| 81 |

MAKE THIS GO ON FOREVER

— **Gayle Knightley** —
— *Thursday* — *Valletta, Malta* —

Each footstep brought with it a stab of fear greater than the last.

She *knew* the Adze had stalked her here.

As she moved through Valletta, she felt their presence. A glimpse of movement in the shadows, or behind the broken windows of the deserted buildings. They were everywhere, their stain ever-present on this once beautiful city.

Gayle wasn't sure why she ever thought she would make it from the racetrack to the fort. She wasn't sure why the Adze let her retrace those steps. All she knew was she had to try. Succeeding in getting this far was a surprise.

Her legs shook as she walked slowly up the steps and onto the roof. It was both familiar and foreign at the same time. A place she felt she should know intimately but of which she couldn't recall the details.

Had she hoped being here would bring it all back?

Return to her the memories she had lost?

As she approached the center of the roof, her legs buckled slightly. She felt sick, her hands trembled, and her breathing was irregular, rapid. Her friends had died here, suffered a horrible and painful end. Was it her fate to join them today?

A tear escaped, running down her cheek as she looked

around. The blood of her friends and the Adze she had slain in retaliation turned the once pale stone of the fort a dozen shades of crimson. They formed strange swirling, stained patterns. A beautiful yet indelible tattoo of death. She had hoped maybe there would have been some tell-tale signs indicating where her teammates had fallen, but there were none. Their blood was now forever merged with that of the monsters who slew them.

I am so sorry. I can't make this right. I wish I could.

The elusive memory of this place had nibbled away at her soul. Filled her with a guilt she clung to desperately to save herself from drowning in her grief. But now the time had come to face that night head-on. She knew what she had done that day was wrong. She would never be able to atone for the disaster she led them into that night.

But maybe it was time to let it go.

Her final few footsteps were filled with apprehension.

Finally, she stood in the exact spot she had been in twelve months ago. This time, however, she was alone. There was no backup for her. No one to protect her. Support her. Conversely, there was no one to pay for her mistakes.

Not tonight.

Under this clear sky and full moon, she would face her demons alone. Her fear, her grief...and the monsters that spawned them.

From the corner of her eye, she glimpsed the first of them. Climbing slowly in their staccato stop-motion gait, up onto the roof to her right. As she turned her head to look its way, she saw more of them. One more, five more, ten, twenty... She lost count. Surrounding her, gradually closing in.

Why so slow?

The way they moved unnerved her. Like being stalked by something not of this earth. Something alien. There were so many now that it would be simple for them to finish the job they started a year ago. Adze had a fearsome reputation as fast and efficiently lethal killing machines, so why the reticence now?

Are they waiting for something?

She tried to summon up any emotion other than fear. Anger maybe. Rage at what these creatures had done to her team. Fury at the pain they had caused her. But all she could feel was the paralyzing terror of being encircled by the black, soulless creatures. All she could see in the moonlight were dozens of unblinking eyes, gleaming dagger-like claws at the end of spindly arms, and those huge, curved fangs protruding from nightmarish mouths.

How many?

There must have been hundreds of them here, forming an impassable wall of inevitable death, and more were still arriving. They scaled the walls and crawled in from over the battlements. Yet they came no closer than about twenty feet. Like there was an invisible boundary none of them were willing to cross.

Why?

In front of her, the ring slowly parted. Adze clumsily shuffled aside, their gangly limbs looking awkward when they weren't in swift death-dealing motion. From within their midst strode an Adze of greater stature than the others. Taller and bulkier. Stronger. Its jet-black skin was marred with scars, wounds of battles fought for supremacy of its hive.

The Alpha.

So, this is it. This is why they waited. He is coming to kill me himself.

He wanted to firmly establish his superiority by killing a legend. So be it, but if he thought she would go down without a fight, he was sorely mistaken.

He advanced slowly.

Puffed up and full of confident menace.

The gap between them closed and with each step nearer, her fear ratcheted up another notch. Death was perhaps seconds away. Her CombatSkin would provide no protection against his claws. The monster could gut her, slash her throat, and leave her to death before she could react if he felt so inclined. One on one, she couldn't match him physically.

Have I come here to die? Is that what this is really about? A death wish?

No. She didn't want to die.

She wanted closure.

If the psychological wounds of the past were ever going to heal, she needed to face *this* moment. This was the closest she could get to reliving Bloody Valletta on her *own* terms. To bring light to the dark nightmares that had haunted her for too long. For a moment, a brief flickering moment, she could have sworn she saw Rio standing there. A ghostly figure. But he was dead. You can't bring back the dead.

You can only join them.

She clenched her jaw, struggling to stop her teeth from chattering with fear. To stop the tears from flowing down her cheeks.

"Do you know...who I am?" she said quietly, but firmly.

Her voice didn't waver, didn't shake.

That surprised her. She was petrified. Honest to God, piss-her-pants terrified. The Adze stood before her, so close she could hear the rasp of its breath, smell the rank odor with every exhalation. Its unblinking eyes stared at her, their milky white vacancy giving her nothing back. Her heart was beating fast, thumping like a jackhammer against her ribcage.

Her nightmares surrounded her, real-world monsters with the tools to tear her apart on a whim. Yet they stood back from her. Wary. Only their leader, the Alpha, had approached, and even that had been with an element of trepidation.

I'm not the only one afraid here.

The thought gave her a sliver of confidence. Just enough to hold on to, so she grasped it. Her throat was dry. Her lips, too. She took a deep breath and clenched her fists, summoning up every tiny bit of courage she still possessed.

"Who. Am. I?" This time her voice was louder, more forceful.

The Adze Alpha tilted its head, regarding her carefully. Its jaws stretched open slowly, the long curved fangs bared, glinting with saliva in the moonlight. Gayle was preparing herself for the attack she feared was imminent when something unexpected happened. Something she had taught her students could never happen.

The Alpha spoke.

It was a mangled set of words, hissed rather than spoken, but it was still recognizable as speech.

"Andrrrreaaaa.... Morrrrss.... Essssss't," it said. "Niiiiigghht...innn gaaaayyelllll."

He knew.

He *knew* her by name.

And he was *afraid* of her.

It didn't matter that she had no recollection of the power she had wielded that night.

It didn't matter...because he did.

"Damn fucking right, I am," she snarled and closed her eyes.

Her own fear evaporated. Transformed to something new.

Gayle had used her abilities without thinking back at the Academy while rescuing Torbar from the burning remains of *Minerva*. The experience hadn't torn her apart or left her debilitated. She hadn't felt addicted, like she craved the experience again. These powers were a part of her, as natural to her as the act of breathing.

For the first time in a year, she let her powers flow through her untamed.

Unchecked.

| 82 |

POWER DISPLAY

— **Michael Reynolds** —
— *Thursday* — *Valletta, Malta* —

"I see our girl," Lana said as she maneuvered *Artemis.*

"Where?" Michael peered through the dropship's windscreen.

"Exactly where I picked her up a year ago. Top of the fort."

In the darkness, it was practically impossible to see Gayle Knightley without some form of assistance. Fortunately, *Artemis* had night-vision built into the front windows, rendering the view in an eerie green backlight. Knightingale was easily spotted standing out in the open, atop the roof of Fort St. Elmo.

"What's she doing?"

"Oh, my God!" Lana exclaimed. "Look around her..."

Even with the aid of night-vision, they were difficult to see, but they *were* visible if you looked closely. The barest of emerald outlines gave them digital form. Adze. Hundreds of them. Scaling walls, coming from seemingly every window and door. Flanking Gayle, circling behind her. Forming a ring of death around the woman who was stood calmly waiting for them.

"She's gonna get herself killed!" Michael whispered. "We gotta do something..."

"Fordith, swing us around and pop the trunk," Amanda

said as she unstrapped herself from the co-pilot's seat.

"What are you doing?" Michael asked.

"What I do best," Amanda stated, exiting the cockpit.

Michael sat down in the seat Amanda had just vacated and strapped himself in. Lana pitched *Artemis* into a pivot, swinging the tail around toward the peninsula. Simultaneously, she reached forward and flicked a toggle on the control panel, turning the image on the central windscreen to a rearward view so they could still see Gayle. On one of the monitors, Michael saw Amanda in the troop compartment approaching the rear doors. A tether-line ran from her belt to an attachment point on the floor. In her hands was her long-range sniper rifle.

"Popping the trunk, Zephyr," Lana said as she flipped the switch on the console that opened the doors and lowered the ramp.

Michael saw Amanda touch the earpiece on her headset and heard her voice through his headphones.

"Keep her steady, Fordith."

As the ramp descended, she walked out onto it, the wind whipping her hair around her face.

Michael had read the reports, the mission logs. He knew what the 137th used to be capable of, how they used to operate. Now he was sat here, a part of them. Lana and Amanda calmly and immediately fell into a practiced routine, referring to each other by call sign as they did so. For the first time since he started working on this project, he felt out of place.

"Zephyr, I'm going to put our port side to Knightingale," she said. "That way I can get Rogue in the nose turret."

"Affirmative," came the reply.

"Can you handle that, Rogue?"

Lana was looking sideways at him. There it was. The subtle invite to the team. Till now, he had been a member of the 137th in name only, but with the use of his call sign, they were confirming his place as a Hunter. Despite the circumstances, it felt good to be invited. To belong.

He nodded and unbuckled the seatbelts he had fastened only a moment earlier. Without another word, he hopped up out of the seat and headed down the steps into the troop compartment. As he turned toward the nose turret, *Artemis* lurched sideways and started to shimmy badly. He grabbed onto the strapping to keep his balance as the dropship continued to shake, its engines whining as if under strain.

"Fucking hell, Fordith," Amanda's voice came over the headset. "I said keep her steady!"

"It's not *me*!" Lana's voice came back sounding strained. "The wind has whipped up something fierce. I can hardly keep us level, let alone steady."

Michael staggered to the nose turret and practically fell into the seat as *Artemis* shook violently again. He seated himself properly and looked out of the plexiglass toward Fort St. Elmo.

What he saw froze him in his tracks. "Y'all...are you seein' this"

| 83 |

MARCH MARCH

— **Gayle Knightley** —
— *Thursday* — *Valletta, Malta* —

Oh, my God...

Her brain was on fire, synapses burning as raw power surged through her.

It wasn't painful.

It was joyful.

Ecstasy.

A bliss unlike *anything* she had felt before. When she had been in the depths of her addiction, chasing the high of her powers as often as she could, she had *never* experienced this. She had always been careful, in control. Not even in the throes of passion, had she ever truly let go.

Not like this.

Every cell of her being tingled with electricity, from her fingertips down to her toes. She wondered if she had felt *this* sensation last time. Here on this rooftop, one year ago, in the blind spot of her recall. The only other time she had, reportedly, let her power course through her unchecked.

Memories flooded her mind. Not the ones she had forgotten; those remained a dark mystery. These were more recent. From only a few days ago...

The sensation of lying in his arms. Feeling his gentle intimate caress. His skin on hers. His fingers brushing lightly over her goosebumps. The heat of their passion. An unrivaled experience she would never forget. Every fleeting second of that night was indelibly tattooed into a memory that seemed to be held in her heart rather than her mind. It had frightened and thrilled her in equal measure.

Yet it also unlocked something deep within her. Elicited an emotional response in her she had never felt before. Or at least not this aspect of it.

Gayle *knew* love.

She felt it for Allyson, Carrie, her mother, and her father.

She felt it for Lana and Amanda.

She'd felt it for Gabriel, for Maggie, and Riku...for all of her fallen teammates.

But this was a subtle yet distinctly different breed of that familiar and comforting feeling. She could see it clearly now.

For the last week, she had been looking for an answer. Vacillating between theories about their night of intimacy and the levitation it created. Years ago, she found the endorphin rush of sex could amplify her powers, so surely this was more of the same? Better sex equals a better high. The equation seemed so simple. So obvious.

Yet she hadn't been able to duplicate that power after that night with Michael.

Because her sisters were right.

She didn't just *feel* love for Michael...she was *in* love with Michael. And that scared her. Her refusal to accept that fact held her back.

But *that* was the key to unlocking her ultimate potential. Acceptance.

Not the sex.

That night in his bed, she gave herself over to him completely. No thought, just instinctually wanting to be in that moment completely.

It wasn't just about conquering fear. It wasn't just about love. It was about *everything*.

It was about realizing that all her emotions were connected. They flowed and merged into one another to create something...beautiful.

She *could* be scared of what the future might hold with Michael while still embracing her feelings of love.

I love you, Michael Reynolds.

She *could* grieve for her fallen friends while not feeling guilty she survived when they hadn't. She knew any one of them would gladly have given their life for her, as she would for them. She could enjoy her memories of them with a healthy mix of joy and sadness.

I wish I could have saved you all. I will try to honor your friendship and your memories for as long as I can.

All along, she had been thinking about this all wrong. Trying desperately to partition and deal with her feelings as individual problems to be solved. They were *all* connected, and to be whole again, she had to acknowledge that.

There was one last burden on her shoulders. The heaviest of all. It was time to let it go.

I miss you so much, Dad.

She felt her feet leave the ground, slowly. Controlled flight. A gentle hover.

The wind whipped up around her, teasing strands of pink across her face as it got stronger. Escalating from a mild breeze to a howling gale and beyond. She seized it, manipulating it, bending it to her whim. It started to spin around her, a slow-moving miniature hurricane with Fort St. Elmo at its epicenter. Her ears were assaulted by the sharp crack of lightning, the baritone rumble of thunder. This was *her* storm. A turbulent and furious manifestation of her power.

Despite her epiphany, Gayle wasn't entirely sure how she was doing this. It was purely instinctual.

The Alpha was glancing around nervously, its head twitching to and fro. She could sense its fear. The other Adze were slowly retreating. Stumbling backward and looking for cover, shelter from this unnatural assault of elements. He was losing control as his brood started to recognize her abject superiority. The Alpha's almond eyes turned back toward her. Gayle could sense he was resolving himself to fight. He needed to impress upon his hive that *he* was the one to be feared. Not Gayle.

It would be a misguided attempt.

Gayle wasn't *close* to being finished with flexing her muscles. Not yet.

The storm was only the beginning of her assault.

She focused her attention beneath them, making the ground tremble and shudder violently. The Fort shook powerfully, cracks appearing like spiderwebs in its walls. The Alpha stumbled gracelessly as his spindly legs buckled, sending him sprawling to the ground. Small rocks and stones bounced as the roof vibrated like a drumskin. Gayle snatched them up with the wind, whipping them around herself, creating a protective shield of rapidly moving deadly debris.

She was shaking all over, trembling from head to toe. Her teeth chattered wildly, and she clenched her jaw in an effort to stop them. Her breathing was becoming ragged and heavy. She wasn't sure what it was. It didn't feel like exertion or fear.

Adrenaline maybe?

Behind her, the sea roiled, crashing ferociously against the shoreline. Violent plumes of water jetted high into the air before falling back to the earth as a mist of rain, twinkling in the moonlight. It soaked her hair, matting it to her head. She felt its reassuring weight. Refreshing her. Cleansing her spiritually.

Her breathing began to slow, steadying. She exhaled and lifted her hands, twisting them slowly in intuitive patterns as if weaving some sort of enchantment or spell. Around her a dozen tiny tornadoes formed, coalescing from the winds and rain. They danced with lethal playfulness, her abilities beginning to work in concert.

An intimidating display of her raw power.

Earth.

Air.

Water.

And finally, fire.

Steam rose from her matted hair. Water turned to vapor by the heat she was suddenly generating. Green fire coalesced, enveloping her hands. Ethereal balls of living flame writhing sinuously. She glanced down at them, surprised by the bright, vivid color. In her peripheral, she could see tendrils of the same jade flame wispily drifting from her eyes, illuminating everything she looked at in an eerie shade of emerald as they dissipated into the night.

Gayle turned her focus to the Alpha.

The anger she had harbored toward him and his kind was still there but felt different now. She remembered the heady mixture of fear, fury, and grief she experienced a year ago. A trio of extremely powerful negative emotions all vying for their place as the primary driver of her newfound destructive capabilities.

Today the anger was a dull ebb in the back of her mind. A memory...nothing more.

And the fear was fading. As the Alpha's terror grew, Gayle's diminished.

The grief was now a bittersweet cocktail of sadness and joy. She would *always* intensely miss her friends, and her father, of that there was *no* doubt. But it *was* possible to move on with your life and remember only the good times.

And there was a good life to be had, if you just reached out and took it.

She was in love with Michael.

There was no denying it. Not anymore. She *knew* what this feeling was.

For too many years her fire had burned red, fueled by intense anger. At the kids who teased her for nothing more than the color of her hair. At the schoolteachers who doubted she would amount to anything. At the Academy leaders who snubbed her team and treated it second best. And at her rival, who she once thought she was in love with but had played her like a fool.

Tonight, that same fire burned the shade of her eyes.

She thought she had come here to face the past and be the avatar of vengeance for her fallen comrades. It would be easy to drown the Alpha under a tidal wave of sea water. Crush him under the weight of a thousand rocks. Summon a tornado to tear him apart. Incinerate him where he stood.

Or any combination of these gruesome methods of death.

And for what he and his kind had done to her team, he would deserve *every* agonizing moment she could inflict.

That is not *who I am now.*

It was as if a veil had been lifted. Revealing a world in true clarity and vivid color. For the first time in her life, the power coursing through her came from a purer place. She was surrounded by love in all its forms. The love of her mother and sisters, coming together in trying times. Of her friends, Lana and Amanda, who had rallied to her side and thrown her a lifeline when she felt she was drowning.

And Michael.

When she had been feeling bitter and broken, and when she had acted childish and selfish because of it, he somehow saw through all of that. He loved her in a way she had never experienced before.

She looked at the Alpha standing defiantly before her.

No. Tonight, Gayle was *not* the avatar of vengeance.

She was something very much better than that.

"Take your people and leave this place. Leave Valletta. Leave Malta," Gayle said firmly. "Do *not* come back here. Ever. Do you understand?"

The Alpha nodded, its head bobbing in a staccato fashion as it started to back slowly away from her. Gayle looked into its milky white eyes and saw the truth. A flicker of movement.

Out of the corner of her eye, she sensed motion.

Gayle smiled, the recollection of a memory from the class she had taught the kids... "There is *one* other thing that stops this from being a completely accurate representation of what it's like to hunt Adze..." she told them during that lesson. "Adze are *never* alone."

It came out of the emerald shadows to her left, a grotesque blur of curving fang and razor-sharp claw, seeking a target to rend and dismember. Against any other opponent, this distract-and-ambush tactic would likely have worked, leaving their victim a bloody, shredded corpse lying in their destructive wake.

But Gayle wasn't a victim.

She was *Andrea Mors Est.*

The woman they called 'The Pink Death.'

With a fleeting thought and smallest of hand gestures, the pouncing Adze was brutally intercepted in midair by a hail of jagged rocks and stones cut loose from the maelstrom encircling them. His end was swift, bloody, and violent as the deadly shrapnel ripped into his body, the storm-force winds sweeping him away into the night.

Through it all, Gayle's stare never left the Alpha.

Now there was genuine terror etched onto the features of the Adze.

Gayle repeated her ultimatum in a low commanding tone. "Leave. Don't come back here…because I *will*. And if I find you or your people here when I do, I will show you the same mercy you demonstrated to my team a year ago.

"Do you understand?"

There was no response from the Alpha, but he understood.

The other Adze had already disappeared into the shadows, and now their leader moved to do the same thing. Backing slowly and deferentially away.

Within moments, he was gone.

As the danger passed, the adrenaline rush started to fade. Gayle began to experience the rhythmic beating of her heart thumping rapidly in her breast. Her breathing was labored; she felt like she had done a few laps of Hyde Park on her early morning run. With a mental nudge, she throttled back her powers, calming the seas, and easing the winds swirling chaotically around her.

As the noise of the elements abated, it was replaced by the pitter-patter of the rocks and stones as they returned to the ground from which they'd been plucked. It only lasted a handful of seconds, then quiet returned to Fort St. Elmo.

Gayle closed her eyes.

Trying to calm herself, she focused on what she could hear…

The sea crashed gently against the shoreline.

The soft crackle of the flames continued to cocoon her body.

And the drone of engines…

They came!

She lifted her head, looking skyward in the direction of this new but instantly recognizable sound, and saw the familiar shape of a DH 442 Dragonfly V dropship.

Artemis.

A smile tweaked the corners of her lips. The dropship hovered overhead with her loading ramp deployed. Gayle could see Zephyr standing on it, her brunette ponytail fluttering like a flag in the wind behind her.

Lana would be piloting, so that left one person missing from view.

She *really* hoped he was here, too.

| 84 |

HELLO, CAPTAIN KNIGHTLEY

— **Michael Reynolds** —
— *Thursday* — *Valletta, Malta* —

"Let me turn *Arty* around, and I'll drop down and pick her up."

Lana's voice was clear as a bell in his ear, a shade too loud now as the noise of the storm had dissipated considerably. As he made his way from the nose turret back toward the troop compartment, he toggled the volume down a little and heard Amanda's bemused follow-up statement.

"Don't bother, Fordith. Our girl seems to have that covered…"

He arrived just in time to see Gayle drift sedately toward the boarding ramp. She looked like he had never seen her before. A goddess. Her emerald eyes burned brightly, literally smoldering. Gentle tendrils of green drifting from their corners, fading into the night air alongside her fluttering candyfloss hair. Her hands were relaxed but engulfed in the same bright flame smoldering from her eyes. She all at once looked both terrifying and ethereally beautiful.

Her face, though, looked serene.

The flames began to dissipate as her feet lightly touched the ramp, and she patted Amanda on the shoulder as she walked past into the troop compartment. She didn't say a word as she moved to one of the seats and sat down, lifting her legs to hug her knees. While the fire was now gone, Michael could still feel the heat radiating off her and see the rapid rise and fall of her chest as she tried to calm herself, controlling her breathing. He didn't want to interrupt her.

Not yet.

Instead, he moved to assist Amanda. She handed him her rifle, then took his outstretched hand to maintain her balance as she unhooked her safety line.

She gestured toward Gayle who looked miles away in a world of her own. "What do you think?" she whispered.

Michael shook his head and shrugged. "Honestly...I don't know. I thought I'd give her a moment to regroup before inundating her with questions about what the hell just happened."

"Did I just see Knightingale *fly* back up to *Artemis*?" Lana's voice came over comms.

Michael glanced at Amanda, who hit the button on the bulkhead to close the boarding ramp. "Your eyes do not deceive you," she muttered.

"Is that a thing she does now?" Lana said. "The flying?"

"Apparently so," Amanda answered. "I take it this is as a surprise to you too, Lana. And the green fire?"

"Nope, not seen that before either. How is she?"

"She's just sittin' quietly," Michael said. "You want to get us out of here to somewhere safe, Fordith? Then we'll set down and have a debrief."

"Roger that," came the response, and Michael felt *Artemis* start to bank gently as the engines rose in pitch and the dropship surged forward.

He didn't say anything about Gayle's newfound ability. He suspected this was connected with their intimacy of a few nights ago. The whole 'hovering' incident. But how do you broach that subject with Lana and Gayle?

'Oh, yeah, I thought she might be able to fly after we bumped into the ceiling during sex!'

Yeah, that wasn't a conversation he was willing to have with them. If Gayle wanted to discuss it with them, that was her prerogative.

Gayle's breathing seemed more stable now, and though her eyes were still kind of distant, he figured now was the time to approach her. He crouched down in front of her, reaching for one of her hands. She offered no resistance to him as he took it and held it gently. It was cool to the touch, not a hint of the heat she'd been giving off only moments ago.

"Hey," he said softly.

Her eyes looked at him, unfocused for a moment before recognition set in. She smiled. "Hey," she responded. Her voice sounded broken.

"Are you okay?"

She simply nodded.

"You wanna tell me about any of this?"

Gayle squeezed his hand and gently pulled him forward. As he leaned closer, she uncurled her legs and leaned into him. Her lips touched his gently as she kissed him tenderly. There was no heat in the kiss, no passion. That was not what it was supposed to be. There was feeling there. Something equally intense but a whole lot calmer.

"I love you," she whispered.

"I..." he started, but she shook her head a little and shushed him.

"It's okay," she said softly. "Tell me when *you're* ready."

After a few seconds, she withdrew from him and tucked her hair back behind her ear. The smile remained.

"Okay..." Amanda said with amusement. "That was not the kind of debrief I was expecting. Do you want me to leave you guys alone for a while?"

Gayle chuckled and glanced sideways at her friend. "Not necessary," she said. "That's what you saw from me a year ago, isn't it?"

Amanda hesitated and then nodded. "Kind of. The fire wasn't green, but...that power, Gayle... Yeah, that's what I witnessed. You remember it?"

Gayle shook her head. "No. I'm not sure I ever will if I'm honest. But it came back to what you said on the range a couple of weeks ago. I needed to face my fear. Problem was I was trying to face the wrong fear. Or fears. But talking to

Alastair...suddenly everything snapped into place.

"Fuck. I feel...like a weight is gone from my shoulders."

Michael frowned and glanced at Amanda. Her expression was broadly similar to his. A mixture of worry and confusion. It was apparently a look Gayle had picked up on. She looked like she was about to talk again when she was interrupted by the entry of Lana, climbing down the ladder from the cockpit.

"*Artemis* is on autopilot in a holding pattern for now," she said. "I thought about leaving, but I figure we should probably retrieve the Banshee our fearless leader took it upon herself to steal. Maybe returning it will influence the court-martial committee to show lenience. What the *fuck* were you thinking, Gayle?"

"Yeah, I probably should return it, shouldn't I?" Gayle said rhetorically.

"That's *not* an answer to my question." Lana raised an eyebrow forcefully.

"She was facing her fears. The right fears," Michael answered. "Though I'm not entirely sure what that means."

"I've been a mess since I got back. You all know it. I knew that I was afraid, but I didn't know of what. I knew what happened, who died. I knew I was responsible—"

"We've talked about this," Amanda butted in. "Gabe or I could have objected. But we didn't..."

"Whatever," Gayle waved her hand dismissively. "It doesn't matter now. The point is, as a result of what happened, I was afraid. Afraid of so many things. I couldn't put the pieces of it all together properly, so I jumped to conclusions.

"Gabe and I had sex right before the Malta mission. I was high as fuck on the power-rush. Both of us were. I made a bad decision, a stupid decision. I read your report, Amanda. What it said I did...but I rationalized it. I was angry, grieving, and high on the rush. I lost control and killed those Adze.

"That was the only rational explanation. Probably the correct one, too.

"But after that, I was afraid of losing control again. How many more people would die? How many more mistakes would I make? I was afraid of using my power, just in case. Afraid of doing *anything* that would cause me to lose control. To *want* to lose control. Afraid of drinking, of sex...of falling in love..."

Her eyes flicked to Michael.

"Then there was the bomb, and I was afraid that I'd wasted what little time I had with my dad by being bitter and angry. I was afraid that he died hating me. Or being disappointed in me for the mess I was making of my life.

"Talking to Alastair gave me the first epiphany. If I wanted to move past what happened here, I needed to experience it. Understand it. I needed to come back here. Face the Adze. Use my powers. Prove to myself I am in control. I don't know if that makes sense to you...but it did to me.

"But that was just the first step.

"A year ago, I think that power was driven by rage. Grief and despair. A whole bunch of negative. Then tonight, while I stood there, I was consumed by fear. Trying to fight it, suppress it. But then I figured it out. It's okay to feel fear and grief, but don't let it rule you. Remember the positives that these things bring to your life, too..." She looked up at Michael. "It's okay to be scared to fall in love with someone. That's kinda what makes it exciting."

It was Amanda who asked the question they were all thinking. "So...did it work? How do you feel?"

Gayle looked at her and smiled. "I feel like myself again. For the first time in...years."

He wasn't sure if he fully understood her explanation, but he couldn't deny there was a change in Gayle. She hadn't let go of his hand the whole time, but she wasn't clutching at him or hanging on desperately. Her grip was gentle, her hand cool in his. From the first moment since he met her, there had been an attitude about Gayle. It shifted and changed, from angry to flirty and every shade in between. But he had never seen her so...in control.

No...that's not the right word. Confident. That's it.

He had seen her demonstrate bravado, but this was just cool, calm confidence.

This was finally the Gayle Knightley he read about in the reports. The leader of the 137th Hunters. He chuckled under his breath, drawing her attention.

"What?" she said quietly, her eyes searching his.

She was beautiful. He had developed feelings for her when she was at her worst; he couldn't deny how he felt. Seeing her now at her best was breathtaking.

"It's nice to finally meet you, Captain Knightley," he said.

Her eyes sparkled and she laughed. "Worth the wait?"

He grinned, knowing *exactly* how to express what he felt. "Abso-fuckin'-lutely."

Her face lit up, and she leaned into him again, putting her head on his chest. Michael put his arm around her, holding her close to him.

"By the way," she whispered, "we need to talk. I need to explain to you why I owe you a new bed..."

| 85 |

CLOSURE

— **Allyson Knightley** —
— *Saturday — Cambridgeshire, England* —

"Fuck, this car is an uncomfortable piece of—"

"Don't you dare finish that sentence," Gayle growled to Carrie who was sat in the back of the Mustang as it bounced down the pothole-riddled backroad. "You say one word against *Sally*, and you'll be walking the rest of the way!"

"I'm just saying, there's not a lot of room back here...and your suspension is not really geared up for off-roading."

"We're not off-roading! Stop exaggerating."

Allyson sat in the passenger seat, listening to the bickering between her two sisters. Not an unusual state of affairs, truth be told; good-natured banter was a part of their sibling relationship. However, today was a little different. There was a level of tension in the car as they rumbled slowly toward the family farmstead down a road that suffered from an overabundance of tractor traffic over the years. She glanced over at Gayle in the driver's seat, her face calm, her outfit black from head to toe.

Matching the colors of her own ensemble. Carrie's, too.

She wished they were taking this road trip as siblings for an altogether happier reason.

Today, under a bleak, cloudy, autumnal sky, they would bury Jaymes Knightley in the presence of family and friends.

She knew her dad would be celebrated by the small gathering of friends and family in attendance, his life and his achievements lauded loudly and proudly. Allyson also knew her day would likely consist mostly of smiling politely, shaking hands, and talking about how proud she was of her father, while trying to hold back the tears until she could find a private moment to vent them.

I am not looking forward to this. Not one bit.

"You okay, Sis?" Gayle said, flicking her eyes across at Ally.

"Mmmm, yeah, fine. Why?"

"Because you're staring at me."

"There's something different about you..." Allyson said slowly.

"Yeah," Carrie chimed in from the back seat. "I can see it, too. You've been, and I mean this in a good way, more normal."

"Normal?" Gayle laughed lightly. "I'll try not to be offended."

As the car turned into the gates of the farm, Ally realized Carrie was right. Gayle did seem more 'normal' than she had seen her sister in a long time. Her face looked serene. Despite the prospect of the day they were about to have, Gayle seemed at peace. The composed confidence that had always been her trademark had been missing for over a year. Today it was evident in her demeanor once more.

"No, Carrie's right. You're back to your old self..."

"And that's a bad thing?" Gayle said.

"Not at all," Carrie interjected. "But you know I have a nose for a story, and there's a story here... I can smell it. So, spill."

"I'll tell you later. Now's not the time," Gayle said as she brought the Mustang to a stop and turned off the engine. "But as a teaser...I went back to Valletta."

"*What?*" Carrie and Allyson exclaimed in unison with identical pitch.

"Later. I promise," Gayle said, and then gestured out of the windscreen at the approach of their mother. "Right now, there are more important items on today's agenda..."

Gayle was right—any curiosity over her sister's new state

of mind could wait, but Ally *definitely* wanted to be filled in on what prompted her elder sibling's return to the place that fueled more than a year of profound nightmares.

She pulled the door release as she simultaneously popped the seatbelt of its retainer, carefully stepping out of the car and smoothing out her long, flowing skirt as she stood up. Reaching back, she pulled the release, levering the passenger seat forward to allow Carrie egress from the cramped rear of Gayle's car. It wasn't the most elegant exit, due to a pencil skirt and the modest heels she was wearing.

The two of them made their way around to the driver's side of the car, where Gayle was waiting. Their elder sibling was wearing a smart pants-suit with what looked like a pair of jet-black sneakers. Her eyes flicked up and down Ally and Carrie, pausing at Carrie's heels.

"Rookie mistake..." Gayle said, shaking her head. "You do realize you're about to be on your feet for roughly the next eight to ten hours."

"I don't do many funerals," Carrie shrugged.

"I've been to far too many," Gayle sighed as she watched her mother approach them from the house, Uncle Norbel beside her "And one I *should* have gone to...but missed."

Allyson knew she was referring to Vaylur. Not that it had been her fault. The flyer accident that claimed the life of Norbel's husband took place while Gayle was en-route to the Malta mission a year ago. Post Valletta, Gayle was in a medically induced coma to aid her recovery at the time of the funeral. Not that she really missed anything. Vaylur had been laid to rest in a mysterious secret ceremony only Norbel and Serlia attended. Allyson assumed it was some sort of Fae thing, but hadn't pushed for details. Herself and Carrie attended the 'celebration' of Vaylur's life, a weird evening event filled with people they didn't know. They stayed a few hours, long enough to politely show their condolences, and then left.

"Hi, Mum." Gayle was the first to greet their mother, embracing her in a gentle hug the moment she was in range.

"It's good to see you back, Gayle," Serlia said softly.

Allyson imagined she meant back on the family farm, but

the look on her mother's face and the tone of her voice seemed to imply something more akin to the conversation the sisters had just been having in the car.

The five of them exchanged greetings and pleasantries, ending up standing silently in a loose circle feeling slightly awkward. They all knew why they were here.

"Do you need us to do anything? Anything to help?" Ally asked to break the silence.

Norbel shook his head. "Though the sentiment is appreciated, Allyson, your mother and I have all the arrangements in hand."

Serlia smiled. "Jaymes didn't want a fuss. It'll just be a private ceremony for us and a few close family and friends."

Norbel turned slightly and indicated down the gravel drive between the barns. "The service will begin in the orchard in twenty minutes, so your timing is impeccably convenient."

"Are you all ready for this?" Serlia asked, her voice full of the empathy Norbel's lacked.

No. No, I am not ready for this. Not ready at all!

As the thoughts were running through Ally's head, she felt Gayle's hand reach for hers, holding it tightly. A silent transfer of support and strength.

Allyson nodded in unison with her sisters.

| 86 |

REST IN PEACE

— **Gayle Knightley** —
— *Saturday* — *Cambridgeshire, England* —

So much for the small family affair...

One by one a series of anonymous individuals paraded past her, all offering their heartfelt condolences and some sharing tiny anecdotes of how wonderful her father had been.

"He was such a kind and gentle soul..."

"He was an inspiration to us all..."

"He was a wonderful man. Always there when you needed him..."

Not a single person had a mean-spirited word to say about Jaymes Knightley. Hardly surprising considering this was his funeral after all, and Gayle was his eldest daughter. What were they supposed to say? Gayle knew they all meant well, but right now she didn't care. So, she shook all their hands, nodded graciously, and gave the same polite smile ad nauseum until her jaw started to ache and her face began to tire of holding back the tears she wanted to cry. It took a Herculean effort to maintain this fragile façade of calm.

Even with her newly regained sense of personal equilibrium.

A sizable part of her wanted to hide away from all these strangers. Run out into one of the many fields of the family farm to scream her grief at a cold and uncaring universe. To swear and shout in the middle of nowhere. To curse at whatever deity up there had decided to take her father away before she'd been given the chance to make amends with him.

Except, that wasn't true.

I was *given the chance.*

When the cosmos offered her the olive branch, she stubbornly threw it back in the universe's face.

Karma could be a complete bitch.

Stood here, out in the orchard where they laid Jaymes Knightley to rest, she had never felt so trapped by open space. This spot was chosen deliberately. The private avenue of fruit trees had been planted when they first bought the farm and had grown tall over the years. It had always been one of her father's favorite places to stroll and think, and many a time had she walked with him. As a pre-teen, she skipped playfully between the apple and pear trees, plucking fruit from the low-hanging branches. When she got older, the two meandered arm in arm, talking about the world at large.

Jaymes never ceased trying to persuade her to follow in his footsteps.

"You understand the way the world *works*," he would say. "The shades of grey. You'd make a wonderful diplomat."

She would laugh, tell him how insane an idea that was. Gayle didn't understand what he meant back then, these 'shades of grey' to which he referred. Now she did. Meeting Mercy had opened her eyes. Yet her father knew years ago she had that capacity within her. He had believed. Had faith she would find her way to the truth. So, he would laugh too, and fix her with the twinkle-eyed stare of a proud parent.

"We'll see," he'd say softly.

The setting sun warmed her tear-stained cheeks as the gentle evening breeze ruffled tenderly through her hair, feeling like the caress of her absent father's hand. It felt reassuring, like he was still there somehow.

As she shook another hand and nodded congenially along with one more tale of her father's everlasting legacy, she stared off into the middle distance, wishing everyone would leave already. The words no longer registered; her mind was somewhere else entirely.

She wanted to be left alone.

Alone with her thoughts and her feelings.

The next person in the seemingly never-ending line of well-wishers extended his hand. She reflexively reciprocated the gesture. Ready to follow the script she had established over the past hours. Shake, pretend to listen, acknowledge, move along.

Lather, rinse, and repeat.

This time, however, it was different.

The new hand slipped over hers, gently squeezing it. But rather than moving on, it lingered tenderly. Her eyes flicked up from the hand to focus on the face. Her heart surged and her mind sighed with relief.

She smiled, this one weary, but genuine. "You came!"
"Of course I did," Michael spoke softly. "I know you said that you'd be okay, but...it didn't feel right staying in London while you were here. Are you okay?"

Gayle nodded and took a deep breath. "Long day. Long...and *emotional* day."

"I expect so."

They both stood for an extended moment, looking into each other's eyes. Eventually Gayle laughed lightly, breaking the slightly awkward tension.

"I'd been thinking, wishing really, I could be alone for a little while," she said. "But now you're here..."

Michael nodded his understanding. "We can take a walk somewhere if ya like? Pretty much everyone's gone now. Or going anyhow."

"I hadn't even noticed. So many people..." Her voice trailed off.

"I saw your eyes start to glaze over after the first fifty or so," Michael chuckled. "I thought maybe it might be a good time to ride in on the white steed. Rescue you. So, for the last few minutes, I've been trying to divert the stream of well-wishers over to your mom and sisters.

Gayle sighed. "Thank you. This was supposed to be a small family affair...but obviously word got out."

"You should be proud. Your father had a great many admirers. I lost count of how many people told me what a great man he was…" Michael hesitated. "I truly wish I'd had the chance to meet him."

"Oh, he would have *adored* you!" Gayle said enthusiastically. "As much as he loved me and let me plot my own course in life, he *always* worried about my career choice and my awful taste in men. You, my dear Captain Reynolds, would have been right up his street."

As quickly as the enthusiasm had surged, it was swallowed up by a wave of sadness.

She would never be able to introduce Michael to her father. Gayle knew that between the siblings, it was she who had shared the closest relationship to Jaymes. The father-daughter bond had always been strong between them. He supported her, advised, and guided her, and most of the time—other than the aforementioned career and men conundrum—she had listened to him.

Gayle tried to stifle a sob as fresh tears began to meander slowly down her cheeks. She squeezed Michael's hand tightly, and a little desperately, in her own. His face changed, suddenly etched with a mirror image of her own sadness as he moved to tenderly wipe the tears from her soft skin with a brush of his thumb. She closed her eyes and felt his fingers move around her neck, past her scar, and beneath her hair as he gently urged her head to his shoulder. Gayle didn't resist, gratefully leaning her face into him as she wept.

There was no place she would rather be right now than safe in his embrace.

She had no idea how long she'd been cocooned in that refuge before she heard the voice of her sister. "Is she okay?"

Allyson's voice sounded hoarse; Gayle wasn't the only one who had been crying today. Not that she had expected otherwise.

She pulled back from Michael's shoulder but remained in his arms.

Ally grinned and gestured at the two of them. "This is a *good* look for you. I think Dad would have loved this."

"I think so, too," Gayle agreed, her voice as broken as her sister's. "And yeah, I'm fine. I just... I needed a moment for myself, y'know?"

"I know *exactly* what you mean." Allyson exhaled heavily. "It's kinda seemed like today was about everyone else, don't ya think?"

"You mean the dozens of people that suddenly descended on our small family funeral?" Gayle said with a hint of sarcasm.

"The last of them are leaving." Ally nodded toward the smaller of the two barns on their parents' farm. "Carrie, Lana, and Amanda are in there. I said I'd come find you. My feet are killing me; you were *absolutely* right about the footwear. Let's go sit down and regroup. Then I'll see if I can scare up some leftovers from the buffet."

"Honestly, I'm not sure I'll ever eat another cucumber sandwich!" Gayle scowled.

"Other sandwich fillings *were* available," Ally chuckled.

"Not by the time I got there after greeting everyone," Gayle moaned. "Just tiny triangular sandwiches with curling corners and a warm green mush inside."

Michael relinquished his hold on her, which gave her a tiny pang of disappointment.

As the golden rays of sunset filtered through the branches of the fruit trees casting long shadows on the grass, the three of them sauntered toward the doors on the end of the ivy-covered single-story brick building with the black wooden roof. Where the other barn had been long ago converted into a multi-purpose venue, this one was still used primarily for storage. It was the perfect place to hide away from the world on a day when that world had invaded your little part of it.

As they approached, Gayle could see her mother saying polite goodbyes to the last of the guests, all smiles as she wished them her best and saw them on their way. The field on which more than two dozen cars had been parked, was now almost empty. Only the stragglers remained, and they would be soon gone, too.

They filed into the barn, and Michael slid the door closed

behind them as Gayle and Ally perched themselves up on one of the workbenches alongside Carrie. Lana and Amanda had seated themselves on an old sofa that had been collecting dust in there for at least a decade. Neither seemed to care a wit about the grey marks all over their respectfully black funeral attire. Amanda looked exhausted, and Gayle wondered briefly about the aftereffects of her surgery.

For a few minutes, nobody said a word.

Gayle understood why.

Conversation fatigue.

The whole day had been an exercise in small talk and pleasantries to people they barely knew or didn't know at all. This was the first chance any of them really had to take a break and grab a moment of peace and quiet. To have a moment of self-reflection.

"I don't think I want to see another cucumber sandwich ever again," Amanda said, breaking the silence.

It started as a chuckle between Gayle, Ally, and Michael, but within moments, everyone was laughing uproariously. Not because it was funny, but because it was the pin that burst the bubble of tension that had been steadily growing all day. Gayle reached out to either side and grasped the hands of her sisters. Her fingers entwined with Carrie on her left, but when they sought a similar connection with Allyson, they found something else was already being held there.

"What's this?" she said, looking down in puzzlement.

"Oh, this? Yes…" Ally said. "It's a letter. To me, from Lyssa. It's…kinda beautiful. Well, maybe you should just read it."

Gayle shook her head. "No, it's a letter to you. I don't want to…"

"Oh, for fuck's sake, Gayle." Allyson rolled her eyes. "Just read the damn letter!"

She pushed the crumpled paper into Gayle's hand and let go.

It was a single sheet, cream in color. Carefully, Gayle unfolded it until the elegant cursive handwriting was evident on the page. The carefully crafted letters were smudged in multiple places, a result of what looked like tears making the ink run.

Allyson,

I only met your father once, on the night of the gala dinner in Nexus. I shall never forget how thrilled he was to meet me and what he said to me that night.

'We need more people in this world who do what is right. It makes our job so much easier.'

Your father gave me a sense of hope for the future. His life was a guiding light showing me the way. Demonstrating to me that Vampyrii _can_ live alongside Humankind. His words have echoed in my mind ever since, giving me confidence in what I am doing that was sometimes hard to find before.

When a Vampyrii dies, we perform the 'Blood to Earth' ritual, to return their essence to the gods who created us. During the ceremony, we quote the gifts that were given to us by our forebears.

My family name, as you know, is Balthazaar.

He, of the Wisdom.

My mother was born of Akhza, She of the Passion.

Jaymes may have been _your_ father, and the patriarch of the Knightley family, but he possessed the traits of both my parents. He was wise and he was passionate. The former was evident in his optimism and view of the future. The latter was clear from his love for his wife and his beautiful daughters.

I see so much of your father in you and your sisters. I know he was very proud of you all. It was obvious from the light in his eyes when he spoke about you.

Please, relay my condolences to your mother, Gayle, and Carrie-Anne. I can only imagine the pain you are all feeling as you bear the weight of such a profound loss. I am truly sorry I cannot be there in person to show my respects.

Until I see you again...

My heart,

Lyssa

x

Gayle finished with a sigh and carefully folded the letter, handing it back to Allyson. Her sister waved it away and pointed to Carrie.

"Let little sis see it," she said.

Their younger sibling unfolded the paper and started to scan her eyes across the text Gayle had just read. As she studied the contents of Lyssa's note, Gayle took a deep breath and looked at Ally.

"I know I've only recently met Lyssa. The first time when..." she paused as the details flooded back into her memory, and she giggled. "When I made my...unexpected night visit—"

"Don't you dare!" Ally interrupted with a teasing tone.

"But...she wasn't what I expected her to be. That night when I burdened you with my little problem," she flicked her eyes unconsciously sideways at Michael, "it kind of felt a little like she was a fourth sister in the room. It's weird because I've spent more than a decade fighting her kind, but that night, it never crossed my mind that I was sharing personal details with a Vampyrii.

"I mean, I guess Mercy had laid some of the groundwork..."

"No," Ally shook her head. "This change started before Mercy. You've been changing for a little while now."

She didn't miss the subtle glance her sister also cast Michael's way. Fortunately, he seemed oblivious to the attention.

"You might be right," Gayle said with a small smile.

"Changing the subject," Carrie interjected. "Did anyone else notice how Mum was today? She didn't seem much like the heartbroken widow. I mean, she *was* much sadder than she's been recently. I saw her cry for what I think is the first time ever... But she looked like today gave her some sort of closure."

"I think it's a Fae thing..." Gayle replied.

Carrie looked confused. "What does that mean?"

Gayle cast her mind back to a couple of weeks prior, when she had stood in her parents' apartment in Nexus, speaking with Serlia about the passing of her father. Even back then, her mother hadn't seemed wracked with grief. If anything, she had seemed calmly philosophical. She thought it a little odd at the time but chalked it up to her being a Fae and pursuing a way of life maybe Gayle herself didn't understand.

"You might be right..." Ally said thoughtfully before Gayle herself could answer. "Do you remember at Vaylur's wake, Carrie? Uncle Norbel didn't look particularly grief-stricken there either."

"Yeah, you're right," Carrie nodded. "I wondered at the time about that. He *said* all the right things but didn't seem especially upset."

"Your uncle has never seemed like the type to be particularly demonstrative emotionally," Michael commented with a shrug. "No offense intended. I know he's family."

"To be honest," Lana said, "he's been like this since Vaylur died."

Amanda nodded. "When we were training at the Academy, the one person you didn't want to piss off was Nasty Norbel."

"God, I forgot we used to call him that..." Gayle shook her head at the memory. She looked at Michael and smiled. "Of all our tutors back then, he was the *toughest*. If we fucked up, and we often did, then he'd come down on us *hard*. He'd never swear, or raise his voice, but you could *see* the anger in him...which somehow felt worse."

"And his punishments were *legendary*," Amanda agreed.

"That's so weird," Michael said, shaking his head in mild disbelief. "He seems so calm these days."

"I was talking to Mum back in Nexus a couple of weeks ago. She said that for her, Dad would never truly be gone. And when I said I regretted not being able to talk to him before... well, she said I'd get the chance to tell him everything when I saw him again. In something called 'The River.'"

"The River?" Allyson asked.

Gayle turned to her sister and shrugged. "Yeah. I didn't know what that meant either. Apparently, it's a philosophical belief or something. She said, to paraphrase, 'It's a way of life that flows toward your destiny...like a river. It guides your fate as you follow it to your ultimate destination.' She ever talk to you about this, Carrie?"

Carrie shook her head at first, and then hesitated. "Nope...but..." She paused for a moment, deep in thought. "When I went to see Ambassador Alzim, he mentioned something called the Song of The Winds. I know it's not the same, but something about it just..."

"You've got that feeling, haven't you?" Gayle asked.

Each of the sisters had an ability a little out of the norm. Carrie had a nose for a story, an eerie sense of seeing beyond what other people saw and making leaps of connecting intuition.

"Yeah... The River, the Song of The Winds..." she mused. "They feel connected. Important. I don't know why, but I feel like I want to find out."

Gayle didn't blame her one bit.

She felt exactly the same.

| **87** |

HER FATHER'S DAUGHTER

— **Allyson Knightley** —
— *Sunday — London, England* —

She fished in her coat pockets for her house keys, eventually finding them and slotting them into the keyhole on her front door. Not for the first time, she wondered why she hadn't invested in the smart-locks that would have detected her approach and opened the door for her. With a turn and a click, the door was unlocked. Pushing it open, she walked into the hallway.

The house was quiet.

Too quiet.

Ally stood in the hallway with her eyes closed. She took a deep breath, then exhaled slowly. Shrugging off her coat, she draped it over the banister while kicking off her shoes before heading into the kitchen.

A drink was required.

She padded to the refrigerator and yanked it open. There was a distinct lack of provisions in the brightly lit compartment, but there was beer. A *lot* of beer. As she grasped one of them by the neck and prepared to pull it from its cardboard packaging, she paused.

The image of the hobo squirrel resurfaced in her mind, and she chuckled to herself as she ran a hand through her hair. Gayle's words from that day echoed through her mind... "You need to look after yourself better than this."

She was right, of course.

Her mind flashed back over the past year, thinking about the number of times she'd been drunk.

Too many.

The night she visited Gayle here in London. The evening she had shared with her sisters. She had been drunk the first time she slept with Lyssa—though to be fair, they'd both been intoxicated that night. She'd been drinking at her last family dinner with her father, and after pretty much every shift in Nexus. For fuck's sake, she'd even asked Michael if he wanted to partake in beers when he'd visited for the security check.

Shaking her head, she released the bottle and slowly, but firmly, closed the refrigerator door.

Maybe tea is a better choice today.

While the kettle was boiling, she slipped out of her clothes and tossed them into the laundry basket. She started sorting through the pile of freshly cleaned clothes she hadn't yet taken upstairs, looking for something to cover her nakedness. Her hands stopped as they felt the soft cotton of an oversized sleepshirt. She gently tugged it free from the pile and held it in front of her. A small smile tweaked the corners of her lips as she gazed at the cute cartoon cat on the front.

There had been too many bad memories recently.

This shirt represented a good one.

A really good one.

She put it to her face and inhaled, hoping maybe it would still retain the scent of her faraway lover. But all she smelled was the flowery aroma of the fabric softener; no trace of Lyssa remained.

It didn't matter—she still had the memory this shirt triggered. That was enough.

Allyson pulled it on over her head and padded barefoot over to the countertop to finish making her tea. Hot water and a teabag. Stir for a minute or two before adding sugar and milk. In that order. The first sip told her the hot beverage was to her liking, so she picked up the mug and headed for the stairs, grabbing what was left of a packet of chocolate digestives en route.

A moment later, she was stood in her makeshift investigation room, thoughtfully chewing on a biscuit and staring ahead of her. Her eyes were following the multicolored strands of string as they moved from picture to picture, document to document. Try as she might, however, she couldn't focus on the reports and photographs that adorned her walls.

Her eyes locked on one particular strand.

It started moving upward from a crime report, and then reached a point where it split.

Two different directions.

Like a choice that had to be made.

The last couple of days had been emotionally draining...not just for her, but for her siblings, too. Both her sisters would cope with the aftermath in different ways.

Carrie was planning to stay at the farm for a couple of days. She was heavily into the planning stage of her next trip, and Ally knew she would throw herself into that prep work with zeal. There was nothing in life Carrie loved more. She wasn't terribly interested in relationships; her career was everything.

Gayle, on the other hand, was extremely focused on matters of the heart. She had driven them all back to London and, after dropping Ally home, was very probably going to spend the night in the arms of Michael, trying to process the weekend's events.

Work.

Or love.

Her father had been so proud of her when she had been hired for the job in Nexus. He bragged about her to anyone who would listen. Chief of FSE Security in Nexus at the tender age of twenty-six. Despite the persistent rumors of nepotism, she felt like she *had* earned the job. Though her experience may have been limited, her record as a detective had been exemplary, and she had the qualifications.

She was pleased she made him proud.

Yet, when she arrived in Nexus, he had still been striving for something more for her. A relationship. She remembered his disappointment when he heard that she and Danni broke up. She recalled his efforts to show her off in order to find a prospective partner.

"Maybe you'll even meet someone at the Gala..." he had said.

She smiled at the memory.

His statement had been prophetic, indeed, though she doubted he would have guessed the woman who would turn out to be the focus of her romantic interest. Jaymes had been the consummate diplomat, as unprejudiced as they come, but even he would be surprised by the fact Allyson had taken Lyssa Balthazaar home that night.

His daughter and a Vampyrii.

While she wished she could have had a conversation with him about it, she knew in her heart he would have been happy about her finding someone to love, no matter who it was. Serlia and Jaymes had a belief system built on the tenet of tolerance. The fact that she found love in the arms of someone of a different race would have made him proud.

She knew *that* for an absolute.

Would he be proud of her now?

How would her father view what she was doing right now?

Wasting her time, staring at a wall, trying to figure out who killed him. While thousands of miles away, the woman with whom she was in love was gearing up to fight a war that would benefit millions of people if she was successful. Lyssa was focused on the big picture, while Ally was obsessed with...what?

Vengeance?

Justice?

Her eyes remained locked on the crimson strand and its forking in two different directions. Was this simple piece of colored string a metaphor for this moment in her life?

Allyson closed her eyes and made a decision.

Grabbing her phone off the table, she activated it and dialed a number.

"Mum," she said firmly. "I need a favor..."

| 88 |

LOVERS IN A DANGEROUS TIME

— **Lyssa Balthazaar** —
— *Tuesday* — *Domaine Saint-Bernard, Pack Nation* —

"Lorelei Skarling's forces have made it into Cleveland and Pittsburgh. They're digging in to establish a defensive line between the two cities. It's a real thin line, though. They won't hold it long without backup."

Lyssa nodded her understanding of what Nykola was telling her. The news wasn't a surprise; it was about what she had expected in all honesty. Skarling was a small House, no more than a couple of thousand soldiers.

"Any word from Allana Haggari?"

This time it was Nykola's turn to nod. "Yes, her army has been establishing a line east of the I-76 as it comes down from Pittsburgh to meet the I-70. Our troops have moved down to Baltimore and are forming a line to link up with her forces about midway between the two cities."

"Can Allana spare any troops to overlap with Lorelei's in Pittsburgh?"

"I doubt it." Nykola shrugged, not willing to commit to a definite answer. "They have a much bigger standing army, double that of Skarling and our own combined. About eight thousand strong. But the territory they're trying to hold is more difficult. The line longer."

"And Jareb? Any movement?" Lyssa asked.

Nykola shook her head. "Nope."

"I'm not sure if that's a good thing or a bad thing," Lyssa muttered.

"Well, considering we're getting all kinds of chatter about StormHall's forces being on the move and heading east, the fact that House Jareb's military seems to be standing down bodes well. It's all moot, though, without help.

"Once StormHall realizes what we're doing and mobilizes his forces...well, that's when the shit will really hit the fan. Especially if he brings the Trampyrii, as you know he will. He'll throw them into the fight as cannon-fodder first, taking the brunt of our defense.

"And I *know* how you feel about Trampyrii, that essentially they're innocents, but if he throws them into the fight, then we're not going to be able to avoid bloodshed. While we physically outclass them, their sheer weight of numbers will give us serious issues. And that's before he commits his proper military might. When he brings the armor and the air force...we're basically fucked."

"What's the timeframe?" Lyssa asked.

"We're talking days," Nykola stated. "At best."

Lyssa said nothing, just stared at the map on the table trying to find a solution. The numbers didn't add up, and she couldn't see her way to an equation that balanced or gave a result in her favor.

"Does it change the outlook if I commit my armies?"

Lyssa and Nykola looked up from the table to see the silhouette of Damian Dane standing in the doorway. He had a wry smile on his face as he entered the room, walked over to the table, and pointed toward Lake Erie on the map.

"I have been amassing my armies here in Toronto, Mississauga, and Hamilton. I can give you around eight thousand of my troops. Spread them along this front you're talking about."

"That would certainly help," Nykola said slowly, deep in thought. "Let's say, optimistically, a Werewolf is worth four Vampyrii in battle. You're effectively putting an extra twenty thousand or so troops on the line. It'll make a big difference, at least at first.

"But, while that brings our total powerbase up to around maybe thirty thousand, StormHall could deploy half of his forces and *still* outnumber us something like seven-to-one. And that's without factoring in his advantage in equipment. It'll extend our time, but only to a few weeks...if we're lucky."

Damian smiled. "All we can do is our best. Even if we fail, at least the world will know we took a stand."

Lyssa raised an eyebrow. "So, you *finally* made a decision."

For a moment, the Wolf King looked a little sheepish, raising his hand to sweep it across his head and his tightly braided hair. "I did," he said finally. "It took someone to remind me of the promise I made. The Oath I had to keep. After that, the decision was not difficult. Speaking of which... If you could both please follow me outside..."

Nykola exchanged a look with Lyssa, one that conveyed the confusion they were both feeling regarding Damian's request.

What's he up to?

He led them from the pavilion toward the lake where his flyer was parked on the grass.

"Okay..." Nykola was the first to let her curiosity get the better of her. "So, what exactly did you bring us out here for?"

Damian smiled and pointed up into the sky to the southeast. Lyssa followed the direction of his finger, and at first, she saw nothing. It was a clear night, black as velvet glittering with a thousand diamond stars. Then she noticed one of the sparkling gems was moving slowly and appeared to be getting larger. She squinted, trying to make out exactly what it was. An incoming flyer maybe? But if so, then why was there no sound?

"What, or who, is that?" Nykola said in a hushed voice.

"You'll see."

Lyssa looked sideways at Damian, intrigued and a little annoyed by his cryptic answer, but now she could also hear something. A whisper of an engine, quieter than anything with which she was familiar. Which could only mean one thing...

"Fae-tech..." Nykola was obviously on the same train of

thought.

The twinkling light expanded rapidly, coalescing into the form of an organic dropship that bore all the hallmarks of Fae design. The seamless construction, the crystal glass, and the incredibly smooth way it maneuvered as it came in for a landing next to Damian's more conventional looking flyer. It settled on its landing legs, and the engine noise diminished until even Lyssa's sensitive hearing couldn't detect it anymore.

A moment later, a hatch whispered open on the starboard fuselage and a ramp opened out, extending from the aircraft to the grass. In the aperture, a familiar figure appeared and started to stride down the ramp. There was a warm smile on her face when she saw Lyssa stood there on the grass waiting for her.

"I do believe you know Serlia Knightley..." Damian said, gesturing at the ramp where the FSE Ambassador had appeared. "She's here because...we think we have a plan for getting some allies for our fight."

"But we'll need your help, Lyssa," Serlia said as she joined them. "It's good to see you again."

"I couldn't have got here without your aid, Ambassador," Lyssa smiled. "I'm eternally grateful for everything you did for me. I won't forget it."

Serlia bowed her head a little in acknowledgment, but there was a sly look on her face as she answered. "I'm glad I could be of assistance, but I daresay that I'm not finished helping you just yet. I may still have a few surprises up my sleeve..." She gestured back toward her flyer, where a familiar figure emerged from the hatchway.

Lyssa felt her jaw drop.

She had feared that with the probable outcome of this little coup she had started, she would likely never see Allyson Knightley again. Yet here she was in Domaine Saint-Bernard exiting the flyer. Ally's face lit up when she saw Lyssa, who moved to meet her at the bottom of the ramp.

For a fleeting moment, the two of them stopped and stared at each other

It started with an embrace.

Lyssa needed to feel Allyson in her arms, to get a tactile sense that this was real. That her love was here in the flesh and this was not just a dream she was having. As her arms slipped around her lover, she put her head on Ally's shoulder and drew in the scent of her hair.

She was really here.

"How?" was all Lyssa could whisper when she regained the ability to speak.

The answer came not with words, but with the gentle press of Allyson's lips to hers. Lyssa's field of vision was suddenly filled with her lover's face and a shock of sapphire hair as she became temporarily oblivious to the world around her.

Finally, the moment was broken as Allyson pulled away slowly. "I decided this is where I need to be right now. Here, with you."

"But what about—"

"It can wait," Ally interrupted.

"But—"

Again, Allyson stopped her in her tracks. "Lyssa, stop. I thought about what my father would want me to do, and while he was proud of my achievements, he also wanted me to be happy. He wouldn't want me to waste my time sitting in a room, staring at a wall trying to solve the puzzle of his death when the woman I love is fighting a more important battle half a world away. My being here would make him proud."

Lyssa frowned for a second.

Did I mishear what she just said?

"Did you just..."

"I love you, too," Ally clarified, blushing slightly as she did so. "Took me a while, but I got there. Three little words, right? Well, four actually."

Lyssa closed her eyes, happiness swelling within her. "I can't believe you're here..." she whispered, still gob smacked.

"Well, I'm not Gayle, but I *do* have power." Allyson stepped back a little and gestured at her outfit. "And I borrowed the CombatSkin again, so I'm at least dressed appropriately. I even converted the color scheme to black and blue, which, correct me if I'm wrong, are—"

"House Balthazaar colors," Nykola confirmed, interrupting their reunion. "I'm Nykola, Lyssa's sister. It is great to finally meet you."

She held out her hand, which Ally grasped while returning the smile in kind. "I'm sorry. We kind of got caught in a moment there..."

"So...you two know each other?" Damian said slowly as he flicked from Lyssa to Allyson and back again.

Fuck!

Lyssa slowly turned to look at the Wolf King, who had what could only be described as a puzzled and slightly hurt expression on his face. She had meant to tell him about herself and Allyson weeks ago. The day he brought her sister Vanessa's body back to her, she tried to broach the subject, but he told her nothing was more important that day than her grief. Since then, life had been a blur. The Blood to Earth ritual, the Summit, the bomb, her escape, and now the planning of their impending coup.

So much had happened, and she had been neglectful in her duty to be honest with her former lover.

"Damian... I'm sorry. I meant to tell you..." she stammered the beginning of an apology.

The look on his face mellowed and changed, the surprise replaced by the warmth of a smile.

"Well, I can't say I'm not a little shocked, but I knew you were looking for something I couldn't provide," he said, shaking his head sadly.

"I'm sorry. It happened in Nexus—"

"—Talking of Nexus," Serlia interrupted. "I'm sorry, Lyssa, but I have something to discuss with you immediately. And time is *very* much of the essence..."

The Ambassador had a serious expression on her elegant features, a departure from the soft friendly face she remembered. Previously, Lyssa had only ever seen Serlia friendly or serene. Always a calming presence. Tonight, there was something more there.

An urgency.

A determination.

"This is about the plan Damian mentioned?"

Serlia nodded.

"Serlia and I had an idea," Damian said, glancing toward the ambassador. "But to pull it off, we need you. And it has to be now. Tonight."

As she flicked her eyes from Damian to Serlia and back again, she wondered what the two of them had come up with. Not that it mattered. If they had a plan, then she would do whatever it took to make it work. She trusted Damian; he had never let her down in the past. And Serlia was the mother of the woman she loved and an honorable person in her own right. The decision was easy.

"Okay, whatever it is…I'm in. What do you need?"

| 89 |

AMERICANS

— Serlia Knightley —
— Thursday — Nexus City, Iceland —

A handful of small spotlights were on at the moment, illuminating the FSE delegate area of the World Council Chamber in a gentle warm glow. The remainder of the room was bathed in a myriad of emerald-hued shadows cast by the light of the aurora borealis dancing brightly in the indigo Icelandic sky high overhead and being gently refracted through the crystal dome.

The once wounded crystal was slowly knitting itself back together, organically healing the cracks to become flawless once more. The wooden beams of native rowan were also recovering nicely, blackened scorch marks fading from their surface. It wouldn't be long before the chamber was fully restored to its former majestic beauty...as if the bombing had never happened. She knew many wondered how this amphitheater of diplomacy had been constructed; the truth was, it hadn't.

Fae didn't build things—they grew them. This building had been cultivated, like a tree from a sapling. It was the Fae way, a philosophy that permeated every aspect of their life. As a race, they were driven to explore themselves, to grow spiritually. From childhood, they were encouraged to establish roots that anchored their souls, and then to expand ever outward and ever upward.

Her husband had been one such branch on the tree of her life.

No, that does my lover a disservice. He was the sturdy trunk upon which my other branches were grown. My career and my children.

Serlia stood in the very spot Jaymes had been when the explosion claimed his life. A tear meandered down her cheek as she realized he would no longer stand steadfastly alongside her. The funeral had been their last moment, her final goodbye. He was now truly one with The River. Body and soul.

Leaving her alone.

The chamber was eerily quiet, a far cry from the usual buzz of hushed conversations, thus it was immediately obvious when the NAA ambassadors entered the room. Exactly on time. The rhythmic beat of Serena Peterson's heels and the soft shuffle of Stephen McAdams' shoes signaled their presence long before Serlia assumed her most cordial smile and turned to greet them.

"So, we're here as requested, Serlia," Stephen said quietly. "Would you mind informing us why you asked us to meet you here in the middle of the night?"

"It's about New Victus," Serlia said simply.

She didn't have to look at Serena to know the young ambassador was rolling her eyes.

"We spoke about this at your home. You know where we stand," she said.

"You claimed," Serlia confirmed, "you did not wish to spill American or Canadian blood to gain territory Grand Chancellor StormHall would give you for free. Is that a fair summary?"

Stephen shrugged and nodded. "Are you looking to try to change our minds?"

The three of them stood before the now restored crystal dome that protected the shallow-dished housing of the AuthaGraphic holo-map, which was also now fully functional. Serlia had already altered the view it was displaying, giving a closer representation of Pack Nation and New Victus.

She smiled. "No. Not me."

Two figures stepped out of the shadows and into the warm circle of light. Both were instantly recognizable to the ambassadors, but no less surprising.

"Good evening, Ambassador McAdams," Damian Dane said warmly. "It's been far too long. And this must be Ambassador Peterson. Ambassador Sabadini spoke about you at great length and in glowing terms." He extended his hand to both in turn, giving each a friendly handshake.

"It's good to see you, Damian. It has indeed been too long." McAdams smiled warmly before casting a suspicious eye toward the Wolf King's companion. "Serlia mentioned you'd struck an alliance with Lyssa Balthazaar...but I have to admit, I was somewhat skeptical it was true. No offense, Serlia."

"None taken, Stephen." Serlia smiled. "It did seem rather...unlikely. But as you can see, it was also true."

"I'm very pleased to meet you." Lyssa extended her hand, which was shaken with a hint of trepidation. "I'm glad you both agreed to hear us out."

Serena and Stephen looked at Serlia, a slightly accusatory look in their eyes. Neither had been told the purpose of tonight's meeting, nor who the attendees were going to be. Right now, Serlia figured, they were likely feeling a little ambushed.

"I think it would help considerably with your final decisions if you were to hear what they have to say," Serlia said, softly. "All we ask is for a few minutes of your time."

Ambassador McAdams walked behind the table bearing the emblem of the FSE and sat slowly in Serlia's usual chair. It didn't go unnoticed that he avoided the seat once occupied by Jaymes.

Ever the attentive diplomat, Serlia thought with a smile.

"The floor is all yours," Stephen gestured to the area in front of the desk with a flourish of his hand.

Damian and Lyssa looked at each other for a moment before Damian stepped forward.

"My surname, quite literally, translates to 'from Denmark.' It is Scandinavian in origin, something I wager we share in common, Ambassador Peterson. 'Son of Peter,' if I'm correct. Tell me, how far back can you trace your family line?"

Serena looked slightly bemused but seemingly decided to humor Damian's question.

"My great-great-grandparents were Swedish. Originally it was Petersson but got changed over time after my family moved to Canada in the 1920s, after the First World War."

"So, your family has been Canadian for a little over 120 years?" Damian asked.

Serena nodded.

"Werewolves," Damian continued, "as a race, are part of a wider classification. Therianthropes. The word, as you may be aware, is derived from the Greek words for 'Theríon' and 'an-thrōpos,' their words for 'beast' and 'Human.' Wolves, tigers, horses, hyenas... No matter the animal, we have been around for centuries, living peacefully alongside Humankind, broadly unnoticed.

"As you may surmise by my skin tone, my ancestors were born in Africa in the 13th century. We didn't stay there. Somewhere in the 15th century, they made their way to Denmark, which is when we got our name. Dane.

"My grandmother, Isabella, led our pack across the Atlantic to the forests of Canada almost 400 hundred years ago. It was ideal for us. We were born to run in nature, and for a long time, life was...perfect. It was a quiet country, and we were relatively few in number. Our kind could pursue life without interference from Humankind.

"More joined us there, all manner of types and ethnicities. It didn't matter to us what the color of our skin was...we were *all* Werewolf. That fact bound us together as a pack. One race living together, growing together. Canada was...is our home. And when Sebastian StormHall instigated The Rising, we *defended* our home.

"We still do."

"You're telling us it was *Sebastian StormHall* who started all this?" Stephen said, leaning forward in the seat. Damian nodded. "If true, then why have none of us heard this information before?"

"Because no one would listen. My brethren and I have all been tarred with the same brush as StormHall and his lackeys. In your eyes, we were all monsters. As the plague swept across North America, you treated us the same as you treated the Vampyrii. Yet, in actual fact, we were protecting you as best we could."

"Protecting us?" Stephen looked confused.

Damian nodded. "We...I...made a promise, many years ago." He glanced at Serlia. "The Oath. I made that promise to Serlia, who accepted it on behalf of the Fae. We tried to fight against the Vampyrii uprising, but we were few in number. The best we could do was hold the line until the Fae intervened. It was their idea for the creation of Pack Nation, the illusion of a Werewolf nation."

"Why would you need to perpetrate such an illusion?" Serena asked.

"So that Sebastian StormHall would never find out we were safely harboring millions of Canadians in the North. He had to believe we were a nation that rivaled his for population. Think of it as a supernatural cold war. There are something like ten million Vampyrii in New Victus. Pack Nation declares a population of three million, but that number includes barely 50,000 Werewolves. The rest are Humans under our protection.

"But StormHall doesn't know that. He *can't* know that."

"I don't understand..." Stephen whispered.

"Because if he *ever* found out," Damian continued, "he would have marched his armies across the border and killed or turned us all without hesitation. And believe me, if we lose this coup, that is exactly what he'll do. He'll hand the western states back to the NAA, and then take advantage of the shortened border and our reduced defensive numbers to invade and kill or turn the millions of free Canadians.

"*Your* people."

Serlia watched as the stunned ambassadors started to process the information they were given. They had been let in on the secret he had religiously kept for over thirty years. It was a calculated risk. Exposing the truth to them now to change their minds about joining the fight.

So that this secret *never* had to be kept ever again.

"Three decades." Ambassador McAdams shook his head slowly in disbelief before looking at Lyssa. "And the Vampyrii never suspected? Never learned the truth? I find that hard to believe..."

"We knew. My house runs the primary intelligence gathering agency in New Victus, and we uncovered this particular secret about five years ago..." Lyssa paused, then raised an eyebrow and smiled. "We simply neglected to relay that little piece of information to StormHall. I saw it as my opportunity to approach Damian regarding my long-term agenda to overthrow StormHall's regime."

McAdams was leaning forward in his chair now, his face showing rapt interest in this unlikely alliance. Serlia could tell both he and Peterson were teetering on the edge, close to tipping over to their side. They just needed a final nudge. Serlia nodded to Lyssa—it was her turn now.

Her long hair was back to its normal raven hue with the distinctive white streaks running down either side of her face. She looked nervous as she stepped forward into the light from which Damian had retreated.

She knew the stakes, and they were high.

"Vampyrii House names are not regional like those of Humans and Werewolves, but each Vampyrii House *was* started in a different part of the world. We may have all migrated to New Victus after The War, but we originated all over the globe. House Izzicar, for example, are Māori. Originating in eastern Polynesia. House Varden, rose in Norway. They are proud and noble Vikings.

"And then...there is House Balthazaar.

"Look at my face. My cheekbones. The shape of my eyes. The straight black hair. My features are distinctive and, dare I say, stereotypical to my race. It doesn't matter what term you use, Native American, American Indian, whatever... The fact of the matter is, I was *born* in what was the United States of America in the year eighteen hundred. My father, Balthazaar, arose in the middle of the thirteenth century...

"Three centuries before *your* ancestors sailed from Europe to colonize the New World. You think of me as Vampyrii...but I think of myself as an American. I was there when the county grew out of nothing. I've lived and worked in New York City since they laid the first foundations. I lived amongst you. I had Human friends, and with them, I laughed, cried, and loved.

"I drank coffee from Starbucks. I ate pie from Joe's Pizza in Greenwich Village. I watched the New York Knicks lose, *a lot*, at Madison Square Garden. I was born under the Stars and Stripes, and I have been an American for two-hundred-and-forty-five years.

"When *I* fight StormHall, it is to take back America. To right a wrong done three decades ago. To restore, to the best of my ability, what once was. And I'm not the only one. There are thousands of Vampyrii like me, who consider what happened a travesty and only want the opportunity to put things right.

"*You* might see us as Vampyrii, but we see ourselves as Americans, and we will gladly fight alongside the flag of the North American Alliance to take our country back from the grip of StormHall.

"Forget my race. What we are here today to ask of you is that you fight alongside your fellow countrymen and women.

"Because *we* are going into that fight for *you*." Lyssa finished there, saying no more.

Serlia wasn't sure if the impassioned speeches would make the ambassadors see past their race. To elevate them beyond petty racism and see them as men and women fighting for the same ideals the NAA espoused. But they had given it their best shot.

Their only shot.

Lyssa and Damian had set the precedent. A Vampyrii and a Werewolf coming together to pursue a higher agenda. A greater good. Maybe showing the NAA ambassadors the truth would set them free of their blinkered minds, allowing them to forge an alliance that before tonight would have been unthinkable.

| 90 |

FINAL SANCTION

— Sebastian StormHall —
— Thursday — New York, New Victus —

Sebastian remembered vividly how Lyssa had denied him access to this vault a few months before, directly challenging his authority. Disrespecting his position as Grand Chancellor. Every fiber of his being hated the woman, yet he bit his tongue and bided his time safe in the knowledge that a reckoning would come. That one day he would have the upper hand.

That day came unexpectedly soon with the bombing of the Nexus Summit.

In hindsight, he wished it had been his idea. It had provided the perfect opportunity to discredit her and, along with her, the cursed Earth Quorum that sat in opposition to him, challenging his every decision. Lyssa Balthazaar had cultivated powerful allies within the Blood Council, hinging on her father being one of the last surviving Progenitors.

A situation soon to be remedied.

He had already managed to stealthily dispatch six of them, a steady weakening of their religious significance. Three decades ago, most Vampyrii considered the Progenitors to be immortal. Even when Yaznuma perished at sea, the fact that his body was never found led to tales of his being in hiding. Or ascending to a new level of existence.

Not Sebastian.

What he saw was vulnerability.

If a Progenitor could drown, then you could kill them in all kinds of creative ways.

Now there were only four left, and their mystique had dimmed. The Vampyrii people were more divided than ever, less impressed by their long absent ancestors. Sebastian had shown them they didn't need the Progenitors—a Vampyrii had all the power they required within their own hands.

Now he stood before the vault doors to which Lyssa had denied him access. She wasn't here to stop him now. His men signaled to him they had cracked the vault's security; the huge, black monolithic doors would open for him when he was ready.

He dismissed them.

He would enter alone to 'pay his respects.'

One by one, they left.

Sebastian was alone.

Reaching his hand for the door, he pushed firmly. It opened smoothly and silently, allowing him entry into House Balthazaar's most sacred inner sanctum. Adrenaline surged and his hand gripped the ceremonial 'Blood to Earth' dagger tightly as he drew it from the sheath hidden beneath his jacket.

Six Progenitors had died by his hand.

He was about to make it seven.

The room itself was almost monochromatic in nature, its ebony wood contrasted gorgeously with the snow-white marble. In the center lay Balthazaar's hibernation chamber. Sebastian couldn't help but admire the craftsmanship, the ornate carvings, and the beautiful ritualistic scriptures etched into its flanks and lid. It seemed almost incongruous with the modern architecture of Hearst Tower. Here beneath the glass and steel façade was a room so traditionally Vampyrii. His finger idly traced the symbols as he considered what he was about to undertake.

Gripping the hilt of the dagger in his right hand, he used his left to push the lid aside, to expose the sleeping form of Balthazaar. He prepared himself to plunge the blade into his enemy's heart and inject the chemicals that would remove any trace of the Progenitor's existence from this world.

The chamber was empty.

Fury burned inside him.

The rage of the cheated man.

He turned and stalked from the room, pulling his phone out of his pocket as he did so. His fingers danced across the screen before he lifted it to his ear. The call connected almost immediately.

"Dr. Shauston... Is he ready? Excellent. Then tell Nathanial I have an important job for him."

| **Epilogue** |

PROJECT: LAZARUS

— **Lyssa Balthazaar** —
— *Sunday* — *Domaine Saint-Bernard, Pack Nation* —

"Welcome back!" Nykola shouted, hopping down from the cab of the black tractor-trailer that had just rumbled into the compound. Her boots kicked up dust as she landed.

"I could say the same to you," Lyssa replied, gesturing toward the trailer. "Did you get it?"

Nykola nodded. "In and out, fast and clean."

"Thank the Gods!" Lyssa exclaimed, closing her eyes briefly.

She took a deep breath before opening them and exhaling with relief.

It was here...at last.

The contents of this truck were vital to Lyssa.

They gave her *hope*.

Nykola slapped her hand on the door of the cab, indicating to the driver to continue onward to park near the edge of the forest before turning to her sister. "So, *I* was fucking awesome, but did *you* get what you went to Nexus for?"

"I'm not sure," Lyssa shrugged. "Maybe. We made our case. Ambassador Knightley seems confident it will work. But...who knows? Their hatred for Vampyrii runs pretty deep."

"Well, if the FSE *does* come on board, then at least we should be able to hold our own on the eastern front. But it would help considerably to bring down StormHall if the NAA could commit from the west or the Gulf of Mexico. I guess it would prevent StormHall from redeploying his forces from those areas and significantly shifting the odds."

"In our favor?" Lyssa asked hopefully.

Nykola shrugged, her eyeline wandering back to the truck driving away from them. "Lys, I'm not the military intelligence expert."

"I know, but...give me your best guess anyway."

"Best guess? Even odds," Nykola shrugged. "A coin toss."

"Really?" Lyssa said, finding it hard to hide the dispirited tone in her voice.

"StormHall has a half-million troops, if you include Trampyrii, which you *know* he will. We can't match those numbers, not even with the Wolves, the Yanks, and the FSE all pitching in. Remember, most of the US armed forces ended up as Trampyrii cannon-fodder serving StormHall. If the NAA had the manpower, they'd have kicked StormHall's ass a lot further east than the San Andreas Line.

"And the FSE is engaged with the conflict with Africa, so they won't be in a position to deploy the kind of numbers that would neutralize StormHall's advantage. We will, however, have access to superior weaponry, and that should go some way toward evening things up.

"Honestly, Lys, this is Mercy's forte. Not mine."

"Well...Mercy isn't here now, is she?"

Nykola looked at her and smiled confidently. Lyssa knew that look. Her sister may not be the military and intelligence expert her niece was, but there was a reason Lyssa had put her in charge of Project: Lazarus, amongst other things.

Nykola Balthazaar was a hell of a scientist, even if it *was* all wrapped up in a distinctly unconventional package.

"Maybe not." She grinned. "But just let me do what I do best."

The Ballad of the Songbird
will continue in Book 3

Tooth & Claw

| **If you enjoyed this book...** |

Firstly, et me thank you from the bottom of my heart for taking a chance on reading this first part of **HUNTERS**. If you enjoyed it, then Part 2 is merely a purchase away!

If you'd like to help, here's how you can.
Indie Authors **need** book reviews.

As self-published authors we rely hugely on word-of-mouth and personal recommendations. If you enjoyed this book, then taking a few minutes to leave a rating, or better still a review, is hugely important to us.

The more reviews we have, the more it helps us gain traction in advertising our books and gaining more readers. It's all about those algorithms.

Here's how you can help:

- Go to where you purchased this book online and leave a rating and a review. It doesn't have to be much, a simple one-liner will do.

- Even if you were given this book as a gift, you can still leave a review on GoodReads. And Amazon will allow you to rate it in stars.

- Easiest of all, tell your friends. Spread the word about a book you liked via social media, and word of mouth.

Thank You

| Also by Jon Ford |

The Ballad of the Songbird—Book 1
Hunters

The Femme Fatales—Book 1
THE SCORCHED SKY
A Femme Fatales Novella
KNIGHTINGALE

| Coming Soon |

The Ballad of the Songbird—Book 3
Tooth & Claw

The Femme Fatales—Book 2
THE BROKEN GROUND
A Femme Fatales Novella
KASAI

| Acknowledgments |

I'd be remiss if I didn't acknowledge a few people, without whom this book would not have been possible. I give my heartfelt thanks to all those who supported me along this journey. Thank you!

Here are a few that deserve an extra special mention.

My Wonderful Wife

After Hunters came out, Wifey *really* raised her support game. She did an amazing job setting up my Jon Ford Author Instagram account and making all kinds of connections on there. So grateful you're my wife, Jess.
Love you always, little Bubba xxx

My Partner in Shenanigans - Nikki Anderson

Honestly can't do this without my Book-Wife, LOL. I know 2020/21 was a tough time for you in many ways, Nikki, but I'm still eternally thankful you're my partner in shenanigans! My books are all the better for your editing, input, and feedback. Love ya, Nik!
(P.S. Buy her books!—'Acts of Closure' and 'Acts of Confession' Available on Amazon!)

Artist Without Compare—Marlena Mozgawa

Think the Hunters cover was fantastic? Seen the one on the front of this book?
Every project I give to Marlena, she knocks out of the park.
She's the perfect artist to bring my vision to life.
Thank you so much for working with me, I can't think of my books with any other cover art but yours!

My Beta-Reader Posse

Chell, Andy, and Sarah. You guys are the old guard, there since Hunters!!
This time there are a few more to add to the list too. Thank you to Emma, Pippa, Malcolm, and Deborah.

The Inimitable Kevin Smith

*"If you're alive, kick into drive. Chase whimsies.
See if you can turn dreams into a way to make a living,
if not an entire way of life." - Kevin Smith*
That quote struck a chord for me, so I did it. I chased my
whimsy, and now you're holding it.

Special Thanks to:

Mercedes Lackey and Judith Tarr, who pointed me in the right
direction.

Finally, I'd be remiss if I didn't also shout out…

So very many Twitter Peeps *deep breath* here goes…
Eaton Krone (@EatonKrone), ALWAYS amazingly supportive.
Anna Mocikat (@AnnaMocikat), an amazing writer and an
even better friend.
Emmy R Bennett (@EmmyRBennett), a source of constant
and wonderful chat and advice.
Halo Scot (@Halo_Scot), one of the most terrifyingly wonder-
ful souls you'll ever meet.
Kayla Hicks (@klrice), superstar writer and fantastic chum!
Dzintra Sullivan (@DzintraSullivan) & **Kia Carrington-Rus-
sell** (@kia_crystal), go buy their books and listen to their fantastic
podcast (What The Book - @WTBPodcast)
AC Merkel (@Blink_Drive), who makes the most amazing
animations!
Anya Pavelle (@AnyaPavelle), Seeker of recommendations.
Ross Young (@InkDisregardit), Master of Beezy & Grim!
EG Radcliff (@EGRadcliff), super-awesome, super helpful.
AND a final shout out to **ME Aster** (@ME_Aster), who was in-
valuable in helping me get Bobbi just right!

PLEASE GO AND BUY ALL THEIR BOOKS.
THEY'RE ALL FANTASTIC AND WELL DESERVING
OF YOUR PENNIES

Easter Eggs Galore!

This book (*and the series as a whole*) has **LOADS** of little nods to my influences, including:

My series title is an homage to **Alan Moore** and **Ian Gibson**'s seminal *'The Ballad of Halo Jones'* which I fucking loved when I was a kid!
The comic writing of **Simon Furman** was also a huge influence. The title of *'Freelance Peacekeeping Agent'* is an homage to one of my favorite characters of his creation, yes?

If you read the chapter titles, you may notice a few references to song titles that I listened to while I was writing that particular chapter. Go check out my website (*www.jonfordauthor.com*) for a track listing of the songs that influenced me.

AND FINALLY...

I'd like to give a huge shout out to my old mucker, Steve Ducker (ooo that rhymes!) who's bought more copies of my book than
anyone who has any sense really should.
He's been a mate for many a year now since we met playing City of Heroes, and he is embarking on his very own writing adventure under the pen name Steve Vimes (@SteveVimes)
Look out for his 'Katie G' series of books, coming SOON!
(See, now I've committed you to getting it out, Steve! Your public awaits!)

| About The Author |

Jon Ford lives in Worcestershire, UK.

He lives with his awesome Wifey, their lovable puppy, Vixen and the demonic hell-puppy, Lyssa. All of them live under the watchful gaze of their cat-overlords Lana and Gale.

No awards to brag about, but he's working on it.
Currently writing two series of books.
The Ballad of the Songbird is an urban fantasy saga with sci-fi overtones. Book 1 'Hunters' and book 2 'Blood to Earth' are out now. Book 3 'Tooth & Claw' will be mid 2023.

The Femme Fatales is an ongoing sci-fi superhero series. Book 1 'The Scorched Sky' and a tie in novella 'Knightingale' are out now. Book 2 'The Broken Ground' will be out later in 2023.

To find out more about the either series - and for my random musings - please visit and explore my expansive website:

WWW.JONFORDAUTHOR.COM

Co-Founder of Tepris Press with NT Anderson.
A little indie imprint label dedicated to putting out high-quality independent books.
Find out more at our website:

WWW.TEPRISPRESS.COM

Also, find me on Twitter at: **@_Knightingale**

And on Instagram at: **JonFordAuthor**